Demon Lord Rising

Jason Farrell &
Michael de Weever

Montauk
BEACH
PRESS

Published by:
Montauk Beach Press
MARGATE, FLORIDA

Copyright © 2019 by Jason Farrell & Michael de Weever

ISBN: 978-1-7334686-0-2 Hardcover
978-1-7334686-1-9 Softcover
978-1-7334686-2-6 Ebook

Editing
Carol Killman Rosenberg • www.carolkillmanrosenberg.com

Cover design
Jamie Noble Frier • www.thenobleartist.com

Interior design
Gary A. Rosenberg • www.thebookcouple.com

Cartography
Sara Stemle • Instagram: @ loud.color

Printed in the United States of America

The forces of darkness burn with a great fire,
a great longing to corrupt and dominate,
and only when the combined well of souls
of all free people unite may such flames
ever be extinguished.

ALGERNON, THE GREAT SAGE OF WRENFORD

The Land

Prologue

Sparks flew as flashing swords glanced off Lark Royale's silver-plated mail armor. His great two-handed sword shattered the half-light, shining frost-white like the diamond set in its hilt as it carved a path through the dozen or more dark-clad knights forming a pile at his feet. Though skilled warriors, their blows couldn't penetrate Lark's thick armor in which he moved with uncanny dexterity. He glanced toward his Druid companion, Kael, who stood stoically with his fist wrapped around his great oak staff. Instantly, two of the dark knights broke away and charged the Druid.

Kael thrust his staff forward and the top exploded in a pyrotechnic flash of greens and blues. The two knights stopped in their tracks to cover their eyes. The Druid held out his free hand and waved his fingers, speaking in a strange tongue. When the knights cleared their vision, they found it difficult to move their legs. Looking down, they watched in astonishment as ice enveloped their black armor, freezing them in place momentarily.

Lark finished off his last attacker with a sweeping upward stroke and ran toward the frozen knights. He dove in a forward roll and came up between the men on one knee, bringing his great sword around so swiftly it nearly severed the first man in half at the torso. Spinning again, he came down in a slicing blow through the thin layer of ice and the second man's chest.

"Functionaries, sycophants, and worshippers," Kael spat. "Is there no end to them? How many must we dispatch to reach our goal? How many will he needlessly sacrifice?"

"He would sacrifice them all down to the last if it gave him one more moment of life," Lark replied. "These were once soldiers. Now they sell themselves with no regard for the cause they serve."

A deep voice entered the room from an opening on the north wall. "Well, if it isn't the Knight-Errant and his old troublemaking fool of a friend. My men are mercenaries, little knight, the most feared mercenaries in all the lands."

The two men turned and saw a huge man enter the chamber, his black robe partially concealing dark armor and a great single-bladed axe. It was Yager Martek, known as "the Red Death" and the dreaded Commander of the Stygian Knights. While Kael stood six and half feet tall, this man stood nearly seven feet. His fiery red hair, unkempt and partially braided, covered both sides of his face and entwined into a lengthy beard and mustache beneath a black-horned helmet. Lark and Kael were well acquainted with Martek's reputation for ruthlessness and unmatched battle skill.

Lark pushed a dead soldier's body aside with his foot. "Forgive me if I'm not quaking in terror." He turned to his companion. "Kael, the spiral staircase there in the corner. Take it to the top. He *must* be there. Retrieve the star and finish it. Let the gods watch over you. This man is *my* task."

"May the Sacred Mother protect you, my friend," Kael said, eliciting a nod from Lark, then he quickly made way for the staircase.

"You Paladins are an impudent, arrogant lot, Royale," Martek spat out as he watched Kael disappear up the stairs. "Do you know why there are so few of you left in the world?" The commander closed the distance between them, but Lark stood firmly rooted to his place. "Most men are too weak and cowardly to live by the arduous, impossible code you all claim to live your lives by. When the time comes, you shining paragons of courage all beg for your lives like stupid women and children." Martek chuckled, low and guttural. "If you wish to beg now, I will consider your plea and show mercy. If not, you will feel every moment before death takes you, and you will have begged for release long before I grant it."

As the last word slithered from Martek's lips, Lark set his great two-handed blade point down before him. He knelt down, gripping the pommel of the blade with both fists and closed his eyes.

Martek laughed furiously. "You do wish to beg!" he exclaimed. "What a disappointment." He stared at Lark a moment. "Oh . . . my apologies. Praying to your false deity for strength. You would be better off praying to me or my master."

Lark Royale opened his eyes and smiled.

The spiraling staircase rose several levels, leading to the top of the tower. Kael stepped off into an expansive rectangular room with a strange crimson hue, created no doubt by the light pouring in through the floor-to-ceiling stained-glass windows. The ceiling was barrel-vaulted with interconnecting stone rafters.

The Druid spotted the lone, dark form some fifty feet away, facing a large oval window. He held a tall black staff that pulsated red with menacing power. Finally, they had found the elusive Shadow Prince, Wolfgar Stranexx. Kael spied the glass encasement between the window and the dark figure, and he moved to the side for a better view. Even through the crimson hue, the bright green gemstone known as the Emerald Star glowed.

"Tell me priest . . . do you know the secret to unlocking the powers of this cursed Elven artifact?" The voice was deep and raspy as if it were being filtered through grinding metal, struggling to escape. *"Long have I labored to discover the secret of its powers, and still I am thwarted by it. Despite all your meddling and trouble, you've cost me you have this one chance. Choose your words carefully. Such knowledge could yet save you and your Paladin protector."*

Defiantly, Kael passed his oak staff across his face freeing one hand, "Even if I had such knowledge, I would gladly die a thousand deaths before helping you. None of your slaves are coming to save you this time, Wolfgar. It ends tonight."

Without seeming to move, the robed figure was now facing him, his eyes shining through the slits of his metal mask. *"That was a mistake, Druid. As far as you've come and after all you've seen, you should have at least tried to make me think there was value in keeping you alive. A thousand deaths would be too good for you. No, one painful death will more than suffice. End him!"*

An inhuman screech from overhead startled Kael, and his eyes shot up toward the winged three-headed reptile descending from the rafters. Though young judging by its size, its 10-foot wingspan still cast an impressive shadow along the floor. The middle head, red, extended further out from its blue-necked companions, opening its mouth as if to screech again but instead released a cone of blazing flames toward the Druid.

Beneath the mask, the misshapen face smiled with pleasure.

Axe and sword clashed and the two warriors pulled in face-to-face with one another, grimacing with tension and sweat.

"You're weak, little man. Your armor may be strong, but it won't protect you for long."

With a forceful shove, Martek threw Lark backwards. The young man smashed into the wall behind him and crumpled to the floor, almost losing his hold on his sword. With blurred vision, he looked up to see the towering warrior drilling down with his axe for a killing blow. Lark ducked to the side, swatting the arm holding the great axe and landed an armored boot to Martek's unprotected side, momentarily knocking him away.

Lark scrambled to his feet and charged with a two-handed strike, but Martek easily deflected it with his elbow plate. With his free hand, he drew out a long dagger from his waist and swiped at Lark's face, leaving a long gash in Lark's cheek.

"Hah!" Martek cried as he drew first blood. "Pray to your god, little man. Fear not, it will all be over soon. I'll carve out your Druid friend's heart with this dagger and place it beside your head in my trophy chamber—if there's anything left of him to carve that is. You don't seriously think your fool priest has any chance against the power of the Shadow Prince?" He laughed heartily and then resumed his attack, blow after ferocious blow with axe and dagger.

Lark parried the attacks but retreated under Martek's brute strength.

"Chance . . ." Lark clenched his teeth, waiting for his moment. "He will defeat your prince and retrieve the Emerald Star."

Martek pressed forward. "Fool! Even you can't be that naive, Royale. What makes you think either of you will leave this place alive?"

"I have faith," Lark said, holding the man's gaze even as they fought. He managed to find a weak spot and shoved Martek back a pace, which in turn caused the warrior to overextend his dagger thrust, and Lark saw his opening. Blocking the axe wide with a two-handed parry, he quickly spun around and slammed his sword down on the dagger, knocking it to the floor, and he leaned in with an armored elbow smash to the face, nearly flooring his opponent, sending his helmet spinning away across the floor. Tightening both hands around his sword, he faced Martek anew. The other's nose had been crushed in, sending a splattering of blood across his face in the shape of an X.

Lark smirked. "Does it hurt? Don't worry, it's an improvement."

Martek looked at him in disbelief at first, then snarled in rage and charged again.

Kael pulled his robe up over his head, and for a moment, the flames bounced harmlessly off the cloth, but they soon ignited, and within moments, the Druid was aflame, writhing futilely against the fire.

The Shadow Prince extended his black staff, releasing an ebony flash of energy, which struck Kael and threw him some ten feet back to the floor where he finally stopped moving. Flames consumed him until they burned low.

"*Fool. I breed Hydras. They are uncompromisingly savage in nature, but a more loyal creature I have yet to find. Feed hearty, my pet. Enjoy the dinner I have graciously provided.*"

The creature hovered just above Kael's body, and the three heads leaned down in unison, anticipating the taste of charred meat. Before they could feast, a green flash exploded from Kael's apparent remains, momentarily blinding the hydra's six eyes.

Wolfgar Stranexx, the Shadow Prince, wheeled about. When the green energy subsided, a hulking creature appeared, nearly eight feet tall. The giant brown bear announced itself with a great roar and swat of its huge claws, severing two of the Hydra's heads cleanly from the necks. The remaining head let out an agonizing shriek and flew in a panic directly toward its master. The dark form ducked just in time as the creature flew over his head, smashing through the great oval window. Wolfgar straightened, holding his dark staff like a shield before him. "*Impossible!*"

Again, there was a flash of green fire, and Kael Dracksmere emerged unscathed having changed from beast back to human. "Who is the fool? Is it the man who knows nothing of his enemy? Druids do not fear fire. The elements are our allies."

Disgusted, the Shadow Prince hissed at him, "*Spare me your pagan religion. It sickens me more than even that fool downstairs who thinks he fights for a god. I have a covenant with dark forces of such power they would consume the likes of you, driving you mad. These are true gods."*

"Then let us see whose are stronger." Kael grasped his oak staff and charged the Shadow Prince.

The two met in the middle of the chamber. Wolfgar swung his black staff so swiftly that it met Kael's and the two weapons locked in midflight, creating of shower of magical energy of such force that the combatants were thrown apart.

Martek charged with such speed and fury it belied his girth. Lark brought his sword up a second too slow and the great axe struck the blade full-on, knocking it clear across the chamber. Without hesitation, Martek swung the great blade before Lark could duck, striking his right shoulder with such force that it ripped Lark's shoulder plate off, penetrating flesh. Martek came back down across the back of Lark's right knee again, tearing the armor off with a spray of blood and causing Lark to crumple to the floor. Lark tried to rise but was quickly felled as an armored boot struck him in the chest, putting him on his back. Martek stood over him, gloating, placing a boot upon his chest and holding him down.

"A pathetic effort, little knight, but I think even you sensed this is how it should end." He spat in Lark's face. "Tell your weakling god how you did your best."

With that, he raised his axe over his head and came down in a terrible stroke, only to be blocked at the last moment by Lark's crossed gauntlets. Martek looked him in the eyes, but was taken aback to discover Lark's eyes had gone completely white as if glowing. Martek's arms started to shake and suddenly he noticed Lark's entire frame was glowing with a golden light.

"This cannot be!" Martek watched in disbelief as Lark seemed to somehow work his hands around the shaft of the great axe despite Martek's strength. In one twisting motion, he flipped Martek over on his back.

The Commander of the Stygian Knights scrambled up on one knee almost instantly, only to see Lark Royale standing upright over him. Lark swung Martek's own axe, burying it deep within the middle of his head.

Martek's body hung limp from the axe blade, held aloft by Lark's grip on the axe shaft.

"Such is the power of faith," Lark said, as he kicked Martek's body off the axe and dropped the axe next to it on the floor. "I shall pray that you are shown the mercy you never showed others in life." He looked to the spiral staircase. "But first things first."

Sweeping his arm in a wide arc, Kael created a shield of blue fire, harmlessly deflecting the darts of deadly black magic the Shadow Prince hurled at him. He thrust his staff forward and green fire exploded from its crown, only to be swallowed by the gloved hand of the Shadow Prince.

"Your powers are inconsequential compared to mine, priest. You should have accepted the merciful death I offered. Now, you will kneel before me and beg for your end!" He raised his black staff and made a slow-clenching fist with his free hand.

Suddenly, an unseen power assaulted Kael. The Druid brought his staff vertically before him to ward off the attack, but his eyes narrowed and he gritted his teeth as he attempted to brace himself, placing one leg behind him. He felt himself being forced to his knees, and he began slowly sliding backward across the stone floor as if he were being crushed. His staff disintegrated into dust before his eyes and he held his hands out in front of him in an effort to fight the invisible power.

"Pain . . . crushing, bone-breaking pain. Beg me for death, Druid! Beg!"

Kael began to scream as he felt his limbs and sinews popping, being pushed ever inward, stretching and snapping to their limit. Just when he thought he would succumb to an agonizing death, the pain stopped. He caught his breath and looked up. Lark Royale stood there, his sword plunged so deep in the Shadow Prince's torso that it protruded out the front of his chest.

Slowly, the dark form dropped his hands still holding on to his pulsing black staff. He turned to face his attacker, his mask only inches from the Paladin's face, red eyes blazing in shock and rage.

"Feel the wrath of the righteous, Stranexx!" Lark shouted. "Your Red Death awaits you in the darkness of the abyss." With that, Lark tore his sword out of the Shadow Prince's chest, tearing flesh as he did so, and spun the Shadow Prince's body around as blood and flesh sprayed the stone beneath their feet.

Kael, still on his knees and gasping for breath, held his hands up and burning, searing jets of crimson flames erupted from his fingertips, striking the Shadow Prince's back. The flames burned deep into flesh and bone. Still, the Shadow Prince did not fall. Stooped over and staggering for balance, Wolfgar Stranexx faced his mortal enemies. He clutched at his chest as his form smoked and the stench of charred flesh permeated the air.

Lark took the momentary opportunity to shatter the glass case holding the Emerald Star, grabbed it, and then rushed to offer a hand to his fallen companion. He pulled Kael up, and they faced the Shadow Prince together.

"So . . . you have the gem and you think you have won. Little do you fools know the price of victory or the meaning of sacrifice. But you will pay and learn."

The Shadow Prince grabbed his staff with both hands, raised it high above his head, and began to chant an unintelligible verse. Suddenly, the staff began to pulse red, brighter and brighter.

"He means to destroy the whole tower—with us in it!" Lark shouted. "Quickly!" He grabbed Kael and tossed him down the spiral staircase. He was close behind. The last thing he saw from the corner of his eye was the Shadow Prince bringing his staff down in a final retributive strike. An explosion erupted, then all went dark and silent.

Flames lit the night sky as the highest spire of the Tower of Darkhelm cascaded to the ground like falling meteorites. From a distant mountain, an old man looked on and tugged at the silver bristles of his beard, wondering what future would yet come of this.

Chapter 1

In a formless prison, beyond space and time, the molecules of consciousness dwelt for time without measure. It was inconceivable that one of such age and power could be infinitely rendered to this state of nothingness by such insignificant beings. Still, nothing was truly infinite, not even himself. Only the vast complexity of his mind kept him from slipping into hopeless madness.

In his resident dimension, he had ruled as a god, immortal, over his demon kin, but it was he alone who had chosen to enter this realm and become subject to its physical laws and dictates. He alone accepted the consequences without hesitation, guilt, or remorse.

From the inception of his imprisonment, he dedicated his mind to a plan of reckoning against the beings of this new dimension he felt destined to rule or destroy. He focused his mind to such single-mindedness of purpose that he became more powerful through sheer force of will.

Revenge was not what he sought; revenge came with the high price of rage that would unbalance a lesser, weaker mind. His far-reaching power of concentration was above anything so petty. His mind became so masterful that he could force minute fractures in the prison, allowing parts of his consciousness to temporarily escape their confines. Outside the prison, the pieces of his consciousness existed in an inert state, at first unable to do anything but float and, through sensory perception, allow him to see, in effect, the world that had imprisoned him.

Through an endless monotony of trials and failures, he soon learned to move more swiftly outside the prison and even to express thought and power and to convey these things to living beings—just enough to subtly influence them, not enough to take control. Despite these achievements, no hint of complete escape existed. Even the briefest paroles of his segmented consciousness drained him. Still, he had inexhaustible patience. Each day his travels brought him farther and his whispers in many ears had set his plan, a millennium in the making, in motion.

Then, a monumental event, one he had dared not hope for, struck him unexpectedly. He instantly sensed the resonating signature of rage, frustration, and an unnatural longing for vengeance. He reached out to this small mass of energy and breathed upon it, temporarily forestalling its imminent fate. In the primitive vernacular of this chaotic world, it was the spirit of a recently destroyed creature, bound for oblivion far more permanent than his own fate.

Do not be frightened. He conveyed his energy into thought and word that could be understood but not necessarily heard. *I have need of one such as you. In life, men called you . . . Shadow Prince. Join with me and you will live again, and those who defeated you will kneel before you or die. Be without any doubt. You must give yourself to me body and soul, and we shall become as one. You will be my vessel, but we will live together again. It will take time to reconstitute your form . . . perhaps years in linear time. I must have your complete loyalty. You will serve my every whim without hesitation or question. Can you give that? Are you willing to serve, or shall I allow you to continue on your present journey?*

This new entity did not have near the power of complexity of thought to convey energy into communication, but the demon's acute sensory perception detected overwhelming acceptance of the terms. Beyond all imagining, he had found the one who would serve as his avatar in the living, breathing world. Through this Shadow Prince, the Demon Lord, Abadon, would one day live free again.

20 Years Later:

The barely audible twang of Elven longbows vibrated through the trees as the archers fired off a volley, filling the confined air with a swarm of arrows that struck their targets with deadly precision. Multiple bodies fell beneath the wooden bridges and staircases that connected the Elven homes amid the great oaks. Still, the attackers came from every direction with the intent of blood and death for this sylvan community of Wood Elves.

From high within the cover of the solid trees throughout the Great Forest of Hilderan, the Elves watched as their wondrous homeland was attacked on four fronts. Within the center of the forest was the golden Shrine of Haloreth, the statue of one of the great Elven wizards of old. A spectacular golden light seemed to perpetually emanate from the statue, touching the trees and filtering up through the leaves to meet the sunlight that streamed down through the leafy crowns of the dense oaks. It was said the servants of Haloreth could manipulate the light, as it was a fraction of the life force left by the great wizard.

The Elves' community had been built into the trees themselves; carved homes with rounded openings, windows, flowers, and vines could be seen throughout the forest. There were several levels climbing ever higher joined by wooden step bridges and spiraling staircases. All the branches and leaves seemed to shimmer constantly, charged by the splendor of the golden light. Normally, it was a place of considerable wildlife, but as the Elves had ascended into the canopy for cover, those animals that were able had wisely followed suit.

The Ogrens, fearsomely large creatures distantly related to Ogres, approached from the north in loose columns approximately one hundred strong. They stomped their oversize feet clumsily causing the very ground to shake and the limbs of trees to tremble. Their dark blue skin distinguished them clearly from their pale cousins. Though they were generally humanoid in appearance, many stood nine feet tall or larger. All were heavily muscled about their neck and arms, with all their excess weight collecting in their stomachs. Large growths and pus-filled warts dotted their bodies, and some were covered with coarse, dark hair. Their huge round snouts housed crooked yellow teeth, and their oversized heads caused them to hunch forward.

The Ogrens had come down from their caves deep in the Morval Mountains, rallied by an unknown evil force. They closed in on the tree houses of the Elves with a speed and agility that belied their girth. Their broad torsos were covered in an amalgam of mismatched armor intermixed with dingy clothing, hides, and furs. Spears were their weapons of choice, yet many carried clubs, maces, and other blunt objects fashioned into weapons.

From the west approached the Goblins—smaller, sinister cousins to Orcs in a hectic disorganized mass but their number seemed endless. They pushed one another forward in wave upon wave. Though not unfriendly to the Ogrens, it was rare indeed for the two races to band together against a common foe. Their greenish-gray skin was covered with dark spots, clearly visible beneath their dull yellow fur. Black eyes squinted out over square snouts and jagged, discolored teeth. Many of them wore segmented metal armor complemented with sharp-edged weapons, mainly swords, axes, and metal spiked maces. Though not tribal like Ogrens, they favored a subterranean habitat where they dwelt in loosely organized bands. Though physically smaller than the Elves, their strength was in their great numbers.

Finally, from the north and east a force of men approached. They were the dreaded Stygian Knights—well known to the Elves but long thought to be extinct—the elite fighting force of the late Pytharian Empire and the Shadow Prince.

From the east, they charged in on horseback, clad in black-plated mail armor under their dark robes. Their metal skins were comprised of heavy, interlocking plates connecting at the joints, and they wore helmets with metal visors. A large, ornate insignia adorned their chests and shields. To those who did not know better, the insignia might appear to be a red dragon, but the Elves knew it to be the symbol of the crimson Hydra, a winged, six-headed beast. It was the symbol of their master who had long since been destroyed. Their warhorses, clad in matching, dark metal-plate barding, were muscular beasts bred for their strength and endurance, and they did not flee despite the arrows that seemed to fly at them from every direction.

From the north, they came on foot, carrying bows with flame-tipped arrows. Firing high from a distance, they set many a tree ablaze. The Elves were not their targets; instead, the Knights concentrated their fire on the magnificent dwellings carved into the great trees. Many of the connecting bridges suffered the brunt of the attacks. Families were separated, and the defenders of the trees could not respond to the danger or come to the aid of the helpless and the unarmed.

Though unprepared for an attack of this magnitude, the Elves fought back with cunning and grace. Volleys of arrows sailing down from high in the branches above found their marks in the chests of beasts and men alike. The Elves could let fly two arrows for every one the humans could fire.

Suddenly, the attackers found themselves prey to ambushes by the unrelenting Elves. Like spiders descending on webs, they swooped down on vines from high within the thick shadows of the leaf-laden branches. With inhuman speed, they dropped down on top of the horsemen, throwing them from their mounts and taking the horses for their own. Once mounted, they nocked their arrows to the string and began rapidly firing back at the Stygian bowmen who assaulted their trees with flaming arrows, bringing down many a Knight.

Wood Elves had fair complexions not unlike those of humans, but their skin was smooth and blemish free. Most had coppery red hair, though golden locks were plentiful among them as well. Though some were tall like men, most were half a foot smaller, but it was their pointed ears, visible even through shoulder-length hair, which distinguished them clearly from humans. In the trees, they were chameleons of brown and green, clothed in bark and leaves, becoming one with their forest environment from any vantage point. Once on the ground, they moved faster than their attackers' eyes could follow, disappearing into the shadows of bushes and trees only to appear from somewhere else, attacking the invaders from behind. Their curved Elven short swords and hunting knives were of such quality that they penetrated even the thickest plate armor of the professional soldiers come to destroy them.

Still, if the legends held true, these dark Stygian Knights were some of the finest fighting men in the lands, and the Elves, while skilled archers and fighters, were not hardened warriors of equal caliber. But the Elves were defending their homes and families, which rallied them together despite overwhelming odds. With merciless speed, they cut the Knights down like they were merely there for target practice. So many fell that the tide began to turn on both the northern and eastern fronts. The human bowmen began to flee, dropping their weapons in their haste to escape.

The Elves had taken dozens of horses, but in doing so, they had made themselves more visible, no longer protected by the concealment and sanctuary of the trees. The Ogrens seized the opportunity and struck, launching spears at the mounted Elves. Though they missed many, the Ogrens managed to create enough of a distraction among the Elves for the remaining dark cavalrymen to hack at them from the rear and from the sides.

The creatures' numbers were vast, and the onslaught of Elven arrows lessened just enough for them to get a foothold at the base of many trees.

Soon the Goblins were in the trees themselves, hacking and slashing their way into the Elven homes. Climbing ever upward throughout the aged trees, the beasts closed on the helpless families of the Elven hunters who had assaulted them from afar.

The Elves could no longer focus on the attackers below. All their attention was turned to the creatures making their way up the trees. Elven archers cut them down from so high in the trees the archers seemed invisible. The invaders took advantage of the opportunity and charged in below, taking axes to many of the trees at their bases.

The smaller trees began to shake violently as the Ogrens shoved and wrenched at them, throwing some of the Elven hunters to the ground. Before they could scurry to their feet, the Elves were slain by hundreds of Goblins that gleefully stabbed them to death and jumped up and down victoriously on their bodies.

The horseman had replenished their ranks by hundreds now. Torches in hand, they thundered through the forest, launching the flaming brands up into the Elven homes as they rode through. The cries of women and children could now be heard throughout the forest. Knights surrounded the base of the trees and handed more torches to the Ogrens and Goblins, who formed a chain about the stairs still unhindered with fire. They hurled torches in all directions until even the brilliant golden light of the shrine itself began to diminish as the flames spread.

It was in this moment—when the enemy nearly had them and the trees writhed in the clutches of the flames—that the golden light sprang to life in defiance of the invaders. The light became an all-encompassing brilliance so strong that many of the Goblins and Ogrens in the trees lost their footing and fell, as they tried frantically to shield their eyes against the intense brightness. All activity seemed to cease as the marauding hordes were momentarily blinded.

In that instant, a single Elf appeared from the center of the largest oak. Clad in white robes, he was unarmed, his hair golden as if one with the light itself and his eyes were like green flame. He spoke in a strangely soothing tone, yet there was mettle within his words.

"You cannot enter here, remnants of the Pytharian Empire," he thundered. "Nor you denizens of the Morval Mountains. I am Lothinir, servant of the Shrine of Haloreth, and while there is breath within me, you shall come no further into this place. Heed my words and withdraw while you still can."

The light intensified. Lothinir raised his hand, and the light shone with such splendor that the invaders could barely take their hands from their eyes. The Ogrens and Goblins backed away, completely removing themselves from the trees. The horsemen began to pull back on their reins, giving ground as well until without warning, a resonating, raspy voice rang out from far behind the dark cavalry.

"*That there is breath within you . . . is a situation that can be remedied, Lothinir.*"

The riders gave way as a lone black horse approached through their ranks from the rear. Its rider was cloaked in a hooded black robe with crimson trim. Upon closer inspection, it was clear that his robe was not composed of fabric, but rather a black chain mesh that protected his back and shoulders and fastened in the center of his chest with a large gold clamp engraved with a red Hydra.

The steed trotted slowly forward, head down, approaching the resplendent Elf. When the fearsome rider reached the front of his ranks, he dismounted and walked slowly forward until he was face-to-face with Lothinir. Traces of gold metal could be seen flashing beneath his hood. Slowly, mockingly he lifted his covered head to face him, revealing a helmet of gold from which hung a mask of golden metal mesh that covered his face.

Lothinir's eyes widened in recognition. "No, it cannot be. It is not possible—"

"*The realms of possibility are vast indeed, Elf,*" the figure replied. An insidious, bitter laugh slid from his lips like acid burning away the air. In the blink of an eye, his arm shot forward and a ray of black energy struck the glowing Elf in the chest with such force and shock that it threw his head back and his arms out to his sides as if he were to be nailed to a tree in that position. His form became completely enshrouded in black energy. The Elven priest remained thus for a seemingly endless moment until, finally, the ebony energy subsided and released him.

Lothinir's head came forward as he fell to his knees. He swayed for a moment, and then fell flat on his face at the feet of the dark-robed stranger. In the same instant that his life left his body, the brilliant golden light completely vanished. There was stillness throughout the forest as all eyes stared at the dark-robed figure.

Smirks and snarls of laughter came from the creatures surrounding the area.

"*Sword*," the dark-robed figure ordered, extending an open hand to one of the humans nearby. The man swiftly obeyed, drawing his weapon and placing the hilt into the menacing figure's hand.

Grasping the sword, the figure placed his black armored boot on the back of Lothinir's head and, leaning his weight forward, immersed the Elf's head in the mud. Then, in one terrible stroke, he decapitated him. A moment later, he bent down and lifted the head by the long golden locks and held it high, turning to the Ogrens and Goblins. Instantly they erupted into cheers and war cries, beating their weapons together and working themselves into a frenzied bloodlust. The dark figure then looked upward and held the severed head high so the muddy face could be seen by the surviving Elves still hiding in the trees.

From deep in the woods, a lone Elven hunter named Lorin Faldor had managed to hide, just far enough away that he had been able to remain undetected. Tears fell from the corners of his eyes as he witnessed the battle and the horror of Lothinir's death.

Lorin overheard as Lothinir's executioner tossed the head to one of the men and said, "*Place his head on their sacred shrine, and kill all the rest.*"

With that, the dark stranger mounted and rode away to the north. A surge of fear and guilt and a sense of betrayal overwhelmed Lorin all at once. He could follow and attempt to kill him, but what chance would *he* have if Lothinir had been so easily vanquished? He was afraid of dying as well, and he hated his fear. There were other lands that needed to be warned and other lives hung in the balance despite his selfish need for vengeance. He would be no good to them dead.

Lorin continued to watch as the remaining marauders slew the families that still lived in the trees, cut off from escape by the fire and the murderous horde. Lorin stood horror stricken, unable to comprehend how the world had spawned creatures such as this.

The Ogrens and Goblins threw Elf children from high in the trees to the ground below or into the fires for amusement. How they all laughed, Lorin could not begin to understand. Any who survived the falls had their skulls bashed in by armored boot heels of the men. A handful of surviving hunters were made to watch as the women's throats were slit, but only after being ravaged again and again.

When Lorin could bear no more, he turned and ran southwest toward Wrenford.

The dark-hooded figure watched from afar as the flames continued to grow, consuming the forest. He listened with an almost intoxicating gratification at the death screams, even as they became fewer and harder to hear. His gaze drifted southwest as if he could see right through the forests and hills to the small Kingdom of Wrenford.

It is not time yet, he thought. *The time will come soon.*

He found himself strangely patient with the idea. He would not even have to be present when it happened. He would have other, more pressing matters to attend to, but all would know it was he who prepared the way for their deaths. This small fire in the woods was nothing compared to what he would unleash upon the rest of the world.

Chapter 2

That same night, two men sat in the corner of a dimly lit tavern somewhere on the outskirts of the city of Wrenford. The comely young dark-haired waitress began to place chairs atop the many vacant wooden tables. A surly, bald-headed bartender wiped a long white rag across the rectangular bar, eyeing the two fellows that were preventing him from closing up for the night. One of them was well known throughout Wrenford and the surrounding lands. Rumor had it he was a hero and had been appointed Baron by the King years ago. However reluctantly, the bartender acknowledged exceptions had to be made for such as him. Heroes were very rare things these days.

Both men sat in a shabby little booth. The table was decorated by several empty tankards, which the men had been merrily draining of their ale throughout the night. The one on the right appeared tall and confident even as he raised his last cup of ale to his lips. His long blond hair fell unkempt in the manner of a seasoned man across his broad shoulders. The flickering light of the dying candle reflected off his brilliant silver-plated mail armor, a metal skin that completely encased the man from the shoulders down. When the light struck it at a certain angle, the armor almost seemed to respond with a glow of its own. A small insignia depicting a town at the base of a massive waterfall—the symbol of his homeland—was magnificently engraved into the right shoulder.

Plated mail as exceptional as his was incredibly rare, even for officers of the watch or guard, the bartender mused. He remembered seeing the famous Captain of Wrenford's Guard a time or two and even he did not have such armor.

His face, well-tanned by the sun, conveyed a pride which shone undimmed through his bright blue eyes. About his neck, there rested a silver cross pendant, representing his steadfast religious ties. At his waist, the beautifully forged hilt of a great sword rested within a jeweled scabbard. A frost-white diamond was etched into the center of the hilt. His name was Lark Royale.

Across from him sat his brother, Archangel. The younger of the two, Archangel was an experienced guide and tracker though he preferred the term "Ranger." His hard features would lead one to believe that he was the elder of the two. His dark brown hair was pulled back into a ponytail. His deep-set dark eyes probed the small establishment as he, too, raised a cup to his lips. Small droplets of ale moistened the short gray whiskers about his chin and neck, which gave him a scruffy appearance.

His brown leather armor allowed him far swifter movement than the heavy, cumbersome plated mail of his brother. He kept two items strapped across his back so they would be close at all times: the first was a long sword sheathed in leather, the second a somewhat fragile-looking short bow.

As the night had passed, the two had reminisced about their most recent journey from which they had just returned. Now Lark, emptying his mug and placing it on the table, gazed upon his brother with a look of affection.

"Archangel, you've helped me in a time of great personal need. I feel this journey has, in a sense, brought us closer as brothers. I shall never forget it. I shall always be there for you whenever you need me."

Feeling uncomfortable with such a display, Archangel did not meet his brother's eyes. Lark had always been more sentimental, doubly so now because of the generous amount of ale he had consumed. *Strange,* Archangel thought, *that while Paladins lived by the strictest code free of vices, the one they are allowed is drink.* However, even that was only allowed in celebration of righteous deeds or quests completed on behalf of their deity or sacred order.

Archangel leaned back and reflected on his brother's words. He knew to be a Paladin took the deepest commitment and the most serious mind. It took the sacrifice of all material wealth and placing your life completely in the hands of your deity. It required an indomitable faith to carry out a life of lawful deeds in order to maintain the highest level of nobility and bravery. Paladins could refuse no challenge or quest put to them. They could never harm the innocent, nor by omission of action, allow anyone less fortunate to be harmed. There were so terribly few of them left in the world; few men could handle the stringent lifestyle. They were forever sworn to the quest of crusading against evil in all its guises. Some were driven mad by this quest, some corrupted, and still others driven from the path of their chosen deities by the fruit of temptation. Indeed, his brother was a rare being. Archangel's respect, admiration, and love for him were unbounded.

But Archangel also knew his brother's love for talking would only intensify unless he did something to forestall it. "Lark, of course you would have done the same for me. We are brothers. You would never have rested until you brought justice to those who destroyed your order. But now that's over with. Your holy brothers can rest in peace, and there is no need to thank me."

The two men smiled wearily at each other. As Archangel took his last sip, he nodded to Lark, who threw a few silver pieces on the table. Both men helped each other to their feet and stumbled outside to their waiting horses.

Archangel watched as Lark struggled to get on his black steed. The animal knew its master well and seemed to bend down in anticipation of Lark's condition.

Once both had mounted, they began a slow trot down the path that would take them home. The warm breeze made it difficult for the brothers to stay awake as they continued north. They spoke no longer, as both men's thoughts were clouded with visions of getting to bed.

Some thirty minutes later, Archangel recognized the border of their land. Their home, built of dark oak, was surrounded by overgrown shrubs, which made the house appear smaller than it actually was. To the left of the house stood a smaller wooden structure, a stable that Archangel had built a year earlier. Both men shared a love of horses and cared for their steeds well.

Lark dismounted. As soon as he touched the ground beneath him, he stumbled, disoriented, but quickly regained his balance. Taking a deep breath, he looked up at Archangel and handed him the reins.

"The ale has taken its toll, brother," Lark said with a chuckle. "Perhaps you could see to the horses for me? In truth, I doubt I could make it to the stable."

Archangel smiled and watched his brother walk toward the house as he led the horses away.

As he neared the front door of his home, Lark became vaguely aware of a somewhat unpleasant feeling in his gut. He thought nothing of it as he fumbled about his waist for the key. As he threw the door open, he was immediately overcome with a strange scent almost like freshly dug earth. He fumbled about for a moment to light the lantern near the door.

Suddenly, he heard movement, and when he looked up, he could scarcely believe the ghastly sight before him. Hanging upside down from the ceiling were two skeletal corpses well past the point of decay covered in dirt. A dark shrouded man stood holding the torch to the right of the grizzly scene. He had a black silk cloth over his mouth and head. Only the man's eyes and nose were visible.

"Greetings, Lark Royale of Osprey Falls," the stranger said in a harsh unforgiving tone. "I thought I would arrange a family reunion for you and your brother. Your parents look pleased to see you, wouldn't you say? You see I've brought them back to you. Rather thoughtful on my part, don't you think? My employer wishes you to suffer like no other man has ever suffered before all is said and done."

Lark tried to focus, his mind was sluggishly racing as this form of a man he'd never met just told him that his parents, killed in a raid that destroyed his town long ago, were hanging here before him now and this was the man responsible for unearthing their long-buried corpses.

"What kind of cowardly animal robs graves in the middle of the night?" He tried to grab his sword hilt quickly but never got it more than a few inches out of the scabbard.

Before Lark could focus to take action, he suddenly felt a cord around his throat and heard a crack of a whip as it wrapped around his legs. The intruder was not alone. Struggling, Lark spied men to his left and right.

The men quickly dragged Lark to the ground and held him fast. Pinned on his back now, Lark could not utter a sound; one of the men clutched at Lark's throat, strangling the life from him. He did not see the form of the shadow-man standing over him as he was fading.

"I have a memento of this occasion for you, Mr. Royale," said the masked attacker.

The dark form drew a short sword and plunged it downward into Lark's right calf, through armor, bone, and muscle and into the floor itself. The intense pain of the blow was the last sensation Lark Royale would feel that night.

Archangel made sure all the horses had plenty of water and feed since he knew they would sleep late the following morning. After securing the stable doors, Archangel made his way toward the front door of his home. A light flickered through the window. Archangel was glad to see that Lark had at least been sober enough to light the lantern within so he wouldn't have to enter in total darkness.

As he reached for the doorknob, he heard a slight shuffling sound emanating from within. As he opened the door, he spoke, "Lark, don't tell me you've fallen. I didn't think you had that much to dr—"

Archangel felt himself being driven to the floor as something struck the back of his head. He was on his knees now, and with glazed vision, he looked upward. All he saw was a sword hilt as it struck him square across the forehead. Somehow, he was still conscious. On his back, he looked up and saw what might have been the form of a man. All that was clearly visible was the color black; the rest was blurred. His ears were ringing loudly, but he heard what sounded like a human voice shouting down at him.

"Not yet, Archangel! Don't you pass out on me yet! First, I want you to know that your mother and father died on their knees, just like you will!"

Archangel felt his right hand go numb and turned his head to see a blade being driven through it. He barely felt the pain. Again, he heard the voice.

"Perhaps we should crucify you in front of your whelp of a brother! You're as worthless to us as your parents hanging up there!"

Archangel felt a gloved hand grab his ponytail, forcing his gaze upward to encompass the two hanging skeletons.

"Say goodbye, now. My employer does insist on 'ruthlessness' and 'thoroughness,' in that order!"

In that instant, Archangel felt as if his head were being crushed, and everything went dark. The faint scent of oil seemed to be all about him.

Algernon awoke suddenly and sat up. The old man put his hand on his chest beneath his silvery beard as if that alone could slow his ragged heartbeat. He concentrated, trying to slow his breathing.

The dreams had started months ago. Each night, they increased in both intensity and sheer dreadfulness. Preparations had begun, but things were escalating too quickly. Still, even he and the King did not know the full extent of the enemy's reach. They did know that, no matter how terrible the outcome they imagined, the reality would be far worse.

Algernon rose, quickly washed his face with water from the basin on the night table, and threw on a brown cloak. Grabbing a gnarled walking stick, he threw open the doors to his chamber and practically raced down the long hallway, rushing toward the King's private room.

As he burst through the single door, to his surprise, he found the King sitting up and awake in his chair by the window. Algernon's sudden entrance in the middle of the night barely caused him to stir.

Thargelion, the Wizard-King, as he was first called so many centuries ago, turned to face Algernon. He appeared as an old withered Elf with the lonely look of an ancient history stored deep in his far-reaching glance. Algernon, who had been with him longer than any other, inwardly could not bear to see him as he was but could never let the old King see it.

"I must leave at first light," Algernon said urgently. "The dreams . . . are so terrible my lord. I must try to save those I can and find what others can be found. I will return as soon as possible."

Algernon waited for a reply, but the King said nothing. Finally, Thargelion's gaze returned to the window, so Algernon slowly made his way across the chamber and collapsed in the armchair across from the King.

"We waited too long," Thargelion all but whispered at last. "We should have acted sooner. Pretend as we may, we cannot stop what's coming. Perhaps no one can. I'm afraid, Algernon."

"But a King *should* be afraid, Thargelion," Algernon replied. "Always afraid. He should be afraid of the darkness creeping in his forests, afraid of the discontented whispers of his people, afraid of plots hatched within his own court and among the men of his own guard within the walls of his own castle. He must learn to live with fear—always—so that his people need not ever fear as he does."

"Must it always be so?" Thargelion asked.

The Sage sat back in the chair. "You asked me that over a millennium ago. Do you remember what I told you so long ago?"

Thargelion allowed himself a hint of a smile as he recalled, "*If ruling were easy, then anyone could do it.* After a thousand years, can you think of nothing original to say, old man?"

"Wisdom has no time limit, my lord," Algernon said with a smile.

The smile left Thargelion's face quickly. "Once again, I must ask a few of the very finest to risk all while I lie and conceal truth after truth from them. And what of my people, the people of Wrenford? How many more must I kill?"

Algernon sat up quickly. "My lord, you've saved this world and brought peace and prosperity to ages of generations. None can deny it."

"None can deny we always knew this day was coming either, can they?" The King sat up and brought his full countenance to bear on his closest friend and advisor. "I wonder, now that we have come full circle in this sordid tale, you and I, will there ever be an end to it?"

"Take heart, my lord. All things have their ending in the fullness of time . . . even you and I. And sometimes life surprises us."

Thargelion eased his head back against the padding of his chair. The two great friends sat together in silence for the remainder of the night.

Chapter 3

Later that night...

Two figures could be seen striding up the center of the main trail that led to the open land just west of the Kingdom of Wrenford. The one on the right, garbed in a flowing brown robe, towered over his younger-looking companion, who was clad in leather armor and browns and greens suited to blending in with the forest. Occasionally, the younger traveler would stop to examine something on the path ahead. The end of summer was nearing, but the dew still glistened upon the night grass.

As moonlight shone upon the trail, the features of Kael Dracksmere were thrown into dim illumination. He stood six and a half feet tall, his thin frame masked well in the shadows of his robe. His brown beard was shot through with streaks of gray, and the creases about his eyes and mouth were indicative of a man near fifty, though Kael was, in fact, well into his sixties. Salt-and-pepper hair comprised his receding hairline, which was additionally marked by the beginnings of a bald spot in the center of the back of his head. In his right hand he held a wooden staff, bound with iron and set with silver rivets. About his waist were various pouches and sacks containing arcane spell components.

Kael was a Druid, a protector of nature. He was a priest of sorts, charged with the care of the wilderness. Druids were responsible for overseeing the lands and all plant and animal life that inhabited them. Mother Nature herself was their deity and granted them special powers through their faith that enabled them to carry out their mission. There were times when the old Druid wished he did not have such powers.

Beside Kael walked his adopted daughter, Elenari Moonraven, a half-Elven girl who had grown up in Alluviam, the homeland of the Elves. She stood almost a foot smaller than Kael, and her chiseled features and pointed ears displayed her Elven heritage. Even half-Elves aged much slower than humans, and while she appeared much younger, Elenari would easily outlive Kael. Fiercely beautiful, she had shoulder-length blonde hair and green eyes. Her dark cloak flowed in the breeze, settling loosely over the feminine contours of her body.

Few people, save Kael, realized just how dangerous this young woman really was. It was Kael who had found her twenty years earlier, alone and starving in Sylvanwood Forest. He brought her to the outskirts of Alluviam to the remote temple of the Kenshari, the sword saints. There she was raised, in a most unique fashion, to master the martial disciplines. The Kenshari, as a rule, accepted fewer than five students a year and taught them ancient combat arts passed down from Elven masters who had lived thousands of years, learning and training. Typically, of those chosen, there was only one student every few years who was allowed to stay long enough to attain the rank of master. Elenari was the first and only student not of pure Elven blood ever to be accepted. She was also the youngest female to ever achieve the rank of master.

The Kenshari only accepted beginning students five years old or younger. Their physical training regimen was said to be more rigorous than any in existence. While the outside world always considered the Elves to be master bowmen, it was the sword that the Kenshari had learned to make an extension of their bodies. The master craftsman of the Kenshari, an individual whose identity was secret to all save the High Master, would forge a sword for each new student, which would be completed before his or her very first lesson. They were showed the blade and told that if they could achieve the rank of master, they would be awarded the sword and offered a choice: to remain at the temple and teach, or leave the temple and be free. Legend said that Kenshari swords could cut through any substance, and were themselves unbreakable. The sacred blade forged for Elenari was called *Eros-Arthas*, which in the common tongue meant "Celestial Avenger."

Elenari, or "Nari" as Kael often called her, was adept at woodcraft, hunting, and all manner of outdoor skills. Additionally, she was exceptionally skilled as a tracker. Having a natural affinity for animals, she often enjoyed their company more than that of most Elves or humans, with the obvious exception of Kael. Though Kael had adopted her, neither of them acknowledged the distinction and referred to each other often as "father" and "daughter."

As the two continued south, Nari turned to her father. "You seem pre-occupied, Father. What's been on your mind the last few miles?" she asked in a melodic tone characteristic of her heritage.

Lost in thought, Kael barely realized he was being spoken to. "Yes, forgive me. I was just thinking of how long it has been since I was able to enjoy the simple pleasures of life." He did not need to look at her to know her face had taken the shape of a curious frown. "The things we take for granted, Nari, like watching a sunrise, seeing rainbows form after a spring shower, simple things, which surround us in everyday life and we all too often fail to appreciate."

He glanced over at her and saw the curious frown right where he had expected it.

"Since when have you thought of sunsets and rainbows?" Nari asked. Her eyebrow slanted in puzzlement. "What of the great adventures you have taken part in? You are a lord and hero in this land."

Kael was, in fact, a Baron of Wrenford, appointed by the King many years ago. Although he did not like titles and would prefer that no one refer to him as Lord Dracksmere, there were always some who did so regardless, out of respect.

Kael placed an arm around his daughter's shoulders and smiled. "Adventuring is for the young and brave, my dear," he replied dismissively.

Elenari stopped and turned toward him. "You're not old, and you have great powers!"

Kael stopped her before she could continue. "Daughter, I'm tired and my power has lessened with time; I fear my great adventures are long over. It's time to rest now. It is the way of things. It is what we talked about. It is as it should be."

Kael continued forward on the trail, leaving a confused Elenari trailing in his wake.

Even as he continued on, despite what he had said, Kael had an uncomfortable feeling within himself. It was a feeling that gripped his very soul. It was a sensation, which he neither understood nor revealed to anyone, even

Nari. It had, in truth, been building for weeks, and he sensed whatever it was would soon come to the surface.

Suddenly, Nari ran ahead of her father, crouched low to the trail, and put up a hand of warning. Kael immediately stopped and waited; he had seen his daughter like this before and knew something was wrong.

Nari moved noiselessly off the trail into the thick brush to the right, disappearing completely from view. She returned only moments later with a look of concern etched upon her face. She spoke in a whisper. "There was a figure in the bushes, but it vanished leaving no discernable trace. I'm sure there's someone watching us."

"Well, my dear," the Druid answered as the two of them continued forward, "in that event, I suggest we proceed with caution."

It was just over the next rise that both would find solace in the comfort of their home. After a few hours, the tense feeling of being watched had eased, and Elenari had openly dismissed the threat as possibly an animal, though inwardly she still had her doubts. Her senses were almost never wrong. Still, she could almost taste the cool ale that awaited them in their stores at home.

Kael, too, was still unnerved. He felt something stirring deep within him, a warm tingling that quickly turned into a sharp, cutting pain. He stopped and held fast to Nari's arm, startling her for a moment.

"Kael! Father! What is it? Are you all right?" Nari pressed for an answer.

"Yes . . ." the Druid replied, even though he knew that he was not. "Yes, everything is fine now. I just became dizzy for a moment. Really, Nari, I'm fine."

Elenari, still unsure, looked over the hill to see an unusual illumination swelling upward from below. Curious, she hastened her father ahead to find the source of the strange light.

From atop the hill, they both overlooked the small valley surrounded by tall oaks and thick brush. Their home was nestled in the center. Underneath the starlit sky of the deepening night, some fourteen men stood inside a wide circle of fifteen standing torches. A huge fire blazed in their midst.

Instantly Kael knew that, although he had never witnessed such a ceremony, a challenge had been issued and must be answered.

Faster than words, Nari went for her bow, only to be held back by her father. "No, Elenari," the Druid said calmly. "You have nothing to fear."

One of the hooded figures broke from the circle, making his way up to where father and daughter stood. Embers crackled and smoke billowed from the great blaze as silence gripped the open clearing. As the stranger neared, a look of recognition crossed Nari's face.

"Galin? What are you . . ?"

Nari lost her words as she saw the look on Galin's face. Galin was the Druid charged with watching over the Kingdom of Alluviam and he had been their friend for some years. Even his handsome youthful face could not hide it. It was a look of fearful remorse. The moonlight shone on the three of them as they reached one another, almost like a spotlight on some bizarre stage.

Galin stood before Kael, and their eyes locked. "Forgive me," Galin said reluctantly. "I am sorry. I've been searching for you for some time. It would seem, however, that I'm too late. I had hoped to warn you of this, but you were nowhere to be found."

Elenari could no longer restrain herself. "What in blazes is going on here? Who are these people and why are they on our land?"

Kael knew the answers to her questions, but he remained silent. There could be no explanation that would ease Nari's concern. He thought inwardly to himself, *No, not now, not here. I don't belong to them, I never have.*

Galin saw the inward torment overwhelming Kael. He was helpless to aid him, which was a feeling he hated above all others. He knew he must now tell Kael that which the old Druid already knew. "The Druids of the council, the Grand Druid, and Oblik himself are below. They wait for us. Talic has been aware of you for many years. You have become much known among the order. Tales of Kael, Baron of Wrenford, have spread over the lands. By our laws, Talic has rightfully issued challenge to you with the approval of the Druid Council."

Nari interrupted. "Druid Council? Kael has never been part of the official order—as well you know, Galin—nor has he any ties to them. What are you talking about? 'Rightful challenge'? They have no such power over him, either!"

Galin continued, ignoring the outburst. "Do you understand the nature of the challenge and the consequences of a refusal?"

"Consequences?" Nari cried. "What are you talking about? He's not answering any challenge!"

Nari turned to her father. Kael, seeing the anguish in her eyes, placed a comforting hand to her cheek. There would be no answer that could comfort her. He knew she must be made to accept whatever was to happen, no matter the outcome. He latched on to Nari's arm with a vice-like grip, startling her. "Come, my daughter," he said sadly. "No more questions, please. Escort me down, for I wish you to be my witness. It is my right."

Elenari escorted her father down the hill in silent disbelief. The Druid, Galin, walked alongside them. When they came within ten feet of the circle, Kael took hold of both Nari's shoulders and brought her face close to his. "This is not what I wanted, but you must do as I say, Elenari, and know that, whatever is to come, you are my daughter and I love you." He kissed her gently on the forehead. "Now, remove all of your weapons and stand back."

Nari hesitated.

"Do it!" Kael commanded. "We will not speak again until what is about to happen comes to pass. And one last thing, my dear child . . . I've always been very proud of you."

With a last look and hint of a smile, the old Druid turned away from his daughter and entered the circle of flame through the narrow entrance the others had left for him.

Like all the Druids around him, Kael was unaffected by the intensity of the fire all about him, though perspiration dripped from his face and beard. He did not seem to notice as Galin calmly left his side to fill the opening in the circle.

As he walked, Kael's legs seemed to be dragging, as if an invisible weight were being placed upon them. *Perhaps it is fear,* he thought, *or possibly just age.*

He stopped several feet away from the two flickering shadows that awaited him near the central blaze. One he knew well through legend. His name was Oblik. He was one of the High Elders, a lofty tree spirit who presided over such ceremonies. He appeared as a gray-bearded, wizened human. All-seeing emerald eyes lit his deathly pale face. He leaned heavily with both hands on a fine-grained, beautifully carved oak staff bound with bronze.

The other man was Talic, the Grand Druid—the highest officiating priest of nature throughout the lands. This man Kael knew by name only, and it was he who was the cause of this gathering. Talic's gaze met Kael's, leaving an imprint of burning ambition and resentment. Kael knew that, over the years, he had attained a certain reputation, a reputation that Talic perhaps perceived as a threat to his power. Kael felt such fear was unfounded, since his distaste for the politics of the Druid society was well known.

Still, all Druids, though not subject to the council's dictates, were subject to the rite of challenge. A refusal meant to immediately be stripped of all granted powers and protections. Upon achieving the rank of Druid, there were only two ways to increase in power: The first was to be the chosen successor to a Druid of the council or the Grand Druid. The second was to initiate the rite of challenge.

How rare, Kael thought, *for a Grand Druid to challenge one of a lesser rank and status*. In fact, it had been decades since a challenge for combat had taken place. Power had been passed peacefully from Grand Druid to successor for some time. The Druids had tried, with some success, to shed the old barbaric days of mortal combat between one another.

Kael continued forward at an agonizingly slow pace as a torrent of thoughts and emotions raced through his mind. He could see Talic clearly now. The Grand Druid stood nearly as tall as he. Unlike the other Druids present who wore robes of black and gray, Talic was clad in a robe of resplendent bronze with gold trim. A coal-black staff of ash rested in his left hand. His hood seemed to envelop his face so that only his pitch-colored beard was visible. He was many years younger than Kael and outweighed him by several pounds. Though his frame was broad, he was by no means cumbersome in appearance.

As Kael came within five feet of the Grand Druid, Talic stepped forward and removed his hood, unveiling his face of polished skin extending to a bald pate and deep-set, penetrating brown eyes. He peered at Kael, sizing him up, probing for weakness.

"You have been a thorn in my side for far too long, Kael Dracksmere," Talic snarled. "I will not wait for you to come against me as you grow more powerful. I wish to rid myself of you and of the rumors and idle chatter amongst our society."

Kael responded calmly, his eyes locked with Talic's, "Is this what our Sacred Mother has told you in the winds that you must do to best serve her? If you believe that, then you prove yourself to be a fool instead of a leader."

"Enough!" Oblik spoke in hallowed tones, "Do you accept challenge according to our ways, Kael of Wrenford?"

The other priests present listened intently for a response, each of them separating so they formed a perfect circle symmetrical to that of the standing torches.

How easy, Kael thought, *it would be to simply walk away*. He would lose his powers, but he might finally find peace of mind. He might be able to be the father to Elenari that she deserved.

Playing with the thought, he unexpectedly found himself meeting the venerable one's gaze with a look of frightening determination. In that instant, something caught hold of his soul, and he knew he was needed again. It was almost as if the land itself called out through him and answered, "I accept the challenge!"

His voice thundered through the flames so that even Elenari, struggling to see what was happening, felt a surge of pride as she heard the courageous cry of her father.

Oblik's raspy voice echoed throughout the clearing. "So be it known to all present that the challenge has been accepted. Combat may be strictly physical, magical, or encompassing both. If physical combat is chosen, shape-shifting will be disallowed. Once combat begins, no outside interference will be tolerated!"

Suddenly the torches died down, and Elenari found herself staring directly into the eyes of Oblik. A chill rippled through her, and she shuddered, knowing the ancient priest was referring solely to her. Though she did not fear him for her own sake, she did fear the consequences to her father if she chose to act.

"Combat will take place within this circle," Oblik continued. "If either combatant breaks the circle, he will be declared the loser and forever banished from our society. Combat is to be non-mortal unless both combatants agree otherwise. Now you must choose!"

The High Elder struck his staff against the ground twice, and the torches seemed to burn quieter in anticipation. The very leaves of the surrounding trees seemed to brush against one another, almost whispering their thoughts in defiance of Oblik's decree.

Talic, a harsh expression on his face, staring at Kael uttered, "Combat will be physical and to the death!"

Without hesitation, Kael responded, "So be it; to the death!"

Kael looked to Oblik, who was unable to hide the look of disgust on his face. "You will allow this?"

"It is done, it cannot be undone," the old tree spirit replied as his green eyes turned their harsh gaze upon Kael.

Oblik then began to speak in the secret language, which no outsider may know, unique only to Druids, "*Sha-Norc-Ra Ne-Testa-Lall.*"

With that, four of the surrounding Druids entered the circle at the northern, eastern, western, and southern points. Each man placed a weapon on the ground: To the north, a scimitar; to the east, a staff; to the west, a club; and to the south, a sickle. These were the ancestral weapons of the Druids.

Kael quickly remembered why his dislike for the Druid society was so strong. This ceremony, shrouded in custom and antiquity, was nothing more than a savage brutal conflict. *Strange,* he thought, *that they care so deeply for the lands, plants, animals, yet they have not evolved beyond harming one another over petty jealousies and power struggles.* The world, though wonderfully full of sacred life, was indeed a strange place. However, whatever he thought, he knew that only one man would emerge from such a conflict.

Oblik motioned with his right hand, and both Talic's and Kael's staves and their spell components were removed from their possession. Talic then took position at the north end of the circle while Kael proceeded to the south end. Both men then looked up at Oblik.

From outside the circle, Elenari watched helplessly as time seemed to stand still in the land of Wrenford. She was forced to remain a spectator, when every fiber of her existence told her she should force her way into the circle and demand of this Oblik why her father must fight to the death, and that, if the answer was not sufficient, she herself should defend Kael, or die trying. Still, above all, her respect for what Kael had instructed her to do restrained her, more so even than fear of Oblik's wrath.

For the final time that night, Oblik's staff struck the ground signaling the beginning of mortal combat.

Talic was a blur as, in one motion, he grabbed the scimitar behind him and sprang forward toward Kael.

Somehow, Kael was faster. Sickle in hand, he rushed to meet his opponent. At the center of the circle, the two opponents met, hands clenched about their weapons, simultaneously swinging and cutting into each other, drawing back bloodstained weapons. Unfazed by the gash to his right side, Talic reeled about for a counterattack as Kael, with a slashed right shoulder, spun around in synchronicity. Sickle and scimitar met and locked together as both men struggled to gain the advantage, neither giving ground. Then, in a show of strength, Talic shoved Kael backward, knocking him to the ground. As Kael's head hit the ground, he felt the sickle slide out of his hand. He looked up to see Talic drilling downward with a lethal swing. Again, Kael was somehow faster, rolling to his right to avoid the deadly blow.

Nari could not suppress the gasp of dismay that escaped her lips as she watched the near-fatal blow.

Even as Talic's weapon struck the ground, Kael was already picking himself up. Before Talic could recover himself, Kael kicked out the back of his left knee, unbalancing the Grand Druid and forcing him to the ground. Kael scrambled to his left, only a few paces away from the club to the west. He quickly snatched the club and turned to find Talic suddenly on his feet and facing him. Kael saw blood flowing down Talic's right leg as Talic, in turn, observed the bloody shoulder of Kael.

Abruptly, Talic attacked, sweeping the scimitar in an arc toward Kael's head. Kael was prepared, and he lifted his club in a blocking position. The impact was so great that, to the surprise of both fighters, the scimitar imbedded itself into the club. Kael did not waste a moment. Pressing his advantage, he quickly swung around to his left with all his strength, throwing Talic, who still clung to his weapon, several feet across the ground so that he landed, headfirst, in the ceremonial fire.

Sticks and embers crackled loudly as the blaze doubled in size. A gust of wind fed the flames even more, so that Talic's form was completely consumed within the fire and Kael lost sight of him.

Kael hastened to free the imbedded scimitar from the club, which Talic had released upon entering the flames. He knew the fire could not injure a fellow Druid; he would only have a few moments. Freeing the blade and throwing the club aside, he began to circle the fire, desperately looking for any sign of movement within the flames.

Without warning, Talic hurled himself out of the inferno, tackling Kael head on. Forcing his left hand under Kael's throat, Talic bent him over in a headlock.

In desperation, Kael, gasping for air, dropped his weapon and tried with both hands to free himself from the strangling grip.

"Perhaps I was wrong to fear you," Talic whispered to him as he struggled in vain to free himself. "You're too old and weak to have ever been any real threat to me."

Talic, closing the fingers of his right hand, landed two sharp blows squarely to Kael's face. Kael staggered as Talic released him from the headlock, and Talic took a handful of the old Druid's hair in both hands and brought Kael's face sharply down, striking it against his knee.

Blood spurted from Kael's face and nose as he felt himself falling endlessly backward to the earth. The collision drove the breath out of him from deep within his chest. Eyes closed, reaching with his left hand, Kael suddenly felt Talic's hands clenched around his neck. He felt himself slipping into darkness.

Talic's hushed words were bitter and burned with resentment. "May you join our Sacred Mother, Dracksmere. Let your death give life to her sacred world around us. You old fool."

It was then that Kael's left hand found the object it so vainly sought. His strength waning, Kael managed to lash out with the singed log he had seized from the flames, smashing it across Talic's right temple.

The log splintered across Talic's head and the Grand Druid rolled away, groaning in pain.

The surrounding Druids watched in awe as the two men valiantly tried to regain their strength. Talic, blood running down the side of his face, struggled to rise only to slip back down to the ground again. Kael, trying to catch his breath, could not maintain his equilibrium and fought even to remain on his knees.

Finding his second wind, Kael recklessly stumbled eastward toward the staff. Talic recovered his senses just enough to spot the old Druid making his move and saw his chance.

Kael's hands found the staff. Out of the corner of his eye, he saw Talic trying to get to his feet. Pushing himself forward, Kael watched Talic fall to one knee, and he quickened his pace. Somehow, he found the strength to raise the staff in anticipation of Talic's vulnerability.

Just as Kael came within striking distance of Talic's head, Talic's right hand shot up in a sweeping motion, releasing a hail of dirt into the air that obscured Kael's vision. Taking advantage of the old Druid's disorientation, Talic rose to wrench the staff from Kael's grasp, bringing the narrow end of the staff into Kael's stomach. As the older Druid doubled over, Talic delivered a crushing blow across Kael's face with the broad end of the staff.

Again, Kael went to the ground. This time, he barely moved, a huge bloody gash on his cheek. After an agonizing moment, Kael bravely pulled himself up so that he was on his hands and knees.

"A fitting position for you in the end," Talic snarled down at him. "Though you fought better than expected, kneeling before me is where you belong."

Kael could barely speak. "A man . . . like you . . . cannot be allowed . . . to head the council."

Kael was no longer cognizant of who he was or where he was when Talic struck him again on the back of the head. As if a bolt of lightning had smashed into him, Kael arched his back and threw his head upward. He felt pain to the core of his being. When he opened his eyes again, his gaze met Nari's.

Nari watched in paralyzed horror as Talic raised the staff again to slay her father. Tears streamed down both sides of her face. "Father no!" she screamed with all her might.

Hearing his daughter's cry, Kael found some final reserve of strength deep inside himself. Rolling quickly to his left, he brought his hands up in a crossed position, just in time to block Talic's killing blow. Still on the ground, Kael wrestled the staff away from Talic and struck a blow between Talic's legs, sending the Grand Druid flying backward, doubled over.

Before anyone could comprehend what was occurring, Kael was on his feet swinging. The second blow smashed across Talic's right cheek, the third blow gouged into his already wounded right side, and the fourth blow smashed into Talic's left knee, shattering it. Talic crumpled to the ground, limp and unmoving, his head resting in an ever-growing puddle of blood.

Kael stood menacingly over the inert body of the Grand Druid. He could feel the rush of adrenaline pulsating through him. He raised the staff for the final blow, a cruel and fierce rage boiling within him.

Suddenly, with staff poised for the kill, Kael heard a barely audible whisper. He hesitated, unable to believe that it came from the pathetic form below him.

"Kael . . ." mumbled Talic choking on his own blood, "I yield . . . to your mercy."

In that instant, Kael remembered who he was and recalled his reason for living: to protect and preserve, an oath he had sworn as an Initiate into the ways of the Druids. Feeling the rush of power rapidly fading, Kael let the staff slide from his hands and collapsed under the weight of the weariness that finally overcame him.

The battle was over and the challenge was complete. Kael Dracksmere was now the Grand Druid of the lands. He neither sought nor wanted the title, but by the laws of the Druids, it was his.

As Oblik, the High Elder, stepped forward, some unseen force extinguished all the flames, plunging the clearing into darkness. Uttering phrases in the secret language of the Druids, Oblik motioned toward Talic. "*Lavesta-Tal-Unfros.*"

Instantly, nearly all the priests present gathered around Talic's unmoving form. Without hesitation, they transformed in a flash of green into wondrous bronze eagles. They lifted Talic off the ground with ease and vanished high into the moonlit sky.

Nari was at her father's side before another word could be spoken. Gently, she held the older man in her arms, raising him to a sitting position.

Galin Calindir, Druid of Alluviam, also went to Kael's side. Galin knelt and laid both of his hands on Kael's chest. Before Nari's eyes, a yellow glow seemed to surround and wash over Kael's form. Moments later, the glow faded, and Kael opened his eyes as the wounds about his face and head slowly closed.

The first thing Kael saw after Nari's concerned face were the burning emerald eyes of Oblik. Unexpectedly, the ancient tree spirit bowed his head gently.

"Remember, my son," Oblik instructed, "it takes far greater courage to preserve life than to take it away. To hurt, kill, or maim is easy for most. To help or heal or preserve is the road less taken. By not taking the life of Talic, you have earned the respect of the High Elders. You are now the Grand Druid. In three full moons, you officially begin your tenure."

Leaning on Nari, Kael struggled to his feet and faced Oblik. "I never wanted this."

"The position and the responsibility are yours until you find someone to succeed you or lose it by the rite of challenge. Do not allow yourself to be corrupted as Talic did. When in doubt, follow your heart and use your power wisely."

Oblik reached forward and touched Kael on the shoulder with his beautifully crafted staff. Green energy flowed into Kael from the end of the staff.

"It is done," Oblik intoned. "It cannot be undone. Those most deserving of power rarely take it for themselves; they instead have power thrust upon them, and out of need, they accept it."

The ancient priest turned and began to walk away.

"Where do I begin?" Kael asked.

"Though you may stray from the path or become lost at times," Oblik replied, "the strength of your convictions will help you find your way. That is all the advice I can give you. The rest is for you to discover."

Kael rushed forward and blocked Oblik's way. "How can the High Elders allow a man like Talic to rule the council? Why is it they do nothing if he or others become corrupted and lose their way. How can our Sacred Mother—"

Oblik raised his hand abruptly, an almost sad smile on his face. "When you take the journey and become an Elder Druid, you give yourself totally to our Mother Nature. We no longer have much interest in the affairs of men. We are there to guide you, to give council in the winds when you call upon us and commune with our Sacred Mother. Sometimes, she uses us to answer." He closed his eyes and took a deep breath, showing his utter reverence for nature. "It is not for us to directly interfere once we have become one with our Sacred Mother." He opened his eyes and fixed them first on Galin for a moment, then returned his gaze to Kael. "You know what you must do. Both of you know. We will be in the wind to aid you. I bid you farewell, Kael Dracksmere."

With that, Oblik transformed into a magnificent white bald eagle and was gone.

Crickets chirped their familiar summer melody as Kael gazed up at their home. The overgrown ivy and weeds, which had accumulated over the months, gave a vacant appearance to their comely little cottage. Now, more than ever, he longed to be in the safety of its structure.

The three of them—Kael, Galin, and Elenari—made their way inside the small home. A dank, dusty room awaited them. Elenari immediately noticed the webs in the corner of the ceiling. She helped Kael to sit down and took it upon herself to prepare a long-awaited meal for all of them.

Galin sat across from Kael at the table that dominated the center of what Kael liked to refer to as the sitting room. Kael exhaled fully, burying his face in his hands. Nari could be heard in the background, clanking about in the basement.

"She must truly be concerned about me," he said softly to Galin. "Milling about the kitchen and pantry is something I thought never to see Nari do in my lifetime."

He caught a glimpse of Galin's polite grin as he stared in the distance.

Realizing that now was perhaps the wrong time, Galin removed the curved scabbard at his hip and placed his scimitar on the table and chose to speak anyway. "Kael, despite all that has happened here tonight, I need you to listen to me now."

Kael slowly lifted his head, leaned back in his chair, and looked across at his old friend. Galin Calindir, at age thirty-eight, was one of the youngest of the Druids on the council. Galin was given the duty to watch over the realm of Alluviam, the Kingdom of the Elves. It was by far the most prestigious position and responsibility a Druid could have, a duty reserved for the best and brightest of Druids. Such was Galin; He had learned to speak fluent Elvish, a beautiful yet difficult language. He was exposed to much magic, lore, and custom from the oldest of races. The Elves were also the race most likely to cooperate with the Druids. The Elves coveted and served nature as much as the Druids did. Kael and Elenari had fought at his side in the past. Galin had solicited their aid in dealing with a group of bandits who were terrorizing villages in the Sylvanwood and knew him to be a man of integrity, honor, and courage.

Kael observed closely as Galin's young face tensed into an unusual seriousness. His blue eyes conveyed a sincerity that Kael had always trusted from the moment they'd met. His wavy, sandy brown hair revealed itself as he removed his hood. His skin was smooth; not a blemish or wrinkle could be found upon his face or around his eyes. He looked clearly ten years younger than he was. Standing barely over six feet, Galin was well built and an accomplished fighter for a priest.

"Six months ago," Galin began, leaning forward, "I began to sense something. I began to almost hear the land calling to me. At first, I thought it only in my dreams, but I soon realized it was something much more. I began to examine the trees, plants, rivers, and forests of Alluviam. And, although nothing was inherently wrong in Alluviam, still the earth was telling me that whatever was disturbing me would soon reveal itself."

"What would reveal itself?" Kael interrupted.

"I did not know at first," Galin replied, "but I decided to expand my examination of the lands during my journey to seek you out. I spoke to hundreds of animals and plants, and time and again they confirmed my suspicions. The lands are suffering, Kael, from something I can only describe as a slow-acting poison. I labored greatly to discover the source of this scourge, only to find it was coming from everywhere. There seemed to be no starting point. Each day I watched it grow stronger as I traveled through the borders of Averon, Cordilleran, Mystaria, as far north as Gallandor, and as far south as Bazadoom. Everywhere, it was the same.

"The presence of evil has always lingered, Kael, but this was unlike anything I had ever felt before. When I was convinced of the severity of the problem, I consulted with the Elven Rangers of Alluviam, and learned that they had sensed something wrong as well. I then made all haste to Arcadia to seek out Talic and advise the council. However, my warnings fell on deaf ears, as all concern was for Talic's challenge to you. Half of the council's members have lost touch with their true mission at the hands of complacency; their purpose has atrophied with age. The other half has come to follow Talic's dictates almost without question. I do not envy you your task ahead."

Elenari entered with ale for all. Galin sat back, exhaling deeply. Elenari took a seat at the table and, having heard the last few minutes of the conversation, arched an eyebrow in curiosity. "What's all this about the lands, now?"

Kael leaned forward. "When you first sensed something was wrong," he said to Galin, "what did it feel like precisely?"

"It was a kind of uncomfortable anxiety, almost," Galin answered. "I remember feeling confused until Mother Earth herself seemed to call to me deep inside and ordered me to investigate."

"Our Sacred Mother knows of this?" Kael asked eagerly. "What does she say it is when you commune with her?"

"She does not know," Galin replied softly. "She only knows something is wrong and that something much worse is coming. She is elusive about answers, but instead I feel her pressing me deep within to find out all I can. Those were not her exact instructions; it's more of a feeling I suppose."

The conversation lapsed into silence as Kael pushed himself up and walked to the window. He stood motionless, staring out into the distance.

"What is it, Kael?" Galin asked, concerned.

Kael was silent for a moment before he replied. "I know these feelings," he said in a whisper.

Galin stared intently at Kael. "You have had these feeling I describe as well?" the younger Druid asked incredulously.

Kael nodded as the room fell silent once again. Nari found herself wary of the conversation. She knew the Druids had an unerring sense of the lands, and the "feelings" they were discussing unnerved her.

Kael stood quietly looking out the window and wondering to himself. What was the meaning of these feelings, and how did he fit into it all? He saw the moon watching over the large oak trees that sheltered his home and almost believed that he saw some kind of sickness within them. It was as if they were calling to him for help.

Kael's sullen mood and their collective fatigue demanded that any further conversation be put off until morning. Without even the desire to clean up, Elenari joined her father, and both retired to their rooms. Nari normally preferred the forest to sleep in; however, this night she knew she would feel more at ease in her own bed.

Galin turned down the kind offer of a roof over his head for the shelter of the forest. He sat in silent meditation until he drifted off to sleep.

Kael woke abruptly to the sound of inhuman howling. Cautiously, he peered outside. Fear seized him, and his mouth gaped open. Within moments, Elenari was at Kael's side as they looked in amazement at the source of the blood-curdling noise.

Just outside the window, his black robe billowing in the wind and a monstrous, grim wolf at his side, stood a masked figure—the Shadow Prince.

Nari, bow in hand, rushed outside. Kael followed frantically at her heels, shouting a warning, "No, Nari! Wait!"

Suddenly, father and daughter found themselves standing not ten feet away from the two creatures. Nari, with an arrow poised and aimed, hesitated to fire; Kael stood motionless to her left.

In the next instant, Galin emerged from the forest to witness the confrontation. Galin did not know the identity of the hooded figure, but the beast was another matter. He knew the creature to be a doom hound, a huge, dark, wolf-like animal standing five feet high at the shoulder. It was said that, once caught in the animal's jaws, the only way to break free was to kill the animal. The beast was a servant of evil.

The Shadow Prince began to raise his hands, and Elenari fired, only to see her shaft bounce off some unseen shield protecting the dark figure. The Shadow Prince's hands began to glow a brilliant red and yellow.

Kael tried in vain to free the proper spell components from the bags at his waist.

Galin, mistletoe in hand, had already been concentrating. Green energy flowed from his fingers, striking the ground surrounding the great wolf. The grass rose up and entwined all about the huge beast. With a raging snarl, the beast bit and tore at the ground with its fangs, easily freeing itself from the entanglement. The beast turned quickly and unleashed its wrath upon Galin, springing toward him in a leaping attack.

Galin lifted his robe and spun around, avoiding the beast's mouth. It landed off balance and rolled away down an embankment, leaving Galin uninjured.

A great swirling ball of fire began to appear in the air before the dark-robed figure. Nari fired several arrows in rapid succession, all of which fell uselessly at the feet of the Shadow Prince. She knew it was too late to thwart him. All she could do now was try to save Kael, who was still struggling to summon his magic. She grabbed Kael violently by the arm and started to run toward Galin.

Unexpectedly, the Shadow Prince hurled the ball of fire at the cottage. It struck with such explosive force that the entire house burst apart. Whatever was left standing was instantly consumed in flames. The explosion flung Kael and Nari to the ground. Debris from what had been their home only moments before rained down upon them. Galin, seeing them fall, half-staggered toward his friends and was relieved to see that they were still alive.

Suddenly, the very earth beneath their feet began to shudder. A rumbling rose up from deep within the earth, and the trees and shrubs throughout the area began to shake violently. The three companions found it virtually impossible to keep their footing as cracks and fissures split the ground around them.

Throughout the disruption, one sound prevailed above the tremors. It was the sound of laughter, a roar of triumph that echoed through the woodlands.

Suddenly, the ground beneath Elenari vanished, and she felt herself falling to the clutches of the earth. She reached out desperately, and Galin caught her outstretched hand.

Kael, who had been thrown some feet distant of the other two in the upheaval, watched as they clung to each other, barely able to hang on. Then, without warning, Galin lost his leverage and both of them were dragged downward into the earth, disappearing forever.

Kael, impaled with a profound sense of loss, lost the will to even remain standing, and he made no move to save himself as he, too, plunged downward into the depths of the earth. The last thing he saw in the world of men was a glimpse of the victorious Shadow Prince, roaring with laughter as the earth engulfed his prey.

A loud clamor wrenched Kael from slumber. His body was covered in sweat. He looked around frantically and realized he was still in his room and in his cottage.

Someone was frantically pounding on the front door. Wiping his brow, Kael peered out the window and saw it was still night. His heart began to pound. He launched himself out of bed and rushed to the front door. Nari had beaten him there, and she threw the door open. It was Galin, visibly distraught.

"I heard a scream," he said breathlessly. "Are you both well?"

Kael looked to his daughter. "Did you dream?" he asked in a whisper.

"No," she replied hesitantly, "but you had a nightmare, Father; I heard you moaning for the past several minutes. I was about to come and check on you when you suddenly screamed."

Wordlessly, Kael stepped past Galin and out into the night. The sweat began to dry on his skin, and he felt a chill run through him.

The nightmare had been sent. He had been contacted, but by what or whom he did not know. *It has been years,* Kael said to himself. *Why in death does he haunt my dreams now?*

Chapter 4

Unable to sleep, Elenari decided to take a walk in the woods surrounding the cottage. This was supposed to be the time of settling down for her and her father, a time of becoming a family, of getting to know each other better than the years and their very separate lives had allowed. Things seemed to be happening much too fast. Kael was the Grand Druid, and even he had little comprehension of what that would mean. Galin had arrived with tales of a strange elusive evil threatening the lands. There seemed to be no way of slowing things down.

She could hear the thin branches rustling as the wind picked up. Nari continued north, cresting a slight incline where the trees and bushes became thin and scarce around her. Her vantage point overlooked a small clearing. What would happen next?

It was nearly dawn; the night had begun to fade into day. Nari's thoughts turned toward the dream that had plagued her father. The Shadow Prince, a creature Kael and the Paladin Lark Royale had encountered many years ago, had returned to her father in the form of a dream. *Why?* Nari pondered to herself. *He is dead and long gone.*

Just then, a distant scent lingering in the wind caught her attention. She turned quickly to see smoke billowing into the sky from down below the hillside. The smoke seemed to be rising from the home of the Royale brothers.

In a flash, Nari was off, running back to her cottage, madly dodging small trees and bushes, which barely slowed her. She moved through the woods like a stag, leaping just in time over broken branches and rocks that might have impeded an inexperienced traveler.

Seemingly moments later, she burst out of the dark woods and emerged into the open clearing near her home. As she ran, she screamed, "Father! The Royales—their home is burning! Come quickly!"

Kael threw the door open just in time to see his daughter running frantically past. As he watched her dart across the field, he caught the scent of burning wood and looked north to see a haze of smoke obscuring the horizon in the distance.

Without a word, Kael closed his eyes tightly. A brilliant green light began to radiate from him, and his robes swirled about his body. His arms lengthened and transformed into feathered wings, and his clothing seemed to melt away as his body disappeared in a flash of green light. When the light faded, the form of a falcon, solid brown and magnificent with the seeking eyes of a hunter, had taken the place of the old Druid's form.

Galin appeared in time to catch sight of Kael soaring away. Without hesitating, he followed suit, shape-changing into a bird of similar splendor.

From the skies, Kael's enhanced eyesight allowed him to clearly determine the source of the flames. At their current speed, he and Galin would be there in moments. From the ground, Elenari watched as the great birds easily overtook her and closed in on the Royales' land.

Kael, reaching the structure first, circled overhead in a wide arc, above the searing heat that emanated from the burning house below. The great supporting timbers of the house were already buckling; the house had been aflame for some time. He landed several yards to the east of the house and looked around one more time with his keen animal eyes before transforming back to a man.

As Galin circled overhead, he noticed something moving below. It was a horse that had broken out of the blazing stable. The animal was still on fire and already horribly burnt. He could not allow it to suffer further.

For a moment, Galin seemed to become ball of green energy as he began to change back into his human form. Still in midair, he began speaking a strange tongue and wildly gesturing with his hands. Suddenly, water poured down out of his fingertips onto the stable and the struggling horse. Gallons of water came pouring down, producing clouds of hot steam as it impacted the burning stable.

Kael, already in human form, raised his hands to the skies. Water shot forth from his outstretched hands in a sweeping arc toward the house itself, dousing the gigantic flames almost instantly. Smoke filled the entire clearing and began to dissipate almost as quickly.

Galin descended slowly, crouching low to the ground where the burning horse had fallen. The animal was dead, its eyes open and staring and body burnt and blackened. Gently, he rested his hand on the animal's head, closing its eyes, and whispered a prayer only Mother Nature was privy to.

Kael trudged through the charred, smoking remains of the house, searching the area desperately for signs of life. He looked up and saw Elenari approaching from behind him, wiping dark soot from her brow.

Immediately, she went over to the bulk of the wreckage, probing with her sword for remains or clues as to what may have happened. It only took her a few minutes to find that which she had prayed she would not. Striking something solid, she bent down to see what appeared to be a human skull, covered in char and ash. Not five feet away, a second human skull, the spine still attached, lay amidst a pile of incongruous bones. Rising slowly, she stood and stared down in mixed despair and puzzlement.

"Father," she said in a hushed voice, "I think you had better come here and take a look at this."

Kael barely heard his daughter. "What is it, Nari?" he asked, still busy sifting through the debris. A moment later, Kael realized she had not answered him, and he turned to see her standing, unmoving, staring down at the wreckage before her. She had found something.

Kael could feel his heart beginning to beat rapidly as he slowly advanced toward her. *Please, don't let it be,* he thought. As he neared her, his heart pounded loudly in his chest. He followed Nari's gaze toward the ground, and saw the remains of two bodies.

Galin hurried to join them, wondering what they had discovered. "Have you found someth—?" His words halted abruptly at the sight of the charred human remains and the pain etched on Kael's face.

Nari bent down and began rummaging through the still-smoking debris with her hands. Her search uncovered a partially burnt, embroidered patch of thick fabric. Brushing the filth from it, she revealed a symbol that she and Kael were well familiar with. Handing the patch to Kael, Nari turned and walked away.

"What is it?" Galin asked. "What is that symbol?"

A sad smile of remembrance came over Kael's face. The symbol was that of a massive waterfall overlooking a small town at its base. He exhaled deeply as he answered, "It is a symbol of a place of beauty that is no more. Like its children . . . it is no more."

Galin realized that Kael and Nari needed time to grieve and walked away, allowing them space. He knew they would answer his questions when they were ready.

Nearly an hour had passed before Kael rejoined Galin. Nari had been carefully studying the remains and scouting around the perimeter of the house.

"Two men lived here," Kael began. "Their names were Lark and Archangel Royale. They were our friends. Lark was a baron and lord in this land, though, like myself, he preferred a humble dwelling on a quiet stretch of land. He had no use for titles, lordships, or castles. The symbol that Elenari found is a depiction of their homeland, Osprey Falls, which was destroyed long ago in a raid by brigands."

As he finished speaking, Elenari joined them.

"Anything?" Kael asked.

Nari looked unexpectedly hopeful. "Strange," she said. "There are only two sets of tracks between the stable and the house. They belong to the brothers. There's nothing else, though. No tracks around the perimeter of the house, no sign of a struggle."

"There's more. The bodies . . . there's no sign of flesh. They are completely burned to the bone. True, the fire had been burning for some time, but certainly not long enough to burn the bodies so completely. Also, one of the skulls is too small to be that of a man. I highly doubt it was either of them."

Before either man could ask a question, Nari silenced them by bringing a finger swiftly to her lips. Her head jerked around. The bushes several yards behind the house rustled again. Within seconds, she had an arrow nocked to the string of her bow, and her two companions turned and looked to see what had startled her so.

Slowly, a hooded and robed figure emerged, leaning on a dark staff. Kael grasped his own staff, feeling the burning sensation of its power coming to life. Galin instantly held his hands out defensively before him, summoning his own power. Elenari drew her bowstring back and took deadly aim at the intruder's heart.

The woods were beginning to stir with life as the sun spilled its first beams of light across the dusty plains of Wrenford. The morning air was cooler than it had been all season, a sign to the foraging animals that another summer was drifting away into the season of colored leaves.

The season seemed to be arriving prematurely; autumn was not due for several weeks. Some trees had already changed, and their leaves were already in the process of falling. Even the feisty squirrels gathered their winter supplies with a queer sense of urgency. The birds, instead of building new warm nests, seemed to be taking them apart, as if they had received a premonition that it was time to move on and search for safer places to make homes in. The animals seemed to sense an increasing state of dread present in the lands.

A rabbit scurried to safety at the rumbling of wooden wheels and the clamor of horses' hooves approaching from down the road. The rabbit watched as the wagon, adorned with various trinkets, fabrics, and antiquities, pressed steadily onward down the trail that ran out of Wrenford and onward toward the mountains of Mystaria.

Two men drove the wagon, both tastefully dressed in the style that suited the typical merchants roving throughout the countryside. They each wore white silk shirts beneath their brown robes. Long gold chains could be seen hanging around their necks below their hooded faces. Several rings decorated their hands as they gripped the horses' reins.

A lantern hung within the housing of the white canvas tarp clanked back and forth as the vehicle maintained a slow but steady pace. A dark-clothed hand reached up to remove the lantern from its hinge, since daylight shone through several flaps cut into the tarp.

It must not appear as if the travelers were trying to hide something. On the off chance that a patrol might stop them, they must appear gaudy enough as merchants, but normal enough not to be closely noticed. They were the most skilled experts at disguise.

The incessant banging of the lantern had stirred another occupant of the wagon to consciousness. The man awoke, dazed and confused. He thought he was lying on his back, but the terrible numbness throughout his body could neither confirm nor deny this. He could see his surroundings well enough, though. He saw articles of clothing, fine dishes of silver, and various small works of art. As his vision cleared, he tried to speak but found he could not.

Suddenly, someone grabbed a handful of his hair and jerked his head upward.

A sinister voice spoke to him in a mocking tone. "Awake so soon, my friend? You're even stronger than I took you for. Well, we'll have to make sure you don't wake up again. Here, I made this myself."

The man gasped as the owner of the voice forced a noxious, thick liquid down his throat.

"Pretty good stuff," the voice said. "Don't worry if you start choking, because if I gave you too much, you'll die anyway." A soft evil laugh filled the vehicle.

The man felt the liquid move down his throat like a bunch of slugs crawling ever so slowly into his system. Just as he felt he would vomit, he fell into unconsciousness.

The sun was still rising as the assassins continued toward Mystaria in their merchant's wagon.

Leaning heavily against his staff, the figure removed his charcoal gray hood, revealing the leathery, wrinkled face of an old man. His snow-white hair fluttered in the breeze as a cool summer wind shot through his lengthy silver beard. His eyes burned like brilliant blue sapphires as he continued forward, undaunted by the defensive postures of the apprehensive trio before him.

Kael had seen the brave countenance of this man before. It was many years ago, in a cave deep within the Hills of Renarn, that their paths had crossed for the first time. Kael knew they had nothing to fear, for this man was Algernon, the Great Sage of Wrenford, and he was known and respected throughout the lands.

For the first time since returning home, Kael allowed himself to smile. He placed an assuring hand on Nari's shoulder, prompting her to lower her bow. "We are in good company, my dear."

"Indeed, young Elenari," Algernon said pleasantly. "If I were the dark lord that haunts your father's dreams, I never would have allowed your aim to be so true."

Kael walked forward and extended a hand to his old friend. "It has been a long time, hasn't it, Algernon, since last we spoke?" said Kael as the two locked hands for a hearty shake.

"Yes, too long," Algernon replied, "and now you are the Grand Druid as well as Baron of Wrenford. Well met, indeed! Too much time has passed, and I fear that, once again, grave circumstances have brought us together, rather than pleasant ones."

Again, Kael could not help but let a slight smile pass his lips in spite of all that had happened. Only a Sage—a man who had devoted his life to the pursuit of knowledge of myriad fields from the scientific to the arcane—could possess such an air of wisdom, and Algernon was a man renowned amongst Sages for his knowledge, travels and studies.

"Please allow me to present my friend," Kael began, but Algernon quickly interrupted him.

"Galin, Druid of Alluviam," the Sage said. "Yes, excellent to make your acquaintance. King Aeldorath speaks very highly of you. I am sorry to meet you under such circumstances."

Galin stared in awe at the legendary Sage who, it was rumored amongst the Elves, had unsurpassed knowledge of long-forgotten Elven magic. The Elves had said that Algernon had traveled to every part of the known world at one time or another. It was also known to very few that he had kept strict detailed notes of all his journeys, which were said to be near his person at all times. Though not a powerful wizard himself or great user of magic, Algernon's magic was in his immense knowledge. He had been chief advisor to the King of Wrenford for many years until rumor had it that he had retired to take up the life of a hermit.

Turning to Elenari, the Sage leaned forward to meet the young Ranger's gaze. "And you, Elenari Moonraven. Your father told me much about you when last we talked. I can see by your beauty alone that even his praises did you no justice. You have grown into womanhood and, I sense, much more as well."

The old man took her hand and kissed it. Elenari blushed slightly and stared back at the man she had heard stories about from her father.

Without hesitation, the Sage continued. "Again, I regret to meet you under these ill tidings." A sullen look overcame Algernon's face as he surveyed the remains of the Royales' property, and his voice took on a harsh tone of bitterness. "A few days ago, I met with King Thargelion in the Citadel of Wrenford. While I was there, I had a vision that what you see before you would come to pass. I made all haste to arrive here in time to prevent this. Apparently, I am too late to be of service."

A perplexed look appeared on Kael's face. *What would bring Algernon out here alone, why did Wrenford send no soldiers?* It was a foolish question, he thought, because he remembered Algernon often seemed to know what others were thinking. He had many unusual abilities, as Kael remembered.

Algernon walked about the wreckage of the house, occasionally poking at the debris with his staff until he came to the two skeletons. Though the winds grew in strength, the scent of charred wood still lingered in the air. "You are wondering why I have come . . . yes?" Algernon said to Kael, looking down at the charred corpses.

Kael nodded. "What have you come to tell us, Algernon? Do you know what happened here? It has been many years since last we met. It is no coincidence that the menace that brought me to you then plagues my dreams now. Nor do I suspect that it is coincidence that you have come to us at the scene of this tragedy that has taken two of our closest friends."

Algernon turned and walked back toward the three companions, holding his gray robe close about him as it flapped in the breeze. "Has it taken them? I wonder." He moved with a slow deliberate gait, using his dark staff as a walking stick. His face was serious as he spoke. "Nor is it chance that the three of you are here together now. You have each been chosen."

"Chosen?" Galin asked, "Chosen by whom, and for what?"

"That shall be explained to you, Galin of Alluviam," Algernon replied. "For now, trust in what I say. It is imperative that we seek an immediate audience with the Wizard-King Thargelion. It is he who has requested your presence. He has sent me to find you. Once we reach the palace of Wrenford, all your questions will be answered. There is much that needs to be said and great tales to be told both ominous and brave."

Kael looked at Galin and Elenari, who each, in turn, wordlessly nodded their approval. In truth, they realized there was little choice. Kael turned to

Algernon, knowing better than to press the old man before he was ready to reveal more. "Then let us be off."

With that, the four of them left behind the memories of old friends and they made their way toward the city of Wrenford to see the Wizard-King.

The sun was at its apex when the group reached the edge of the city. It had been nearly four hours since they left the smoldering ruins of the Royale brothers' home. There was little conversation during their trek, only personal thoughts of the mysteries that would be revealed during their audience with the king.

As they entered the bustling avenues, Kael could not help but see the city as he had remembered it, the way it had been many years ago. It seemed only yesterday that he and Lark Royale had walked the streets with ragged beggars and hungry children tearing at their clothes. But today, the city of Wrenford thrived with commerce and trade as was evident in the varied merchant wagons that passed in and out of the town on the cobblestone streets.

One might never have imagined that, at one time, the people of Wrenford had nearly abandoned their homes, Kael thought to himself, *victims of famine and drought brought forth by the theft of the mystical Emerald Star. But now, the magic of the sacred stone flourishes and protects its people. Peace and prosperity had reigned for years since the defeat of Wrenford's ancient enemy, the Shadow Prince.*

Kael turned to see the Dragon's Breath Inn, which even at this noon hour was crowded with patrons. It was here where Algernon had taken both him and Lark to solicit their aid, and their quest for the recovery of the Emerald Star had begun. A melancholy feeling invaded Kael's thoughts as he remembered Lark. The old Druid was so deep in thought that he did not hear Elenari calling to him to move out of the way of an approaching cart. Galin grasped Kael's robe and quickly pulled him to the side, allowing the horse-drawn vehicle to pass.

"Kael, it has been long since you last visited the city," Algernon commented. "I'm sure there are many memories here for you, both good and bad. Be patient, my friend. There will be plenty of time for reflection soon enough."

Kael nodded in agreement, but found himself remembering that sometimes the old man's abilities could be somewhat unnerving. He lost himself in thought nonetheless as they continued down the ever-crowded main road that led to the Citadel of Wrenford.

After the better part of an hour had elapsed, the spires of the Citadel of Wrenford came into view of the party. The Citadel was a large, square building of stone, surrounded by four towers and a fifteen-foot wall crowned with battlements. The four towers each had two guard stations between them, riddled with arrow slits and each mounting one catapult and one ballista. Patrols of four, all crossbowmen, marched along the north, east, west, and south walls. Their gleaming helmets could be seen from some distance, as well as their tunics of gold and green. There was only one entrance: the main gates on the north wall. Four tall men armed with polearms flanked the gates, while four on horseback, clad in light chain mail, came to greet anyone who entered the perimeter.

Algernon abruptly took the lead, waving to the men on horseback while still several yards away. Instantly recognizing the Sage, they rode out to greet him.

The Captain of the Guard, a huge stocky man broadly built at the shoulder, dismounted and hailed the party. "Algernon," said the Captain, "twice you visit us in one month. Surely this is a bad omen."

"Perhaps even more than you dare guess, Garin, but be sure you whisper your suspicions to no one. Instruct the others, no one is to know our business."

Captain Garin listened intently to Algernon, and the others could see by the soldier's face that the Sage's words would be followed without question.

Elenari was taken aback by Garin's appearance; his armor must have been specially crafted to cover his mighty frame. Garin wore his long gray hair tied in a ponytail in much the same way Archangel Royale wore—had worn?—his hair. She had no doubt that this man would be a dangerous opponent.

Garin turned his attention to Kael. "Hail to you, Kael Dracksmere, hero of our people. We are honored to have you amongst us once again, my lord. Indeed, the king's need must be great."

The Captain rode alongside the party, escorting them up to the main gates and paying special attention to the robed man and the young half-Elven woman who accompanied Algernon and Kael.

"Fear not, Garin," said Algernon as he quickly led them through the gates, "for they are each as strong an ally to the lands as Kael or I."

Beyond the main gates was a steel portcullis, which was quickly raised to allow them access through small courtyard. Within the confines of this yard, patches of daisies and tulips lined the walkway to the giant bronze doors of the Citadel.

To the left of the walkway was a small stone fountain fashioned around a statue of a multifaceted gemstone representing the famed Emerald Star of Wrenford. Twin white doves rested together atop one of the pointed edges of the statue. Water cascaded down the sides of the representation like raindrops.

To the right of the passageway grew one of the most magnificent gardens Galin had ever seen, comprised mainly of red and yellow roses growing together. Galin hesitated, in awe of the garden's beauty.

"The roses have not been planted, my friend," said Algernon, "for this is the one place in all the lands where they grow wild in such a fashion."

Shaking his head in wonder, Galin followed after his friends. As they approached the great bronze doors, they noticed the doors were inscribed with Elvish runes and strange characters. According to Algernon, the symbols were a magical ward of protection, placed on the doors by Thargelion at the time of their creation. They opened on silent hinges.

They entered a brightly lit hall where two guards approached to greet them. These men were different from any soldiers they had yet seen. They were heavily armored in shining plated mail, and each carried a great broadsword at his side. Their faces were completely concealed behind their finely crafted helmets that seemed to join with the rest of their armor where the shoulders met the neck. They wore flowing gray and green robes fastened at the shoulders that complemented their royal bearing. Acknowledging Algernon, they motioned for the rest of the party to follow them to the main audience chamber to await the arrival of the Wizard-King.

As they walked down the golden hallway, Galin gazed up at the ornate tapestries that hung all about the smooth marble walls. Throughout the length of the hall, antique chandeliers of sparkling crystal hung from the ceiling. Though the size of the Citadel was not great, the attention to every little detail of the décor lent both a noble and ancient feel to the place.

Kael watched as Algernon quickened his pace with a look of eager anticipation for the coming meeting. Kael himself felt a queer anxiety, much the same as that which he had felt years ago just before his first meeting with Thargelion.

Finally, they reached the end of the long hallway where a much smaller set of marble doors blocked their way. Instantly, the doors swung open and a refreshing, cool breeze struck them. The guards stood at the doorway and bade the party to enter.

They found themselves in a rectangular chamber, within which the first object of interest was a huge, polished-oak table. It was over twenty feet in length and nearly half that in width. Many finely crafted oak chairs, cushioned with padded backings, outlined the length of the great table. Garnished candelabras of silver lit every section of the table.

Elenari immediately turned to take in every inch of the room, noticing the four walls decorated with shields and racks of various weapons. Even she was awestruck by the wondrous mural that encompassed the entire ceiling, a massive depiction of an unimaginable battle scene. One half of the image was a dark mountain range under a raging storm in the night-darkened sky. Spilling out of the mountains were thousands of dark horsemen raining down upon and besieging a small city. In the sky, above the dark hordes, a lone figure rode a giant red dragon with many heads and watched the onslaught from the sky. Elenari quickly realized the beast was a hydra and the small city below was Wrenford. A small defending force of soldiers, clad in gray and green and carrying huge battle standards of the same color, rode out of the city. In the midst of this hopelessness, a defiantly brilliant green glow seemed to outline the city. Bolts of green lightning, emanating from the city itself, forked outward into the onrush of dark invaders. The final image depicted the invaders withdrawing north to the Morval Mountains and the flying figure pulling back the reins of his fearsome mount, escaping back to the dark realm from whence he had come.

Elenari realized that this work of art told the story of the bygone time when Wrenford had been at war with the remnants of the Pytharian Empire, and how the magic of the legendary Emerald Star had saved the people of this small kingdom.

As Nari finished contemplating the mural, a pleasing voice snapped her out of her daze.

"Alas . . . we need constant reminding of our history lest we forget it to our utter doom."

Nari turned to see the most aged Elf she had ever met. He seemed little more than a frail scarecrow of a figure, leaning on a polished black staff. He wore a simple silk robe of gray and green. He stood slightly hunched over, and his face was riddled with wrinkles, especially around the eyes. His hair was a stringy white, and he had a short white beard. Elenari suddenly became aware that, but for this stranger, she was standing alone in the room.

The ancient Elf pointed toward the open door on the east wall. Nari turned for a moment to look at the opening, but when she turned back to face him, he had disappeared, gone as swiftly as he had appeared.

Quickly, she moved toward the open door that led into the throne room. As she entered, she saw her party standing within the center of an octagonal chamber. On the north wall was a throne of ivory, upon which maroon satin cushions rested. Above the throne hung an iron chandelier set with burning incense, which gave off a surprisingly pleasant fragrance. As she looked about the chamber, she noticed her companions' gazes were locked on the space to the left of the throne. She moved to stand beside Kael to see what had so attracted the attention of the others.

There, encased in glass, lay the magnificent green emerald known as the Emerald Star. It rested on a four-foot pedestal of chiseled marble. Though only the size of a man's fist, its presence gave it greater magnitude.

"The Emerald Star, my friends," said a lyrical voice from behind the throne. "The very same gemstone, crafted ages ago by my own hand with the help of the Elven Wizards of old in what is now the Great Forest of Hilderan, and finding its home here in Wrenford ever since."

Two fair-haired young men came into view from somewhere behind the throne, guiding the royal figure of an ancient Elven man. A crown of gold set with three precious stones—ruby, emerald, and sapphire—rested atop his thinning white hair. The King, slightly over five feet, was arrayed in a silk robe of gray and green. His short white beard did not conceal the many creases and wrinkles covering his face. From beneath bushy eyebrows, he peered at the party with blue eyes much like Algernon's. For an

Elf, even one so ancient, his skin showed unusual signs of age. The two young servants eased his fragile form onto the throne. At the weary, dismissive wave of his hand, the young boys retired back behind the throne out of view.

Many remarkable legends were told about the old Elf King. The truth of all the legends had long since become entwined with myth, and only a very few now lived who knew the reality of such tales. The most prominent of these tales told of how he and the ancient wizards of old had rid the lands of an ancient demon lord and his army of foul creatures that sought to dominate the world.

Kael and Algernon knelt before the old king, and Galin and Elenari quickly followed suit behind them.

Rising at the King's bidding, Kael saw that the years had indeed taken a great toll on Thargelion. Never had the King looked older or more fatigued. Kael solemnly regretted not visiting him for so many years. It pained him that he should be summoned before his King—his friend—solely because of matters that would no doubt be disheartening.

Gazing upon Thargelion, Galin knew he was in the presence of an Elf who had very nearly lived his full life span. Thargelion must have been well over a thousand years old. Perhaps he was one of the elusive Gray Elves; their life spans were said to be far beyond those of normal Elves. But Gray Elf or no, all Elves were said to be stricken with rapid aging toward the end of their life span. It was the price they paid for appearing ageless and young for centuries. Aging caught up with them only toward the very end.

Galin, hailing from Alluviam, had heard stories of Thargelion in his youth. It was said that Thargelion had cleared the parcel of land now known as Wrenford of monsters, brigands, and rogues almost single-handedly in order to establish a community. It was said that he possessed the skills of both a legendary warrior and great wizard.

Only a man of extraordinary will and vision, Galin thought, *could have ruled an area so long, thwarting every attempt at invasion.*

Thargelion was a humble man who could have easily ruled a vast portion of the world, but instead he chose a small, quiet kingdom to live out his remaining days in peace and prosperity. It did not matter to him that its inhabitants were predominately human. He could have ruled the Elves but for reasons of his own he chose a life apart. Still, most Elves did not show such drastic signs of physical age even before their end. Many wondered what could possibly have caused his terribly frail appearance.

Elenari felt a sense of pride at being summoned by a man of such nobility as Thargelion. This was the same monarch who had summoned her father years ago to the quest and deeds that had made him famous.

Algernon moved to stand at the King's right side and rested his hand on the old Elf's shoulder. The bond between the two men was clearly evident in the gesture. The King motioned to Kael, who bowed and stepped forward to face Thargelion.

"Greetings, Lord Dracksmere, my good friend," the King said. "It has been some time since we last met. Although we have not spoken in many years, I—we, the people of Wrenford, have not forgotten what you have done for this great land. You are truly, now and forever, one of the saviors of Wrenford."

The king's tone softened. "I deeply regret the loss of Lark Royale and his brother, more than you can know. I grieve with you, as do the people of Wrenford, for we have lost a great hero and friends of our homeland."

Algernon turned to the King. "My Lord, the charred remains of two bodies were found at the Royales' home, but there was no conclusive evidence that they are the Royales."

Elenari suddenly stepped forward, interrupting. "King Thargelion, it is my belief that the Royale estate was purposely destroyed and set afire though for what reason, I cannot guess."

Kael and Galin quickly turned to Elenari with surprised glances that conveyed to her that her behavior was inappropriate. Thargelion saw the exchange, but smiled; he liked a direct woman who was unafraid to speak her mind.

Elenari caught herself and bowed. "Forgive me, Your Majesty! I . . ."

"Most intriguing," the King replied. "Do continue, Ranger."

Thargelion's melodic tone of authority seemed to rejuvenate Nari's confidence. "I know this," Nari continued, stepping closer to the throne, "or rather I believe this, because I discovered traces of oil throughout the interior of the house." Her voice steadily rose in tone and power as she went on. "The oil was spread out in such a manner that the fire could have been deliberately set. Also, the bodies were found in the same room, right next to each other. I, too, know the Royales, Sire. They are excellent warriors and experienced men. Why would two warriors such as these men stay in one room, beside each other, as their house burned down around them? Also, consider the patch of Osprey Falls, gentlemen; how convenient that it was found yet no armor, weapons, or any of their possessions were recovered."

"So what is it you are suggesting, Elenari?" Kael asked.

"Nothing for certain," she replied, "but I am convinced that the fire was no accident, but I believe it was meant for us to think it was. Nor am I convinced that those were the bodies of Lark and Archangel."

"Indeed, Elenari," Algernon said firmly. "These suspicions have merit and require further investigation, but for now they must wait. As hard as this may be to accept, there are matters at hand even more urgent than this unsettling tragedy." Algernon's tone suggested that further inquiry on the subject should be avoided for the moment. "Unfortunately, we have little time and much to discuss."

With that, the Sage rummaged through a tattered brown pouch about his waist and pulled out what appeared to be a handful of sand. Suddenly, his arm shot forward as if to hurl the dust at the party. All three of them instinctively cringed, raising their arms protectively in a reflex action, but, to their astonishment, a glittering cloud of gold and silver hovered in the air between them. As the dust particles descended, they began to swirl in circles and coalesce into a cloud. Images began forming in its midst.

"Hark," Thargelion commanded, "for there is much to tell, and though some of the tale will be familiar, it is crucial that it be told anew for all present to hear. Many years ago, two brave heroes came to Wrenford to seek out and destroy an evil that was looming over the kingdom, like a dark storm cloud waiting to burst with all its fury."

The dust settled into an uneven circular backdrop. The assembly watched, spellbound, as the images of Kael Dracksmere and Lark Royale appeared before them. The images faded into a thick fog, only to reappear seconds later, facing a hideous, towering blue dragon that swooped down like the wind itself, breathing bolts of lightning upon the brave warriors.

The King continued, "These men faced great dangers, including this one we see here. The blue dragon and servant of the evil Prince Wolfgar Stranexx, later to be known as the Shadow Prince, was destroyed by the Druid Kael in a fierce battle that almost cost him his life."

Elenari was mystified. She'd heard this story told in taverns, bars, and from Kael himself more times than she could recall. Nothing she had ever heard compared to seeing the events played out before her eyes.

"And so the adventurers continued their journey to find the mystical Emerald Star—the protector of Wrenford—and to destroy the diabolical Stranexx." The image faded and reappeared with the two men battling dark horsemen depicted earlier in the mural of the main audience chamber. "They battled the dark Stygian Knights, the elite and greatly feared fighting force that comprised the heart of Wolfgar Stranexx's army."

Again, one image vanished to be replaced by another.

"Kael and Lark are now seen engaging a large black Hydra and although its acid-breath weapon almost finished Lark, the young Paladin showed his bravery when he defeated the sinister guardian of the city of Branix Major."

The vision disappeared and slowly transformed into the image of a large tower surrounded by a noxious yellow cloud.

"It is here, in the once-great city of Branix Major in the northern part of the Pytharian Empire, that the two warriors first confronted the dreaded Wolfgar Stranexx. Here, they regained the stolen Emerald Star and Stranexx retreated from the superior prowess of Lark and Kael."

Kael found himself staring into the dust cloud, remembering the conviction and feelings of righteousness that had burned through him years ago as he surmounted each of these obstacles with Lark at his side. His feelings were mixed, and he found himself yearning desperately for the security of those feelings once again.

The tower disappeared and reshaped itself into the image of an ancient fortress.

"Behold Darkhelm," Thargelion said quietly, "the eastern seat of Stranexx's power in what remained of the Empire's lands. It was here that Stranexx called upon the powers of darkness in an effort to prolong his life span and increase his power. He contacted an entity of such unadulterated evil that it changed Stranexx forever. Instead of gaining immortality, he became horribly disfigured and slipped into an existence rivaling undeath. His power did increase, however, in that he gained a strange influence over other undead creatures, but for all intents and purposes, he was no longer a man. He became the Shadow Prince, a name born of fear from his own people no less."

The image shifted again and was replaced with the images of Kael and Lark combatting the dark-robed figure of the Shadow Prince.

"The two heroes tracked the dark lord to his lair. A battle ensued, and the combatants found themselves locked in a deadly struggle for survival. The Shadow Prince fended off the magical attacks of Kael while exchanging blows with Lark, only to counterattack both men with renewed fury. With indomitable spirit, the two men turned the tide of the encounter with unrelenting attacks of spell and steel, forcing the dark prince to admit defeat. At last, the dying Shadow Prince broke his black staff across his leg, releasing its retributive powers in hopes of destroying his two opponents along with himself."

They watched as the highest spire of the ancient fortress exploded in the night sky. Algernon's dust then simply dissolved into the air itself.

One of the servants had brought water for the King in the interim. After a few quick sips he continued, "Over the last several years, since the Emerald Star was returned to us and peace restored to our lands, Wrenford has thrived and is still thriving today." The King paused and looked out the circular stained-glass window on the west wall, a look of pain registering on his face. "But something is wrong; a poison has infected the lands. This poison is so potent that it is seeping into the very essence of all life. Plants and animals alike are slowly being drained of their vitality. The process is so very slow, they are barely aware something is wrong. A creeping death has been loosed upon them."

Galin, like Elenari, had heard many renditions of Kael and Lark's story, but never had he experienced the sensation of living through it as he just had; he was still reeling from the experience. Hearing this, his eyes widened, as he whispered, "I know of this poison."

Thargelion nodded and continued. "This poison is not only within the lands, but without as well. Dark forces are stirring once again in the north, but this time there is something . . . *different*. There is far-reaching wisdom and purpose beyond anything we have ever encountered. There is a dark intelligence, as yet unrevealed, which guides all that is occurring from afar, beyond the eyes of seers and the wise alike."

Waiting for Kael to meet his gaze, the King continued, "Some of these forces are not unknown to us, my friends, though we thought them to be extinct."

Algernon disappeared behind the throne and returned moments later, holding what appeared to be a soldier's uniform, comprised of a pitch-black robe and tunic. A large red insignia depicting a Hydra was emblazoned on the breast of the tunic. It was the uniform of a Stygian Knight.

Kael stared blankly at the uniform, hoping he were only present as an observer in his own nightmare and expecting any moment to be awakened by Elenari in the sanctuary of their small cottage, but this was all too real. He knew there was no escape.

In solemnity, Thargelion turned his weary eyes to rest on Kael. "I understand how you must feel right now, with all that has happened to you these past few days, but we need you once again. You and your companions are all the people of Wrenford have, and quite possibly all the hope of the surrounding nations."

Algernon, sensing the old elf's fatigue, soothed the King once again, placing his hand on Thargelion's shoulder. Algernon then turned to the party of three. "Kael, you and Elenari have been away traveling for quite some time. Many things have changed in your absence. Your friend Galin, I'm sure, has told you about some of these changes. Perhaps I should tell you more. First, know that much of what I am about to tell you has been confirmed by King Thargelion's long-range scouts. The scouts in the service of Wrenford, as you know, have an impeccable reputation throughout the lands."

Algernon clutched his robes close about him as he moved to the west window. The luminescent rays of the sun outlined his shadow, making him appear larger in stature. As he walked, the party no longer saw a withered old man; his gait seemed to be that of one born of nobility and unhindered by age. He began to weave a tale, which mesmerized all present so that they could do nothing but drink in his words.

"Many things have changed all at once," he began, "yet with such subtlety as to barely warrant notice. The pieces begin to fill the great puzzle, which the shortsighted and the complacent might never decipher until it is too late and already upon them. As you know, Koromundar has always been somewhat of a nervous twitch to the other nations. Allied to none, yet prepared to war with all, its barbaric tribesmen have often been known to be aggressive toward the nations of the known world. Primary amidst their objectives of conquest have been the lands of Mystaria and the Republic of Averon. The Golden Khan, Moglai, was overthrown six months ago. Koromundar's new ruler is Antar Helan, a warrior known to have dealings with the Shadow Prince years ago. An edict from Helan has stated that their nation will no longer engage in trade or any negotiations with the surrounding lands. I believe Antar Helan to be the puppet head of a government, and that he is being controlled by an outside hand. Even now, as we speak, there are rumors of their armies forming on the borders of Cordilleran, the homeland of the Dwarves."

"In the dreaded, ruined wasteland of Bazadoom, many changes are occurring and rumors of war are once again on the horizon like a far distant storm. From these lands, Orcs, Ogres, and other vile races are massing and making attack runs on border forts of Averon, penetrating into Alluviam. The reasons for this are unclear, as the creatures of Bazadoom have never known such unity of purpose as to ally against bordering countries. Such an organized force has not been assembled in these lands as far back as memory can conceive.

"Jarathadar, historically a peaceful desert country, has recently undergone a radical transformation. In recent years, civil war raged through the country with the terrible swiftness of a sandstorm. In this war, the Emir, Rodenshah, was killed, along with many others of the royal family. Beyond all belief, a new government took over three months ago in the form of a dictatorship. It is also rumored that, within the Soren Desert, there exists a training camp where the deadly Stygian Knights are training the nomadic desert dwellers for war. More troubling than this, the new dictator, who is still unknown to us, is rallying the people against Cordilleran in particular of all nations. Again, the reasons for such actions are unknown."

Algernon paused for a moment, carefully planning his next words as his probing eyes scanned the party from beneath thickets of snowy eyebrows. His gaze stopped on Galin as he measured the Druid's own self-worth.

"Galin, as you may know, Alluviam, the ancient homeland of the Elves, is having its own problems. Once again, rumors are rampant that the mythical, pale-skinned cousins to the Elves are infiltrating the city of Alluviar. I am referring, of course, to the underground people called White Elves by their surface-dwelling brethren. Due to the resentment these White Elves have against their kin, it is rumored they have joined this dark alliance in an attempt to regain what was once theirs thousands of years ago. However, since so many question the very existence of the White Elves, these rumors may be naught but bedtime stories told to frighten the Elf children."

Galin returned the Sage's gaze with thoughtful concern. He looked away after a moment, unable to hold the other's intense stare. "The White Elves are real," he stated suddenly. "That much Aeldorath himself admitted to me personally."

Algernon, his hands clasped behind his back, paced in a circle around the glass case that held the Emerald Star. "Cordilleran, the kingdom of the Dwarves, appears as if it will take the brunt of the mounting imminent attacks. With an army of close to twenty thousand, it possesses the largest standing force of any nation. Although there has been no formal declaration of war by either side, Cordilleran has been in several skirmishes along the Koromundar borderland already. And, there is information that Mystaria, the implacable nemesis of Cordilleran, is supplying the tribesman of Koromundar with magical weapons and armor. The Wizard Council of Mystaria has officially stated that they will remain neutral at this time, though our scouts have indicated there are dark factions at work manipulating their government."

Algernon stopped and let his hands come to rest atop the glass display case. "The only countries that we have had no direct observation of or communication with are the faraway island kingdoms of Arcadia and Bastlandia. Communication has come via winged messenger that, despite their mighty fleet, Arcadia has had increasing amounts of trade disputes on the water with their eastern neighbor, Bastlandia. There is fear that open hostilities could break out at any time. Though perhaps beyond the enemy's looking glass for the moment, we fear even they will have some part to play, for good or ill."

Kael, beginning to feel despondent and somewhat overwhelmed by Algernon's narrative, could contain himself no longer. "What does all this mean, Algernon? What is it you wish to say? Do not camouflage it under rumor and bureaucratic guile."

Algernon hesitated. "That which you fear most my friend," he said at last. "The Shadow Prince has returned!" He quickly evaluated the reaction of the three companions before him. Shock and disgust were spread across Kael's face, and wonder seemed etched upon the faces of the others. "Make no mistake: this is no longer the necromancer, Wolfgar Stranexx, but an enhanced spirit creature whose avarice and lust for power know no earthly bounds. The creature desires not only revenge upon Wrenford, but upon all free nations. His undying wrath will make itself known to all corners of our world and he has returned with a power and single-mindedness of purpose that will allow nothing to hinder him. Furthermore, he is not solely driven by anger and vengeance as he once was. He plots and plans carefully with patience beyond measure, controlling all the strings in unison like a great puppet master. He has grown more cunning and powerful than any imagining could ever have predicted."

Galin was astounded. If he had only acted sooner or tried harder, perhaps the Druid Council would have heeded his forewarnings. He looked at Thargelion, who sat restlessly in his throne, helpless before the menace brought about by his archenemy, the Shadow Prince. The King had called upon them, this small party, telling them that they were the hope of all nations. Algernon had made reference to their being "chosen," and called him and Elenari allies to the lands as strong as Kael himself. What did these two old men know about him that he did not? The answer to this question was foremost on his mind.

Elenari, standing at Galin's side, had listened earnestly to the tales of both Thargelion and Algernon. If what the old Sage said was true, it would take a lot more than the three of them to bring together the free peoples of the land to stand against whatever this dark alliance was sweeping across the countryside.

A bitterness seized Kael's soul as he considered the ramifications of what Algernon spoke of. The Shadow Prince, Wolfgar Stranexx, who he had thought had been destroyed forever, now returned with a vengeance. *How could it be?* Kael thought, barely realizing he was speaking aloud when he said, "I saw him die! What proof do you have of this?"

"Perhaps you did, Kael," Algernon replied, "but there are many dimensions and planes of existence that we know nothing about. There are different states of being and consciousness outside our own; we may only guess at how such things come to pass. The forces of darkness burn with a great fire, a great longing to corrupt and dominate, and only when the combined well of souls of all free people unite may such flames ever be extinguished." He squeezed his fingers into a fist.

"We have a witness who saw him," Thargelion interjected, his face downcast. "I'm sure you recall the Wood Elves of the Shrine of Haloreth who awarded you the staff you carry for saving them. They have all been killed—massacred, down to the last child. A lone Elven hunter, the very last of their kind, witnessed a figure in black possessed of powerful dark magic kill Lothinir, the servant of the shrine. For his own protection, we sent him to Alluviam to recover. The figure wore a golden helmet; however, Lothinir recognized him, a look of astonishment and fear was said to be present on his face before . . . he was murdered."

"That's no proof of anything," Kael protested. "How do you know for certain that it was him?"

"He led a force of Stygian Knights," the old King said, managing to meet Kael's eyes, "allied with creatures of the Morval Mountains."

Kael closed his eyes and winced as if in pain. He remembered the beauty of the home of the Wood Elves. He remembered their kindness and the faces of the children as they played in the trees. He remembered when Lothinir himself had presented him with his enchanted staff after Lark and he had rescued them from the magical limbo the Shadow Prince had consigned them to years earlier. The thought that they were all dead was beyond believable.

"You spoke of a dark alliance?" Elenari prompted gently.

Algernon's sky-blue eyes gleamed back at Nari. "Indeed, by all accounts, the Shadow Prince hopes to turn the nations against one another, so that eventually all the lands will owe him fealty. Should this come to pass, all races will suffer an eternity of pain and torment."

Humidity settled in the chamber as Thargelion wiped his brow with an unsteady hand. Kael waited patiently, staring blankly at Algernon, for the Sage to tell them what was required of them.

Feeling the burning desire of Kael's eyes pressing upon him, the Sage walked slowly as if gathering his thoughts. Suddenly, he turned to face them, his robe reeling behind him, and spoke to them in hushed tones. "My friends, if there is going to be an all-out war, as the King and I sense there must be, it cannot be fought without an alliance of all the remaining free nations. We, as a whole, must unite!" Algernon again walked between them; their eyes fixed upon him as he stroked his long silver beard. "Therefore, my friends and allies, the Kingdom of Wrenford reaches out to you.

Its only hope of regaining eternal peace lies with you and your abilities. Join me, and venture out to the distant nations, which need the guidance and skills of experienced warriors. Help me unite those countries that yearn, as we do, for everlasting harmony. Rekindle their values of freedom, and resurrect alliances long thought dead and buried. It is high time they were brought forth out of the growing dark."

The sunlight seemed to stream more brightly through the stained-glass windows. Algernon continued with renewed passion, stirring them to believe that they truly were the chosen ones for this journey. "By creating an alliance with our neighbors, we will have the forces to combat this dreaded disease and prevent it from massing its destructive powers. For one man defending his homeland is more powerful than the strongest mercenary.

"The second part of our journey might possibly be even more vital to our ultimate victory and survival," Algernon continued. "Help me carry the Emerald Star to Cordilleran, our neighbor to the south, which seems to be the primary concern of the evil forces that threaten us all. For only the Emerald Star, forged by Thargelion and the Elves, has a chance to save Cordilleran and its Dwarven inhabitants from extinction. Its powers of protection may yet rid Cordilleran of its unwanted trespassers."

The second Kael heard Algernon speak of removing the mystical gemstone from Wrenford, an uneasy fear struck him. Wrenford would be little more than defenseless and surely would fall quickly to the dark hosts forming outside its borders.

As if reading Kael's mind, Algernon spoke, "Yes, the Emerald Star is truly the only defense Wrenford has against such evil. The sacrifice of Wrenford is a small price to pay for the survival of our world. Have no illusions that is what we are now discussing."

As Kael met Algernon's eyes, full of such impassioned remorse, it so moved him that he found himself feeling undesirably vulnerable.

Galin listened in silent anger, thinking to himself how outrageous it was for the ruler of Wrenford to decide such a fate for his people. Who were these men to condemn their countrymen in the slim hope that a viable alliance could be formed to preserve what they euphemistically called "the free peoples of the world"? What made the nation of Cordilleran more deserving of preservation than Wrenford? Galin turned his head, and his gaze pierced the colored window to the west. In disgust, he tried to drown out Algernon's words as they echoed in his mind. Galin had always believed that life in any form was the most precious gift the world had to offer, and to risk disposing of it in such a manner was unthinkable to him. Brushing his hair out of his eyes, he again considered all that had been said that morning.

Still lost in thought, Galin did not even notice that Algernon suddenly stood beside him to his right, peering straight ahead through the window. Still looking into the distance, Algernon spoke in a strange voice that almost led Galin to believe the others could not hear him speak. "In any war, battle, strife, or contest, something is always won, be it a prize, money, freedom, survival, or just the knowledge that you met the enemy and defeated him. Therefore, every fight is worth fighting to some degree, and every sacrifice to arrive at those ends is viable and necessary."

Galin replied, though he knew his words were spoken in vain, "You know this Shadow Prince will look to destroy Wrenford first, especially without the protection of the Emerald Star. What's the garrison here? A few hundred? They have no chance against the numbers you are talking about. What of the people in the Citadel and outlying villages? What do you plan on telling them? The end you seek with your grand plan cannot justify the means!"

"Unless there is no other way to preserve the good," Algernon replied in a whisper. "If Wrenford falls, the race of men will continue on; if Cordilleran falls, the Dwarves will be extinct and their race forever wiped from this earth." He moved silently away to join the others.

"It was my decision to take the Emerald Star to Cordilleran," Thargelion said suddenly, his head bent and eyes staring at the floor. All eyes turned and rested upon the old King. Thargelion closed his eyes tightly. "It was a decision . . . that was not, by any means, made lightly."

In that instant Galin felt ashamed in spite of himself. He had failed to consider how difficult the decision must have been, both for the King and for Algernon. Both of them already felt the pain of losing Wrenford and grieved a thousand-fold for each death that would come. No souls would suffer more torment about the possible future than theirs. Galin knew he must unequivocally commit himself to whatever lay ahead, no matter his personal beliefs and opinions. *Perhaps*, he thought, *the end may somehow justify the means*. He turned and rejoined the others.

"Why would Lark and Archangel be attacked and/or kidnapped?" Kael asked suddenly. "Algernon, you said that you foresaw the danger to the Royales and hoped to arrive in time to prevent it. Would the Shadow Prince seek to attack Lark and me first because he considers us a danger to him? Do you think he was behind what happened? Why Lark first?"

Algernon and Thargelion passed a glance between them, which conveyed an understanding and reluctance. Kael saw the exchange and wondered if they knew more than they were revealing.

"I know why," Thargelion said. "Lark and Archangel are of my bloodline. Though quite distant and somewhat removed, their lineage can be traced back to my house. No . . . they do not know, but it was how I found Lark years ago when the Emerald Star was stolen and you first came before me, Kael. It was better for all that no one knew. It was safer for Lark. The Shadow Prince labored endlessly for years to discover the workings of the mystical emerald, and time and again, the knowledge to wield it eluded him. Now, I fear it is possible that he had discovered that which I hoped he never would."

"What is it you fear he has discovered?" Kael asked, still somewhat in shock after learning his best friend was a blood relative of the King.

"That one of my bloodline whose heart is pure and righteous can tap the powers of the Emerald Star," Thargelion replied gravely. "Algernon can wield the gemstone because long ago I imparted the ability to him magically. The side effect of such magic is that it has granted him an unnaturally long life. I'm sure by now you have guessed he is far older than any human man ever could be. At any rate, if the Shadow Prince were ever to gain possession of the Emerald Star with someone to wield it for him, he would be unstoppable even unto the ending of all things. That, above all else, must never come to pass."

"Lark would gladly die before helping the Shadow Prince," Kael stated flatly. "You must know that."

"If Stranexx has found a way to cheat death," Thargelion responded, "he is no doubt in league with evil powers beyond our understanding. His power and influence are being felt throughout the lands, spreading like a disease. It is possible that even a man as strong as Lark may not be able to resist it."

"What about Archangel?" Kael asked. "Could he wield the Emerald Star as well?"

"No," the King answered. "Though a good man, he had not dedicated his life to piety as a Paladin forsaking all else. . . . Well, that is all the tale I wish to share for now—and perhaps even this is too much—but for my part, I can only beseech you to aid us in our time of need. Algernon begins his great and perilous journey on the morrow, and I can only hope you will join him for all our sakes, and even for the sakes of those who do not yet know the great service you undertake in their names."

Sensing the old king's weariness, Algernon decided that further discussion would wait until morning. He assured the party he would outline the details and the order of their destinations during the morning preparations. For the night, Kael and his companions were offered every luxury the Citadel of Wrenford had to extend.

That night, each of them went to sleep with their own aspirations, questions, and thoughts of what would be waiting for them when they awoke.

Chapter 5

He hung loosely by the wrists in a cold, moist concrete cell, with his hands and feet chained to the wall. Blood dripped from his wrists, and his hands rested lifeless in iron shackles. A single oil lantern dimly lit the west wall. Its light danced in response to the cool breeze, which blew in through unseen cracks from the innermost recesses of the chamber. He was stripped down to his undergarments, which were now well soiled with blood and dirt. Drops of blood trickled down his right calf and splashed into the growing red puddle beneath his body. His blond hair, stringy from the dampness, covered his face and eyes, which were tightly closed caused by the potions he had been forced to ingest earlier.

A wooden door opened slowly to the right somewhere, scraping against the stone floor. A figure holding a large fiery torch entered the square-shaped chamber.

Slowly, the shadowy form edged closer to the chained man. The form wore a black hooded robe, elegantly tailored to fit the features of his body. A brilliantly forged dagger, its hilt studded with diamonds and sapphires, was strapped to the right of his waist alongside pouches of herbs and roots. The gems glinted in the half-light, capturing the illumination and bouncing it back upon the prisoner. Adorning his neck was a tightly wrapped, black silk scarf.

The man removed his hood, revealing a long scar running down his right cheek. His lengthy black hair was slicked back, displaying his almond-shaped eyes, which appeared blood red when the light of the torch struck them. A relaxed, mocking grin formed at the left side of his mouth. He and his men did excellent work. He had been warned that this pathetic mess in front of him was capable of easily defeating all six of his men. He could hardly believe it.

He spoke to his unconscious prisoner. "Fortune has surely smiled on you this day, my friend. The Shadow Prince has use for you yet. But when he's finished with you, I intend on slaughtering you like a helpless lamb, Lark Royale."

Elenari woke just before dawn. Escorted by a guard, she took her short sword and a sharpening stone and went to the courtyard. Her thick ebony cloak protected her from the chill of the early morning hours. Her timing was perfect; it was nearly an hour until the sun rose. The familiar purple and pink blotches had begun to appear in the sky along the horizon line, signaling the birth of a new day.

She sat on a smooth marble bench near the rose garden, pretending to sharpen the magic blade of her weapon. True, her sacred blade, *Eros-Arthas*, would never dull—the blades forged for the Kenshari would never lose their edge—but the exercise, though moot, always helped her think. The sword reflected dull light as the darkness of night fought to linger on.

Nari could not help but wonder what would be expected of her during this journey. None of them, even Kael, had ever traveled with Algernon before. The old Sage seemed relatively fit, but what would happen if they were hard-pressed in battle? What if they had to run and their lives depended on their swiftness? What would this wise old man do then?

The more Elenari thought about it, the more she felt Algernon's presence would only slow them down. True, Kael was getting well on in age, but Druids had the luxury of always being in the most vigorous prime of health, regardless of their age. It was one of the many benefits of devoting their lives to the service of Mother Nature. She knew Kael was more than capable of meeting the physical demands of such a perilous journey.

Still, she couldn't help but like Algernon. If nothing else, he was charming, and she knew they could find solace in the Sage's soothing words.

Galin stared up at the stone ceiling of the lavish room afforded him by the hospitality of the King. The great brass-framed bed made no annoying squeaking noises, and the pillows were not filled with itch-inducing feathered stuffing. The King's decorator was indeed both meticulous and tasteful.

Galin smirked, thinking to himself how odd it was that, with all the day's events, he felt it necessary to opine on the furniture of his overnight lodging. If only times were such that something so mundane could be thought of as important. In a few hours, he would quite probably begin the greatest, most significant journey of his existence. He couldn't help wondering what special part he might play. Despite his misgivings, he resolved to himself that he would join this quest with Algernon and the others. If for no other reason than for his own righteousness, he would do it to serve the will of Mother Nature.

Kael did not sleep at all. He lay motionless for hours, going over the final moments he and Lark had spent with the Shadow Prince years earlier in his mind. He remembered the Shadow Prince's staff shattering and releasing enough power to destroy the entire top of the tower. *There could be no escape*, he thought. *Nothing could have survived within the heart of that blast.*

Try as he might, he could not discern a logical explanation for what he had learned from Algernon the previous evening. If only he could accept the truth and move on, but he couldn't. He knew he could never truly rest until he confronted Wolfgar Stranexx again. Only this time, would they have enough power to destroy him?

Several hours later, Elenari, Galin, and Kael assembled in the main audience chamber. They indulged in a brief breakfast provided by the king's servants. Conversation was hollow at best, and cursory. They each eagerly awaited Algernon and longed to begin the inescapable journey ahead of them.

At that moment, Algernon burst through the doors. Lingering in the doorway for a moment, he gestured to them that it was time to leave.

"Come," he said. "We've lost precious time already which is my own fault but we can afford to delay no longer. Your horses are saddled and waiting. Be sure that you have all the equipment you need. There will be no turning back once we begin."

The party checked their packs and weapons and secured the generous rations of food and water given them by Thargelion's servants. Within a matter of minutes, the three companions followed the Sage out into the courtyard.

There, as promised, four saddled horses waited patiently for their new masters. A slight wind rustled through their cloaks and under their tunics as the small group made their way toward their steeds. The horses grazed upon the brilliant green grass, which flourished in the beaming morning sun. These were truly magnificent animals. Two of the four horses had stunning manes of white, while the other two had manes as black as coal. There was no doubt that these mounts, with their toned, muscular legs and crystal-clear, dark eyes, were healthy and swift. A large oak tree, which Galin identified as centuries old with a mere glance, sheltered the animals from the direct sunlight.

As the three drew close to the horses, Elenari, moving slightly more briskly than the others, noticed a figure lying beneath the aged oak. The man wore a long green robe made of finely tailored, rich fabric. Leather armor could be seen covering his well-tanned skin. A shining silver cross-bow lay across his legs, and a scabbard of a long sword rested beside his right arm.

Curiosity moved Galin now, and he walked away from the horses to take a closer look at the man resting in the shade of the tree. Slowly, the stranger pushed himself up from the earth and dusted himself off. Despite the fact the most of his face was covered by dark brown hair, Galin knew who he was. Brushing his tangled hair aside, the man looked at Galin. His brown eyes sparkled, even in the shade, as he watched the others gather around him. It was difficult to discern his age though not less than forty seemed a safe guess.

Algernon, holding a large, leather-bound tome with metal fasteners in his right hand, went to shake the stranger's hand. Elenari knew immediately that this man knew the art of woodcraft and tracking as she did, and that, like her, he was a Ranger.

Algernon smiled as he began to introduce the outsider, "My friends, I would like you to meet—"

At that moment Galin cut him off, finishing the sentence for him. "Hawk," the Druid exclaimed, "of the Freeholds of Gallandor!"

Algernon raised his eyebrow in rare surprise, "Do you know our guide, Galin?"

Kael looked on with sharpened interest, awaiting Galin's response; neither he nor Elenari had ever seen this man before.

"Well," Galin responded humorously, "there is some comfort in knowing you can be surprised, Algernon. Know him? I saved his life many times over."

Hawk let out a deep, bellowing laugh, which seemed to shake the ground they were standing on. Straightening, the party could see he was broad but exceptionally lean-muscled, which made him well suited for the art of tracking.

"You, save *me*?" Hawk mocked him. "It was I who saved you, my Druid friend. Were it not for me, you would still be digesting in the stomach of the Goreth we encountered unexpectedly those years ago."

Still laughing, both men embraced tightly, and then pushed each other away to have a better look at one another.

"I see time has been good to you, Galin," the Ranger said, patting his friend on the back. "But that is the way of Druids, is it not?"

"I find it astonishing you are still alive to insult me," Galin responded with a smirk. "I thought your dangerous escapades in the Freeholds would have finished you off years ago."

"No, my friend," Hawk answered. "Even I have somewhat mellowed with age, believe it or not. What about you, Galin? You were young and bold in those days—an initiate priest out to save the world."

Galin smiled. "Not anymore, I have . . . settled down and took a turn at the quiet life these past years." Out of the corner of his eye, Galin noticed a distinct change in Algernon's face as he spoke.

Kael and Elenari looked on, smiling. Without further hesitation, Galin quickly took his friend by the arm and introduced him to his other companions. "Kael, Elenari, I would like you to meet an old friend of mine.

This is Hawk, a Ranger and—how does one say it?—a soldier of fortune, from the Freeholds of Gallandor."

"Well, that's one way of saying it," Hawk responded as he vigorously shook first Elenari's hand, then Kael's. Although his grip was tight and uncomfortable, Kael continued to smile politely at the newest member of their group.

"Yes, Kael," said Hawk reverently, "the Grand Druid. I am honored. The King has told me of you and your daughter. It is a pleasure to meet you both."

Elenari nodded reassuringly to Hawk and moved away to tend to her horse, deciding to keep out of conversation's way.

"So, you have spoken to Thargelion?" Galin questioned as he pulled his cloak about himself to protect him from the cool morning breeze.

"Of course, it was King Thargelion who summoned me here," replied Hawk. "I was most recently doing some tracking along the outskirts of Alluviar, the Elven capital, when I encountered a man in what is virtually the wilderness. He identified himself as a scout of Wrenford in service of Thargelion. I was amazed when the remarkable fellow stopped me, called me by name, and informed me that King Thargelion of Wrenford required my service at once. At first, I thought the man a lunatic, but after hearing what he had to say, I no longer doubted him. I've done services for Thargelion in the past, and he has always paid handsomely. So, here I am, part of your merry band."

"Hawk is one of the best guides in all the lands," Algernon added. "We will need his abilities to see us through the mountains and into Mystaria beyond. Fortune has smiled upon us that he arrived in time. He will be an invaluable asset."

"The King himself has briefed me," Hawk said to Galin. "However, there is still much I do not understand. At any rate, I agreed to guide your party through the Andarian Ranges. Beyond that, we shall see."

"Forgive me, gentlemen," Algernon interjected flatly. "I do not wish to break up your reunion but we are losing valuable daylight. The time is now. We must begin our journey."

One of the guards brought Hawk's steed to him. It was an older horse, but Hawk refused to ride any other. The gray steed, which he had named Silvermane, with his cracked leather saddle, moved close to its master as

Hawk stroked the animal's thick mane. A large, black sack hung from the back of the saddle. Hawk touched the animal with such unusual gentleness that it seemed as if the horse and whatever it carried were all Hawk had in the world.

Elenari took discreet notice of the exchange; she could not help but respect any man who knew how to treat an animal. She smiled as she mounted.

Algernon looked to the sky, shielding his eyes from the glare with his right hand; he noticed the small puffs of clouds that dotted the ocean-blue heavens like cotton. The sun appeared high, nearly undimmed and completely visible. He pulled himself atop his white steed and looked to the others, who were already mounted and awaiting his order.

The air about the courtyard grew suddenly thicker, as if in that moment the wavering summer humidity had chosen to spread throughout Wrenford. All eyes were on Algernon as he positioned his horse in the middle of the others. The morning birds chirped their songs of hope in unison at that moment, as if bestowing a blessing upon the party. Algernon looked up, and the others turned to follow his gaze upward.

It was Thargelion who had caught Algernon's attention, standing atop one of the towers. His robes billowing in the wind, he seemed like a scarecrow set upon his fortress to frighten away those dark things that threatened his land. He waved to them in a gesture of farewell.

Algernon nodded and smiled to his King and friend of so many long years. He found he had to look away, quickly, so the others could not see the sadness in his face as he collected himself. "Goodbye, my King, my dearest friend," he said in a whisper that went unheard by the others.

"Friends," Algernon said, "let us begin our trek. The roads we will travel will be long and rife with danger, for the people and customs we encounter within each country will be much different from those most of us are familiar with. The first leg of our journey will be to cross the Andarian Ranges. These ancient mountains to the west, with their sharp rocks and dangerous paths, will lead us to the lands of Mystaria, home of the magic users. I will not mislead any of you: Mystaria holds nothing but danger for us."

Kael knew of Mystaria from stories he had heard over the years. He knew of the many weird and dangerous dwellers of that land. He also knew that Mystaria despised priests of all kinds; in fact, any priest discovered in Mystaria was arrested and quite possibly executed as a heretic. It was illegal for priests to even enter within the borders. He wondered how Algernon had planned to deal with such an eventuality.

Once again, as if Algernon were reading their minds, the old Sage spoke. "Kael, Galin, as Druid priests your presence in Mystaria will be extremely dangerous. This land of wizards and magic has but one strange religion, unique to itself, and all priests not of that religion will be seen as heretics and executed. Therefore, to protect yourselves, you must remove your holy symbols of mistletoe and never reveal them again, no matter the cost, until we leave Mystaria."

Galin and Kael looked at each other and did as the old Sage requested.

"For our purposes," Algernon continued, "Kael and Galin will be under the guise of magic students. Should anyone ask, I am taking them on a pilgrimage to the Great School of Magic. We have hired you Rangers"—he pointed to Hawk and Elenari—"as our guides and protectors. No one shall reveal their true name until we stand before Prince Maximillian, Chancellor of the Wizard Council of Mystaria. We will follow the Alband River south to Mystaria City. May luck and hope be with us and take us there safely. Let us be off."

Algernon led his horse alongside Hawk's, and they turned westward, moving at a slow trot.

As Thargelion watched them ride from the Citadel, he closed his eyes and winced as if struck by pain. There was so much they did not know. There was so much guilt that he alone must bear the burden of. He knew Algernon had felt that he, too, shared a measure of that guilt but the reality was that Thargelion alone bore the mantle of responsibility. The time had come, at last, when the demons of his past might yet come to chastise them all before the bitter end. He had no more tricks or magic left to save any of them. All he had was hope and he could not be certain he even had that.

The black figure stood upon the jagged rocks and stared into the darkness, unmoving. As the intense heat whirled about him, his dark robes whipped about violently in the hot wind.

He stood alone atop a molten heap of rock and lava, enduring the scorching air that no human could withstand. Suddenly, he raised both his arms above his hooded frame, and the earth's crust responded with agitation. Bubbling fire and volcanic soot shot upward hundreds of feet, only to splash down into the fiery pit below him.

The twisted figure began his chanting.

The shadows were darker than night now as they began to spin about him. As the powerful winds picked up, a swirling pool of lava formed in front of him. The intense heat and wind became stronger and stronger. As he chanted, the lava raged with a fury no longer driven by earthly forces. Rocks and fire spewed outward and lava poured forth as he gesticulated wildly with his hands. Using arcane gestures, he called upon an ancient evil.

The hot wind blew back the hood of the creature to reveal a mask of iron beneath a golden helmet. His deep voice became more thunderous and his chants more garbled.

In that instant, the entire east side of the volcano exploded outward with unbridled fury. Chunks of molten lava burst forth and fell to the earth below. From a distance, it appeared like a bright crimson shower of falling stars.

The dark figure's robed arms swung with renewed fury as the molten embers surged into the pitch-black sky. Shrieks of laughter somehow overcame the wrath of the rumbling mountaintop as the Shadow Prince moaned and wailed. He brought his hands down to his chest and there, cradled in his arms, rested a brilliant, magical diamond.

The stone encompassed the width and volume of a man's hand. It sparkled red from the molten lava beneath the Shadow Prince's feet. His helmet of gold reflected the tumultuous lava, which continued to bubble and burst.

Suddenly, he shot forth his hands out into the night and threw the diamond into the waiting lava. Just before the gemstone reached the pool of molten rock, a streak of lava discharged upward and engulfed the gem, pulling it deep within the pit of fire.

The Shadow Prince brought his arms down to his sides and awaited the outcome. Black robes still swaying in the hot breeze of the volcano, the dark form stared out through the dark eyeholes of his mask, his gaze penetrating into the fiery lakes of boiling rock.

Moments later, the volcano began to settle. The violent shaking had ended abruptly, and lava ceased to boil over the edges of the shattered mountainside.

As he looked downward, a small tributary gently snaked off the river of lava, which had settled around the base of the volcano. Slowly, the thin stream of lava made its way to the Shadow Prince. It flowed in a perfectly straight line, effortlessly, as if some unseen force was controlling it. It began to circle his feet.

Suddenly, the brilliant diamond surfaced within the lava before him. The Shadow Prince laughed as the lava continued to form into a man-like shape. It stood some ten feet high with discernable legs and arms. Within the center of its oversized head was the diamond.

"*Seek*," he commanded in hushed tones. "*Seek the Emerald Star.*"

Instantly, the molten creature turned away and began its hunt.

Chapter 6

Late morning came with dark clouds that pushed northward like invaders, making way for the crystal blue sky and warmth of the late summer sun that greeted the party as they traveled northwest.

Although the end of summer was approaching, the air and heat, which were usually unbearable around this time, were instead comfortable and somewhat relaxing. A moderately cool breeze blew from the south, tugging the massive pines and oaks that lined the trail to the Andarian Ranges. As the wind blew through them, the leaves gently brushed against one another, creating an ever-so-slight rustling.

Their trail, well-trodden between grasslands, was composed of arid dirt with sparse patches of weeds, which darted along the dusty path. To the east and west grew enormous pine trees and venerable oaks, appearing by their grain and roots as if they had been growing there since the beginning of time. Their leaves were wilted and dry due to the apparently chronic lack of precipitation.

Here in the western portion of Wrenford, traveled mostly by merchants, the surrounding landscape was comprised of rolling hills full of life. Small multicolored birds swooped down from high above, searching for insects or any sign of their late-morning breakfast. Meanwhile, raccoons and squirrels alike crossed paths often, foraging in the darkness of the trees on either side of the trail.

The party of five, led by Hawk, moved swiftly and in single file. Galin, riding second, found himself frequently looking behind him to eye Algernon. He was impressed at how the Sage rode his white steed with competence and pride.

Kael rode behind the Sage, keeping his gaze fixed on the old man's back. He wondered if Algernon had told them everything or if he had chosen to keep some things to himself. He could not be sure. He also gave thought to his new title, Grand Druid, which he had otherwise given almost no thought to since he acquired it. That, too, would be a troublesome dilemma for him when the time came, but for now he could give it no further thought.

Elenari brought up the rear at a distance. She was the anchor of the group, her eyes constantly probing deep within the thickets of the woods around and behind the party.

Kael and Galin agreed between themselves that, for safety's sake, Algernon would ride between them when the trail allowed. After all, he carried the magical Emerald Star.

Elenari's half-Elven senses benefitted them greatly. She constantly watched the rear to ensure they were not being followed. At times, she faded back and waited for the party to move out of sight before she would catch back up to them.

Conversation was light and uninteresting for the most part. Now and then, Hawk would point in the direction they were heading and make reference to specific plant or animal life that he thought may be of interest.

Galin continued to look toward Algernon, who always returned the glance with a nod and a smile. Despite the old man's pleasant demeanor, Galin could not help but question if the elderly Sage was truly capable of such a journey. Interestingly enough, he somehow found comfort in the presence of the old man. Was it the knowledge and wisdom he had shared, or was it his unerring optimism and belief that all would work out for the best? Either way, Galin maintained a constant curiosity about this wondrous elder. *What stories he could probably tell,* Galin thought as he patted his dark steed and rode onward.

As the morning shifted into afternoon, the party glimpsed the peaks of the mountaintops to the west, towering over the small trees below. By nightfall, they would be nearly at the foot of the Andarian Ranges.

It was afternoon now; the yellow sphere of sun beat down upon both the land and the travelers. Occasionally, it would sink behind the clouds, which dotted the sky like enormous masses of cotton, allowing them brief periods of respite from the intense rays of heat.

Kael, feeling assaulted by the hot rays of the bright sun, took refuge in the brown hood atop his head. Thoughts of all that had occurred continued to race through his mind—the battle with Talic, the painful feelings of insecurity within his scarred soul, and the potential loss of his friends. Lark Royale, his best friend of many years, was either dead or captured. Why?

Kael thought back to his first meeting with Algernon when he and Lark had arrived at the Dragon's Breath Inn of Wrenford. Most people's first impression of the young Paladin had been that he was pompous and self-righteous, and there could be no denying he had been so at times. Kael smiled as he recalled fonder times.

Over the years, Kael had learned to block out his memories of their encounters with the Shadow Prince, but on occasion, he would remember. Whenever he got together with Lark, the Paladin always managed to bring the subject to the surface somehow.

"Good against evil, my old friend," Lark would say to him. "Good shall always overcome in the end, Kael; have faith, and trust in that."

The smile fell from Kael's face as he let slip an inaudible whisper, "How will it overcome this time?"

In the midafternoon, the clouds became few and far between, and their fleeting protection from the sun all but disappeared. The dark clouds that had approached earlier in the day had receded like unwelcome guests, and the heat from the sun continued unchecked. The trail, still arid and dusty, had not seen rain for some time now. As the horses passed, whirling clouds of brown dust rose up from the ground to stick to the perspiration on the travelers' bodies.

They continued primarily in tight single file, given little choice by the narrow confines of the trail they followed. Hardly a meaningful word had been spoken since they had left the Citadel of Wrenford; no one had the strength to speak. The heat consumed their power and drained them of their will to talk or move too much.

At times, Hawk would briefly stop the party to rest the horses. The dwindling shade of the thinning pines and oaks that towered above them was a welcome haven.

As Algernon dismounted, he spoke quietly to Hawk, out of earshot of the others. "You know your trade well indeed," said the old Sage with a lighthearted chuckle. "You had us continue on farther, I think, than any of us wanted to go only so we would appreciate our rest here in this densely shaded area of our path. Excellent."

The companions gave water and oats to their mounts and removed their saddles to ensure that they were indeed well-rested—all save Elenari, who turned her horse and rode back from whence they had come.

"Where's she going?" Galin asked Kael, gently stroking his horse.

"She is going to mask our tracks and make sure we are not being followed," said Kael as he re-secured his saddlebags.

"You know, Kael," Algernon said with a shake of his head, "she is quite something, that daughter of yours." He swallowed a piece of bread, opened his leather-bound book, and began to scribble down his private thoughts.

Several minutes later, Elenari returned noiselessly into view. She nodded to Hawk and they began to saddle the horses to continue on.

Thankfully, they traveled through a more densely forested area now and maintained an increased pace with the setting of the sun, but the forest gave way to mere patches of trees as they approached the base of the mountains. They felt cool and refreshed for a change. They were more relaxed, and each seemed ready to continue for some time until they would camp for the night. Then, suddenly, Hawk stopped the party. Algernon and Elenari rode to the front to confer with him. A moment later, Hawk signaled for them to dismount. They gathered close and remained standing while Algernon spoke.

"We shall camp for four hours, after which we shall travel for the remainder of the night until morning before we stop again. Those who would hinder us will assume that we will travel by day only. If we travel by both day and night, resting at specific intervals, we will gain twice as much ground while still remaining well-rested. There will be no fire. We shall have to endure without cooked food until such time that we have sufficient cover. There shall be no watch; the animals will alert us if anyone comes. Sleep now, and rest well, for we are still within the safety of Wrenford's borders."

The Sage then took Kael and Galin aside and spoke to them briefly before lying down to rest. Hawk watched as Galin and Kael went to each horse in turn and spoke into their ears in a soft language unlike any he had heard before. Realizing what they were doing, he understood that the horses would indeed alert them of danger. He had forgotten the advantages of traveling with Druids. Their task complete, the Druids took to their earthen beds, and soon all of them were asleep.

The hours passed quickly but comfortably. In no time, Elenari was back in the saddle and off scouting into the darkness as the others prepared to continue. As before, she returned within minutes and spoke with Hawk. It was decided that, during night travel, Elenari would lead the party because, due to her Elven heritage, she possessed a keener sense of vision in the darkness than Hawk. She had the ability akin to Elves to see into the infrared spectrum, which enabled her to see anything at night that gave off heat energy. In the dark, Nari's vision could see comfortably at nearly sixty feet what the others could barely make out at twenty feet.

The party continued on like the shadows that glided through the vanishing woodlands. Elenari would stop the party frequently to confer with Hawk about signs on the trail and directions; however, this did not impede their progress in any fashion. They traveled throughout the remainder of the night and straight on until dawn. At daybreak, they stopped and rested.

"We shall sleep five hours," said Algernon, "Not a moment longer. Rest well." He curled up beneath a tree and fell instantly to sleep.

At noon, they awoke and the journey continued. This day, the sun showed no mercy. The trees cracked in agony, and the leaves seemed to wilt before their eyes. The noise of their horses' hooves trampling the fallen leaves was reminiscent of a damp fire. The trees were much smaller now and rapidly thinning as they climbed the mountain trail.

Kael couldn't help but think that the scorching heat seemed to be a catalyst for the poison that already infested the lands. There were no birds chirping, no animals scurrying across their path; there seemed to be no living things anywhere around them. It was too hot, too draining.

Galin wiped the dirt and sweat from his brow and looked to the east. A moment later he found himself coughing as a thick cloud of dust rose from Hawk's horse in front of him. The dirt seemed to settle in layers upon him, but he smiled nonetheless, glad his old companion was here with him once again.

But the smile slowly left his face as he further contemplated things. Galin brought his gaze to bear on Algernon behind him. Once again, the old Sage, his long white beard now dotted with dirt, nodded and smiled. He seemed to have the answers to all unanswered questions.

Hawk sat with a proud posture astride his horse. He rode handsomely with the grace of a nobleman, yet to the others he was still little more than a mercenary. His green cloak hung loosely now about his broad shoulders. His sword rested snugly within its brown leather scabbard across his back.

Hawk found himself reflecting on his own life for a moment. He had chosen the adventurous life long ago, selling his skills and sword to the highest bidder. He became a pursuer of thrills and knowledge. Like all Rangers, he was a loner. He never stayed in one place too long, never getting too close to anyone—save, perhaps, for Galin. Sometimes, these things were his regrets, his nightmares. There was no longer any place he could call his own. Once, long ago, he had a great name, a fine home, and plenty of wealth. But he had given it all up—or, to be more accurate, it had been taken away from him. The prospect of having a family also seemed impossible to him.

The sight of the looming Andarian Ranges in the distance brought him back to the present. Hawk knew these mountains well. Many considered him the best tracker in the northern lands. Despite this, he was highly impressed with Elenari's skills. While his skills as a Ranger seemed more natural and hers more practiced, hers were certainly no less efficient or effective. Additionally, she had extremely heightened senses, even for one only half Elven. Throughout the length of the afternoon he contemplated his place within their group.

Kael removed his hood; his head pounded, and his sweat stood out against his dark robe for only a moment before the heat swallowed and absorbed it, like summer's dew upon a fertile plain. Droplets of sweat streaked jaggedly across his dry lips. His eyes remained on the old man in front of him. His thoughts, however, continued to drift back to his encounter with Talic, and the fight that had changed his future once again. Oblik had increased his power to that of the Grand Druid, but he struggled within himself for the courage he would need. He had never experienced such an inner struggle before. Perhaps it was because he had resolved to retire from a life of adventure before all this had happened. He might even have refused Talic's challenge and given up his powers had he not sensed the evil poisoning the lands. Inevitably, he knew that he must face the Shadow Prince again, and this time he must utterly destroy him. Why then was this all so difficult to come to terms with?

The purpose of his journey continued to consume Kael's thoughts as he rode on. It was a journey to find himself, to learn, and even to rediscover himself. But how, he wondered, could they destroy a being such as the Shadow Prince, who had somehow returned from the inescapable realm of death? If, indeed, his powers transcended mortality, then their journey might well be in vain.

The relentless sun rained suffering down upon the dried lands. Somehow, perhaps through force of will alone, the companions continued forward on their almost impossible quest filled with unknowns.

Save the lands, save Cordilleran, stop the Shadow Prince—all of these thoughts raced through Elenari's mind. The young half Elf rode behind her father, the stoic anchor of the group. Her eyes never stopped moving. She saw everything. The heat bothered her to a lesser degree than the others. After all, the Elven part of her granted her far more endurance than her human half. Her straight blonde hair seemed to repel the rays of the sun, rather than absorb them.

Born from a mix of races, Elenari grew up with Kael, never knowing her real parents and always wondering why they left her. Never, in all that time, had she shown anger at them openly; in truth, she felt none. She considered her life, such as it was, a great gift, and she was grateful for all she had and all she had accomplished.

Elenari decided to fall back a few paces behind the rest of the company. Although she was behind them, she could still observe everything. She heard the jingling of Hawk's hand axe at his side, saw the patterned movement of Galin's reins, felt the restlessness of her father ahead of her, and heard the deep measured breaths of the old Sage. She patted her steed on the neck and urged him on, always peering into the shadows of the trees and rocks on either side of them, always prepared for the unexpected.

Most men underestimated Elenari because of her slight appearance. For weeks on end, she would go off alone in the woods, away from her adoptive family, to hone and sharpen her skills. She knew the full range and extent of her abilities, and knew her limitations better than others might think. She knew this and was proud of it. Aside from Kael, her skills were all she had.

Elenari admired her father. Kael was the only person she would trust . . . could trust. He was the only person she wanted to be with. He was the only person she ever needed. But things had changed. Since Kael had been forced to become the Grand Druid, he had withdrawn within himself. Elenari was wary of this, and it concerned her greatly.

The brown peaks of the Andarian Ranges towered grimly over the horizon. They radiated a sense of foreboding, a feeling that warned travelers not to enter. They had reached the foothills and the peaks drew nearer with every mile. Despite any foreboding, in time, they would enter the darkness of those looming mountains.

On the trail, the air about them seemed almost too heavy to breathe. A warm wind shot through them incessantly, searing their faces, chapping their lips, and increasing their fatigue. The trees hissed like serpents as their desiccated leaves rustled. Dust clouded the air in their wake as they pressed onward.

By mid-evening, Hawk thought it best to set up camp to give the horses and themselves some much-needed rest. They turned left off the trail into a clearing, where they unsaddled the horses and released them to graze on what grass they could find.

The men each drew from their store of rations some dried meat, ale, and bread and sat together under the crystal sky. Elenari, however, chose to enter a small thicket of trees south of the camp, informing Kael that she would soon return.

With Algernon's permission, Hawk had built a small fire out of broken sticks and dried leaves. Although a fire was not necessary, and knowing the dangers, Hawk reluctantly allowed it, resigned to the fact that a camp without a fire was not a true camp. Since they had gained so much ground, thanks to Algernon's plan of travel, they were entitled to quietly enjoy themselves as they sat about the crackling blaze and ate their meal.

Algernon sat contentedly on his knees, a seemingly uncomfortable position to the others. He ate at a large piece of cheese, which he followed with gulps of ale. As the crickets chirped nearby, the old Sage's eyes darted back and forth to each of his companions as if he were trying to read their minds.

"I remember a time," he said, breaking the silence, "when the very land on which we sit was cold and desolate."

Pushing himself up from the dry ground, he brushed his white robe free of dirt, groomed his silver beard, and walked away from the fire. A large rock formation stood near their camp, and he approached it, his hands grasping at the aged rocks as if he needed their support. The others noticed his touch was a gentle caress. He looked down at the ground and then up into the darkness of approaching night. His low melodic tone caught hold of each of them in turn.

"Many years ago," he said, "before there was a time that mattered to most, these lands were inhabited by dark creatures—creatures of loathing. What we now call Wrenford was nothing more than a waste of space, wasted on monsters dwelling in darkness and feeding on horrors. They were deformed creatures that walked, crawled, flew, and even burrowed. Dig deep into the well of your imaginations and you could not conceive of such foul-looking things."

He strolled over to Kael, whose eyes were wide with interest. "No man dared try to live here." He turned quickly to Galin. "No race at all dared to venture here."

Hawk, who had been lying down half-conscious, pushed himself upward to listen. He found himself strangely attracted to Algernon's voice.

The elderly Sage wet his lips and crossed to Galin's side. "Soon these creatures began to push outwards into the neighboring lands where the other races dwelled, such as they were."

The young Druid looked up at him, wondering how old he truly was. He had heard Thargelion say that, as a side effect of his magic, Algernon had been granted longer life, but how much longer?

"Then," the Sage continued, "In a time when the moon was full and the lands were quiet, it was decided. Something must be done. In what is now called the Kingdom of Alluviam, a council of free peoples decided that these creatures must be destroyed where they lived and bred. They decided to send an army full equipped. A young Elven Prince, one of many sons to the King, was chosen to lead this army. He was a powerful wizard even in his youth. His mystical prowess was matched only by his tenacity as a warrior.

"But . . . he was a visionary, which placed him in disfavor with his father and siblings. He believed that people had an innate right to freedom and that no man or species should be subject to the rule of another against their will. However, despite this, none could deny his abilities or their love for him.

"He was a natural leader," Algernon said affectionately. "Charismatic and righteous, he inspired fierce loyalty among his men. So it was that he was sent to the lands southeast of Mystaria to rid them of the scourge, which thrived there."

Algernon paused and scanned the group of faces about him. He had captured their interest entirely; they hung on his every word. The burning embers of the fire floated up and disappeared into the darkness. The crickets and grasshoppers no longer made their music. Everything, even the horses, seemed to be listening to Algernon's tale. The wind swept across the lands, and he moved closer to the campfire, trying to regain his thoughts. As he spoke, the Sage gestured with his hands so that it appeared he was spinning thread, a tale that entwined all who listened.

"The army, twenty thousand strong, was armed with the finest weaponry in the known world. Each was courageous, strong, and highly skilled. However, it was the exceptional strength and determination of their commander upon which they all relied."

He stopped for a moment and walked away from the fire, looking out of the clearing and beyond into the trails ahead. He stood at the edge of the campsite with his back to the rest of the group, fidgeting almost nervously with his fingers.

"As they entered the Andarian Ranges," he said, "they were ambushed by the evil creatures I spoke of earlier. Try as they might, there was no escape. They fought bravely, hacking away at the claws that reached for their throats, but there were far too many—more than they could have possibly imagined. The young prince pulled his men back out of the mountains for a full retreat."

Algernon turned and faced his companions once more. "In the end, several thousand were lost. Those few that remained fled back into Mystaria. The young prince took sole responsibility for the loss and placed the misguided blame upon himself. From that moment on, he charged himself with the task of forever ridding the lands of those dreaded monsters. The next battle would be a personal one."

Again, as if reading their minds, Algernon spoke, "Thargelion never forgave himself for the loss of those men. Yes, that young officer and prince is the now–King Thargelion who occupies the throne of Wrenford."

"An excellent story. Well told indeed, however, that story has been passed down from generations. No one knows if it ever happened and certainly even an Elf is not that long-lived. Your hero, old man, was not Thargelion but I do love a good fireside tale," Hawk said as he downed another ale and poured another.

Algernon merely smiled, "Perhaps, but I thank you for the compliment."

"How did the lands eventually become free from the creatures you spoke of?" Kael asked quietly, perplexed.

The old man sighed and sat himself down in the spot where he had been earlier, took a sip of ale, and looked at each of them in turn. "That is a story, I fear, which will have to wait for another night."

With that, Algernon lay down on the ground, pulled his robes close about him, and went fast to sleep.

A rustling rose up suddenly from behind Kael, within the trees, startling the party. Elenari emerged, returning from her nightly hike.

"That was a short walk, my dear," said Kael as he reclined. "You must be a bit tired tonight."

Elenari looked down at him quizzically. "Short?" Nari asked. "I've been gone the better part of the night."

She shook her head and moved to the warmth and comfort of the campfire. While the others turned in rather quickly for the remainder of the night, Elenari stared into the fire, her mind preoccupied.

The others were soon asleep, save Hawk, who appeared to have had a generous amount of ale in her absence. Suddenly, he dropped his mug, and its contents spilled into the fire. As he reached for it, the fire momentarily grew and bit at his hand. He pulled it back quickly, and Nari could tell from his face and the way he cradled his hand that the burn was considerable.

"Hawk, are you hurt?" she asked sincerely.

"Hurt?" he slurred, looking up with a wink. "What I am . . . is drunk! What *you* are is hurt." He pointed a finger at her.

"I don't know what you mean," she replied sharply, and withdrew from him.

"Hurt," he said again. He produced a piece of cloth from his belt and began wrapping it around his injured hand. "Troubled, child; you are troubled . . . come, what's the matter? Anyone with a good eye could see it. Sometimes it's easier to tell a stranger."

Nari looked at him for a moment and could not help but be impressed. She had never realized it was possible for humans to have such instincts, especially intoxicated ones; she had been wanting to talk to someone.

"All of this . . . has happened so fast," she whispered. "This was supposed to be a time for my father and me to get to know each other again. We've been apart for some time, you see, and we both wish to become a family again."

"Family?" Hawk exclaimed, using a stick to save his mug from the fire. "Why in the devil would you want that? Strike out on your own, I say. Travel the world; it's yours for the taking. No ties, no responsibilities, no obligations to hold you back. There are only the wonders out there, somewhere ahead of us. Families leave . . . they die."

"Have you never had a family of your own, Hawk?" Elenari asked intently. "Do you not think of them ever?"

Hawk stared deep into the fire for what seemed like an eternity. "Me? No," he said finally. He shook his head as if the idea was ludicrous. "Never. But I knew a man once who did." He motioned with his fingers for Elenari to come closer.

"I knew a man who had a family," he said sadly. "It was a small family, mind you, just his wife and son, but they were more precious to him than all the gold and jewels ever discovered. He was noble and strong with a great name and the means to protect them and keep them safe . . . and he loved them more than life itself. But the Jade Fever came upon them, a foe he could not fight with his strong sword arm, and infected both mother and son. Have you ever seen what it can do, that terrible affliction that strikes down both King and beggar alike? It liquefies your organs and literally boils your blood until the agony becomes so great that you die, and your corpse becomes an almost jade green. Poor man . . . poor unfortunate man. No . . . I do not think about my family."

With that, he turned over and soon began to snore lightly.

Elenari watched him. There was much more to this man than any of them had dared to guess. She felt his pain and saw the honesty etched in the lines of his forehead and face. Very few men of any race ever said anything worthy enough to move her so.

Hawk awoke to the blanket of a starlit sky. He leaned forward, feeling the sweat trickle down his face, and suddenly realized that he was alone. The others, the horses, all of them—were gone. It was the same patch of grass in which the five of them had made camp in earlier that night, yet now there had been no sign of their passing. He reached for his weapons only to discover that they, as well as his possessions, had vanished. He remained calm, for surely he was dreaming. However, there was something dreadfully real in all of this. The wind died, and the air became uncomfortably hot. An acute smell suddenly made his nostrils flare. The scent was not discernable, but a touch of death lingered in its wake.

Hawk awoke with a start to Elenari holding him fast about the shoulders. He was about to cry out but Elenari covered his mouth, calmed him and whispered in his ear, "It's all right . . . you had a nightmare."

She shook him once more and assured him that he was awake, but her intensity conveyed a deeper meaning. Instantly, Hawk realized something was wrong. Elenari silently motioned for him to get up and follow her. Slowly, casually, he reached for his sword and quietly strapped it to his back. He picked up his belt, which held his hand axe, and secured it as he followed her.

Hawk could see the others now as well. They appeared as little more than glistening silhouettes in the moonlight. It was enough for him that they were there, and he was free of the nightmare that had plagued him. The others stood in a circle, holding the reins of their mounts. As Hawk joined the circle, Galin handed him the reins of his own horse.

"There's something out there, behind us," Elenari said in hushed tones. "Whatever it is . . . it's not human. I can't track it."

"And it knows we are here," added Algernon reluctantly.

Elenari and Hawk conversed briefly in whispers and then bade all the men to mount their steeds. They began traveling at an agonizingly slow pace with Nari and Hawk riding in the rear, side by side. They had gone approximately fifty yards when Hawk gave a short yell and rallied the horses onward. Simultaneously, he and Nari let themselves fall back off their horses and disappeared into opposite sides of the woods. The other three men sped off into the night, racing into the nearby mountains.

Elenari crouched low to the ground and moved stealthily through the trees and brush. This patch of woods was rich with small trees, a perfect sanctuary for their intruder. She already had an arrow poised and ready as she searched. She was now hunting their stalker . . . silently.

Hawk crept soundlessly, hand axe grasped tightly, in the trees on the opposite the side of the trail. He sensed a presence now. He read the signs of the land around him, but they yielded no indication of any strange passing. He stopped, half-kneeling, and listened. He had an uneasy feeling; they were in imminent danger.

Dawn would soon be approaching, but a strange, dying half-light filled the area as the moonlight began to lose its power, and the land where they were hunting darkened.

Elenari was close. The creature began having trouble eluding her. She had no track or sign to go by, but she knew instinctively that she was directly on the creature's trail. All her feelings and senses told her so, and she trusted them implicitly. Still, her probing infravision saw nothing through the darkness. She was glad Algernon and the others had escaped to safety, because anything that could elude her Kenshari senses posed a deadly threat. There was more than just instinct present. There was a sense of intelligence about the thing as well.

Hawk cautiously made his way past the trees, shrubs, bushes, and weeds to enter a clearing approximately twenty yards in diameter. There, he sat and listened, hoping what was left of the waning moonlight would aid him and shed light on the intruder. He knew danger was very near because all the animals and insects had gone mute at a time when they should be releasing the sounds of life. He knew he must use an old technique to find these things. He closed his eyes and slowly tuned out the sound of his breathing, heartbeat, and thoughts, and listened for the sound that did not fit.

Suddenly, across the clearing from Hawk, a twig snapped. Instantly, he saw a bipedal figure across the clearing. In the second it took for his eyes to focus, he saw it was Elenari. He took a deep breath and nodded to her. She returned the gesture. Suddenly, Elenari made an unusual motion with her right arm, almost as if she had thrown something at him.

Hawk was astonished when it hit him like a rock hurled by a giant. He staggered back and looked to see a knife, buried to the hilt in his left shoulder. Without thinking, he was off and running through the high grass, pursuing his attacker, roaring, "Elenari!"

Nari appeared immediately across the clearing, right behind her imposter, and joined the pursuit. Faster than the human eye could follow, Nari fired three arrows at her imposter, who evaded them with phenomenal agility. Hawk reared back and let his hand axe fly. It soared like a guided arrow past the real Elenari and directly toward the back of the imposter. At the last moment, the intruder crouched to the ground and the axe struck and split a small tree.

Hawk collapsed and watched as Nari dropped her bow and quiver and began to run after their attacker, faster than humanly possible, and disappeared into the night.

A few minutes later, she returned, carrying a figure over her shoulder. Hawk, slumped up against a tree near the spot where he had collapsed, tried clumsily to reach for his sword, but Nari threw the creature to the ground at Hawk's feet.

Its loathsome, leathery carcass was riddled with stab wounds from Nari's curved short sword. Nari turned its bloody body over with her boot. It had thick gray skin that bunched at the joints of its lean bony frame. Huge lifeless eyes rested in the sockets of its oversized head. Hawk looked down at the creature whose blood was spilling out, soaking the earth. He looked up at Nari, whose hands were stained with crimson, and he knew in that moment, young woman or no, she was a skilled warrior who had more than earned his respect. The creature, he thought, must have felt astonishment at the time of its death, for it had met a hunter even deadlier than itself.

Elenari bent down to examine Hawk's wound, which had bled profusely and had not yet stopped. Hawk had already removed the knife leaving a circular black wound, which appeared to be swelling rapidly. Quickly Nari ripped the fabric of his tunic and began putting pressure on the wound.

"I'm sorry, I shouldn't have left you," said Nari sincerely.

"No . . . I'm glad you got it," Hawk replied weakly. "What is it?"

"It's a doppelgänger!" The exclamation came from behind them, and before the word was fully pronounced, Nari spun around with sword unsheathed. To her amazement, the figure of an old man emerged out of the waning night. At first, she thought it to be Algernon, but the peculiar accent confirmed that it was not. The newcomer was clad in dark robes. His hair was white, not as long and silvery as Algernon's, and he had no beard or mustache. His face was less wrinkled than Algernon's, his eyes deep-set. His skin was pale as if it had not seen the light of day for some time. The hair of his head resembled straw both lengthy and rigid, as if he were a scarecrow. There was a genuine quality about him, something non-threatening.

"I say there, girl!" he exclaimed. "Hold on just a minute now—didn't come here looking for no trouble. Can't handle much trouble at my age. Name's Rex, Rex Abernackle. Live up in the mountains. Make it my business to travel at night. Been seeing too many strange things lately. Say, your friend's bleeding there." The old man bent down to examine Hawk's shoulder.

"How do you know what this creature is?" Elenari asked without lowering her sword.

"Got me a few of these nasty beasts living up in the mountains," he replied without looking at her. "Have to be careful; they use their powers for two things: gold and food. They're intelligent, make no mistake, but evil to the core." He turned back to Nari. "Girl, if you can kill that monster, you got nothing to fear from me. I'm gonna look after your friend here."

Elenari sheathed her sword; though she did not like the way this old man had just shown up without warning, she sensed there was little to fear from him despite all.

Hawk's breathing had become unsteady. "That's bad poison," Rex said. "Works fast. You're going to have a fever, chills, shakes, delusions, the whole thing. Don't mean to give you bad news, son, but I believe in bein' honest. If we can get you to my cave, you'll be just fine. You hang in there now, son."

Elenari hurried away and reappeared moments later with their two horses.

"Do you know anything about poisons?" Nari asked. "Can you help him?"

"Sure, I know about poisons . . . used to make enough of them. You let me ride one of them horses, and you can take your friend on yours and follow me to my cave."

Nari looked down at the cracked, lined face and thin eyebrows and detected sincere caring in the old man's demeanor. She helped Hawk to his feet and up onto her horse.

Rex smiled and mounted Hawk's steed, Silvermane. "Stay close now. We're takin' a narrow trail into the mountains. Don't worry about the animals; they'll make it even though you'll think they won't."

With that, she followed Rex on horseback, holding Hawk tightly in the saddle before her. In what seemed like no time, the trees and forest cover had vanished and they were on a jagged, winding trail that steeply inclined at points, winding ever upward. Many fears raced through Nari's mind, not the least of which was the result of Hawk's irregular breathing. She believed he had lost consciousness, since he no longer responded to her. She also worried about the others; if, as the old man had said, there were more creatures roaming these mountains, what would become of them without their guides? She finally consoled herself with the thought that, as soon as she knew Hawk was safe, she would venture out to find Algernon and the others.

Within minutes, they arrived at a large dark orifice in the base of the mountainside. Elenari could tell there was torchlight beyond in the cavern.

They dismounted and together, Nari and the old man carried Hawk to the sanctuary within. Upon entering, Nari was amazed to see the old man had an extensive amount of possessions, supplies, food stores, and other oddities she had not expected a cave dweller to possess. The floor of the cave was almost totally lined with furs, blankets, and pillows. The entire back of the cave was taken up with large tables, holding several different glass containers of liquid in various colors. Beakers and tubes of all shapes and sizes were present along with several candle-operated burners. Still another large table contained a collection of powders, herbs, plants, shrubs, and a multitude of foreign substances. Lining the walls were row upon row of shelves of books and tomes. There was a small table set aside apparently for dining. In the alcove in the east corner of the chamber, she could see eating utensils, wineskins, several canteens, and a host of other supplies, presumably food stores.

They laid Hawk on a large pile of furs and covered him in blankets.

Elenari eyed Hawk carefully. He was already soaked in sweat and suffering from chills. It was the first time she had ever been this close to him, in truth. He really was a good-looking man—in his late thirties, she guessed. She put her hand to his forehead and felt he was burning up. The fever had set in exactly as the old man had predicted. His condition had deteriorated at such speed that he may well have been dead by now if she had taken more time pursuing the creature. She looked around for Rex, who was quickly skimming through a large tome with a metal binding.

"That's no ordinary poison your friend is infected with. It's laced, tainted with magic. Makes it work faster and makes it more resistant to antitoxins."

"What does that mean?" Nari asked, almost desperate. "Can you help him?"

"'Course I can help him; wouldn't have brought him up here if I couldn't. Just got to be careful is all. The antidote for this poison's got some volatile ingredients. Meaning there's no room for error."

Rex's hands moved as he spoke. He mixed several ingredients in a small bowl even as his eyes continued skimming the book in front of him. Without looking away from the book, he added several liquids and pinches of powder to the mix. Abruptly, he closed the book, picked up a small knife, and returned to where Hawk lay. Rex bent down and removed Hawk's vestment to reveal the wound. The swelling had increased considerably, as had the dark discoloration around the wound itself.

"Just need one more thing," he said. "You see, to make most cures complete, you always need a small sample of the disease or toxin involved." Gently he pressed the knife to the wound and removed a sliver of diseased skin from Hawk's shoulder. Then he stood up and returned to his table. "What's your name, girl?" Rex asked suddenly.

Elenari hesitated, unsure what to say.

"Well come over here, whatever-your-name-is. I'm going to need your help for a minute. Here, light this, and hold this beaker directly over the flame."

Rex poured the blue mix he was working on into a beaker, which he handed to Nari, after she had lit the burner as Rex directed. Hawk began to moan. Rex went over to his side to comfort him. He wet a fresh rag and put it to Hawk's forehead. He then covered him with more furs and tucked the blankets tightly about his neck.

Nari watched as the powdery mix she held liquefied and became crimson in color. Rex returned to her.

"Good," he said as he took the beaker from her. "That's the color we need. Come with me now."

Together they knelt beside Hawk. Rex looked at Elenari and made sure he had her attention before he spoke. "Now, I need you to hold his nose. He's not gonna like the taste of this, but I don't want him to miss a drop. Then I need you to hold him down. Likely, he'll have a violent reaction to it, but that's normal, you understand?" Nari nodded. "All right then, here we go."

Elenari pulled Hawk's mouth open and held his nose as Rex quickly poured the contents of the beaker down his throat. She closed his mouth immediately before he could spit and held his nose until he swallowed. Instantly, Hawk lurched, screaming in pain. Twisting and turning violently with a sudden surge of strength, he tried to get up. Elenari used her entire body weight to hold him down until the reaction ceased.

"All right," Rex said as Hawk relaxed, "we've done all we can for him. The rest is up to him. Wouldn't worry though; this boy's as strong as an ox. Expect his fever will break around dawn. Come on, girl, I'll pour us a drink."

Elenari looked at Hawk, who appeared to be resting somewhat comfortably though he was still sweating fiercely. She put the blankets back over him, moved his hair out of his face gently with her fingers, and got up to join Rex.

Elenari sat down at the table wiping her hands and face with a dry towel. "Tell me about this Doppelganger. What is it, and where did it get magic poison from?"

"Apologies," Rex replied. "*Doppelganger* is an old-world term. Not surprised you haven't heard it before. It didn't make the poison; that poison was either given to the creature or it took it off someone it killed. Doppelgangers don't have a need to use poison. 'What are they?' you ask. They're chameleons, changelings, shape-shifters, deceivers—whichever term you like best. Only difference is they got sharp claws and inhuman reflexes. Thing about them, though, is they have limited extrasensory perception, which allows 'em to sense the surface thoughts of their victims so as to become the likeness of someone that person feels comfortable with. They can exactly impersonate whomever they choose. Usually they use the power to lure humans or others to their lair for food. Like I say, only two things they care about: gold and food. You youngsters are lucky. You must be some kind of fighter, young lady." He took a deep swallow from his mug. "Never heard of no one catchin' no Doppelganger running, much less killin' one afterwards."

"How do you know so much about poisons?" Nari asked.

"Used to be an alchemist," Rex answered. "Made potions, poisons, and cures, whatever."

"What do you do now?" she asked.

"I mine," Rex responded. "Mine for gold, platinum, electrum, all sorts of precious gems. Dwarves got tons of the stuff buried in these mountains. Just a matter of time before I stake my claim and find my fortune."

Elenari smiled. "I never heard of anything precious being in these mountains my whole life."

"Nonsense," Rex scoffed. "Don't you ever listen to rumors or legends? Always just a little bit of truth in every one of 'em. Way I figure it, if there's a little bit of gold in every one of these mountains, then I'm destined to be a rich man."

Nari laughed in spite of herself, now very pleased to be in the company of this cheerful old man.

Rex returned her smile and poured them some wine. "Now, more interestingly, just what in the name of a Bug-Bear are you two doin' up in these mountains?"

Strangely enough Elenari did not like the idea of deceiving this old stranger who had been so kind to them, so instead she evaded the question. "I've three other companions out there who are looking for us. I've got to find them. You'll watch him?" She looked over at Hawk.

"'Course I will," said the old man.

"I should go and find them." Elenari grabbed her weapons, started to walk toward the cave exit, stopped, and turned to look back at the old man. "Thank you, Rex. Thank you for what you are doing."

Rex raised his glass toward her and winked. With that, Nari turned and was gone.

As Hawk opened his eyes, he saw the morning sun streaming in through the mouth of the cavern. Then a dark shape obstructed his view. His eyes slowly regained focus, and he recognized the glistening silver beard of Algernon. He saw the old Sage clearly now, and, for the first time, up close. Though he barely knew Algernon, he couldn't have been more pleased to see him than in that moment.

"How do you feel?" the Sage asked.

"Alive," he responded, "but not like the man who had your confidence days ago."

"Do not be foolish, my friend. I know a great deal about you, more than the others. Have no fear, your secrets are yours and safe. You are all the man and more who had my confidence and trust. Never forget that." Algernon placed his hand on Hawk's uninjured shoulder reassuringly. "Rest well; we leave by midday."

As Algernon walked away, Kael appeared at his bedside to greet him.

"Let me see your wound," he instructed, removing the bandage to reveal a now much-smaller stab wound. "The old man's potion was powerful indeed. Nari told me of a deep wound infected with rot. There is no infection, and the wound has already begun to heal. Sit back and relax for a moment."

Kael eased him back to a lying position. Hawk took a deep breath as Kael placed one hand on his wound and, with the other hand, drew forth a small plant from a pouch at his waist. Kael spoke a few words in a strange tongue, and suddenly yellow energy came from his hand and covered the length of Hawk's body. In the next moment, the energy faded, and Kael removed his hand. The wound had disappeared completely.

"Your wound is gone," Kael assured him. "Your strength will return very shortly."

"Thank you," said Hawk, as he felt the new skin.

During the night, Elenari had located the others waiting in the mountains and had brought them to Rex Abernackle's cave. Rex had offered them food and drink and assured them that Hawk's fever would break by dawn. During the night, they spoke of the Doppelganger, and Algernon explained that the creature could have been a minion of the Shadow Prince. Elenari informed them that whatever the creature had learned would be buried with it.

Algernon was openly distraught, however, and told them there would be many more obstacles along the way, some far deadlier than this. He seemed anxious for the first time and in a hurry to get underway.

By noon, the men and Nari gathered outside the cave. Hawk came out to meet them. Galin was the first to clasp his hand and greet him with a smile.

"Good to see you up and around. You know perhaps you're getting too old for this kind of thing, my dear fellow," said Galin jokingly.

"Perhaps," Hawk replied. "I'll give it some thought the next time I'm saving your life."

All of them laughed. Rex approached Hawk and handed him a parchment.

"This map will show you trails that your horses can travel through the mountains safely," he explained. "I understand from your friends that you're headin' to Mystaria. Dangerous country. Feel I should tell you, a lot of strange things been happening on the Mystaria border. Mostly at night, seen a lot of activity. Strange, very strange. Seen folk, white folk, kinda like Elves only completely white-skinned, white as my backside. They travel only late at night. Seen armies, too, marchin' across the border—barbarians, Ogres, and other monsters from Bazadoom. They always march by night and camp occasionally on the border in tents and such. Never seen activity like that in these parts in all my years. I'd advise you people to be careful."

Hawk shook Rex's hand. "Thank you for saving my life, Rex. I'm forever in your debt, sir."

"Well I won't hold you to it; forever's a long time, son. Never did hear your name though." Rex looked at him sharply and then at the others. No one replied. "There's that look again. What's got you people so spooked?"

Hawk dropped his hand and looked at Algernon, who walked over to Rex.

"We are deeply in your debt; however, it's much safer for you, my friend, if you never know our names. Such knowledge could put you in mortal danger. Those who seek us would kill for such information as well as our location. I would suggest you consider leaving your cave and finding a new dwelling. I regret that we have been a burden to you," said Algernon.

"Appreciate your concern," said Rex, "but these are my mountains. Sounds like you people got enough to worry about with the trouble following you. Wish you a safe and speedy journey."

Algernon shook his hand, then mounted his horse and signaled the others to do the same.

Elenari guided her horse to Rex's side and nodded to him. "One day I'd like to come back and tell you my real name," she said. "If that's all right with you. Thank you for your kindness. I enjoyed my time here."

Rex bowed. He spoke as if recalling something from long ago. "I look forward to make your official acquaintance, young lady. Hell, if I were fifty years younger I'd be beggin' you to stay so as I could attempt to court you proper. Nice having a beautiful young lady around again. It's been a very long time."

Elenari smiled and waved goodbye along with the others as they rode off to continue their journey through the Andarian Ranges. They would not soon forget the hospitality and kindness of Rex Abernackle. He gave them a cheerful wave as they rode away.

The hours passed slowly as the winding trails became steeper and their altitude increased with each mile. Hawk, once again, led the company. At Algernon's urging, they maintained a gruelingly rapid, uphill pace. He was concerned, as there would be little vegetation or water in the mountains, and the thinning air would take its toll on all of them, save Elenari. The only thing in their favor was the jagged slopes and cliffs above them, which fortunately provided adequate shade from the power of the sun.

As the sun began setting, the companions finally stopped to rest. The trail was narrow so there was little room to camp. They sat huddled against the rocks. They planned a four-hour rest, and they would travel during the night.

Kael sat gazing at the sky as darkness made its way quietly across the lands. He thought of the Druids. Surely some amongst them must have recognized the poison that had infected the lands. The Druid Council, as he had always understood it, was formed to guard nature and the lands from such afflictions, but their petty squabbles and differences apparently occupied too much of their time; the Council had lost its way long ago. *If they could be united*, he thought, *surely, they could find a cure for this plague, which might destroy all plant, animal, and even human life.*

Perhaps he could unite the council before it became too late. *I must get a message to them soon. There are so many uncertainties in the future*, he thought. *I may never live to see the Druid Council. Would they even listen to me if I could contact them?*

Kael's mind, unable to rest, continued to wander. What would happen to them in the realm of Mystaria? Where would they go next? He started to wonder if even Algernon knew the answers anymore. He took a deep breath and cleared his mind. *One day at a time*, he thought. *That is the only way to live right now.* He finally drifted off to sleep.

Galin, however, could not sleep, and he noticed that Algernon as well was awake.

"Algernon, what are our chances really?"

"Chances?" Algernon said quizzically.

"What will happen in Mystaria?" Galin continued.

"The mysterious unknown of Mystaria . . ." the Sage replied. "There live the most powerful wizards of the world. There lies the Great School of Magic. There dwells the most powerful sorcery of all. There, all things are possible. Our chances, as you say, are as good here as anywhere else. We must create an alliance of the lands. We must reach Cordilleran before their army falls, and most of all we must never give up hope. Hope, my young friend, is our most powerful ally, and it will bind the free peoples of the land to unite. The powers of evil will never know victory as long as there is hope in some part of the world. Remember that . . . *always.* Think no more of chances, and instead fortify and reenergize your hope so that it may never be quenched."

Galin felt his eyes closing after Algernon's last words as, almost against his will, he too went to sleep.

Elenari and Hawk fell asleep discussing their travel plans for the following day. They had gained a mutual respect for each other as well as a fast-growing friendship. Elenari was amazed at Hawk's senses and skills at tracking and reading sign. Never had she thought it possible for a human to possess such keen senses. He carried himself with an air of pride and confidence, which inspired the trust and loyalty of those around him. Hawk, in turn, felt Elenari to be a Ranger equal if not superior in skill to himself. He also considered the possibility she may well be the most powerful warrior in the group, though he could not come to terms with how that could be. She was a slight young woman, yet she had hunted down in short order the creature that had almost killed him.

When Hawk had first met Elenari, he had sensed that she did not much like people. She was somewhat aloof and often stood apart, but as their journey had progressed, he had come to consider her a close friend and hoped to be thought of as the same by her. She had saved his life and, perhaps, touched a part of him he thought long dead in the process.

Algernon was the last to fall asleep. He produced a small metal box from the many folds in his robe. This was the powerful magic that placed them in danger. This was the power the Shadow Prince could sense and yearned so greatly for. This was the reason they must press forward to distant lands and into danger. This was their hope and or their doom. It was the Emerald Star.

Chapter 7

Startled, Lark awoke suddenly. Darkness was there to greet him. He could neither see nor feel anything. Perhaps it was yet another dream. Dream . . . or nightmare; he could not be certain of either at that instant. His thought processes were muddled and confused at best. A harsh taste still lingered in the back of his throat, down to the furthest reaches of his stomach. A result, no doubt, of the noxious liquid he had been continually forced to ingest.

He could hear now. Slight sounds of dripping water echoed in his mind. Soft at first, the sounds grew to an unbearable thundering echo when he sensed it. If he concentrated, he had the power to detect the presence of evil within a certain radius, and, although he could not focus, it was there somewhere nearby in the darkness. Definite and painful, the feeling was sharp, indicating a strong evil of enormous power. There was something vaguely familiar about the presence, and then, as suddenly as it had appeared, it was gone. He no longer detected anything.

His eyes suddenly felt heavy, as if an invisible weight were being placed upon them. As quickly as he had come awake, he fell back into the realm of sleep.

When he awoke again, the bright light of a nearby torch off to his left greeted him. He was in a different position than last time. Now, he stood with both arms shackled to the wall above his head. All his clothes had been stripped away, save for the loincloth about his waist.

Before him, a huge, muscular figure, presumably human, stood unmoving. Lark could see the sinews rippling throughout the neck, shoulders, and chest of the figure before him. Its face was masked with a dark hood.

Then, it came again, the incessant dripping that maddened him. Even if the hulk before him were there to administer some form of torture, he thought, it would be a welcome diversion to the endless pattern of the watery drops. Three drops, then silence for several seconds, then three drops again continually on and on.

"*Greetings, Lark Royale,*" said a hollow voice from out of the darkness.

"Who are you?" Lark demanded, raising his voice. "Who is that speaking?"

"*Shall we begin?*" Again, the grim voice came at him from all directions in the darkness.

"Who are you?!" Lark screamed. "Where is this place?!"

"*How many drops do you hear?*" the voice asked.

"Who *are* you?" Lark cried again.

This time his outburst was answered with a sharp kick between his legs from the giant, whom he'd almost forgotten upon hearing the voice. The blow left him desperately gasping for breath.

"*Let us try again. How many drops do you hear?*"

"Why . . . does . . . it matter?" Lark said in sarcastic contempt as he struggled to catch his breath. "You planning . . . on fixing the leak?"

This time, he was not prepared for the strength of the blow. The brute's closed fist slammed into his left ribs. An echoing snap now filled the emptiness of the chamber beyond his sight.

Lark released a short grunt of pain as he sagged heavily downward, relying on the strength of his shackles to support him. He knew that he had likely lost at least one rib now and that his tactics would have to change.

"*How many drops do you hear?*" the voice asked again in the same tone with no hint of impatience.

Regaining his breath, Lark responded, "I . . . hear three drops."

With that, a swift uppercut to the muscular part of his stomach prompted Lark to forcefully cry out.

"*You are mistaken.*" The voice remained irritatingly calm. "*There are four drops. Now, how many drops do you hear?*"

"I only . . . hear . . . three drops," said Lark recovering from a fit of coughing.

Another uppercut from the masked giant struck him, changing the coughs to gagging.

"*How many drops do you hear?*"

"... three ..." Lark was able to spit the word out and this time, a third blow to his stomach came, causing him to vomit.

Without mercy, the voice continued, *"How many drops do you hear?"*

Again, Lark came to his senses suddenly. He found himself shuffling backward, raising his hands in defense. As his vision cleared, he realized he was in the corner of the chamber. In that instant, he also realized he wasn't chained. He was free. Then, he felt it, a biting, searing pain from his stomach to his chest. His breathing was ragged and unsteady. He remembered his broken rib, and it seemed as if he could now feel it cutting into his lung.

His other senses soon started to respond. The putrid stench of dung and vomit hung in the air around him. There was something else, a faint odor of food. His eyes adjusted well enough to the blackness that he could see the outline of a dish on the floor near him. Immediately, he told himself not to touch any rations that his captors would offer him. Then he realized that if they'd wanted to kill him, they could have easily done so already, and it would be almost impossible to weaken him any further without killing him. In light of these facts, he concluded it would be safe to try the bread and water they had left for him.

Slowly, feeling the stretching of his already bruised stomach muscles, he reached for the food. Cautiously, he ate and sipped. It was then that he heard a key turning in the lock of the far-off door to his chamber. He heard two pairs of booted feet enter the room.

Lark could also hear his heart pounding. It was still completely dark; he knew they were somewhere in the chamber, and he hadn't heard the door close. This was his chance. He would surprise them with an unexpected display of strength and make it out through the door.

"Stand up and turn around!" It was another voice that was vaguely familiar to him. He quickly made the connection and recognized it was the voice of his original captor.

A torch was lit. Lark hurled himself into the man who held the torch, startling him for just a moment. Before Lark could make a break for the door, the second man kicked him in the stomach, and he doubled over in agony. Then what felt like an elbow smashed between his shoulder blades and brought him to the floor. The next sensation he felt was a boot on the left side of his face, pinning him down, allowing his other tormentor to shackle his hands behind his back.

"That was very foolish, Royale," his captor said. "For that, we shall have to hurt you as you've never been hurt before."

As they lifted him up from the floor, he saw the two men clearly now. The first was the man who had captured him; the second was the hooded hulk responsible for his broken rib.

"Now then, Royale, my name is Navarre, and strangely enough, I may be a better friend than you realize. However, just now, you betrayed that friendship and so you must be punished."

Navarre was a tall man, as tall as Lark. He seemed to have dark shoulder-length hair. Though his features were not completely visible, Lark could make out a deep scar from his right temple down to his chin.

The giant to his left guided him now, and the two men moved him from his chamber to somewhere else. As they entered the hallway, Lark barely had time to see what was around him before the man calling himself Navarre blindfolded him.

They then guided him down several corridors, turning right and left, passing through multiple doors until finally they stopped. The blindfold was then removed, and it took a moment for Lark's vision to clear. His heart sank as he viewed the instruments of torture now surrounding him. He saw several devices he recognized—an iron maiden, a rack, several vises, a guillotine, and many more devices of pain that were foreign to him. They were in an octagonal chamber some sixty by sixty feet across. The walls were black and rancid with mold. Lark could make out what appeared to be fresh blood on several of the instruments. There seemed to be no air in the room. There was a dark, foul smell about the place. Lark could sense the presence of death. It lingered here, waiting always for its next victim. At that moment, he felt for sure he would be that victim.

"You're going to be very disappointed if you expect any of this to frighten me," Lark said confidently. "A Paladin fears no evil."

Without warning, the giant threw him up on the rack. Within moments, his arms were bound above his head and his legs were tied and stretched apart.

"And you're going to be very disappointed as well," the assassin replied in a pleased voice, "thinking we care what frightens you. All we care about is the pain we can inflict upon you."

Trying to relax, Lark steadied his breath in anticipation of the voice. Oddly, several moments passed, and he heard nothing. Suddenly, he felt his limbs being stretched in different directions, the pull on his arms and legs slow and gradual but steady. He twisted about and tried to see Navarre and the giant, but he could only hear noises behind his head and out of sight. One of them, presumably the giant, he thought, was turning the wheel that eventually would tear his limbs apart.

"Where are you?" Lark said in raised tones.

The rack continued to turn.

"Where are you?" He screamed it this time.

The pull on his limbs grew uncomfortable as he released several accentuated breaths as his body fought against the pull.

"Only base cowards . . . and fools . . . hide behind masks and tools to do the tasks . . . their manhood lacks!" Lark exclaimed. "Navarre, face me in combat! Prove your worth . . . or slink away into the fear . . . that rules your life. You . . . are . . . less . . . than nothing, and I pity you and . . . your great oaf of . . . a servant. Please, by all the gods . . . if I am to die . . . let it be . . . at the hands . . . of men!"

The clanking of the linked chain, which connected the rack to the control wheel, was his only answer. The pain had become unbearable now, but still, he refused to cry out in agony. They would get no satisfaction from his death. The searing, burning pain ripped through him as he felt the stretching and tearing of muscles, which he could no longer bear. Everything then became lost in darkness.

A skeletal hand tapped in a smooth rhythmic motion on a large, rectangular, ash table within the bowels of Dargonath Keep. Deep within the eye sockets of the skull burned the red eyes of Prince Broderick Voltan. He wore a black cloak and robe, and atop his head sat a shimmering crown, for he had no need of illusions to conceal his appearance here, in his own castle. Voltan was one of the princes of the ruling council of Mystaria, a title that made him one of the most powerful wizards in the known world. He was also, unknown to even most of the ruling council, a *lich*—an extremely powerful undead spirit, which through an unnatural lust for power and eternity transcended the boundaries of mortal life to an undead state of immortality. It also required evoking the practice of necromancy, the arcane area of magic relating to death. Only the most powerful wizard with an insatiable hunger for eternal life could make the journey to lichdom complete. Voltan was such a wizard, and now, he was much more. He was an entity of enormous power and evil.

A dark figure obscured in a cloud of mist moved through the stone corridors, gently rapping the pulsing red staff against the earthen floor. He thought about Dargonath for a moment as he continued moving through the ancient fortress. Perhaps this should be his capital and seat of power, but he quickly dispelled the idea, relying on the perfection of his previous plans. Voltan, also, would oppose it, though he cared nothing for the Prince's likes and dislikes.

However, Voltan possessed great power, and he was wary of it, but it was still no match for his own. There would be a need, though, at least in the beginning, for a general in the new order. Voltan would be a general, his commanding general and second-in-command. Though his ambition and lust might prove to interfere, Voltan would serve or be destroyed.

The figure stopped before a huge iron-bound door. He raised a gloved finger and, noiselessly, the great door opened to admit him.

The huge iron-bound door creaked open on steel hinges, preparing the way for the Shadow Prince. An impatient Voltan rose from his seat and lit the four torches of the room with his very thoughts.

Speaking in an ancient language with an eerie tone beyond death, Prince Broderick Voltan greeted his ally, studying him carefully. He wore brown robes, trimmed with gold and decorated with an ornate crimson multi-headed dragon on his chest. In his gloved left hand, he held a pulsating red staff. Etched into his mask of iron was an expressionless gaze, without mercy.

The Shadow Prince, as well, measured Voltan. A skeletal being clothed in blackness, a crowned white skull whose ivory face was animated only by twin red orbs of energy set far back in the darkness of black gaping eye sockets—he was the personification of death. Much like himself, Voltan's lust for life and desire for more power had made him into something more than human. They had both defied natural death, the timeless enemy of man, to exist in a different state, drawing their energy from the negative material plane. Retaining their knowledge of sorcery, their arcane powers had become greatly enhanced. Voltan's were so because of his ascension to Lichdom, while the Shadow Prince's power became greater by an ancient evil, which had transformed and resurrected him to a unique undead spirit.

They sat together alone and faced each other in the square stone chamber. The iron door closed with a deafening echo. Here, in this windowless, airless room, they would discuss the future of the world they had been consigned to exist in and to conquer.

"*All the pieces have fallen into place as I have foreseen,*" said the hallowed voice of the Shadow Prince.

"What of the Emerald Star?" Voltan asked, unable to conceal his impatience.

"*The Emerald Star is my concern,*" the Shadow Prince replied. "*Soon, it will be in our possession. The one who will wield it for us is being held in Shadowgate.*"

"The Paladin called Lark," Voltan spat out in disdain. "His will is great. His spirit cannot be broken . . . as well you should know." With this last statement, a daring hint of sarcasm entered Voltan's voice.

The Shadow Prince's tone was calm and unwavering. "*He will break and become a living servant to my every whim. Before such time . . . he will suffer a hundredfold for the torment I endured because of him. He shall live out his final days as my personal slave until his usefulness ends. It is only then that I shall personally kill him as he begs, cries, and pleads for mercy for those he cares for. I will revel in the ecstasy of extinguishing his soul forever. Then I shall do the same to his Druid friend.*"

"These are but trifles," Voltan stated. "There are more important matters to be settled. Your past attempts to utilize the mystical gemstone have all met with failure. Why do you expect to succeed this time?"

"*I was not then that which I am now,*" The Shadow Prince replied. "*I sought to make use of the object myself, ignorant of the fact that only one whose heart is pure and mind is lawful can tap into its power.*"

Voltan leaned forward. "It is a talisman of Elven magic. It is an anathema to us. Why not seize it and destroy it so its power of protection no longer aids those who would stand against us?"

"No." The Shadow Prince stood up and began to pace. "*It must not be destroyed until. . . . There is one who has called to me. It is he that discovered my consciousness, little more than a mass of particles, drifting forever in limbo, and breathed life into me. He reshaped my form and filled me with his power in exchange for . . . no. The Emerald Star will not be destroyed unless he wills it. In our brief and intermittent contact, at least that much has been indicated to me.*"

"Who is this entity, and where does he call to you from?" Voltan asked.

"*It is he whose coming and power are beyond reckoning, whose life force can never be ended. That is all you need to know. Let us begin.*"

The Shadow Prince let his open hand drop to the map on the table between them and fall upon the Kingdom of Wrenford.

Lark awoke in an upright position. He was seated up against the wall. Although he was in complete darkness, he knew by the putrid stench that he was back in his old chamber once again. Both his ankles were shackled to the wall but his arms were free. He was thankful for that. Every breath and even the slightest movement caused him pain now.

He thought of Archangel. He had been very careful not to mention anything of his brother. *With any luck, Archangel escaped the night I was taken,* Lark thought. If he dared inquire about the presence or condition of his brother, whether they knew of him or not, Lark feared he would only put Archangel in more danger.

Kneeling, he put his hands together, closed his eyes, and bent his head in prayer. He begged that his brother might still be alive. Then he gave thanks, as always, and asked for help with his own plight.

His eyes flew open. Why had he not prayed until now? Perhaps something in the food had kept him too drugged to think of doing so.

He heard the dripping again. He had almost become accustomed to it by now. He didn't know whether it was in his mind or the pain, but he was unable to drown it out. His thoughts were still foggy, pain and fatigue biting through him; he tried to focus on answering some pivotal questions. First, where was he? Next, who were his captors, and why were they doing this? *These three things,* he thought, *must be established as soon as possible.*

"How are you feeling, Mr. Royale?" The voice was back, echoing throughout the chamber, coming from nowhere and everywhere at the same time.

"Who are you?" responded Lark, faintly, giving the impression he was in worse shape than he actually was, though only barely.

"How are you feeling?" the voice repeated.

"Who are you?" Lark asked calmly, but with more conviction.

"Mr. Royale, how are you feeling?" The voice's tone never changed.

"Who are you?!" Lark burst out with all his strength.

Now the voice seemed to hold the slightest hint of satisfaction. *"You have answered the question. Excellent, we are making progress. How many drops do you hear?"*

"I hear three drops, then nothing, then three drops again," said Lark calmly, though he was thoroughly disgusted with himself for losing his temper.

"There are four drops," the voice replied. *"How many drops do you hear?"*

"Where is this place? Why am I here? And who are you? Answer just one of these questions, and I'll consider answering yours."

"What do you think became of your brother?" the voice asked suddenly.

Lark's heart began pounding again; he did not know what to expect next. He opted not to answer.

"You will see him soon."

The bearer of the voice's footfalls became distant, leaving Lark to believe he was alone again.

Lark sat completely motionless. Fear crept into his mind. He let several minutes pass in silence. When he felt certain the voice was truly no longer there, he allowed himself to cry.

Hours passed and his eyes became more and more used to the darkness, yet still he could see nothing.

Archangel was dead. The thought tortured him worse even than the unrelenting voice. Was it the truth? He fully expected his tormentors to enter the chamber at any moment, dragging the dead body of his brother before him. Why had he not been told about him until now? Had they possibly been holding him all this time as well?

He knew that he could not trust his captors, so he settled to himself that he must continue hoping that his brother lived until he found out otherwise. He had to focus. If he was not careful, his mind could be a greater enemy here in the darkness than the voice or any of them, if he allowed it.

It was then that he felt a weight on his left leg and an almost itching sensation in his calf. It was a rat. It had come upon him several minutes ago, but he had not felt it until now.

Instinctively, he swatted the animal aside and watched it scurry into the cracks and crevices of the stone chamber. He looked down at his exposed calf muscle and a flashback of Navarre thrusting a blade through his leg shook him. It was an entry and exit wound several inches long, but it was burnt and blackened on both sides. They must have burnt it with a torch while he had been unconscious to prevent him from bleeding to death. *How compassionate of them*, he thought bitterly.

The idea suddenly struck him. Again, he put his hands together and prayed for guidance. Bleeding . . . blood . . . he looked to the cracks and crevices of the wall.

Lark stirred to life, struggling to rise as the chamber door swung open. The hooded giant and Navarre entered.

"Stand up!" Navarre ordered.

"What do you want now, coward?" Lark said in a low tone of fatigue.

Swiftly, Navarre drew the dagger from the front middle of his waist, sweeping across and slicing into Lark's left breast.

The giant moved with exceptional quickness and kicked Lark's legs out from under him, causing him to fall flat on his back.

"Fool!" Navarre hissed. "You may die in this place, Lark, but not before you learn respect."

Lark tried to maintain one breath after another, bracing himself for whatever was next. He was at their feet and at their mercy. Navarre snapped his fingers, and the giant removed a powder from his waistline. He bent down over Lark and emptied the pouch of salt into his pulsating wound. Lark responded with a low groan of pain.

Navarre watched Lark's face as he raised his right leg and let his boot rest softly right on top of Lark's wounded chest.

"How does this feel, animal?" Navarre said, grinding the heel of his boot into the salted wound with all his might. "We could have been friends, you and I, but I much prefer it like this."

Lark could not hold the scream within him back, and he cried out in excruciating pain.

"Shut up!" Navarre yelled, as he brought his boot down on Lark's face. Again and again, he stomped Lark's face with his boot until the screaming stopped.

The giant pushed Navarre back for a moment, restraining him, and looked down at their prisoner.

Navarre, Viscount of Shadowgate and Guildmaster of Assassins of Mystaria, straightened his shirt and fixed his collar. He looked down at Lark and when he saw that his chest was still moving and that he was breathing, he felt a moment of relief. The cut he'd given Lark was deeper than he'd intended, but he was glad of it. Blood flowed from the left part of Lark's chest down to the floor. Then he bent over Lark's head and spat in his face. With that, he and his giant companion left the chamber, leaving behind the bloody mess that was Lark.

Lark woke again. He suspected a day or two had passed while he had been unconscious. His left eye was swollen shut, and he felt the sensation of his cracked lips and parched throat.

Trying to raise his head, he experienced difficulty as his hair was knotted down to the floor and stuck in his own dried blood. He had no idea when he had last drank or been fed. He knew he was barely alive.

The voice, as he should have expected, was there to greet him in the dark.

"Lark, I have a plate of the finest mutton and cold ale waiting for you. My healer waits to tend your wounds. Please let me help you. Let me be your friend."

The voice was almost a whisper. For the first time, Lark heard the voice in a different tone: compassion. Perhaps they had been trying to help him all along. He remembered how Navarre had said he was a better friend than Lark knew.

NO! his mind screamed. What was he thinking? What was wrong with him? He had been tortured like an animal. His brother had possibly been captured or killed. There must have been something in the food and drink they were giving him to even cause him to hesitate. He brushed such insane thoughts aside as they crept into his mind, one by one.

"All you have to do is tell me how many drops you hear, and this all ends." The voice was becoming alluring, almost seductive.

Lark hesitated a moment and then exploded, "No! Never! I'll never tell you, never!"

The outburst was furious and unexpected, even to Lark. It had cost him dearly, but he had the uncanny feeling that the voice had shrank away in fear for one brief moment.

Lark had been blindfolded and moved again. Judging from the distance he had been forced to go, he estimated he was going to a new chamber, though he could not be sure.

When they stopped, they shackled him at the wrists, standing and facing a wall. The dried sweat of his body started to give him the chills as he waited for what would happen next. His blindfold was removed. It was still dark, though he sensed there was some light source several feet behind him.

He heard movement behind him as well—the heavy steps of one man, the giant. The walking stopped a few feet behind him. Now, he waited for the voice to come. He knew that it must.

The incessant dripping of water began throughout the new chamber. It must have been a chamber similar to his previous cell, because the terrible stench was present, along with the rats—he could hear them scuttling.

The voice began from nowhere. *"How many drops do you hear?"*

Lark did not respond.

"How many drops do you hear?"

Again, Lark did not answer.

This time the crack of a whip slashed across his back like a sword slicing through him, yet he did not let out even a wince of pain.

"Each time you do not respond, you will receive one lash. Each time you respond incorrectly, you will receive five lashes. Shall we continue? Now, how many drops do you hear?"

"None," said Lark without fear.

Immediately, the giant whipped him once, twice, three times, up to five.

Lark threw his head back, grinded down hard on his teeth, and still made no sound.

The voice calmly continued, never losing patience. *"How many drops do you hear?"*

"None!" Lark exclaimed.

Again, the giant struck ferociously. On the fifth lash, Lark grunted in pain, unable to bear it any further.

"How many drops do you hear?"

"Three," said Lark, breathing heavily.

The giant attacked, quicker and stronger than the last time. Each lash made Lark wince in pain, though he still refused to cry out.

"You are lying, Lark. A Paladin must always tell the truth. A true knight's integrity must always be beyond reproach." the voice softy admonished.

"Paladin"—Lark clung to the word like a lifeline. He was a Paladin, a holy knight, a nobleman, and Baron of Wrenford. He had powers, which for some reason, until now, he had forgotten. He had hardly prayed to his god at all since his capture. There was clearly an unseen force working on him all this time, keeping thoughts of who and what he was hidden from him. Was it magic, something in the food, or a combination?

Paladin. He concentrated on the word and its sense of identity. The voice had finally slipped and made its first mistake.

However, the incessant snapping of the whip against his back brought him back to the matter at hand. He had to think now. He had to concentrate on the strategy he had been forming in his head several days ago. As the voice continued to ask the same redundant question, Lark did not respond, and suffered only one lash at a time. This would hopefully buy him the time he needed.

He began to focus. As a Paladin, he had the innate power to heal his own wounds through a special magic. He could feel the magic starting to work. It was more difficult to summon now than it had ever been before, but he could feel it working.

He must be cautious. He thought about his broken rib. He let the magic wash over it and soothe it. Slowly, he mended the bone and stopped the internal bleeding. It had taken almost ten lashes, but he opened his eyes and looked down at his stomach. The large purple splotch had marked the break, and it was no more. His breathing was easier and no longer a labor. Much of the constant pain he endured had been due to that injury, and now it was gone. He had healed it, as he should have long ago.

Still, the lash bit at him and the voice taunted on, but whatever day it might have been, it had been a day of personal victory for Lark Royale.

After he had lost count of the lashes, the questioning finally stopped and the giant left the room.

Lark was left shackled with his face flush up against the wall. His back felt like a practice target for a rapier. It was raw and pulsing with an unbelievable pain and itch. He would have to be very cautious. Slowly, he concentrated. Gently, the magic began to heal.

Days passed and each day, Lark used his power a little more, though it seemed to be more of a stress to him each time. Each day he managed to heal himself a little more without notice. It had been days since the voice last plagued him. His behavior, as well, had been exemplary, so he had endured few beatings as time went on. He was fed on a regular basis. He continued to eat and drink the food, though he became more convinced it was drugged.

Finally, his day came. He sat in his chamber, ankles chained, and he waited. He waited for the rat. Purposely, he did not eat his food and waited for the rat to show itself. Then, without warning, it appeared just within arm's reach from him.

The door to his chamber swung open, and the giant entered. As he got closer to Lark, he held a torch over him and saw that he lay motionless with his eyes glazed over, and blood appeared to trickle from his mouth. Quickly, he stowed the torch on the wall and bent down and unchained Lark's ankles. The master had told him that, should the prisoner ever die, so would he.

The moment he was free, Lark took action. He sat up and forcefully spat a mouthful of blood directly in the giant's eyes, unsettling him. He then kicked the huge man between the legs with all of his might. The giant let out a great cry and fell to his knees. Without hesitating, Lark began smashing his head against the wall until he heard it crack. As soon as the giant stopped moving, Lark took his keys and broadsword and was off.

He rushed down dark hallways and finally up a set of stairs. As he reached the top of the stairs, he saw Navarre standing across the hall with his back turned to him. Lark moved toward him, tightening his grip on the sword.

He did not see the crossbowman behind him. Instantly, two bolts struck the back of his shoulders, sending him to the floor. Navarre turned and sauntered forward, kicking the sword away before Lark's hand could find it. He lifted Lark up by the hair and viciously struck him in the face with his fist. He then began kicking him in the ribs over and over again.

"*Enough!*" It was the voice, which stopped the beating. It was the first time Lark had heard a different tone in the voice. The voice itself sounded different . . . familiar, almost.

In a half-conscious state, Lark saw the shiny leather boots, which must have belonged to the owner of the voice. They walked right up to where he lay, and then he lost himself to darkness.

When Lark awoke, he found himself chained back against the wall with his hands shackled above him. He was in a different chamber. There was quite a bit of light, which he struggled to adjust his eyes to. All he could see initially was a bright blur. It took several minutes for his eyes to start seeing shape and form. He was weak. He knew he'd been severely beaten.

He tried to summon the magic. There was no response. He could no longer do it. He found even remaining conscious was a difficult task at the moment. He no longer thought of magic or plans or anything, except how to sleep and be rid of the pain. It was then that his eyes focused just enough to see his worst nightmares come to fruition.

Two men were dragging Archangel into the chamber. He was either unconscious, too weak to move, or dead. They held him by each arm, dragging his feet on the floor. He too had been stripped of his clothes and severely beaten. He saw his brother's face and barely recognized it. The eyes were purple and swollen; his nose was bloated and likely broken. They held him fast in a kneeling position.

Navarre appeared in Lark's peripheral vision. He was wearing his usual white silk shirt, but no vest or cape, as was his typical attire.

The voice came to him as if from the wall behind him.

"*I am sincerely sorry for what must happen now, Lark.*"

Lark's heart found the strength to start pounding. Clarity and fear came to him at once. Helplessness was his only resolve.

The voice seemed compassionate, almost trustworthy. "*You could have prevented this, Lark. You have it in you to prevent the death of thousands. You will see that soon. You will see you are on our side. We are on your side. Understand that all we do is for your own good.*"

"No," Lark pleaded desperately. "Leave him! Take me . . . leave him be . . . please! No!"

"*Fear not, Lark,*" the voice said. "*Your brother's brave sacrifice is for the greater good. It is for you . . . to help you understand.*"

Before Lark could protest further, Navarre removed his jeweled dagger, walked up to Archangel, grabbed a handful of his hair, lifted his head and drove his dagger into Archangel's left eye. He held it there and then rotated it, gouging the eye out of the socket.

Archangel let out a ferocious scream for a moment as blood spurted forth from his eye, and Navarre struck him on the back of the head with the hilt of his dagger, knocking him unmoving to the floor. The blood flowed freely out of him.

Lark cried out, wailing in pain and grief. He hung limp, sobbing, with tears running down his cheeks.

"*Release him,*" said the voice with the slightest hint of satisfaction.

Navarre and two of his men approached and released Lark's arms from the shackles.

Lark fell at their feet, devoid of pride; he crawled on his stomach, between their legs, slowly toward Archangel. Without looking, he knew they were smiling and snickering, looking down upon him. When he had almost reached his brother, Navarre's men quickly picked Archangel up and removed him from the chamber.

Suddenly Lark saw the shiny leather boots of the owner of the voice, standing in the place where Archangel's body had been lying.

"*Lark . . . Paladin.*" The voice suddenly sounded very different. It was hoarse, bitter, and sadistic. Yet, at the same time, it now seemed familiar. "*You will never know how I have enjoyed hurting you and watching your pain. I wish to go on hurting you; however, perhaps Voltan was right. Despite torture, magic, and potions, you still do not break. I took your brother's eye and still you did not give in. Unfortunately, I no longer have the luxury of watching and waiting. The time has come to resort to a powerful magic that even you, with your indomitable spirit, will be powerless to resist.*"

Lark looked up to see the iron mask of the Shadow Prince looking down at him.

"No," Lark breathed, "it cannot be you . . . you're dead. We killed you."

Lark was so weak he could not discern if his vision was accurate or a product of his incessant torture. The dark shape of his old enemy bent down, holding a medallion in his hands. The medallion bore the red hydra, the symbol of the Shadow Prince and his army of Stygian Knights.

As the Shadow Prince placed the medallion around Lark's neck, it burned his skin. Suddenly, it vanished from sight; Lark still felt it around his neck, invisible to the naked eye.

"*How fitting,*" the Shadow Prince whispered, "*that one of Thargelion's bloodline will prepare the way for the ascension.*"

Lark awoke to find himself unchained, back in his cell with the ever-present dripping in the background. He was dazed and confused.

The Shadow Prince waited for Lark to fully awaken. "*Lark, even the most powerful magic could not turn you to aid us willingly, but it can persuade you to see things differently to help you aid us through your own beliefs, your*" beliefs and convictions in our right and just cause. Lark, how many drops do you hear?"

"I hear four drops, master," answered Lark.

"No, Lark . . . I do not wish to be your master, only your friend. I am on your side, and I want what you and your friends want: to bring peace and justice to the lands. I wish, as you do, to rid the world of all the evil that would plague it. I want to protect those who cannot protect themselves."

The Shadow Prince continued on and on. Now that he had convinced Lark to believe he heard four drops when there were only three, it would be easy to convince him of many other things that were just as untrue. With the help of the medallion's magic, Lark believed all that he was told with innocence and conviction.

Within the following days, he established a rapport and dialogue with the Shadow Prince, whom he now knew as a friend and staunch ally.

When the time was right, the Shadow Prince took Navarre aside in private after one of his sessions with Lark. "Clean him. Feed him all that he can eat and move him to a chamber on the second level. Give him plenty of exercise. I want him back in fighting shape. Give him access throughout the castle, except for the dungeon levels. Tell your men."

"I will not," Navarre answered calmly, with a look of disbelief that the Shadow Prince would even ask such a thing.

The Shadow Prince took a step closer to Navarre, bringing his mask of iron close to the Viscount's face.

Navarre saw the blackness of the empty eye slits bearing down on him and realized he'd made a fatal error.

The Shadow Prince addressed him slowly, mockingly, "Your master, Voltan, serves me, which means that you, by extension, are my slave. Does it not?"

Navarre suddenly felt a burning and shortness of breath in his throat. A sharp tightness in his chest constricted his lungs, preventing him from speaking. An unseen force now controlled his muscles. He was driven to his knees, then forward on all fours.

The dark form towering over him lifted one of his boots off the ground and put it to Navarre's mouth. Struggling and fighting against the unseen force, Navarre found himself licking the bottom of the Shadow Prince's boot.

"*Ahh . . . It pleases me that you know your place, Viscount. Forget it again, and you will die horribly, without the benefit of another lesson.*" With that the Shadow Prince released him and stepped back. "*When you create boundaries and restrictions, Viscount, it promotes unhealthy curiosity. I shall return in several days; do not dare fail me.*"

"Yes, master," said Navarre, sincerely bowing lowly and abjectly.

Chapter 8

A heavy mist came with the next morning, despite strong gusts of wind which snapped throughout the air. It was an unusually cool morning in southern Mystaria.

The company had finished their descent through the mountains the previous night, successfully surmounting their first great obstacle, the Andarian Ranges.

The companions packed up their belongings, ate a meager breakfast of bread and cheese, mounted their restless steeds, and continued northwest through the majestic countryside of this land toward the mysterious magical city of Mystaria.

For a brief time, Hawk and Galin rode side by side and spoke once again about the old times. Hawk had fully recovered from his injury, and the burly Ranger seemed more comfortable now, surer of himself, as he trotted alongside his friend and his other companions.

Galin, as well, seemed to have forgotten the many uncomfortable feelings he had about this journey; they had been chased away by the beauty of the day. In reality, they should not have been feeling so at ease, since they were entering a country where both he and Kael could be executed if they were found out, but there was something about the day that made that prospect seem nonthreatening.

The lands through which they currently traveled were lightly forested, covered in light green pastures of silky grass and rolling hillsides. The morning dew clung to the ground, glistening in the sun like a frozen pond in wintertime. The sky above was clear and fresh with few clouds passing by with the wind. A brisk breeze shot through the delicate grass like currents through a docile body of water. Though none of them voiced it aloud, inwardly they thought that it was indeed a glorious day to be alive and free.

Algernon looked ahead, eyes straining to find the Alband River, which ran south throughout Mystaria and even reached into the foreboding lands of Bazadoom. The Sage listened keenly to the very land itself, and in response, he heard the rushing waters of the mighty river ahead in the distance. He smiled, for he could hear the sound of lapping water over polished rocks. Few things were more soothing to him than the sound of rushing water. His smile, however, concealed many of his true feelings. He alone was cursed with the knowledge that this wonderful day and seemingly peaceful journey might soon turn into something more horrible than the others dared expect.

In fact, he could not reveal many premonitions he had about the future or the emotions which they stirred in him. Instead, he must continue to masquerade a sense of comfort and confidence for the others. It burned him inside to keep them hidden, but he knew it was for the best.

In any event, he thought, *nothing is set in stone. It was always changing, the future; there were always emotions there to sway it.* He reached inside his ivory robes and held fast to the metal box, which contained the Emerald Star.

Elenari and Kael also rode close together, discussing the beauty of the land ahead. Neither had ever been to Mystaria, naturally, nor had they ever truly expected to visit it. Kael held fast to his reins as he surveyed the lands around him. As a Druid, his first and best love was the land. He marveled in its beauty and grace, its peacefulness and innocence. Mother Nature, too, never ceased to amaze him, as she balanced all things in life and yet made powers beyond reckoning available to those who knew how to harness them. It was on this power that he himself had drawn many times before in his life to defend the land, nature, and her charges, thereby preserving the balance of good and evil. He closed his eyes and breathed deeply. Today, he was confident such power would never fail him against the forces of evil.

As the morning crept on toward noon, the weather gradually became warmer. The party made their way toward Mystaria City one mile at a time. The early afternoon brought the Alband River along with it to cross their path. The crystal-clear water was so inviting that the group quickly dismounted to share in the river's bounty. The horses plunged their muzzles deep into the river, sucking up as much water as they could. It had been some time since the animals had been treated to such fresh water.

Kael bent down at the riverside, removed his hood, cupped his hands, and slowly dipped them into the rushing water. It felt cool and refreshing as it streamed through his aged fingers. The water seemed to massage and relax them, and he lifted them to his mouth.

The others filled their canteens and mounted their horses. Algernon warned that it would not be wise to stay stationary out in the open for long. The less time they wasted, the faster and safer they would be traveling.

As they began their trek south, along the river, Hawk spotted a band of riders approaching from the west. He knew they most likely spotted them already. Quickly, he turned to Elenari for an opinion. Without hesitating, she urged them on to ride at a swifter pace.

Algernon feared there would be no escape, but he rode on quietly with the rest of them.

The band of riders moved closer every moment on a direct line for the party. Perhaps, hoped Hawk inwardly, they were only travelers, but that thought quickly dissipated as he kept turning back to check with Elenari, who had far better vision. She finally signaled him to stop, and so he halted the party.

As the party turned, they all watched the band of riders come closer into view. Their horses were large and black, with silver armor draped over them; heavy reins covered their sturdy frames. The riders wore glistening silver-plated mail armor and carried long pikes. Their uniforms were brilliant silver with finely crafted helmets. These were not travelers. They were professional soldiers, approximately twenty in number.

Hawk brought the party close together in a tight circle. Kael felt they were a border patrol out on a scouting survey of the lands. Elenari and the others agreed.

"None of you say anything," said Algernon suddenly as he trotted forward to take the lead position, adding calmly, "I shall speak for us."

The lead rider approached alone, stopped before Algernon, and then slowly circled the party. His visor was down, concealing his face and eyes. Kael noticed, as he passed, the insignia of a tower on the armor with the letter *M* engraved thereon. As the lead rider completed his circle, he stopped and spoke.

"I wish to see your traveling papers." His strong voice echoed within his helmet, making him sound almost mechanical.

Hawk kept his gaze fixed on the rider, his expression even-tempered.

With that, Algernon slowly moved his steed very close to that of the lead rider. Casually, he reached into his robes and, much to their surprise, produced a folded parchment closed with a foreign seal.

"I think you will find our papers are in good order, sir," spoke the Sage, handing the scroll over to the rider.

The black-gloved hand of the rider snatched up the scroll and quickly unraveled it.

Hawk breathed easily, hoping his unease would go unnoticed. It was just a border patrol, as they'd thought. It was a good thing the old man was prepared. He'd expected as much, however; Algernon and Thargelion had planned this journey and would have taken whatever precautions possible.

Kael and Elenari held fast to their reins, and Galin's gaze was fixed on Algernon, trying to read the old man's expressions.

The lead rider lifted his visor, revealing a very human face. His ruddy complexion beaded with sweat that ran down his chin. His hair was black and matted to his forehead from perspiration. His dark, bulging eyes studied the scroll carefully.

A breeze of warm air shot through them from the west, blowing their hair from left to right. Algernon held his beard until the air became still and musty again.

No one spoke. Silence filled the air except for a flock of small brown birds chattering as they flew overhead in a standard V formation.

This is taking too long, thought Galin, as his eyes wandered until they found Hawk, whose fingers nervously tapped on the pommel of his saddle.

At that moment, Elenari's horse let out a sigh and buckled forward a bit, bringing the lead soldier's eyes up from the parchment toward the young half Elf. Nari patted her horse on the neck, quickly calming him.

Five other soldiers rode up and joined their leader, curiously eyeing the party. The lead rider began folding up the scroll, all the while looking at Elenari's eyes closely. Elenari, wary of the soldier's stare, gazed outward over the grasslands, careful never to meet the other's gaze.

Algernon held out his wrinkled hand in anticipation of being handed back the parchment.

"I would like you to follow me," spoke the lead soldier as he flipped his metal plate back down over his eyes and placed the folded scroll inside his own saddlebag.

"Is there a problem, my friend?" the Sage replied in a cracked voice with a strange tone. "I'm quite sure our papers are in perfect order. They bear the seal of the Great School of Magic!"

The Sage's tone had become powerful and menacing, making for a most unusual contrast with the prior tone he had used. He went from the epitome of courtesy to scolding the rider for being disrespectful. A large cloud brushed across the sun, masking all of them in shade suddenly. Algernon appeared great and powerful, shining in the sudden darkness.

Though the lead rider's face was veiled behind his helmet, the party got the sense he was nervous and suddenly unsure of his next move. "You will follow my men and me to our post . . . where we will stamp your papers and confirm that they are in order. I apologize for any delay." The iron in his voice had all but vanished as he watched to see how Algernon would react. His men closed and encircled the party, none of them knowing what to expect next.

Elenari found herself reaching for her sword, but Kael quickly caught her eyes with a stern look and shake of his head. Slowly, she removed her fingers from her scabbard.

Hawk and Galin looked toward each other, knowing what the other was thinking. It was like old times. Each one of them knew the other was ready to take immediate action.

Just as Galin was about to move, Algernon spoke. "We shall, of course, honor your wishes; however, we are not of a mind to be delayed. These men are on a journey to the Great School of Magic to meet their teacher. I promised to deliver them in just a few days. So you see, we are expected."

Algernon placed heavy emphasis on his words, but the shadow passed away as suddenly as it had come, and once again, Algernon appeared as a wrinkled old man.

The lead rider responded to Algernon with a barely discernable nod of the head. He quickly pulled his reins, turning his horse about, and forcefully pointed west in the direction they were now all to ride. They turned their steeds westward and began at a slow trot.

Galin brought his horse up alongside the Sage and whispered, "What just happened there?"

"I tried a small trick of light and shade, hoping to intimidate our young officer," the Sage responded in a whisper. "Unsuccessfully, I might add. He is either very well-trained or protected against such weak magic."

"Is this a normal procedure?" Galin asked.

"The word *normal* has little meaning in this land. We must hope that it is only what it appears. In the future, ensure you take no action unless I do first." Algernon's tone was commanding even in whisper. "So be patient and trust my judgment until the time for action comes."

The Druid sighed heavily and forced his gaze forward, pondering the old man's words.

The group, led by Hawk and surrounded by soldiers, trotted along through the almost virgin grasslands of southern Mystaria.

Elenari looked closely at the lead rider. His silver armor gleamed in the brilliance of the sun. His sword hung concealed inside a fine leather scabbard. The handle was golden, smooth, and polished. *Likely crafted by Elves,* Nari thought. A large ruby, which seemed to give off a slight aura, was set in the pommel of the sword. She peered about at the other soldiers; they too, possessed weapons of similar craftsmanship. These men were indeed warriors, the likes of which she had never seen.

They continued through the lush landscape, passing small brooks and numerous ponds that dotted the Mystarian countryside. Ahead, over the next hill to the west, mountaintops jutted out above the horizon. Gigantic peaks shot into the sky, stretching above the clouds, reaching into infinity. The beauty of the breathtaking landscape was nearly lost on the companions, who continued to follow their escort southwest, moving deeper into Mystaria.

Late afternoon came, and Hawk began to wonder if they would ever reach their destination. Though he was somewhat familiar enough with the country to get them to Mystaria City, he had no desire to learn more about the geography, since a man was never truly safe in Mystaria unless he was a wizard. It was a fact that meant all of them, save possibly Algernon, had much to fear. While Algernon was no wizard, he certainly seemed a kindred spirit to the people of Mystaria whose lives seemed centered around magic.

As the sun began its descent and twilight approached, a lone structure appeared ahead on the trail. Overshadowed by looming mountains, it was a circular black tower nearly a thousand feet high. Its width and depth were at least half that. The top was shaped like a crown riddled with small slits designed to allow arrows or crossbow bolts to be fired out of the structure should it come under attack. The structure was fortified with heavy stone battlements from top to bottom and seemed all but impenetrable. A moat completely surrounded the tower, making it appear as if there were no way in.

The backdrop of the mountains protected the tower from wind and most certainly shielded it from sunlight. The mountains also protected from invasion from multiple sides. Any force would have to assault the tower from essentially the direction they were approaching from.

Galin felt a chill as they entered the shadows cast by the mountains. The shadows around the tower had an unnatural darkness about them and an odd loneliness as well.

The group moved closer until they were only a few feet from the moat, which prevented them from going any farther. There was no longer any grass, only dried dirt all around the moat and base of the tower.

As they continued forward, a large wooden drawbridge was slowly lowered from the base of the tower. The chains rattled as the bridge came down over the moat. All of them crossed over the creaking planks in turn and disappeared into the blackness of the tower. When the last rider had entered, the bridge was brought up again, sealing the tower shut.

The foyer of the tower was quite large, but the air seemed somewhat musty. The floors were damp and covered with gravel. Torches, secured by metal brackets, threw flickers of light into the hallway beyond.

It was still difficult for most of them to see, save Elenari, whose infravision allowed her to see all that was around them. She saw paintings dotting the walls of the hallway. They were pictures of prominent-looking men in military uniforms. She saw a suit of plated mail armor propped up against the wall to the right. It stood alone, as if it were guarding something. As she looked up, she saw the barrel-vaulted ceiling was at least seventy feet high.

The carved gravel floor gave way to cobblestone, and the echoing footfalls of the horses became greatly pronounced. They continued forward through this tremendous entranceway.

Elenari alone continued to see things in the dark, hanging upon the walls to the left and right. They were images, paintings of various depictions of a man in different stages of his life. There were wall-mounted tapestries as well, purposely kept in the dark of this cold cavernous hallway. Each showed the figure of the same nobleman dressed in armor or finely tailored clothes, or holding various weapons, symbols, and instruments. Some depicted him hunting, some riding, and even some had him appearing as if he were casting arcane magic spells. Yet Elenari noticed there was a constant characteristic in each of them: He was always alone. Perhaps that was why this huge foyer was so cold and devoid of light.

They traveled another fifty feet until the lead soldier finally signaled for the party to dismount. The soldiers, save for their leader, stayed their mounts.

The party dismounted in turn. Each was still in possession of his or her weapons. With that, the other soldiers guided the horses off to the left and into the darkness. Hawk hesitated; his horse, Silvermane, was more than merely a steed to him. He had to make a decision quickly. Before he came to his verdict, however, Galin was at his shoulder and in his ear.

"It's all right," said the Druid softly. "He'll be fine. Let's go."

Hawk looked back once more toward his gray steed and reluctantly followed.

The flickering torchlight, until this point, had illuminated very little, but suddenly two miraculously carved double doors appeared before them. It was difficult to tell what material they were constructed of at first, but it appeared to be a finished wood containing myriad carvings of various animals and creatures, so fine and lifelike in their detail that it seemed as if they could jump out at any minute from the doors to attack the newcomers. Within the very heart of the doors, indented in the center, was a spectacular shield, no doubt the family crest of an ancient and powerful clan. The minute carvings in the wood were so complex that a magical aura seemed to emanate from them, while at the same time the sword that crossed through the shield gave off the feeling of great power through force of arms.

The fixed gazes of the party were interrupted by the slow opening of these doors, which released a stream of light and warmth that invited them inside beyond the threshold of this magnificent portal to whatever waited within.

Unable to imagine what to expect, they entered the chamber. The double doors swung abruptly closed, unsettling the party for just a moment. Within that moment, a new and stranger stimulus began working on them—music from a stringed instrument flowing into them from everywhere and nowhere all at once, soft and without harshness but played with such unbridled passion that it touched their very souls. All of this, and more, they felt in the passing of a moment.

They focused their eyes and attention now, enough at least to realize that they were in a place far different from the dark, aloof foyer ever could have indicated. Hanging from the ceiling of this place, perhaps a hundred feet above them, was a chandelier, the likes of which was said to adorn the legendary palaces of Arcadia. The colored spectrums of light, which darted through the prisms created by the fabulous crystalline glass, were a wonder to behold. The chandelier seemed to possess an infinite number of arms and candle holders jutting out from one another like roots from an ancient tree. The chamber, some two hundred feet wide, surely did this device no justice. With all of its different appendages, it was at least that long and wide. Somehow, all of them suspected that this wondrous device provided light for the entire tower.

The next object of interest also boasted size as its outstanding feature. It was a beautiful mahogany table, fifty feet long by half as much wide. Every inch of it had been sanded and treated with a finish that made it shine. Adorning it was a lone place setting comprised of the finest china and utensils.

Elenari was the first member of the party to tilt her head in a direction other than forward. Lining the walls, which surrounded this amazing place, was the most exotic collection of creature, not animal, trophies she had ever beheld. They were grandiose, mounted on enormous plaques and frames. There were literally hundreds of creatures. As her gaze traced the circumference of the room, she saw such monsters of legend as the Minotaur, Owlbears, Giants, and even increasing in size to various types of dragons. It was beyond comprehension. There were creatures that appeared to be demons or devils, and as she looked beyond them, she saw creatures so terrible and unrecognizable that she prayed there would never be reason to know of them.

The others, as well, were awestruck, save Hawk, whose eyes never left the source of the eloquent music, which had greeted them. He keenly watched the musician, who sat opposite them deep within the chamber with his back turned toward them. He was tall and broad, dressed in an evening robe of amber with black trim. The shine and texture of the fabric indicated it was silk. His coarse black hair was perfectly combed down to the middle of his neck. His head stayed tilted to one side, as he appeared to be resting his chin on the stringed instrument, which he caressed with the bow in his right hand. The music flowed from a powerful crescendo down to such dulcet tones that it was actually chilling. It did more than move Hawk. It carried him away to other places, other times, both happy and sad, his journey dictated by the force of the music. He identified with it almost immediately. The stranger had given the music character, making it wondrously full of life. He imbued the music with so much of himself that it almost seemed as if he were trying to make the music into a living thing. *A man would only do this,* Hawk thought, *if he himself were so terribly alone.*

The lead soldier, who until this point had remained stationary, now moved forward behind and to the right of the table. As he passed the blazing hearth on the east wall, he cast a shadow amidst the flames that roared and danced, sensitive to the differing tones of the music, likened to a patch of dandelions shimmering in the wind of an open field. This was one of many images the music triggered in their minds as they listened.

The soldier walked right up to the musician, whose now somber melody continued uninterrupted by the intrusion. It appeared as if the soldier spoke a few brief words, and then retired down the west side of the room, leaving the five companions alone with their unusual host.

They were all completely captivated with each stroke of his instrument, not unlike the inanimate creatures, which encircled the walls of the room. Then, unexpectedly, the musician stopped playing. One moment, a wave of emotions bombarded them, carried to them by musical tones that seemed to soar through the air, and the next moment there was nothing, as if the rendition of the entire piece had been meaningless to him. Gently, he restored the delicate instrument to a small wooden case, which lay near his place setting.

In a fluid motion, he turned and faced the party.

Kael noticed the pale complexion of the man and the smooth solid lines that traced the perfect bone structure of his jaw and face. He was a handsome man, though somewhat eccentric in his mannerisms which were meticulous from his deliberate gait to the way he moved his fingers. His features were exquisitely detailed, down to the curls of his finely trimmed mustache.

He faced the party, gazing momentarily at each of them. Slowly, he brushed out the wrinkles in his jacket and produced a curved black pipe from his breast pocket. He struck a match, unseen to them, and nonchalantly brought the pipe to his lips and proceeded to light it. Puffs of smoke rose above him as he exhaled, surveying his guests. He then removed the pipe from his mouth with his right hand and placed a monocle over his left eye with his left hand.

Casually exhaling again from his pipe, the man spoke. "Good evening," he said, nodding toward the party. "Please be seated." His voice was deep and loud. Disguised in his geniality was an air of authority, which could not be concealed.

Algernon replied for them. "Thank you, my lord," said the Sage as he seated himself and gestured for the others to follow suit. "You are most gracious in your hospitality. I trust you will find our papers in order."

"Indeed," said their host. "I understand you've been traveling. Please, join me for my evening meal."

A moment later, several handsomely tailored servants appeared from the west side of the chamber from an opening which led to a connecting chamber, carrying large, covered silver serving trays.

As Kael and the others took their seats, suddenly before them appeared place settings with china and utensils to match their host's down at the other end. They had appeared out of nowhere, as if they had been there all along, concealed somehow. All were surprised, save Algernon.

The servants, all of whom were young men, brought out five huge trays and placed them, still covered, before the travelers, and returned from whence they came.

Next, three beautiful young women appeared, carrying decanters of wine. One of them exclusively served the man at the head of the table while the other two served the party. In turn, they poured each traveler's wine and removed the covers to their trays, revealing a king's feast for each. Roast boar took up the center of each plate flanked by carefully sliced potatoes and stalks of carrots. A rich sauce glazed over the pork, making it appear succulent beyond belief. Steam rose from every plate, and everything seemed cooked to perfection.

Even more inviting than the ambiance of the meal was the perfume the three ladies wore, which blended in the air like a rose garden on a summer's day. Each of them wore a flowered dress cut tastefully about their neck and shoulders. Two of them had shoulder-length ebony hair, while the one who served their host had long, flowing auburn hair.

All of them, save possibly Kael and Algernon, were obviously captivated by the women and food provided by their mysterious host.

"Please," said the man, in a much gentler tone than he had used earlier, "forgive me. In my haste to provide a good meal, I have forgotten my manners. I am Gideon Crichton and allow me to extend the hospitality and protection of Mordovia Tower to you all. Now if I may, sir, can I inquire as to your name and those of your friends?" Crichton looked at Algernon.

"I am Alizan," answered the Sage, bowing his head, "a humble mage, and these men are my apprentices. We are making a pilgrimage to the Great School of Magic as is clearly defined in our traveling papers. The two Rangers are our guides and protection."

"Again, you must forgive me," said Crichton as he leaned back in his chair, puffing on his pipe and calmly exhaling through his nose. "I am of an old family. We do not place much faith in written parchments. In my experience, iron from a man's words comes from the man, not the papers he carries. That is why I instruct my patrols to bring all travelers through my lands here so that I can speak to them personally."

"Do you receive many travelers on their way into Mystaria?" Hawk asked as he raised a goblet of wine to his parched lips.

Crichton hesitated for a moment as he pulled the pipe from his mouth and looked toward the blazing hearth. "Unfortunately, only a very few these days," he said somberly.

Hawk nodded and looked to the others, wondering how these wondrous trays of food were prepared in moments for them. He feared there was far more to this man than any of them dare suspect.

"My lord," Algernon said, "our compliments to your cook. The food and wine and the company have been outstanding, and we thank you for your gracious generosity. May we enjoy the protection of your tower for the night and leave at dawn?"

Crichton was quiet for a moment. He let his eyepiece fall and slowly reached for his wine. As he swallowed, his gaze locked upon Algernon. It seemed to the others that Algernon's question had somehow struck a nerve, irritating their host.

A moment later, Crichton smiled. "Of course you are welcome to stay the night. However, I wonder if I could intrigue you gentlemen and the lady with a game of sorts before you turn in for the night?"

"What kind of game did you have in mind?" asked Hawk.

Crichton leaned forward in his chair and returned Hawk's stare with burning eyes of coal.

"The most amazing and dangerous game of all, my friend." Crichton stood up and began to walk slowly around the table. "What types of games have you played in your lifetimes? Games of chance, cards, dice, darts, but have any of you ever experienced a game so intense your very lives depended on the outcome? Look at the walls around you. Obviously, there is no greater sport than the hunt. It is during the hunt that we see the animal at its best and worst. We see how strong its instincts for survival truly are. We see how clever or deceptive it can be. We see it frightened, and we see it at its most ferocious." He stopped and looked into the fire again, hesitating. Suddenly, he spun around.

"Don't you see? It's not the kill that we desire when we hunt; it's the chase, the challenge, the intrigue about your opponent that lets you know you are truly alive. The emotions that seize you as you close in for the kill, almost feeling sorry for your prey . . . but truly you are sorrier that the hunt in all of its enigma has come to an end." He looked to the fire again.

"Excuse me," said Kael. "Please forgive me for interrupting, but we have traveled a long distance and are quite tired. We would probably be very little use to you hunting at night for game."

"No," Crichton replied. "On the contrary my friend, two of you can be of invaluable use to me. I only need two of you to join me—the two best hunters in the group." He placed his eyepiece on and studied Hawk and Elenari for a moment. "Yes . . . you two are the ones, unless anyone else would care to volunteer."

"I am sorry," said Hawk, catching the moisture on the rim of his goblet with his finger. "But unfortunately, we are both too tired to join you and must respectfully decline your invitation."

"Their teacher will be expecting us early tomorrow and will not be pleased if we did not get a good night's rest," said Algernon. He stood up from the lavishly decorated table with a mind to retire for the night.

"Come now, old man," Crichton said jovially, "I think we both know your papers are not in order, and there is no teacher waiting for you at the Great School of Magic, either." Crichton withdrew the papers from inside his robe and examined them. "Still, this is a forgery of unequalled skill. Only a true scribe of Mystaria or one of the princes might have seen through it. My compliments." Crichton nodded to Algernon. "However, I will overlook this if two of you would simply take my invitation to join me on a most exciting hunt."

Crichton's eyes glared and nostrils flared as he spoke of the hunt. Hawk reached beneath his green robe and gingerly placed his fingers about his silver hand axe, waiting cautiously to see what Algernon's response would be. Galin pushed his plate away and quickly stood erect. None of the others moved as all eyes came to bear on Algernon.

"Prince Crichton, what is it exactly that you require of us?" the old Sage asked, his patience waning.

"Ahh . . . excellent. You know of me. I believe I know you as well, old man," said the prince. "It has been a long time since last you and I met."

Elenari clenched her sword, as she was certain Crichton's answer would determine her next course of action. Unexpectedly and without warning, Crichton moved toward Elenari, stopping inches from her face. He looked down with amusement at the young half Elf, saying, "Do you truly possess the courage to draw your weapon? We shall indeed see of what worth your spirit is, young woman, before the night is over."

Elenari smiled. "We shall indeed."

Algernon raised a warning hand to Elenari and again addressed Crichton. "What are your terms?" asked the Sage.

The prince turned back to Algernon. "My terms are painfully simple," he said with a mocking smile. "You will choose from amongst you two who will compete in the hunt. If you cooperate, join the hunt, and survive until the end, I shall give all of you safe conduct from this tower to Mystaria City and anywhere within the borders of Mystaria. If you refuse or both die during the hunt, then none of you shall ever leave this tower again."

"What do you mean, *if* we survive?" Elenari demanded.

Crichton smiled. "You see, young one, I will be hunting the two of you, and if I find you, you will not survive."

"You plan on killing all of us if we refuse?" Hawk asked arrogantly.

Crichton faced him with an icy stare. "It would mean less to me than killing any creature you see on the walls around you." His voice lingered in the air with deadly earnest.

In that moment, Hawk and the rest of them knew the prince was a man of his word, and no matter what else, he would not hesitate to kill them all.

"The rules are simple," said the prince. "You will have twelve hours to elude me. You will leave all of your weapons here, and you will each be allowed one sword. You will have a one-hour head start. At the end of the twelfth hour, the tower bells will ring twelve times. If both or even one of you is still alive by the last ring, then all will be set free with safe conduct. If both die, then all will be killed. Now you must choose who will face me."

"Elenari and I will challenge you," said Hawk almost immediately.

Galin could not contain himself. "Hold on, Hawk! You don't speak for all of us, nor do you decide indiscriminately who lives and dies in this group!"

"Oh no?" Hawk said. He grabbed Galin with both hands and pushed him up against the wall, whispering so the others could not hear. "But I do decide who the best hunters are and who among us is better suited to protect Algernon, and I trust that to no other save you. Please . . . trust me, my friend." He released him.

"Enough, all of you," Algernon ordered. "The decision has been made." He nodded to Hawk and Elenari.

Elenari removed her weapons, piled them on the table, and waited for Hawk to do the same. As Hawk did so, Elenari looked at Crichton with open disdain.

"Yes indeed, my dear, that's the look I am after. That is the look and feeling that will either give you the edge to survive or foolishly lead to your death. I know it is not fair," said the Prince with the most sincere sympathy, hinting nothing of sarcasm, "but nor is life . . . and so the hunt must be analogous. Now, you will excuse me while I prepare. This will give you some time alone; I will see that you are not disturbed."

With that, the Prince bowed his head slightly and left the room.

Galin immediately turned to Algernon. "First," he snapped accusingly, "you allow us to be taken here, next, you intend to cooperate fully with this madman and sacrifice two of us in the process. We're getting out of here right now!"

Galin turned on his heels and started toward the door.

"Galin! Galin, stop!" Algernon exclaimed in a deafening tone, causing the Druid to stop and turn with anger on his face. Algernon walked close to him so their faces were but inches apart. "That man is Prince Gideon Crichton, Supreme Commander of the Mystarian Army, and one of the ruling princes of Mystaria. His power is beyond all of you. Even the most skilled would be hard-pressed against him in open combat." His gaze turned upon Elenari. "We are not leaving this tower unless he wills it. As to our participation in his hunt, we have little choice. The prince has brought us here to serve his own ends, whatever they may be. Unfortunately, for now, we must each play the part he has intended for us and hope for the best."

Algernon placed his hand on Galin's shoulder for a moment. He did not speak, but only looked deep into his eyes. Galin could not see his lips moving but still he heard the Sage's voice in his mind: *"You will find yourself in doubt many times from now until the day we part company and beyond. Never doubt that any action I have taken is for the good of the party and those who depend on us."*

Algernon then turned away from Galin and walked over to Hawk and Elenari. "No man or woman has ever survived the prince's hunt. Each of you will need all the skills and abilities you have acquired throughout your lives to do so. Do not give up, even if you think the end is near. Our lives are in your hands. Good luck my friends." The Sage took their hands in his, bowed his head, and muttered something they could not understand, then added, "May Thargelion watch over you."

Hawk turned to Galin, who appeared deep in frustrated thought. "Well," Hawk said with a smile, trying to make light of the situation, "knowing no one has ever survived this certainly gives me a goal to shoot for, wouldn't you say?"

Galin could do nothing other than return the other's smile, marveling at Hawk's spirit in the face of such danger. He clasped Hawk's hand tightly. The look the two men exchanged told the story, for words were no longer needed between two old comrades such as these.

As Elenari and Kael embraced, the old Druid said, "It seems our roles have reversed. When I had my trial, you were helpless to aid me. Now, I am helpless to aid you in yours." He placed his hand on her cheek and then moved her hair behind her pointed ear.

"I'll see you in twelve hours, Father," said Nari, with a spark in her eye that marked a determination Kael had seen in her many times before. He prayed it would be enough to see her through this as well.

At that moment, Prince Crichton burst through the door. "Forgive me for interrupting, my friends, but if you would accompany me into the next room, we can begin."

It raced through branches, down veins and roots, and ran into the earth like a stray tributary of a mighty river. Grass, weeds, and dirt bowed to it, vanished, and gave way to its power. Animals and plants dissolved in its wake, and even rocks and stones softened under its magnitude. In its volume and scope, it penetrated mountains and dried up whole rivers in its pursuit. For they were nothing to it; all of the objects it indiscriminately destroyed were nothing. All of the living things it effortlessly killed were nothing. All of them meant nothing. Only one thing would ever have meaning. Only one thing gave it purpose, the very thing it sought—the Emerald Star.

Hawk and Elenari followed the prince to a small, barren adjoining chamber. It was square approximately ten feet by ten feet. There were no other exits or windows, only a large rectangular rug in the middle of the floor.

A moment later, two young boys, similar to the servants from the dining hall, appeared. The first pulled up the rug, revealing a large trapdoor in the floor. The second servant carried two long swords. He knelt before Hawk and Elenari and offered them the blades.

"The blades are Elven craft," said the prince. "They are exceptionally light and more powerful than most other metals. I think you will find them to be quite effective."

As the two inspected the swords, the first servant opened the trapdoor, revealing a set of stairs going down.

"You have one hour," the prince said unemotionally. "I suggest you not waste it."

Elenari went down the stairs first, followed by Hawk, who hesitated halfway and turned around to look up toward Crichton.

"You'll forgive me if I don't say 'good hunting,'" said Hawk with a mocking grin.

"Of course," the prince answered. "I admire your spirit. I have no doubt I'll enjoy hunting both of you."

In the next moment, Elenari and Hawk vanished into the darkness.

Crichton and two of his soldiers reentered the room where Kael, Galin, and Algernon waited. The soldiers fitted the prince with his plated mail armor, as young squires brought it in one piece at a time.

Crichton stood erect as four of his men tended to him. First, they put on his shin guards and slowly worked their way up his legs and torso. The armor was crafted exquisitely of gold and made the prince appear huge and menacing. Two more soldiers brought a huge red cape, which they attached to his shoulder plates.

Algernon watched with keen interest. Crichton, by all accounts he had ever heard, was a powerful wizard yet he had somehow found a way to wear metal armor, which was normally forbidden to wizards. In fact, no self-respecting wizard would ever entertain the notion of armor. Most wizards felt their magic should be sufficient to protect them and that those who wore armor were weak and unable to use magic. Yet the prince was the commander of their entire army; whatever his limitations or intentions, he was a dangerous man of many talents.

Galin stood watching him for several minutes and could no longer restrain himself. "Why are you doing this?" he demanded. "Is this how you prove your manhood to your men?"

"The question, my friend, is why I should not do this?" answered the prince in a curious tone. "Manhood, as you put it, has nothing to do with life. The hunt is everything. The hunt is life and death. It is all that is left."

After giving the prince his helmet, his soldiers brought him a huge, glowing, two-handed sword. He held it outward, making sure all could see it. "Dwarven craft," he said by way of explanation. "Exquisite, is it not? It also contains several enchantments. It has never failed me in battle, yet for all things, there is a first time. Well, gentlemen, I'm off to begin the hunt."

Crichton turned away from them and went once again to exit the room with his men.

Algernon stood up. "It has not been an hour yet." He walked close to Crichton and spoke in a whisper. "You are the last descendant of a proud and noble order. Its like shall never come again; there will never be another. That you have come to this, I would not have guessed."

Crichton looked at him intently for a moment; indecision was evident upon his face for the very first time. He moved close to Algernon, so close their eyes were but an inch apart. "What I have come to, old man, you could not possibly imagine. Pray you never have to."

His tone was ice. A moment later, the intensity left his face, and his expression was as confident as it had been just moments earlier. "Indeed, surprise is an integral part of the hunt. Not only does it prove interesting for the hunter, but the effect on the animal is equally stimulating." Crichton turned and smiled, speaking in a strangely sincere tone. "Fear not, they will be given a fighting chance. On my oath."

A moment later, he was gone.

Hawk and Elenari found themselves running down a maze of stone corridors, turning right then left, choosing one passage over the next. The pair seemed caught up in the huge, labyrinthine dungeon that extended well beneath the tower. They passed many doors as well. Some were wooden, some stone, and even some iron. This was the prince's hunting ground.

They had been running for over thirty minutes, until finally the path they had chosen ended at a wooden door. They took a moment to rest. Elenari went ahead a few feet down the corridor to listen for any sign of pursuit while Hawk listened intently at the door.

"I don't hear anything, but there's a strange odor," said Hawk.

"We have to go in," answered Elenari. "We don't have time to go back."

With his sword poised, Hawk cautiously edged the door open.

"No, Hawk, wait!" Elenari exclaimed unexpectedly. "Something's moving in there!"

Suddenly, something grabbed Hawk by the throat and pulled him inside the darkness of the chamber.

Elenari quickly ripped a torch off the wall and rushed into the room to see a huge white creature hurling Hawk like a doll against the wall. She could see they were in a large, octagonal chamber. In one corner were piles of hay, and strewn throughout the rest of the chamber were piles of fruits, vegetables, and plants.

The creature turned to face Elenari. It reared up on its hind legs to a height of eight feet. It had a huge muscular chest, and it was completely covered with white fur. Its long powerful arms rested loosely at its sides. It must have been one of the great apes from the jungles of Arcadia. She had heard of them but had never seen anything like it. She knew it possessed the strength to literally tear them apart.

Elenari managed to hold the creature at bay with the menacing flames of the torch and spoke in the direction Hawk had been thrown. "Hawk, are you okay?"

"I'll live," he answered, sounding as if he were scrambling to his feet.

"Open that door on the far wall, and we'll get out of here!" Elenari exclaimed.

The creature, growing brave, began swinging its long arms at Elenari, trying to knock the torch from her grasp. It let out a battle cry and began pounding its chest.

"Come on, Hawk!" she screamed.

The next moment, she heard the door unlatch, and light streamed into the chamber. As Elenari made a break for the open door, the creature lunged forward and slapped the torch from her hand. Instinctively, Elenari slashed back with a sweeping stroke across the animal's chest, sending it howling backward in pain. She bolted through the door to escape the chamber.

Hawk slammed the door shut behind her and produced a small metal spike from his waist, which he wedged into the doorjamb.

"That should hold him a little longer . . . maybe," said Hawk. "Let's go."

They took off down the new corridor at a run. Again, they turned east, then west, constantly running. The corridors sloped up and down; some were lit, some dark, and others still were sectioned out in such a way that they formed a hopeless maze. Once again, the path they had taken ended at a door—oak with metal hinges and locked.

Together, they threw themselves against the door, hacked at it with their swords, and kicked it until they grew tired.

"He must have . . . started . . . after us . . . by now," Hawk said, gasping but quickly gained a second wind. "Well, I guess it's time to stop wasting time standing around making noise."

He stepped back a few paces. Realizing what he was planning, Elenari braced herself, sword ready, though she did not expect Hawk to succeed. Hawk rushed forward and threw himself against the door with terrific force, smashing the lock open and, carried by his own momentum, falling through the open doorway.

Elenari found herself gazing in awe, not only of Hawk's amazing feat, but of what lay inside the gargantuan room. At first, it appeared to have no ceiling, but after a moment, it became clear there was some type of glass dome hundreds of feet overhead. Trees and plants of all types filled the space. It did not seem even remotely possible that such a place could exist—an indoor underground forest.

Sunlight appeared to provide the illumination, though they both knew this could not be the case. They could not see where the room ended—only trees as far as their vision could go. It was fantastic.

Quickly recovering from their bout of wonder, the two entered the arboretum, rushing headlong through the huge trees and plants that populated the space. Elenari always ran a few steps ahead and faster than even she could see.

Suddenly, a branch appeared in front of her from nowhere. Hawk watched, horrified, as the branch struck Elenari in the throat, throwing the lower part of her body up into the air in front of her. When she fell to the ground, the back of her head absorbed the brunt of the blow. Her sword dropped to the ground beside her, and she lay motionless.

Before Hawk could bend down to reach her, he felt something strike him from behind—a quick blow to the back of the neck. It sent him down to his hands and knees, dazed. He felt for a moment as if he might lose consciousness, but he knew all would be lost if he allowed that to happen. Releasing a cry of rage, he picked up his sword, spun around full speed, and from a kneeling position, swung at the enemy behind him. A huge branch slammed to the ground in front of him, severed from the tremendous tree that towered over them. The trees—the very trees themselves—were alive and attacking them.

Like a man possessed, Hawk flung himself at the great trunk, hacking and slashing all the branches around him as they came for him. They began to pile at his feet, until soon, the tree itself could take no more and began to back away. Still, many other trees now approached them from both sides. He whirled about just in time to see Elenari being dragged by several branches toward another, smaller tree. This tree-creature was different—it possessed an immense gaping maw lined with razor-edged teeth. Eagerly, the monster dragged the inert body of Elenari toward its mouth.

Without hesitation, Hawk ran forward, leaping into the air to come down with all his fury, plunging his sword hilt deep into the creature just above its mouth. With an inhuman cry, the creature shrank back. Hawk knew he had only seconds. Frantically, he dislodged his blade and bombarded the creature with fierce thrusts and cuts, which rendered it little more than a mass of twigs.

Abruptly, in one motion, he slung Elenari on his back and took off. Holding her over his right shoulder with his right arm and wielding the sword with his left, he cut and severed all that barred his way like a wild man. Nearly a dozen of the tree creatures fell to his indomitable strength before he finally broke through them. Still, he ran on with his friend on his back.

Ahead, he saw another wooden door in the distance. Somehow, he made himself run faster. Leading with his left shoulder, he roared in anger and exploded through the door, shattering it almost to bits. Still he ran, bearing the pain, the weariness, and the strain of Nari's weight. Nothing could hinder him.

He found himself running through a long corridor when, inexplicably, the stone floor beneath him gave way. It was a trap. The echoes of his scream still lingered in the corridor long after he and his companion had fallen into the darkness.

The creature halted atop a ridge. It gathered its mass together and slowly rose, expanding and forming a bipedal shape that stood nearly ten feet. From a distance, it appeared as a mass of fiery molten lava. It had almost discernable arms, legs, and a head. The large ruby embedded in the center of its head gave it a bizarre, cyclopean appearance. The grass, trees, and leaves within its immediate radius crinkled back, becoming brownish-black.

Suddenly, five Mystarian soldiers on patrol rode up behind the creature. Momentarily startled, they pulled back their reins and stopped. The creature slowly turned to face them. The five men wore heavy plated mail and carried pikes and long swords.

"What do you think?" one soldier said to the others.

"No doubt some failed experiment of one of the princes," another answered.

The creature moved close to one of them. Proudly, the soldier went to prod the creature with his sword. As the blade touched the creature's shoulder, lava shot out from its body and ran up the length of the blade and up to the soldier's right shoulder, engulfing his entire arm. A moment later, the lava returned to the creature's body, and the soldier's right arm and sword were gone. The man howled and fell off his horse.

The nearest soldier rushed forward on horseback and attacked, swinging his sword high and landing it in the creature's neck. The weapon halted and remained stuck in the creature. Seconds later, the blade dissolved. Instantly, the man dropped the empty sword hilt, his jaw dropping with fear.

Within a heartbeat, the creature condensed its mass and volume and became a stream of liquid, flying through the air and right into the soldier's mouth. For a split second, the other three watched as their companion showed no change. Then, he exploded into a thousand bits. His blood sprayed them like a fountain. In sheer terror, they broke apart and rode away in different directions.

The creature's arm shot forth, launching a molten missile at the first man, striking him in the back and carving a tunnel through his torso as it exited out through his chest. His lifeless body fell to the ground, not slowing his galloping horse from escaping.

In no time, the creature liquefied again and raced along the ground until he was underneath the second man's horse. Rising up and expanding, it covered the animal, incinerating it. The rider was thrown, facedown, to the ground. Before he could move, the creature towered over him. It stepped on the man's head, crushing and melting it off the rest of his body.

The last soldier rode like the wind, not looking back, feeling safe enough to realize he had escaped. Unbelievably, the creature formed suddenly before his horse. It seemed impossible that it could have moved so fast. With a backhand swing of its arm, the creature struck the soldier across the face of his helmet, sending him flying off the horse. As quick as the soldier rushed to his feet, the creature was on him. It lifted him up with one molten hand around his neck and watched as his armor and flesh melted away and crumbled to the ground.

The creature surveyed the area. All were dead, and none of them had the Emerald Star. It turned, and the ruby in its head began to pulsate. The Emerald Star was northeast. Instantly, the creature liquefied and was gone.

Hawk awoke to a strange half-light shining on him from above. His head was pounding. The blow he had suffered earlier was now taking its toll. He realized he was slumped across Elenari, who was still unconscious.

They had fallen down a trapdoor, as he remembered. He saw the opening above them. Every muscle, bone, and fiber in his body screamed in pain. The fall was some twenty feet. Amazingly, he didn't feel as if anything was broken. He desperately hoped it was the same for Nari. There were no outer signs of injury, but he could not be certain.

Perhaps it's better this way, he thought. He had no idea how many minutes or hours had passed. Perhaps, if they just both lay quiet down here, time would pass and Crichton would never find them. However, as much as he wished it to be, he feared luck was something he could not factor in as being on their side.

He was barely able to push himself up without falling back down. *One thing is certain,* he thought, gazing up, *without Elenari's help, we will never get out of this pit.*

He moved Elenari to a sitting position against the wall and gently turned her head from side to side. He found himself staring at her for a moment; she was incredibly beautiful. "Come on, girl, wake up. I need you to help get us out of here. Can you hear me?" Hawk continued this until he heard a barely detectable moan emanate from Nari's lips. "All right, that's it . . . come on."

Hawk gently smacked Nari on each cheek, bringing her closer to consciousness.

Elenari came around slowly and muttered, "What happened? Where . . . are we?"

"Let's just say we had a little accident," he said, "but now you have to wake up. Come on, we have to get out of here."

"I don't . . . remember . . . what happened," said Nari. She seemed to be coming around much better now.

"Probably better that you don't. How do you feel?"

"My neck . . . and head. Must have happened during the fall in here."

Nari began looking about their surroundings. Hawk helped her to her feet and explained the nature of their situation by pointing out the opening above, which allowed for the little light they did have. Though she was tired and dazed, she explained to Hawk that if she stood on his shoulders, she could jump to the opening. Hawk had his doubts, but he also had no other ideas. He gave her a boost, and she stood on his shoulders.

As he was bracing for her leap, an odd thought occurred to him. "By the way," he said conversationally, "I've been meaning to ask you about your last name. How did you come to be called Moonraven?"

Standing atop his shoulders, Nari put her hands on her hips and looked down at him. "You want to hear about how I was named *now?* You were just rushing me to wake up so we could get out of here, remember?"

"I'd been meaning to ask you, I suppose now is as good a time as any," Hawk replied.

Smiling in disbelief, with hands on her hips, Nari replied, "My father found me when I was a child in the forest at night. He said had it not been for a raven he noticed on a branch above me and the bright moonlight shining on that spot, he would have passed by me."

"So he chose that name for you?" Hawk asked.

"No," she replied. "If you must know, I chose it, now if you don't mind I think we should be concentrating on getting out of here."

"Yes, I suppose you are right. Did I ever tell you my last name?"

"No," said Nari, looking up, judging how she would make the jump.

"It's a very similar story to yours, only my name is Sunsquirrel," Hawk said.

Nari hesitated and looked down at him for a moment, expressionless. Neither said a word, and in the next instant, they both burst out laughing.

"Well," Nari said, smiling, "as amusing as it would be to remain stuck in this pit with you, I think that's my cue to leave."

She bent down low as Hawk struggled to hold himself still, and then launched herself up and grabbed the stone around the opening. Hawk cheered from below as she made it.

"Impressive!" he called up to her, as he gathered their belongings. "You are full of surprises, I see."

"Of that you can be certain," Elenari said as she pulled her legs up and climbed out of the pit.

Directly across the opening from her sat a huge black wolf, completely silent, as if awaiting her arrival.

Elenari froze in a crouched position, arms extended out before her.

"We may have a little problem up here!" she exclaimed. "Pick up the sword, Hawk. Now!"

"What do you say, girl?" Hawk yelled up to her.

At that moment, the wolf propelled itself forward over the pit into Elenari, forcing her onto her back. Jaws snapping, the animal went for the throat. At the last second, she got her foot against the animal's stomach and kicked it back down into the pit. The wolf fell with a violent impact. The last sound it made was a high-pitched yelp as Hawk brought the sword down across its throat, killing it.

"I hear more coming! Now would be a good time to throw me up the sword!" urged Nari.

Hawk quickly threw the sword to her.

"Now throw me your robe!" Nari ordered.

"Will it be my britches next?" Hawk shouted back to her, but he quickly removed his green robe, balled it up, and tossed it to her. Elenari grabbed the robe, opened it, and extended it down to him like a rope.

"No, Nari!" Hawk cried. He could now hear the sound of more wolves and men running toward them in the distance. "Save yourself and get out of here!"

Elenari was nearly flat on her stomach, arms hanging down into the pit. "I'm not moving from here without you. Now jump for the robe, and I'll pull you up!"

With his remaining strength, Hawk jumped, grabbed the robe, and wrapped it around his hands. He held on tightly as Nari hauled him upward, astonished that she had the strength to lift him up and out of the pit.

As both of them straightened to a standing position, they saw Crichton at the far end of the corridor, holding a team of wolves by chains and leading a group of fierce looking well-armed men. As they locked gazes, the prince handed the team to one of his men, drew his great two-handed sword, and took off after their retreating forms.

Hawk and Elenari were becoming fatigued and struggling against the pain inflicted by their fall, but they continued following the winding corridor as quickly as possible. They could hear the prince, his men, and the wolves still close behind them.

The corridor then turned straight for a great distance. The prince stopped, dropped his sword, and turned back toward his men. "Quickly!" he ordered.

One of the soldiers handed him a great black crossbow. He took deadly aim and fired. The bolt struck Hawk in the back of his left thigh, causing him to drop to one knee.

Elenari stopped as well and, without thinking, ripped the bolt from Hawk's leg, causing him to cry out through gritted teeth. She put her arm around Hawk's neck and urged him on.

The prince smiled as he replaced the crossbow with his sword and continued running after them. *It will be soon now,* he thought.

Hawk stumbled, causing both of them to fall. Valiantly, Elenari tried to raise him up, but Hawk pushed her away. "Go now, Nari. Here is where I stay. Leave me the sword. I can hold him off longer than you would think."

"No, Hawk," she snapped. "I'll fight him here and now."

Hawk grabbed her arm and swung her around. "No, you aren't hurt. I can buy time for you to escape. You think I'm a good Ranger; I was born to fight with a sword."

"No, Hawk," she pleaded. "He can't beat me; you don't understand."

"Please, Nari . . . let me do this. Go—now!"

Elenari looked back. In a moment, the Prince would be upon them. They had only one sword left between them. With a last look at Hawk, she put the sword in his hand, turned, and continued running.

Crichton stopped about three feet from where Hawk lay. "Forgive me," he said. "I must make this quick so your friend doesn't get too far. You led a noble chase."

Swiftly, mercilessly, he brought his great sword above his head and came swooping down at Hawk, who unexpectedly parried the blow to the side and managed a kick between the prince's legs to the unprotected part of his mighty armor. However, the prince recovered within a moment and, with his next swing, wrenched Hawk's sword away from him. He raised his own blade a third time for the killing blow.

He did not see Elenari standing right beside him, sword in hand. As Crichton's blade reached its apex, Elenari stepped forward and delivered a two-handed blow to the prince's head with such brute force that it knocked the helmet off his head and doubled him over. She considered pressing the attack but his men would be on them in moments.

Elenari did not waste a second. She pulled Hawk to his feet, handed him the sword again, and they were off running.

Crichton slowly stood up, gathering his senses. His men stood paralyzed in disbelief. The prince, his hair a mess, did nothing but stare at the two attempting to escape him.

"Astonishing!" Crichton said with genuine bewilderment, a wide smile on his lips. After a moment's hesitation, he continued the pursuit.

Hawk and Elenari came to a fork in the corridor where they could choose to go right or left.

"We have to split up here," said Hawk.

"If he goes after you, you can't outrun him!" Nari protested.

"No, but if at least one of us lives, then so do the rest. Go on now, girl, no more arguing!" Hawk pushed her away.

"There is much about me you do not know," Elenari said firmly. "Believe me, he will not kill me."

Hawk faced her calmly, almost quietly. He removed his green robe again and wrapped it around his right hand as if it were a shield meant to protect him. He took the sword from Nari's hand.

"There is more about me than you know as well, Elenari Moonraven. May we both live to learn such things."

He bowed his head and abruptly turned away from her. Elenari saw the prince approaching and reluctantly departed down the left corridor.

Without hesitation, Crichton went down the right corridor, seeing the blood trail on the stones that certainly belonged to the wounded man. *Excellent*, he thought; he would still have time to get the other one. A moment later, he saw Hawk about twenty feet ahead of him. He faced the prince with an en-garde salute.

"Come on!" Hawk challenged defiantly. "Come on, Crichton!"

The prince stopped for a moment, looking carefully at him. His poise and stance was that of a swordsman, a skilled swordsman. This was more than he could have ever hoped for.

They clashed swords. Crichton lunged four times, only to be blocked each time by Hawk's skillful swordplay.

Then, with inhuman speed, Crichton swatted Hawk's blade away and slashed his left shoulder. Again, the prince rolled his blade off Hawk's attempted block to slice into his right shoulder.

Hawk was completely exhausted and out of breath, with blood running down the length of both arms. Crichton was a superior swordsman and was now toying with him.

The prince struck yet again, thrusting into Hawk's right side. Edging ever backward, Hawk shuffled across the stone, just trying to remain standing.

At that moment, a thunderous bell rang out with a deafening force, which caused even the corridor they were in to vibrate slightly.

Hawk's face came alive with the bell's first toll. *Nine more rings*, he thought, *nine rings away from life.* He decided, in that instant, that he still had nine rings left within him.

As the prince swung his final blow, Hawk ducked with blinding speed, turned, and began running again.

"Impossible!" the prince exclaimed; he had been determined to end this quickly.

The bell tolled twice, three times, and a fourth, and Algernon's voice echoed through Hawk's mind: *Do not give up, even when you feel the end is near.*

In a moment, the prince was on him, about to strike. Without warning, Hawk stopped mid-stride and turned, swinging his sword with all his power. The blow caught the prince's blade in midair and batted it down. Incredibly, his second blow struck the prince's chest just below the neck, driving him backward. Hawk struck a third time to his chest, then a fourth time to the prince's stomach, doubling him over. His fifth and final blow smashed into Crichton's back, driving him to the ground. Hawk found the prince's sword with his foot and kicked it back behind him. The bell had tolled four more times during the battle, making eight.

The prince shuffled forward on his knees and lunged for his sword. On the ninth toll, he picked his weapon up, rose from his knees on the tenth, and arched the blade back just in sync with the last toll.

When the echoes and vibrations stopped, Crichton stood two feet from Hawk, who was using every bit of his remaining willpower just to keep from falling. Slowly, gently, the prince lowered his blade.

Hawk's blade slid to the floor. Hawk leaned back until he felt the corridor wall against his back and let himself slide down with gravity into a sitting position. The sound of his deep inhalations filled the corridor.

Crichton looked down at him, shaking his head and smiling. "Outstanding! Never have I faced a man with your spirit, courage, and strength. The woman as well . . . remarkable."

Hawk wearily lifted his head and saw the prince was not out of breath and none of his blows had penetrated the armor, though they had left considerable dents. Oddly enough, he thought, *The prince is indeed a man of his word.*

At that moment, Elenari appeared, running down the corridor ahead of the prince's men. She saw Hawk and screamed. "Hawk! If you killed him—"

"Hold, young one!" said Crichton hastily. "He is alive. I have kept my terms. The hunt is ended, and you are victorious. I salute you both."

In military fashion, Crichton brought his blade to his shoulder, clicked his heels together, and bowed his head. He clapped his hands and pointed toward Hawk. Immediately two of his men lifted Hawk off the ground. Elenari burst in between them.

"Where are you taking him?" she demanded.

"Fear not, my lady. My personal healer will tend his wounds. Now, if you will follow me, I shall take you back to your friends." Crichton gestured with his hand, indicating she follow.

Elenari let the men carry Hawk and reluctantly followed the prince.

The weary travelers were each given a room to rest for as long as they wanted. In the afternoon, they were all reunited in the great audience chamber. As Hawk entered the room, Galin rushed first to greet him.

"It appears I'll outlive you yet," Hawk whispered to Galin. "Another life you owe me. I wonder when the shame will become too much for you." The two men warmly shook hands.

Elenari met Kael with an equally warm embrace.

"Well done, my young friends," greeted Algernon as he placed a hand on each of them. "Well done indeed."

A squire then entered the room and handed Algernon two sealed parchments. Before he could inquire about them, a familiar voice filled the room.

"The first, are your original traveling papers," said Crichton in an eloquent melodic tone. "The second are papers signed and sealed by me, which will guarantee you safe passage to Mystaria City if that is your destination. I must humbly thank you, gentlemen and lady, for the unparalleled sport you provided. I hope you enjoyed your stay at Mordovia Tower. Farewell, wherever you may go."

Crichton bowed and turned away, taking the seat upon which he'd sat when they had first observed him. Again, his back was to them, as he took the bow to his violin. He began to play the wondrous piece he had left off with.

They each had strong emotions concerning Crichton, and there were many things they wished to say, but they silently took their leave of the tower and their most unusual host.

Their horses and possessions were waiting at the front gates. Hawk was indeed glad to see Silvermane again and patted him vigorously.

The Captain of the Guard advised them to to follow the Soubia River southeast, then due south, then veer southeast toward Mystaria City. They rode away from Mordovia Tower with renewed confidence that their next destination would be the council chambers of Mystaria City.

Chapter 9

The last units of the colossal army penetrated through the darkness, emerging from the treacherous slopes of the Andarian Ranges. The night shrouded their immense gathering; the moon and stars were cloaked by the ominous clouds that had mysteriously arrived earlier that morning. The invaders came from the northwest of Wrenford, from the mammoth neighboring country of barbaric tribesman called Koromundar. Like sand through an hourglass, they filed into the bordering woodlands surrounding the peaceful villages, town, and Citadel of Wrenford.

Soundlessly, they crept through the thick forest and grasslands, growing ever closer to the sleeping city. The noise of the insects of the night became muffled with the anticipation of the impending slaughter. All that stood between thousands of barbarians and the keep of Thargelion was but a few scant miles of grassland.

This army, clad in animal skin and armed with an array of axes, clubs, swords, and bows, looked more like wild beasts than men. Many wore furs and armor of leather with metal helmets painted black. They stopped and waited for the signal to commence their attack.

The forward ranks, consisting of five thousand infantry mostly armed with swords, were flanked by several rows of cavalry, thousands strong, waiting to reinforce the initial siege. Many rows of archers took position on several surrounding hilltops, preparing to quell whatever resistance the people of Wrenford offered. There were to be no prisoners.

Within the Citadel of Wrenford, Captain Garin strode down the long hallway that led from the audience chamber to the throne room. The passage seemed particularly lengthy this night. As he saluted the king's personal guards, the huge double doors swung open to admit him.

Across the chamber, King Thargelion sat nestled deep within his throne. The flickering torch on the east wall permitted barely enough light to even see the King from the doors. The atmosphere was unusually sullen.

"It is done my lord. All those who would leave from the city and surrounding villages have been evacuated. We spared what few horse soldiers we could to escort them south toward Averon. Still, there were many who chose to stay despite the danger." The captain bowed.

The King seemed distracted as he looked toward the window. "Well, that's something I suppose."

Still shrouded in darkness, the King spoke, "Yes, my friend. See to it both the watch and guard are doubled in strength. There is a foreboding in the air tonight. Be sure they are alert at their posts." The aged Elf stared to the empty glass encasement to his left, which had once housed the precious Emerald Star.

"But your highness," Garin began to question, "the hour is very late, why?"

"I learned something long, long ago as a soldier, Garin, and I was a soldier centuries longer than you have even lived." He spoke not admonishingly, but with almost sad reluctance. "Though no truly wise sovereign wants men to blindly follow his orders all the time, it is sometimes wiser to obey than to question."

"Yes, my lord. It shall be done."

The broad soldier left with a queer expression across his face. The king's mood disturbed him; he rarely gave orders without reason, and Garin disliked the tone of despair in his voice. It was something he could not remember hearing ever before.

Thargelion held fast to his throne, trying to gain strength from its cool sturdy structure. He gazed at the double doors, wondering if he owed his loyal captain and men the truth. Perhaps he did. But perhaps this was his burden alone to bear. Still, with so many truths kept hidden throughout his life, would revealing one make any difference?

They all knew the risks. Most of the garrison had known the Emerald Star was gone and still all had remained, down to the last man, and not just out of loyalty to him. This was their kingdom as well, their home, and they felt responsible for it, the same as he. He looked to the window to the east and waited for it to come.

The night breeze, which drifted calmly through the plains of Wrenford, swiftly grew stronger as the smell of rain became present in the air. Abruptly, in the distance, faint rumblings of thunder reverberated, causing the lands to tremble. The lands hungered desperately for precipitation. Droplets of rain fell, swallowed at once as they struck the ground. The trees groaned as gusts of wind pulled and tugged at them. Thunderhead clouds forced their way over Wrenford at impossible speeds.

Suddenly, a forked streak of light connected the sky and earth for one soundless moment, only to be followed by a harrowing explosion of deafening thunder. Atop the walls of the keep, the crossbowmen of the watch fell hard against the battlements as the entire fortress seemed to vibrate.

The warriors of the tribes of Koromundar, having turned away from the blinding flash, raised their heads skyward to see a mounted, dark stallion racing through the night. The horse rode upon the very currents of the air itself, using the intense winds to carry itself even faster. Astride the back of this magical beast, a cloaked figure rode over them, reveling in the growing fury of the raging storm. This was their signal.

Like hungry dogs purposely left unfed, they ran, weapons drawn, howling in rage, through the grassy plains that separated them from their prey. Undaunted as the sky opened to release an unholy downpour of rain, they pushed forward, rapidly closing the distance. For them, no mere force of nature could dissipate the desire for blood, which they could almost taste and so desperately hungered for.

Above them, the rider raised his arms, revealing his skeletal frame, and lightning shot forth again illuminating the Citadel of Wrenford, exposing it to the attackers. The darkness of night would offer no protection for them or their king. There would be no escape for any of them.

At the keep, soldiers mobilized within seconds. All catapults and ballistae were manned and stores of ammunition made ready. The main gates were immediately sealed by a huge, iron portcullis. Within the courtyard, archers and crossbowmen scrambled for the battlements, hoping to set up a deadly crossfire should the main gates be breached.

Over two hundred mounted cavalry formed up before the keep, preparing to ride out and defend the city and surrounding villages. Through the wind and rain, Captain Garin yelled instructions to a young officer named Del, who would lead the cavalry. After their brief exchange, Del faced the horsemen, drew his sword, and cried, "For the King! For Wrenford!" In unison, they repeated it back to him with pride.

With that, the cavalry galloped toward the city, and Garin disappeared through the main gates of the keep, which were swiftly secured and bolted when he reentered.

In the courtyard, the infantrymen of Wrenford took their places as the pounding rain obscured their vision to near blindness. The wind caused the rain to pour down almost horizontally, striking their faces. All they could do was wait for the inevitable now. Somewhere, deep within their hearts, they knew, without the Emerald Star, their fates were sealed.

Garin raced frantically through the halls, shouting orders to the king's guards, instructing one of them to watch the audience chamber, leaving only one to guard the king. As he burst through the double doors, he found the king sitting, just as he had left him minutes ago.

"My King, we are under attack!" Garin warned urgently. "You must escape the fortress; we cannot protect you if you remain within!"

"You are needed by your men now, my friend," the King said. "Go . . . I release you from your service to the crown. Each of us will face his destiny tonight."

"No!" the captain answered. "Only death can release me. My sacred duty is to defend my land and my King, as my fathers had before me." Even as he spoke, the screams of howling barbarians ringing in the distance turned his head.

"Then follow my last order to you, Captain of Wrenford," Thargelion commanded in the most menacing tone Garin had ever heard him use. "Go and support your men. Go *now!*"

Hesitating for a final moment, Garin disappeared back down the hall. The double doors closed behind him.

As the rain battered down upon the dryness of the lands, the thundering hooves of the Koromundarian soldiers rumbled through the towns of Wrenford. The land shuddered as if in the wake of an earthquake's tremors.

Through the towns and villages, the barbarians slashed and burned anything in their path. Women and children were slayed instantly, without a thought, as their homes were reduced to ashes. All were claimed in a terrible wake of death and destruction. The army never slowed, racing toward their primary target—the Citadel. Even the pouring rains could not extinguish the fires, which seemed to draw on the power of the invaders' rage and hatred.

From the keep, Garin, standing atop the highest tower, watched as dark smoke billowed into the air from the villages surrounding the Citadel. Although the wind-driven rains made it difficult to see, he could tell that a huge army was drawing ever closer to the keep. Then, cutting through the night, he caught a clear glimpse of the invaders. It was difficult to tell how many there were, their numbers were so great. Like an army of ants swarming over an animal corpse, the howling barbarians pushed through the blackness. They covered acres of grassland, moving at an incredible rate.

Garin watched from on high as Del led the cavalry of Wrenford out to meet their enemies. Before any of them had time to fully comprehend the scope of what was occurring, they were mauled, no match for the thousands upon thousands of barbarians. Many were dead before they hit the ground, while the rest were trampled underfoot. Even their horses were killed and trampled upon. They were all dead.

Thunderclaps erupted in the darkness of the night. The sounds made even the force of the pouring rain obsolete. The death cries of the cavalry were never heard by anyone.

It was at that moment a surge of hopelessness overtook Garin. The city and villages of his homeland were no more—people and children murdered, homes and shops destroyed—and he could do nothing to help. Nothing. He looked down now at the men of the garrison, standing within the courtyard of the keep. Torches flickered, suffering from the rain as they awaited the onslaught. Garin knew they did not have a chance.

He took one more brief moment to picture how beautiful the lands of Wrenford had been, how peaceful. The wild roses of red and yellow, unique only to Wrenford, had often made him smile. Now, all of that was gone. Looking out over the kingdom one last time, Garin unsheathed his glistening silver sword.

Quickly, he turned and ran down the stairs of the tower. Garin emerged, racing into the courtyard, his men watching as he passed through the ranks. *They are so young,* Garin thought, *Most of them have never seen battle.* He stopped within the center of the courtyard, turned, and faced his men. Raising his sword to the night sky, pointing it at the keep, he screamed, "Victory for the King! Victory for Wrenford!"

His courage was so great, his troops became seized within the rapture of the moment and almost felt victory was possible.

In that instant, a spray of arrows spilled over the walls of the keep, killing half a dozen archers on the ledge of the Citadel's upper battlements. The main gates shuddered suddenly; the invaders had managed to lift the portcullis and were attempting to batter down the gate.

The Citadel archers on the battlements launched a hail of arrows at the invaders, killing dozens, but for every one barbarian that went down, ten others took his place. There were too many. The archers reloaded, vainly, and their arrows rained down upon the attackers again, disappearing into the night.

The main gates weakened as Garin and the men waited breathlessly for them to give way and the murderers to enter.

Too suddenly for any of them, the gates collapsed, allowing the barbarians to funnel into the courtyard. Their black helmets and animal-skin armor were like nothing the soldiers of Wrenford had ever seen. They were savages, slashing and stabbing at anything, clambering on top of one another to get into the Citadel.

On the other side of the yard, Garin and his men were there waiting for them. Just as the impenetrable line of invaders was about to reach them, the crossbowmen fired. As Garin had planned, the enemies were caught in a deadly crossfire from the scores of men hidden behind arrow slits in the walls to the east and west of the courtyard. Garin did not hesitate, ordering the infantry line forward to force the invaders back. After gaining a few feet of ground, he would quickly order their retreat and, as the barbarians gathered in the courtyard, the hidden missile fire from the walls would cut them to pieces, and the next infantry rank would move forward.

Finally, the archers could no longer reload as fast as the barbarians could replace their ranks. With that, Garin ordered all ranks of infantry forward. Swords clashed and the smell of blood filled the air as the two armies met.

Immediately, three barbarians went after Garin, nearly climbing on top of him and battling him with all of their might. With terrible quickness and precision, he dropped two of them with one slashing swing. The third he killed with a counter thrust. Turning, he swiftly ran to the aid of one of his infantrymen who was already badly injured. Pushing the young man to the ground, Garin faced the attacking enemy, thrusting his blade through his foe's heart, all the while screaming, "Victory for the King!"

Again, Garin was off and running through the turmoil. He jumped atop a small ledge and flung himself into a pile of barbarians, forcing them to the ground and stabbing through their chests, then raced to face the next group of enemies.

His men fought gallantly as they were pushed deeper and deeper toward the back of the keep. Their swords swung frantically, fighting off impossible odds at every turn. The invaders fell, but more always took their place, fresh and hungry for blood.

Throughout the courtyard, Garin rallied his men on. He was everywhere, his sword constantly sweeping through the rain, killing enemies on either side of him.

Suddenly, five barbarians were on him, their swords anxiously seeking his veins. They hacked at him, but still the broad captain was too quick. He slashed one in the throat, another in the chest, and severed another's arm, but there were too many even for him. A dark blade penetrated Garin's upper chest and collarbone as he let out a yelp of pain. He immediately turned and cut the attacker to pieces.

Blood poured from his right shoulder as he listened to the screams of pain and death echoing throughout the yard. He saw dozens of his men lying all about on the ground. The enemy had forced them back against the south wall and had surrounded them all. The battle was lost.

Anger completely consumed Garin, and tears filled his eyes. He lifted his sword, crimson with blood, and rushed screaming into the enemy. He slashed, parried, and stabbed, killing all in his way, never seeing the faces of the lives he took. He was a madman, swinging his weapon into the invaders around him.

Suddenly, he felt something from behind. An axe had entered his back, then another sword into his side, then another blade into his stomach. Blood flowed from his body, pouring out from his mouth and nose, as his sword finally fell limp from his hand. He collapsed to his knees, covered in his own blood. He tried to push himself back up to his feet, but he couldn't. He lifted his head one final time to see a bludgeoning sword take his life. His body fell to the ground, lifeless, and the invaders ran over it, forcing it down into the mud.

The barbarians overtook the remainder of the Citadel, encountering minimal resistance. They gathered a handful of the king's surviving soldiers and rounded them up in a small circle.

Casualties from both armies lay strewn across the compound. The garden, once full with life and beauty, was torn up and destroyed like everything else. The green grass of the yard was burnt and muddy, covered with corpses. Blood stained the earth heavily. In some areas, weapons and arrows were stuck in the ground, belonging in large to the soldiers of Wrenford who'd never hit their targets.

As the barbarians moved through the courtyard, checking for any additional survivors, a lone horseman rode through the broken-down main gates. His steed was black as pitch with brilliant red eyes, and puffs of gray smoke billowed from its evil snout.

The rider was little more than a skeletal being, once human and now encapsulated in a cloak of pure evil. A black robe covered his ghoulish form and a shimmering, surreal crown of gold and gems adorned his skull-like head, white as ivory. His blood-red eyes had an aura of death about them. It was as if the Grim Reaper had come to gather his minions from the dead. After all, he was undead—a lich.

Voltan rode his cursed steed, a demonic species of horse never seen by human eyes, up the pathway, leading toward the entrance to the inner keep. His eyes darted left to right, surveying the death his followers had left.

The rain continued to fall, though not as strong as before, but enough to create puddles of water within the courtyard. Blood mixed with the rain, creating a maroon river that streamed toward the entrance to the keep. It would take a long downpour to remove lingering bloodstains throughout the Citadel.

The Lich rode with pride and sense of victory. Long had he waited for such a day. The people of Wrenford had been no match for the barbarians of Koromundar. It brought him great pleasure to see them all dead. He was satisfied with what he saw, though greater satisfaction would be his before the night ended.

Voltan stopped his horse only a few feet from the entrance where the survivors of the garrison of Wrenford were being held. He looked down at them and he was pleased; only six remained. He extended his hands slowly down toward them, and a dark green gas flowed from his fingertips. Within moments, the young soldiers found themselves choking and gasping for air. Another second later, they all collapsed, dead, with a green hue about their faces. Voltan enjoyed seeing them die.

He dismounted from his dark beast and moved toward the keep's portal, pushing a dead soldier's body aside. Before him were the great bronze doors which led inside the keep. Green fire erupted from Voltan's eye sockets, melting the Elvish runes which protected the entrance. With that, he pushed the doors open.

The young guard, heavily armored in shining plated mail, removed his robe of gray and gold. He held his great broadsword out before him and waited. As he watched the other end of the golden hallway, suddenly, a figure appeared that had not been there a moment earlier. He saw the being, which appeared to be nothing more than an animated black robe, slowly moving forward, closing the distance between them. The figure's head was shrouded in a hood, concealing his face from view.

"Halt, in the name of King Thargelion!" the king's guard exclaimed.

The skeletal being did not halt until he was within arm's length of the soldier. Suddenly, the robe's right arm shot forth. With unbelievable strength and speed, the skeletal hand ripped the soldier's helmet off, and, in the same motion, bony fingers gripped the soldier's neck.

Voltan drew the man close to him and forced him to meet his gaze. The young soldier's face became stricken with terror, and his sword dropped to the stone floor. His scream rose at an inhuman pitch, and he knew fear to the core of his being. He flailed about wildly in the viselike grip of Voltan.

"Cold . . . so cold!" the young guard was able to gasp between screams. Voltan now lifted him off the ground, enjoying seeing the soldier struggle. Nothing pleased him more than the effects of his touch on mortal flesh.

He watched with glee the grotesque transformation that took place before him. The young soldier aged at a wickedly cruel speed. His brown hair lengthened and became stringy and gray, the skin of his face and eyes withered to wrinkle upon wrinkle. The tissue of the young man's eyes melted and fell back into the sockets as the skin continued to deteriorate until nothing but bone remained. The last cry of the once-brave, once-young man was an unearthly gurgling noise, which ended the terrible death throes the soldier had been forced to endure. Voltan now held a complete skeleton encased in plated mail armor before him.

Voltan's death-defying laugh echoed throughout the hall, as he let the bones and armor crumple to the floor before him. Kicking the skull aside, Voltan proceeded through the double doors to the throne room beyond.

The doors exploded off their hinges almost in tune with the raging storm outside. Voltan entered triumphantly, only to stop several feet away from an empty throne.

"*Come out, old one! The end of your time is at hand. Look upon me! I am the death that had finally come to claim you. I know you are here . . . I can feel your life force waning away with each passing moment. I can hear your heartbeat. I can sense your fear . . .*"

"My time may well be at hand, but your time is coming!"

The grandeur of Thargelion's voice filled the chamber, and suddenly, light poured in from all directions, brilliantly illuminating the throne. Voltan shrank back, covering his eyes and face. His undead state predisposed him to a hatred of bright lights.

The intensity of the glare decreased just enough for Voltan to bring his hands down to see something beyond belief. From behind the throne, Thargelion emerged clad in resplendent mithril armor shimmering with the colors of Wrenford. He drew a gleaming blade from a multi-jeweled scabbard with one hand, and with the other, he held a mighty shield with the protruding emblem of the Emerald Star upon it. Even more incredible was Thargelion's physical appearance. He had long flowing red hair, and his skin was as pure as ivory. There, in all his vitality and glory, was Thargelion, the Wizard-King and sovereign of Wrenford.

Unsettled, Voltan took two steps backward. He felt something enter his back. He looked down and saw a glowing blade piercing through his chest. Impaled, he let out a cry of surprise and pain, and he spun around quickly to see Thargelion in his true form—that of a withered old Elf.

Thargelion's sword still within him, Voltan managed a wickedly mocking laugh. "*Very good, old man, but truly there is no escape. That the legendary Thargelion should be reduced to such petty illusions. Yet few things are more pathetic than an Elf who has outlived his youth to decrepitude and dotage. Is it not a kindness to relieve you of your misery? You die this night. Enough!*"

The undead prince waved his left arm and instantly dispelled what was left of the illusion, simultaneously summoning a swirling ice storm which filled the chamber with its fury. Raging winds and snow attacked Thargelion as he tried valiantly to stand his ground, not giving way, as Voltan expected.

When the lich was sure the old Elf King could see him, he slowly grabbed the front of the mystic blade and effortlessly pulled it through his body as if unaffected by the intrusion of the enchanted weapon. He then tossed the sword behind him.

Thargelion held his hands out defensively before him. Voltan watched his hands as they took on an amber glow. Then, searing, burning jets of flame shot forth from his palms, through the ice storm at the evil creature.

Not amused, Voltan blocked each blast with an outstretched hand, which swallowed the flames as quickly as they struck.

A well-directed gust of wind then swept Thargelion off the ground and threw him several feet away, smashing the old King into his throne. Thargelion bravely managed to get to his feet, holding on to the throne for support. The frost and snow obscured his vision so that he could no longer see the lich clearly.

Voltan, however, saw him, and he thrust his right arm forward in a snapping motion, releasing a lightning bolt that struck Thargelion directly in the chest, slamming him back into his throne again.

The storm quietly ceased as Voltan slowly approached, gliding on the very air that led to the throne. Thargelion still stirred with life, barely moving as he sat on his throne.

The Lich hissed in anger as green fire burst forth from his eye sockets, enveloping the old King. Thargelion's body twisted and contorted, as the flames held him fast like a vise. A moment later, his body convulsed once more as the flames released him. Voltan had climbed the stairs now and reached the throne. He looked down and saw that, still, Thargelion was not dead.

"*All the better,*" whispered Voltan, slowly sliding a pair of leather gloves onto his skeletal, white hands. He grasped both sides of Thargelion's head and brought him upward until his eyes were level with Voltan's own. Then, with a final gaze, Voltan inserted his thumbs into both of Thargelion's eyes, gouging and digging deep into the sockets until blood poured from them. Thargelion's body writhed and trembled three times and then moved no more. Voltan let the body fall at his feet.

A warrior of Koromundar burst into the room, taken aback a moment by the grisly sight before him. Voltan turned to him.

"*Toss me your sword,*" the Lich hissed.

Quickly, the barbarian complied, giving up his blade. Voltan rested his right foot on Thargelion's chest and looked at the old elf's face, savoring his death. Then, with an air of contempt, he brought the sword down in an overhead swing, severing the king's head. Then, he violently kicked the king's body down the stairs.

With that, he turned and eased himself into the throne. The sound of settling leather echoed in the chamber as gloves rubbed against the cool metal.

He gestured with his hands and spoke. "*Rise, my pets. I have food for you.*"

Rats of various sizes emerged from cracks and corners, scurrying from everywhere, covering the inert body of Thargelion, tearing and biting at the clothes and flesh, swarming over him.

Voltan turned to the barbarian. "*Take the head as a trophy for the Shadow Prince.*"

"What of those still in the city and surrounding villages?" the man asked.

"*Burn the city!*" Prince Broderick Voltan turned to the window, saw the flames burning outside, heard the distant cries of the dying, and hissed, "*Indeed . . . it has begun.*"

Chapter 10

The determined party traversed the rocky trail, slowly making their way to Mystaria City. They trod carefully but with a sense of ease as well. Algernon explained that the papers of safe conduct from Prince Crichton were better than an armed escort in this part of the world.

The day was chilled with a heavy moisture building in the air. They saw few trees and bushes in this part of Mystaria, and even those they saw seemed to be wilted and dying. Hawk speculated that it could have been the cool weather and lack of sun that was causing the plant life to appear as it did.

However, the Druids seemed to know better. When they stopped to rest for a moment, both Kael and Galin moved away and touched the trees and bushes. In the eyes of the others, they seemed to be establishing some sort of link with them, which was initiated through physical contact. Once established, that link went much deeper; they were, in fact, communicating with the plants, but not in the way the others would think of it. It was more of a primitive process. They in essence became one with the trees and plants. The Druids could feel what the plants felt and through those feelings were able to interpret what the plants were communicating.

After only a few minutes, they were both of the opinion that it was not a natural decay they were witnessing. It was the slow poisoning of the land that seemed to affect different plant species at different rates of speed. However, it was a condition that the plants and trees themselves could neither understand nor account for.

At times the terrain was not conducive to riding on horseback, so they would dismount and lead their horses on foot by hand. Hawk would look back frequently to see Elenari bounding from rock to rock, always steady, like a confident predator, moving through the trails created by convoys and caravans. She continued to guard the rear of the party. She would, at times, fall out of sight completely, only to reappear just as swiftly, as if she were taking an invisibility cloak on and off.

Hawk, tall and burly with his great two-handed sword strapped to his back, was not as agile as his half-Elven counterpart. He was still well balanced in this type of terrain, but his mind was more focused on the sights and sounds around him. His head was always moving it seemed. They were his natural movements, which might tire an observer to watch, but he was quite unburdened by them. He walked at a quick pace and would often suddenly stop, bend down, and put his ears to the rocks to see if they warned of nearby movement.

This had been a far more difficult task thus far than he had signed on for, more so even than he could have imagined. However, he was not one to run away from any danger; in his mind, any chance to rid the world of evil was worth fighting for, whether he would admit it to the others or not. He was also becoming comfortable with the members of the group. He was glad to be traveling with Galin again.

Hawk wondered if the others knew how lucky they were to have his friend along. He was a fearless warrior for a priest and well-studied in the arts of Druid magic, which Hawk had seen him employ on more than one occasion. Then, there was Kael, the Grand Druid, who had been famous even before becoming the head of the Druid order. Though much older than most of them, he was tall and powerful. Still, there was something not quite right about him. Hawk could not put his finger on what it was exactly. Algernon was old, wise, and mysterious but always had a kind word and a resourceful mind.

Finally, there was Elenari. The only thing that matched her beauty was her tenacity as a warrior and skill as a Ranger. There was much he did not know about her as well, and despite how he fought it, he found himself increasingly drawn to her.

The day transformed into night as Elenari took the lead and Hawk fell back to cover their flank. The night air was fresh and brisk, though not uncomfortable. Hawk could make out the lights of a large city just beyond the horizon. It was Mystaria City, capital of the wizards' world. It was perhaps another half-day's journey. Hawk did not think much of this country, especially after what he and Elenari had just experienced at Mordovia. The men of Mystaria were pompous, arrogant, and self-righteous. Most of the wizards were probably some of the wealthiest people in all the lands. Hawk knew they lived in massive castles and strongholds with enough extra gold to melt and use in the creation of magical treasures.

Hawk reflected upon his own life. He too had once known a life of privilege, title, and wealth long ago in a land far from where they traveled. His life of solitude had taken a toll on him. Too many years, he thought, of living alone, trekking from land to land, selling his sword and service. He was always in search of something he felt he could never find again; in truth, part of him never wanted to find it. That something was love, and it had cost him everything he'd once held dear. Wealth and love were both overrated as far as he was concerned.

Still, he wondered, if that were so, why he could not stop thinking about Elenari. Thoughts of pity and anger rose from deep within him. He hated himself for feeling this way. He was looking back in life when he should be looking ahead. He was feeling sorry for himself.

Hawk shook his head as if to rid his mind of all these foolish thoughts completely. He looked up and squinted through the darkness to see the rest of the party had gone nearly a quarter mile ahead of him. His bout with self-pity and anger had caused him to slowly fall off the trail. He rushed to catch up.

When Hawk caught up, Galin was first to approach him. "Perhaps it would be best if we stopped here to rest for the night before we lose you completely. We will need to be well-rested and in good form for our council meeting tomorrow."

Hawk agreed and could tell by the look on Algernon's and Elenari's faces that a break would not be argued. Kael, too, wrapped himself tightly in his cloak and agreed it would be a good time to rest. Elenari departed to scout ahead for their morning journey. The remainder of the party took off their gear and sat on the grass to rest.

The night air became cooler, and few animals could be heard, save for a bird or two chirping in the distance over the buzzing of the night insects. The dark firmament above them was black and speckled with tiny white stars. The moon rose and shone brightly upon the land.

Without a sound, Elenari returned to the group and sat resting beside

Kael, whose eyes were shut with a faint hum breaking through his lips. She locked her hands behind her head and found herself staring at the stars.

It was the fall, Elenari's favorite season. It reminded her of one of her first memories of when she came to Kael as an orphan. She could remember the smell of decaying leaves on the ground as Kael carried her to the Kenshari Temple within Alluviam. She recalled the gloomy sky, and she could hear the sound of the leaves crackling beneath Kael's boots. The thought that she was safe with him is what she remembered most. Sometimes, when she became scared or nervous or even lonely, she would think back to that time so many years ago. She remembered how warm she'd felt, held up against Kael's body. She thought back to how, in his quiet but deep voice, he would assure her that everything would be okay.

"You're safe now," he would say. "I won't let anything happen to you, little one."

She found it so strange that, after all these years, that memory was still so vivid and so very comforting to her. She drew from Kael the strength she needed to get through those early difficult times. Being a half-breed had been difficult on her as she had grown up. Never accepted completely by the Elves and dismissed by humans as fairy-kind, Elenari had never truly been able to find her place. However, as long as Kael was with her, she knew there was always a home for her, and it did not matter what country that home was in.

Unfortunately, Kael had rarely been present for Elenari as she grew to womanhood. During her younger years, she came to resent him for leaving her for such long periods of time. Somehow, she would always find a way to make sure he knew it as well. She was never disobedient to him, but she had ways of letting him know of her anger.

She looked over for a moment at him while he slept, then she turned her gaze down to the ground, almost ashamed of how she treated him through the years. She remembered once when Kael left her at the Kenshari Temple, without a visit, for nearly a year. Her anger had flared during those times. The constant teasing from the other disciples or students had been almost more than she could bear in the beginning.

There was one Elven boy, especially, who had tormented her constantly. Milben Eloend was his name, and he represented everything that Elenari resented about the Elves. He came from a wealthy family. His grandfather, who had fought in many of the old wars, was himself one of the Kenshari masters. His father, Paudner, was an ambassador to Averon and was well respected among the royal council. Milben also happened to be an excellent swordsman. Milben and Elenari were the two most-skilled students, yet he had always seemed to be just a little better than she.

She remembered when she had first seen High Master Quentil Reyblade. When he would emerge from the temple to the training field, all the other masters would kneel before him. He was one of the Gray Elves. Some said he may have been the oldest living Elf in Alluviam. He was an ancient, almost stick figure of a fellow, well over a thousand years old, but to watch him with a sword was more like watching an expert dancer or artist performing at the pinnacle of their craft. After taking an immediate liking to Elenari, he would almost always spend extra time with her. He taught her how to make the sword an extension of her body. She learned how to breathe so she could fight for hours without tiring. She had practiced day and night on the Grispond Tree, an ancient magic tree which could withstand even Kenshari blades, in the courtyard of the temple. She would swing a great two-handed sword in each hand until it became effortless, and the strength in her arms endured beyond pain and fatigue.

She sent her thoughts even further back to being brought before Master Reyblade for the first time as a small child. He was sitting with his legs crossed and eyes closed, apparently meditating. A full head of white hair crowned his small frame. Elven skin did not age the way human skin did; while clearly showing signs of immense age wrinkled about the eyes and forehead, he still had a smooth, polished look about him. Though frail in appearance, as if a strong wind could blow him away, she eventually came to learn in time that he had unseen power and strength beyond her imagination.

She asked him what he was doing, and he answered, "I am listening for the quiet voice within me. When you can quiet your mind, child, you can hear your inner voice. Within your inner voice is an energy that neither tires nor lessens with age. I see a great future for you, my child, but it is clouded by the strength of your emotions. They are powerful indeed. They do you credit, but they will do you harm."

Suddenly, his eyes opened and stared at her. She saw a raging blue fire within them, and she shrank back from him as he continued speaking,

"When you fight, child, it shall be as if the heavens sent you down to earth to avenge some terrible wrong. Hence, the name of the sword we shall forge for you shall be *Eros-Arthas*, the Celestial Avenger. If you live and learn long enough, the sword shall one day be yours."

Elenari had grown into a most promising disciple. She and Milben were selected for the *Verrin Corros*, an event held but once each year where the two finest students from the temple would demonstrate the Kenshari disciplines and techniques. No outsiders were permitted, only Elves; however, the participants were allowed to invite those closest to them. Elenari obtained special permission to invite Kael because he was a Druid and friend to Master Reyblade. She had eagerly anticipated his presence.

When the day of the event arrived, Kael was nowhere to be seen. Milben's parents were there, along with his grandfather. Before the event began, Master Reyblade took her aside and said, "This is a great honor; do not let your emotions rule the day, child. Display what you have learned with skill and pride, and listen for the quiet voice within you. Do not think about those watching, about Milben, or about anything else. Only act where your inner voice guides you."

With that, she stepped onto the field and faced Milben. He was a lean, powerfully built Elf with shoulder-length locks of red hair.

They turned their swords so the tips of the blades were touching the ground and their hands grasped the pommels of their weapons. They bowed to each other. Milben leaned forward and whispered, "No half-human will ever beat a pure Elf. Remember that."

Elenari's anger boiled into an unnatural frenzy. She did not know whether it was the result of Milben's comment alone or Kael's absence, and it didn't matter; she no longer cared. Her sword moved and struck faster than the wings of a hummingbird. Milben did not have a chance. None present were prepared for what occurred next.

Her blade cut through the air, and before anyone knew what had happened, Milben was on the ground, stunned, still gripping his sword. The observers, still quiet, tried to figure out what they had seen.

Elenari's breathing was heavy; her chest pumped up and down as if she had just run for miles. Her sword tip was fixed against Milben's throat.

A sharp pain throbbed in Milben's left ear. He felt something warm dripping down his cheek, forming a puddle on the ground. He reached for his ear as the pain became suddenly intense. As he held his ear, he could feel something strange through the warm blood. His eyes widened and his mouth fell open; Elenari had sliced off the tip of his left ear.

"Now who looks more human?" she asked mockingly through labored breaths, standing over him. In the next instant, Master Reyblade appeared and ripped the sword from her hand.

The campfire crackled in the breeze as embers blew up into the air. Elenari stirred to consciousness and watched as sparks from the flames disappeared into the darkness. She looked over at Kael and saw that his eyes were open now. They met her eyes with a soothing look of compassion. A calming overtook her body as she lay on her side and closed her eyes, wishing for no further memories or dreams.

Galin was poking the fire slightly with a stick, as Algernon wrote feverishly in his tome.

"Algernon?"

Algernon stopped writing. Hawk opened his eyes momentarily as the scratching of the quill ceased and then slowly closed them again. Algernon looked up from his script and caught Galin's eye. Galin could tell he did not yet have the old man's full attention, as the Sage seemed deep in contemplation.

"Algernon," Galin said a second time.

This time, Galin's voice shook Algernon free of his thoughts. "Yes, Galin?"

"How long have you had this . . . book of yours?" Galin asked.

Algernon smiled and closed the great tome and fastened the two metal clasps, sealing it. His smile was contagious, and Galin too began to smile, awaiting an answer to his question.

"Young man," said the Sage, scratching his head, "my writings date back to when I was an apprentice seeker of knowledge to a man named Corinthian, Sage and advisor to the King of Alluviam more years back than I care to remember."

The memory made Algernon smile a little larger in spite of himself. Galin found it difficult to believe that Algernon was ever an apprentice or even ever a young man for that matter.

"My young Druid, it is true that I have been throughout the known world and beyond. I have seen empires built and crumble in my lifetime. I have seen good men die horribly and evil men rule prosperously. I have lost dear friends to age, battle, and passion. I have lived the life I was born to live, and soon, like all of them, I will be laid to rest, returned from whence I came. When that time comes, I will leave this tome behind—not as a remembrance of me, no, that is not why I keep this book—but of the world that I lived in and the world . . . that could be once again. Perhaps the people of this world will see this book as a history and choose to learn from it, perhaps not. It could fall into evil hands and become an instrument for the ruination of man, or it just might end up in a cellar somewhere, surrounded by empty bottles of ale, collecting dust."

With that, Algernon chuckled and settled himself to sleep for the night.

Galin was intrigued as he too lay down for the night, thinking of the mysteries contained in the Sage's book as he drifted off to sleep.

The night came and went, and the morning brought with it clear skies of blue and modest sunlight. The group packed up their belongings, had a breakfast of soft rice and cheese, fed their steeds, and continued toward the magical city that was their destination.

Hawk took the lead, traveling about a quarter mile ahead of the rest while Elenari served as their steady rear anchor. Galin and Algernon traveled side by side, chatting about the common rumors and mysteries of Mystaria City to pass the time. Kael rode behind them, reminiscing about Lark Royale, wondering if he were still alive, and wishing he were there with him like old times.

The hours passed quickly and morning along with them. Afternoon was upon them before they expected. They did not stop for lunch; instead, the group slowed and ate in the saddle. They did not have the luxury of taking their time, since the incident at Mordovia Tower had delayed them over a day.

It was a natural transition for them to trot at a faster pace as Hawk explained the city would be over the next rise. Elenari rode up to quickly scout ahead over the rising hills. She stopped and was the first to point out the shimmering top of the metropolis that was Mystaria City. She waited until the others caught up and stood with her, overlooking the wonder that was the capital of the lands they were traveling.

Algernon seemed genuinely happy about finally reaching the outskirts of the city. "Friends," he said, "this is the most magical place I have ever encountered. Behold, a vibrant city of trade, magic, and excitement. It is a city ruled completely by wizards of every level of power. Be on your guard, though; beneath its veil of magic lies a subculture of plots within plots. Secrecy, political intrigue, and great danger lurk around every corner."

Elenari pointed to the enormous rounded building with varying layers of brass, silver, and gold. It seemed to be styled after the pointed hat of a wizard, only it was larger than most castles she had ever seen.

"That, my dear, is the Great School of Magic. It is a place where nearly every wizard has visited at some time in their life. Some of the greatest wizards still living have taken residence there to retire and teach. Every kind of magic is taught there, from rudimentary conjuration to dark necromancy. It is a fantastic place devoted to knowledge and learning, or . . . at least it was, once."

Algernon stared at the structure until Elenari pulled on her reins and started them moving again.

Within the hour they found themselves entering the city. The streets were lined with glass lamps, in each of which burned a light that danced even during the daytime. The streets themselves were lined with what appeared to be gold bricks as far as the eye could see. Hooded mages filled the streets, going about their various businesses. Occasionally, a skeptical glance would come their way, but only for a few moments.

They were entering into the late afternoon, approaching early evening, and Hawk was surprised to see that there was still commerce going on at such hours.

As if reading his mind, Algernon spoke, "Indeed this truly is a city that never sleeps. Vices of flesh and games of chance rule the night here for those who know where to look and have the means to indulge in them. They have become a necessary evil for many, including the aristocracy. There are many mages, you see, who peak at a certain point. They reach a point where there is little more they can learn in their particular school of magic. They are stunted by either age, lack of ability, or limited powers of understanding. Their vices are a much-needed diversion from the continued doldrums of existence in which they will never become more powerful or acquire new knowledge."

Algernon quickly pointed them to a large stable. "The local laws do not allow horses through the city unless attached to a merchant caravan. We will have to leave them here and walk the rest of the way. Stay close, and do not speak to anyone if it can be avoided."

They walked in a close group, constantly looking all around at the oddities that made up Mystaria City. There were several shops they passed that appeared interesting. The first was called Mystaria City Magical Mementos. Within the window was a sign that read: DECORATE YOUR CASTLE WITH OUR MAGICAL MEMENTOS. Elenari peeked through the window, and to her utter amazement, she saw stone gargoyles of various shapes and sizes actually walking around in the store.

As they continued, Hawk paused at a shop called *Mystaria City Magical Blades*. Two swords were on display behind the storefront windows. At first glance, he thought they were affixed behind the glass, but upon closer inspection, the two large swords were actually dueling in midair. He continued to peer in and spied a magnificent, golden two-handed sword with a hilt made of dragon scales. Galin had to nudge him past the window so they would not fall behind Algernon, who was walking through the city as if such wondrous things were an everyday occurrence.

Even Kael became distracted by the store window of *Staves and Stuff*. Three staves made of strange polished wood shone brightly through the glass, floating in the air and dancing around a cauldron of fire.

Algernon called to all of them, as they were falling behind, "Please, friends, stay close! If you are not attuned to this culture, you could find yourself in trouble faster than you might think."

He reached into his tunic and pulled out a few old bags of various powders, suddenly stopping at a store called *Powders and Potions*: Wizard Hagmend Presiding. He walked into the store with the others in tow.

It was strange for them to step from the hustle and bustle of the city streets into the dark stale air of a store. Once the door had closed behind them, everything went suddenly quiet. The walls within were lined with dozens and dozens of boxes, some with as much as an inch of dust on them. Even the floor had a strange appearance to it; it looked as if it had not been walked on for years. Algernon approached the counter and waited.

After a few minutes had passed, Elenari whispered, "Algernon, what are we waiting for?"

At that moment, a tall black-bearded man slowly descended the stairs as if on a cloud of air. His feet did not seem to move. He floated down behind the counter and stared at the group, his interest suddenly lighting on Elenari. Slowly, the man brought his hands up to his ears and stroked them.

"Ah . . . a half-Elven girl," he sighed, like a giddy, hungry child at the breakfast table. "Do you have any idea, my dear, how rare a specimen you are? Perhaps I could interest you in a deal." He produced an empty beaker from under his robes and handed it to her.

"I doubt it," she replied with apprehension, returning his intense stare for a moment. "I'm not quite what you think. What kind of a deal?"

"Your blood is extremely rare . . . what a Prince would pay for it! My . . . one just thrills at the thought of it." He shrugged his shoulders as if he had the chills. "I've run out of half-Elven blood, you see, for some of my more . . . dark potions, shall we say? I will pay most handsomely, however, for a beaker full of yours."

In an instant, Elenari drew her blade and leveled it at the man's neck. "And I will give you a beaker full of your own blood, completely free of charge."

The man looked at her nervously, astounded. "My, you *are* a unique specimen."

With that, Algernon tapped on the counter to get the man's attention. "Mr. Hagmend, we are not here to trade, but instead to purchase some ingredients I require. These people are with me, and I am in no mood to wait."

Hagmend forced himself to turn from Elenari to look at Algernon.

"I see," said Hagmend, as he slowly nudged the tip of Elenari's blade away with his hand. "The usual for you then, I suppose?"

"Yes, thank you, Mr. Hagmend," the Sage replied.

Hagmend pulled from his robe five small cloth bags, which he handed to Algernon, who in turn handed over to him what sounded like a small bag of coins.

"Good day, Mr. Hagmend," Algernon said as he motioned for the others to follow him out of the store.

"Half-Elven blood," Hagmend said in a low sigh as they walked out. "I could have purchased a fortress in the clouds with such nectar."

It was nighttime now and the darkness seemed to be picking up the pace behind them. The streets were still full of robed mages hurrying about. Some were on street corners, dealing out of carts selling potions, spell components, and even other unusual materials the travelers did not recognize.

The buildings around them were made of the finest materials, mostly base precious metals in a contemporary design with silver hues at the base and gold and brass at the crown. Galin noted that the architecture here in the city certainly lacked an earthy quality. Some of the buildings were composed of a combination of marble and gold leaf, while others were made of strange metals that most of them had never seen the like of before. Always in the distance, towering over all else, was the Great School of Magic.

After what seemed like hours, the group, led by Algernon, came to a large building of a more ancient design. It appeared much older, in fact, judging by the stonework, than any building they had yet seen. Before them were hundreds of marble steps leading up to a massive set of metal double doors.

"Behold, the oldest building in Mystaria, where the ruling body, the Council of Princes, meets to deliberate on those matters that they alone deem worthy of their attention—the *Calthredzar,* as it is known in the old Mystarian speech, or Great Council Chamber. There are five hundred steps to the great doors. We must make haste ere the council concludes for the day."

"They are still in session at this late hour?" Galin asked, astonished.

"They do not reckon time here quite the way they do in other countries," Algernon replied, as he leaned upon his staff for support in navigating the steps.

As Galin began climbing behind Algernon, he looked back at Hawk, who seemed somewhat disgusted at the prospect of climbing so many steps. "Come on, Hawk," he said with a smile, "it's only five hundred steps ...a good stretch of the legs."

Hawk's distaste for this land was building as each second passed. He was giving serious thought about waiting at the bottom of the steps but realized Galin would torment him to no end when they returned, so he began climbing with the rest of them.

Sometime later, with Elenari and Kael taking Algernon by the arm, they all finally made it to the top. There, before the doors, were three men. Two were clad in golden-plated mail armor with a white Pegasus adorning the breastplates. They each carried large swords, and their faces were hidden behind the visors of their helmets. The third man was wearing a crimson tunic, puffy about the shoulders, as well as a crimson beret. White tights adorned his legs, and he wore red shoes with the tips curved upward.

This third man took two march-like steps forward to meet them and, in an officious voice, greeted them. "I am the Herald to the Chancellor. All who pass through these doors must announce themselves and their cause to me, lest they be denied entry into the Calthredzar forthwith."

After taking a moment to restore his breath, Algernon replied, "Know you that I am Algernon, Sage of Wrenford, and Chief Advisor to the King of Wrenford. These men and women are a special envoy of ambassadors from the sovereign nation of Wrenford. We seek an immediate audience with the Council of Princes on a matter of the gravest importance that threatens the very survival of Mystaria itself. Know also that we speak on behalf of Thargelion, King of Wrenford, and with his authority, and if you attempt to deny us entry than you do so at your nation's very gravest peril."

He then handed the herald the sealed parchment of Prince Crichton.

The herald bowed, a gesture to which Algernon replied in kind. A moment later, the massive metal doors opened to admit the Herald and quickly closed again, barring their way and leaving them with the two large guards.

"Somewhat of a tedious procedure, I grant you," Algernon whispered, "but nevertheless, this is the way things are done here."

"Will they see us?" Kael asked.

"The chances are slim in truth," the Sage replied. "We must trust to hope."

It was then that the massive double doors slid open again, revealing the herald on the other side. He bowed once again. "Know ye that the ruling Council of Princes of Mystaria will see you now. You have been properly introduced and, on behalf of Chancellor Maximillian and all of Mystaria, I bid you welcome to the great council chamber. You may approach."

Algernon entered first, followed by the rest. The herald brought them into an enormous chamber, shaped like an indoor coliseum, which appeared to be constructed of pure gold. Four ascending tiers of golden seats, lavishly decorated with various cushions and pillows, stood before them. There were many nobly dressed officials seated there. At various divisions between the seats were trays of fruits and appetizers, complemented by decanters of wine and water.

Immediately before them was a silver platform with a platinum podium. The platform seemed just big enough to fit all of them. The herald pointed to it as an indication that they should stand there.

As soon as the last of them stepped upon the platform, it suddenly rose into the air midway between the tiers. Before them, an explosion of prismatic colors erupted, leaving in its wake a three-dimensional, full-color map of the world, as they knew it, before them. Colored lights formed nations, boundaries, and borders. Even mountain ranges and forests were given scope, depth, and color to scale. Seamless lines of animation even indicated the directions in which the rivers flowed. It was the most amazing representation they had ever seen, breathtaking in its beauty.

Without warning, the very floor beneath them vanished, giving no indication that it had ever existed at all. They appeared to be floating over an endless abyss.

"Do not look down, and focus your eyes straight ahead," Algernon whispered. "Make no sudden or rash movements."

"Ambassadors of Wrenford, you may now plead your cause before the Council of Princes." It was the herald's voice echoing from someplace behind them.

With that, Algernon moved to the podium, cleared his throat once, and began.

Chapter 11

"My lords, my ladies," Algernon said loudly and supremely confident, "we have crossed the Andarian Ranges and traveled far through great risk and peril to speak with you. In truth, to warn you of a monstrous evil that threatens to consume us all."

Algernon paused. Smirks were drawn on several faces at this point, sighs and even giggles escaped through some lips.

"I am not a wizard. Nor am I a citizen of Mystaria, though some of you know me. Those that do, I hope to trust that you will sway others that I am not one who fancies at practicing my story telling skills for naught. Some present in this chamber have employed my services in years past. I implore you only to listen and consider what we have come to tell you."

With that, Algernon directed his gaze to Kael and nodded as if the Druid would continue speaking their case. "Allow me to introduce Kael Dracksmere, newly ordained Grand Druid of the lands. He shall provide you with the appropriate background information. His presence is necessary as he has had first-hand experience with the evil that threatens you. Additionally, he is here first and foremost as an ambassador from Wrenford and he is protected as such. I implore you, do not allow your prejudice to cloud your reason. I beg you to hear his words."

Upon the mention of Kael's title, roars of protests came from the council. Many aides stood up and strenuously objected.

The aide to Prince Broderick Voltan spoke above all other voices, "We protest vehemently this . . . heretic! His very presence is an affront and insult to the council and to us all. The Council of Princes will not be converted to heresy by any priest!"

"We are not clerics!" Galin burst out, filled with pride and rage, "We bring no gods, no religion, or holy crusades here to sway you. We are humble priests of nature and we bring only the truth!"

Kael grabbed Galin's arm and pulled him back. He knew there was little to be gained by trying to justify their Druid's ways with this crowd.

"Forgive me, Grand Druid," Galin said as he bowed his head to Kael.

Kael stared at him in disbelief. There was no hint of jest or sarcasm; Galin was truly, officially deferring to him as the head of the Druid order. Though surprised and flattered by such a show of respect from such a headstrong man as Galin, Kael also felt unsettled by his display.

As the harangue of dissent continued in the council, Kael whispered to Galin, "I was your friend long before I became head of your order. Kael will do well enough between us my friend. Within a political arena or any other."

A sincere smile came over Kael's face. Galin returned the smile with a slight nod of the head.

"Enough!" Chancellor Maximillian raised his hand. "The Sage Algernon and the men accompanying him are here as ambassadors from the sovereign nation of Wrenford. They will be accorded every courtesy as such. Clear the council chamber . . . immediately."

Without hesitation, all advisors and aides quickly left the chamber without argument or another word. Only the Princes themselves remained.

"Grand Druid, please continue," said Chancellor Maximillian.

Kael cleared his throat, seemingly unable to summon a strong enough voice. "Several years ago, the young prince Wolfgar Stranexx, heir to the throne of the Pytharian Empire northeast of Wrenford, made a pact with the dark powers to become something more than a man. A skilled sorcerer even in his youth, Stranexx was able to raise a great army of followers who were totally enthralled by him. Their loyalty was beyond question."

Kael hesitated; he was clearly uncomfortable speaking. He surveyed the council. Many of their eyes wandered, and some of them held their heads in their hands and looked in the distance, uninterested. He was losing them.

Algernon, too, noticed things were going badly. They needed to change the mood in the room, and quickly. Suddenly, it hit him—an overwhelming wave of strong thoughts. He could never control his limited powers of extrasensory perception—it was never a switch he could turn off and on.

The thoughts and emotions bombarded him over and over. The

thoughts were clouded by hate. So much hate, he could barely stand it. Scenes of destruction, death, and murder harassed him; it was Wrenford he saw. He leaned heavily on his staff, swaying and almost falling over. Elenari quickly grabbed hold of him, steadying him.

Kael had no choice but to continue, even though he was faltering and embarrassment caused him to stutter and occasionally lose his train of thought.

"Though consumed with increasing his power," he said hesitantly, "and lusting to conquer the surrounding lands, Stranexx was no fool. He believed the key to his destiny was in a highly trained army whose skill and prowess on the battlefield would be beyond reckoning. He spent every gold piece in his treasury to hire the finest mercenaries to train his men." It was then he first saw a slight nod of approval from none other than Prince Gideon Chrichton.

"His first conquest would be the southern Kingdom of Wrenford. However, King Thargelion had been wary of the threat and had prepared. His advance scouts had been monitoring the enemy army. When the attack came, the protection of the mystical Emerald Star defeated Stranexx and his army."

Kael watched as the assembled audience arrogantly scoffed at him and his history. *Lark Royale would have known how to speak to such men,* he thought. Pompous and righteous, Lark would shove their arrogance right back at them and force them to listen.

This image of Lark became the rock upon which Kael would build. He found his strength. His confidence would be in his arrogance and sheer righteousness. He slammed the butt of his staff against the floor and waited until he had all their eyes.

Kael had a strength in his voice now; his speech no longer wavered, and he seemed to have regained the council's attention. "Many years later, Stranexx tried again, but he was no longer Stranexx; he was an undead creature known as the Shadow Prince. But powerful though he had become, like so many arrogant fools who think their power is absolute and great, the Shadow Prince was insecure. He feared losing; feared his old enemies. This insecurity led the Shadow Prince to steal the Emerald Star. He snatched it away like a common thief and foolishly attempted to use it.

"But his arrogance and ignorance backfired. Together with a Paladin named Lark Royale, I sought out and destroyed the Shadow Prince, recovered the Emerald Star, and returned it. He was not all-powerful; he was impudent and conceited. These are the qualities that ultimately led to his downfall."

Prince Claudius rose from his seat pulling the wrinkles from his robes. "Priest, do you have any idea where you are? You are in the great council chamber of Mystaria addressing the Council of Princes. Do you think to lecture us about the petty history of a kingdom of ants? How dare you. We know more of history dating further back than you are ever likely to learn. Let me save you any further patronizing speech. We know this tiresome little story. I for one have heard enough on the subject." He sat to the silence of several approving nods.

Algernon stepped forward as Kael concluded. "What does any of this have to do with you or Mystaria?" he asked the assembly. "The Shadow Prince has returned. Through his own power or something greater, he lives, as surely as we do. He no longer plans to conquer Wrenford alone; he plans to conquer all nations and free people everywhere."

With that, several of the princes rose and began shouting various questions. Prince Crichton was able to quiet them. He addressed Algernon. "What is it you seek of us?"

"We seek to form an alliance of free nations, while there is time to thwart—"

A deafening laugh filled the chamber suddenly as Prince Broderick Voltan rose, straightening his robe and sash which loosely covered his frame. "Finally, Chancellor," he boomed in amusement. "I commend you on providing not *one*, but *several* court jesters for our entertainment. I always thought we should have a royal fool at court, but you have truly outdone yourself. All that is missing is the colorful motley they should be wearing!" He turned to face Algernon with a look of disgust. "You dare come here, offer not one shred of proof of this great threat—from some fool who couldn't take over a town of ants after years of trying—and suggest he would be a threat to us? You offer no proof that this Shadow Prince even exists, yet you know what he thinks and plans. How interesting."

He looked away from Algernon dismissively and lowered himself slowly into his seat. "Once again, my compliments on the entertainment," he said to the chancellor. "Most appetizing."

"If you think we are lying," Galin said forcefully to Voltan, "why don't you use your great powers to search our minds to find out?"

Voltan leaned forward and locked his gaze with Galin. "If you are not careful with your insolent tongue, my priest friend, we may do much more than that." There was ice in Voltan's tone; his accent faded into hollowness, devoid of any semblance of humanity.

Galin took a good look at Voltan and realized that his face was very difficult to see. He could make out all the features, the angular lines, the eyes, the nose, hair, and mouth but not all at once. His face was almost in a haze, somewhat out of focus. The eyes, however, burned red, almost as if they were aflame. Galin felt a chill as those eyes caught hold of his. Something was wrong with Voltan's eyes, and they caused a sharp painful response in Galin's mind. He had felt the feeling before. It was the feeling of evil.

"Enough, Voltan," Chancellor Maximillian spoke. "What does your Shadow Prince intend to conquer us all with?"

"Yes, indeed," joined the Princess Octavia. "With his ill will and bad wishes toward us, perhaps?" She laughed, and several of the others joined her.

Algernon stood straight, and his voice was powerful. "He is currently forming several armies in Jarathadar, Koromundar, Bazadoom, and perhaps even underground among the White Elf nation. If he joins these armies, their number will be beyond your comprehension."

Prince Voltan laughed immediately, an evil cackle. "And are we to blindly take your word for this, old man, and boldly join your alliance against this phantom threat you've proved so convincingly?" He scoffed, "White Elves, indeed!"

Algernon reached deep within his robes and produced a scroll, which he held aloft for all to see. "Yes, I thought you may require proof of this, so King Thargelion instructed his advance scouts to commit to paper all that they have seen in their recent travels to the aforementioned countries."

Hawk, standing in the background, looked to Elenari and smiled. Once again, to their surprise, the old man had been pleasantly prepared—one step ahead of the crowd.

As Algernon handed the documents to Chancellor Maximillian, he continued. "Yes, the numbers listed there are from the better part of a month ago; they could be double or triple that by now."

All the laughter had ceased as the council very seriously reviewed the documents in question. Many even left their seats to read the documents over Chancellor Maximillian's shoulder. One thing that was not in doubt was that Wrenford, small a country as it may be, had the finest scouts of any in the known world.

All seemed concerned, save Voltan. "This is ridiculous, Chancellor," he spat, clearly frustrated. "These documents could have been forged. They have no more merit than this drivel we have been forced to endure here today."

Chancellor Maximillian, now clearly annoyed, looked to Voltan and replied, "Prince Voltan, these documents carry the personal seal of King Thargelion. He has ruled his land for centuries in peace. There was even a time he studied here in the Great School of Magic. His deeds are legendary. Are you calling this man a liar in open council? If so, then provide your evidence."

There was no more laughter or even a hint of smiles now as the remainder of the council looked at Voltan and awaited an answer.

Voltan rose slowly, looking at the party from Wrenford. Though it was difficult to clearly see the expression on his face, once again Galin saw the burning red eyes, filled with hate and disgust. Voltan quickly turned and exited the council chamber without a word.

Algernon looked to the council. "You are the first nation we have come to. We hope you will consider being the first to forge an alliance to stand against these armies and offer what aid you can. As you can see, the information indicates that the bulk of the armies are massing near the borders of Cordilleran. An invasion there is imminent. They may already be under siege and—"

Prince Claudius interrupted, "Cordilleran, you say? About to be attacked? Perhaps this Shadow Prince is not as dark as you portray him."

"The only good Dwarf is a dead Dwarf," added Princess Octavia. "Disgusting creatures."

"Don't you understand?" Galin implored. "If Cordilleran falls, all other nations will fall, including Mystaria, as surely as we stand here. Cordilleran has the largest army of any nation. If they fall, what hope is there to stop this army—this dark alliance—should they become bold enough to attack your borders?"

"No force would dare attack Mystaria," scoffed Prince Claudius. "Our magic would destroy them."

"Can you take the chance, in the name of all your people, that your magic can withstand the numbers that Algernon has provided you with?" Galin asked sincerely.

It was a question that clearly provoked much thought among the council.

"Even if we successfully ally all the free nations together," Kael added, "it is likely we may not have the numbers to combat such a force. Can Mystaria stand alone against such a threat?"

"We will consider all that you have told us," said Chancellor Maximillian with a slight bow of his head. "We ask that you wait outside, while we decide on our answer."

The party was moved to an adjacent antechamber. The chamber was lavishly decorated even for a small waiting area. The presence of the mystical was not absent even here. Amid the cushioned seats and ornate tables was something else for their viewing pleasure, a fountain in the corner of the room. But it was like no fountain they had ever seen. It was in two parts. The first was a marble basin upside down, coming from the ceiling and its twin resided right side up in the floor. Water flowed from each of them and met in midair between the floor and ceiling. Suspended in the air were rock formations and the miniature of an intricately detailed galley sailing through the tumultuous waters. It sailed around the rocks, avoiding them, as water crashed against them creating a soft mist.

There was little conversation. Elenari finally broke the silence. "How do you think they will vote, Algernon?"

"It is difficult to make a guess," replied the Sage. "I would not dare to venture one. These walls, no doubt have ears. I would suggest any discussion wait until we are no longer inside this place."

The better part of an hour had gone by when the silence was broken by the double doors swinging open to admit Prince Gideon Crichton. He wore an expressionless mask on his face, giving no hint of the council's decision. He waited as they formed in a circle before him.

"My friends . . . you put forth a most impressive argument—better, I would think, than most among the council expected. However, I regret to inform you that we voted not to be part of your alliance."

He watched for their reactions. Algernon looked to the floor, sighing. "There was little hope."

"I would offer that there was little hope that we would all make it here in one piece," said Galin, placing a reassuring hand on Algernon's shoulder and offering a smile, "and yet we have. Perhaps there is more hope than we think."

"Well said," Hawk offered.

The party gathered close around Algernon and offered great hopefulness in the face of this first setback.

"Did any of them vote to join the alliance?" Elenari asked.

"Yes, indeed, some did," answered the Prince, winking at the young Ranger. "Not only did some vote your way, but even more are concerned about the information you provided. Walk from here with your heads held high. Your cause is just and important. I sense if you are proven right, our paths may cross again in the future. Perhaps sooner than you think."

The Prince looked to the floor for a moment before he addressed them further. "There is another matter. I regret to inform you that Wrenford has been invaded. The Citadel has been destroyed, and King Thargelion is dead. You have my sincere sympathy, and I grieve with you. The world is a lesser place without him. Farewell, my friends."

With a short but sincere smile, the enigmatic prince quickly turned to exit the chamber.

"The council knew that, and still you voted against us?" Elenari cried.

The prince hesitated and turned his head, "Yes."

He quickly departed, closing the council chamber doors behind him.

Kael placed a hand upon the old Sage, steadying him as he leaned heavily upon his staff.

"In truth," Algernon said wearily, "I saw it in a vision but hearing the words aloud have made it strangely more real. He was not only my King; he was the greatest friend I could have ever imagined. The world is so less fortunate. We have known each other since long before any of you were born and beyond, and still it was not long enough."

The Sage's lips quivered, and he could no longer speak. Upon exiting the Calthredzar, he beckoned them through a small grove to the base of a large oak. He bade them to sit at the roots of the ancient tree. A look of great dismay suddenly crossed his face.

"Algernon," said Kael, as he took the Sage's hand in his, "you said yourself our chances were slim here. You must not abandon hope. . . . Thargelion would not want you to,"

"No, my friend," Algernon replied. "It is not our diplomatic mission that currently troubles me. Come close and heed what I say: While inside the council chamber, I began sensing powerful thoughts of hate and evil. The thoughts were masked by magic, but such reckless hate as I sensed seeped through the magic meant to guard it. I sensed death and torture. I saw the destruction of Wrenford. I saw . . . I saw . . . the death of Thargelion."

Algernon's voice cracked, and he could not help but put his face in his hands. Both Kael and Galin grabbed his arms, trying to comfort him, trying to absorb his pain. Hawk and Elenari looked away in solemn remembrance of the old King.

Algernon took a moment to compose himself. "So passes Thargelion, first and only King of Wrenford."

A long moment of silence passed through the group before Algernon spoke again.

"There is more I must tell you," he said. "I believe Lark Royale lives."

Kael, dumbstruck, squinted his eyes and listened intently.

"I saw him alive and being tortured," Algernon continued. "He was in great pain. I sensed someone derived great pleasure from his pain. I tried to understand, to feel where he was being held. One word penetrated before I lost contact: *Shadowgate*."

"What is Shadowgate?" Kael asked eagerly.

Algernon stopped to gather his thoughts. "Shadowgate is here in Mystaria. A viscount named Alastair Navarre rules it. He resides in the fortress of Shadowgate. He is also the Guildmaster of Assassins of Mystaria. In addition, he is rumored to be the head of a secret sect or cult known as the Brothers of the Shadow."

"Guildmaster?" Elenari inquired.

"Yes, the guilds are extremely powerful more so than even the princes in some matters. They rule the darker parts of Mystaria." Algernon replied.

"Hold on a moment, Algernon," Galin said flatly. "I don't remember any viscount at the council chamber."

"No indeed," Algernon replied. "These thoughts were emanating from Prince Voltan. Navarre is known to be the political ally and servant of Prince Voltan."

"There is something about Voltan, Algernon," Galin said. "Something not right. I felt cold when he looked at me. I felt pain, and . . . I daresay, I felt fear. There was something about his face and his eyes."

"Yes, Galin; I felt it as well. I fear there is something sinister about Prince Voltan that is hidden from us. There is great evil within him."

Hawk joined the conversation. "What is this Brothers of the Shadow you spoke of?"

"Rumor has it they are trained in the arts of stealth and assassination since childhood. There are said to be very few of them. They are often employed for assassination or kidnapping missions of great priority. Assassination, kidnapping, and ransom are a thriving business here in Mystaria. Wizards pay in gold. Assassins belonging to the guild, strangely enough, are the only other non-magic users, aside from the military and a few mercenaries, who are able to attain citizenship here. If the Brothers of the Shadow exist, they will be in the fortress of Shadowgate as well. The fortress is where I believe Lark and possibly his brother are being held."

Algernon concluded, and there was silence, uncomfortable silence.

"We must go to this place and try to free them," Kael said.

"Now hold on a minute," said Hawk. "I don't know about the rest of you, but I signed on to guide you people through the wild to the surrounding countries. I didn't sign on for suicide rescues on some premonition. Do you know for sure they are at this place? Do you know for sure they're even alive?"

"No," the Sage answered mildly, "I do not know whether they are still alive, but the thoughts I intercepted tell me that they are. And no, I do not know for sure that they are at Shadowgate."

"I'll take my chances on Algernon's premonitions," Kael said firmly. "Lark and Archangel cannot just be abandoned to torment. We must do something. We must try."

"I agree with Kael," Elenari said suddenly. "Lark and Archangel are my friends as well. We need them. We need all the help we can get. If any one of you were captured and taken to that place, would you want us to abandon you?"

"I submit we still do not have all the facts," said Galin. "However, if we have the chance to add two to our number such as the Royales, we cannot pass them by."

"You're right, my friend," said Hawk. "You don't have the facts. You're all ready to risk your lives and your mission based on senses that Algernon himself admits are not totally accurate. I've heard a lot of talk for days of all the lives that are at stake, and you're ready to risk all that for two men?"

Hawk stood, shaking his head, and walked away from the group.

As Galin followed after Hawk, Algernon faced the others. "There is one other thing to consider. If the enemy did not know our purpose or location when we set out, he surely does now. We will be hunted every step of the way from this point on. I'm afraid I'm inclined to agree with our guide. This is a risk we dare not take."

Kael was beside himself with anger. "How can you of all people say that? I thought for sure you would encourage us to try to rescue them. This is *Lark Royale* we are talking about—the same Lark Royale you employed years ago to find the Emerald Star and defeat the Shadow Prince! How can *you*, Algernon, turn your back on that man and his brother? I thought I knew you. Apparently, I do not." Kael stormed off in another direction, trailed by Elenari.

Algernon was left alone with only his own troubled thoughts to keep him company.

Within the Mystarian council chamber, the ruling princes had convened in a secret session. Strict orders were given for no interruptions on pain of death.

"We may have made a mistake in dealing with this Antar Helan," Princess Octavia said. "If this Shadow Prince is behind his forces and is gathering such an army, why would they not march against us once Cordilleran and the others have fallen?"

Prince Voltan, who was among those in the secret session, answered, "*Shadow Prince* . . . hah! Princess Octavia, your reputation has never been that of someone who fears a bedtime story. Surely that is all this Shadow Prince is."

"I think it is most interesting indeed, Prince Voltan," Chancellor Maximillian said shrewdly, "how you, having barely spoken a word in council for the last decade, suddenly find yourself so concerned with the affairs of our nation. It was at your great insistence that we agreed to supply magic arms to Koromundar for their war against the Dwarves. Now, today, we heard your lengthy objections to the statements of the Wrenford ambassadors. One would almost think you were hiding something or defending something."

"My thoughts exactly, Chancellor," Prince Crichton said, folding his arms and looking at Voltan.

Prince Voltan shifted in his chair, almost bored by their remarks but clearly angered. "I see nothing odd in making sure our country does what is in our own best interest. The Dwarves will be destroyed as a nation, a nation which could have threatened us in the future, and the surviving prisoners will be shipped to us as slaves and subjects to experiment on. None of you can deny this is in the best interest of our country. The Dwarves, with their natural resistance to our magic, are a threat to our way of life. . . . As for this *Shadow Prince*—if he did exist, he was destroyed, and the notion that he has unified an army of men and monsters in the broken lands of Bazadoom, as well as underground Elves? Nonsense."

Voltan rose and sauntered toward the double doors, leading out of the council chamber. He turned before exiting to face them. "I am ashamed to call myself one of you if you even entertain such nonsense."

He left, shaking his head and laughing a loud mocking laugh.

Kael and Elenari returned to the tree where Algernon now stood.

"Forgive me for losing my temper," said Kael calmly. "You know how close Lark and I are. I do not wish to risk the mission, but I will go after them myself."

"Not without me, you won't," Nari interjected.

As Kael let his arms fall in protest, Algernon cut in before he could make any further statements. "I lead this group, and I will make the decisions concerning this group. Whatever decision I make will be final." As Kael began to shake his head again, Algernon continued, "And I have decided that we will all go to Shadowgate to ascertain if Lark and Archangel are there. We will free them if we can, but if we can't, we will go on and honor what they have always stood for by completing our mission."

Kael took a deep breath and nodded his head approvingly this time. As he moved toward his horse, Algernon grabbed him in a viselike grip above the elbow. The old Sage's face was iron. "Understand that this is the one and only time I will take such a risk. Such an operation will take considerable time, effort, and power to plan and carry out. We have none of these to excess. If they are too heavily guarded, we must walk away. Do you understand, Kael?"

Kael met his gaze. "I understand."

Hawk and Galin continued talking even as the others came within earshot.

"I was hired on to guide this group," Hawk whispered fiercely, "not to join suicide missions to rescue people I've never even met." He stalked away and led his horse back toward the others.

"You know, perhaps you're right." Galin increased the tone of his voice so the others could clearly hear them. "A rescue like that would be far too dangerous for a guide of your stature. You'll be much safer if you hide in the hills and wait for us." He motioned toward the hills.

Elenari was already on her horse, and she guided the animal closer to Hawk and Galin. "Hawk, you're not coming with us?" she asked incredulously.

"No, he's not," Galin replied loudly. "He's staying behind."

Hawk saw the look of disbelief in Nari's eyes, and it pained him greatly to let the young woman down. "Of course I'm going!" he said hastily. "He's just putting you on, dear lady. Who else is going to watch your back if not I? Certainly not this gentle, kindly priest you see before you."

Galin rode away toward Algernon and Kael, laughing to himself.

Chapter 12

Shadowgate rose out of the ground like a blight on an otherwise pristine plain. Moss grew along its sides and towers like capillaries bypassing a malignant tumor. Outcroppings of quarried rock and stone lay at the base of the north and west walls, signs of a siege long since passed.

The fortress was no stranger to physical damage but was by no means weak in structure. A large rectangular keep rested within the heart of two distinctive protective walls. The outer wall, reinforced with battlements, had towers at each corner as well as siege artillery. The inner wall was even sturdier, despite its age, and its design was greater in height and strictly for protection of the inner keep.

Hardly an inviting edifice, but beneath the years of overgrown moss and cracks stood the remnants of a once noble sanctuary.

The party saw it for what it was—the base of operations for the Assassins Guild of Mystaria. It was the prison in which Lark and Archangel Royale were being held. It was the greatest obstacle they had yet to face. They knew that no matter what else occurred, tonight they must succeed.

Against all argument, Algernon insisted on infiltrating the castle with them. He maintained that without his aid, the mission could not succeed. Despite all evidence to the contrary, he won them over, and reluctantly they agreed.

It was nighttime now, and the party crouched low within a lush, dense thicket of trees not more than one hundred yards away from the castle. Each of them was making their separate preparations for what was to come.

Elenari raised the hood of her forest cloak. The outline of her shape began to shimmer and immediately blended with the dark overgrown landscape in which they hid until she almost disappeared from view completely.

Algernon fumbled with several packets about his waist until he produced one he was satisfied with. He beckoned Hawk to come closer to him while he emptied the contents of the pouch in his hands. Slowly, he began to sprinkle the dust over his own head as well as Hawk's. Hawk watched as his own hand became more translucent by the second until it vanished completely.

The only members of the party that could still be seen were the two Druids, their gazes intent upon the ebony curtain of night above them. There was magic in the air; they each felt it without needing to explain or acknowledge it to one another.

Suddenly, red sparks burst forth from seemingly everywhere. In the next instant, Elenari, Algernon, and Hawk could see a reddish hue outlining each of them.

"Stand fast!" Algernon warned, realizing that the others thought that they had been found out. "It is a temporary magic that will allow us to see each other so that we may work in concert. Kael and Galin will also see us, but no other. It will not last long, so we must make haste. We are taking a great risk. We cannot fail, and I will not allow the Emerald Star to be taken." He looked to each of them, and they understood clearly what he meant. "May the spirit of Thargelion be with us."

Algernon looked to the Druids. "Begin."

The Druids stood, unmoving, and called to the forces of the prime material plane. They pulled and coaxed, using words and gestures known only to priests of nature, to unlock the powers and mysteries of Mother Earth. But she was slow to respond, even to two of her servants, for she had been greatly taxed of late and her life force weakened. Still, the natural powers were not entirely dormant.

Kael and Galin were attempting to influence and control the skies, winds, clouds, and rains. The Druids felt the elements struggle against them, and they were wary of it, but the energies of the sky, which had been summoned slowly, began to strengthen. Against the coolness of the night, the Druids began perspiring.

A summoning of this magnitude took unbroken concentration, and the expenditure of such power would come at a cost. They felt the winds first, and then the raindrops. The clouds responded, racing in from the north like smoke from a far-reaching fire. The coming storms rumbled in the distance, reverberating throughout the ground, announcing their presence so that all creatures could beware.

Below, the party started toward the castle wall. They increased their pace, knowing they needed to make it to the ramparts of the castle before the lightning became too fierce.

Elenari led by several yards, her instincts and physical prowess allowing her to move with the swiftness and agility of a cat.

Hawk and Algernon followed her at a slow run. Hawk was pleased the old man appeared ready for such a pace and found him to be right on his heels, not lagging. However, he dared not take the chance. He grabbed Algernon by the arm and supported him as much as possible during the long sprint.

The rains came in drenching sheets, hitting the ground like a stampede. Hawk found himself fearing it would wash away the magic and their veneer of concealment, but to his comfort, it did not.

The magic held, and they made it to the cool stone walls just as the lightning started. The first bolt hit, illuminating everything, cutting through the darkness like a jagged sword. As the flash of light died, several seconds passed before the thunder roared, causing the ground and the very fortress they leaned against to tremble. Flashes of light connected the heavens to the earth for all to see, quickening in their pace and frequency, relinquishing nothing to the thunder that followed them.

Elenari heard activity now from the walls and spires above. The rain had become hail and assaulted them without mercy. One of the captains called out to members of the watch patrolling the walls and catwalks which connected the towers, authorizing them to leave the battlements and take shelter within the towers.

Though this is what the party had wanted to hear, Hawk cautioned them, "We must wait. They must also move all heavy siege artillery from the walls to alcoves near the towers." What seemed like a whisper came across loudly over the pouring hail and rain.

Again, Elenari heard conversation and scrambling of men. As she peered up, she saw several soldiers doing as Hawk described, hustling to move great catapults and ballistae under cover to escape the rage of the storm. While the rain and hail posed no threat, a stray lightning bolt would.

The storm doubled in magnitude and intensity as each minute passed, spurred on by the will of the Druids. They focused in deep concentration, physically weakening as they attempted to hold the weather conditions so they would not lose their resolve and move away from the castle.

The rain fell from their eyebrows furiously as they continued to wait, backs pressed firmly against the outer castle wall.

Algernon quickly produced three small glass vials from within his tunic and handed them to the other two companions. They put the vials to their lips, draining the contents. Moments later, they felt it beginning to take effect.

Galin and Kael stood erect, arms still outstretched above them, robes flailing about wildly in the wind. They continued using their powers to invoke the storm, unleashing its forces to the point where it was nearly uncontrollable. Bolts of lightning shattered the darkness like glass. They attempted to glance forward from time to time to search for the others, but it was fruitless, as they were blinded by the storm. They would need to see soon, though, if their plan was to be carried out.

Hawk felt a tingling sensation in his stomach, reaching down to his legs. He looked down a moment, and even through the rain, he noticed they were no longer on the ground. They were rising, floating like bubbles, adjacent to the castle wall. As they ascended, lightning struck in multiple spots along the surrounding plains. The thunder was deafening here, as if the storm had localized just over the castle. When they reached the appropriate height over the battlements, they eased down to the stone surface beneath them.

At this point, Elenari led the party; her superior vision would guide them even through the rain and darkness. Several dozen yards ahead stood the southeast tower, and below its spire was a great metal door. To their luck, the door was open. About six feet to the left, an unknown number of soldiers were still securing the siege artillery in the tower alcove.

Nari continued guiding them forward at an even pace, closing the distance between themselves and the tower doorway. Just then, a dark-armored soldier appeared from the alcove, blocking the doorway. He was giving orders for the men to hurry with their task. He placed one hand on the open metal door. There were markings on his dark armor, but even Elenari could not make out the details with the rain slamming into her eyes, courtesy of the raging winds. She stopped the party not ten feet from the burly soldier. In a few moments, the men would complete their task and the entrance to the tower might be cut off before they could sneak in.

Hawk and Algernon looked on intently through the deluge at Nari, waiting for her to do something. Seconds passed, and still she did not act. In the next instant, several soldiers appeared out of the alcove and moved past them and toward the tower door. Nari shot forward, shoving the closest man into the others, knocking half the men down. Immediately, not knowing how the altercation began, the men started pushing one another. Nari looked to the officer who had been blocking the doorway. He quickly stepped forward and away to quell the argument, exposing the opening. Instantly, Nari, Algernon, and Hawk darted through the narrow opening and plunged themselves deep within the castle proper.

Galin and Kael eased their concentration just enough so that they could see the castle through the rain. They were each exhausted, barely able to stand comfortably. They did not see the red glow of Algernon's magic and assumed the others had been successful. Now, it was time for them to make their move. They nodded to each other and bolstered their remaining strength, standing still rooted into the ground. Bolts of forked lightning came down from the sky, striking their hands and they, in turn, redirected the lightning so that it attacked all about the castle as if the heavens themselves lay siege to it in retaliation for some unholy offense.

During the next flash of lightning, Galin and Kael disappeared themselves in a flash of green fire. Their arms sluggishly fell and their legs shortened along with their entire bodies. In a moment they reformed and came out of the fire in the form of pigeons. It had been Algernon's idea; he knew that pigeons were used to send messages from one province to another in Mystaria. There would be nothing unusual in seeing pigeons flying into the castle.

The rain let up just long enough for them to fly, streaking like arrows through the night. They glided right through one of the many crossbow slits adorning the tower battlements and into the castle.

Kael and Galin found the others waiting for them almost immediately. Algernon's magic had worn off faster than expected, and they were completely visible again. They were all in the tower now, but getting inside as they had was hardly the most difficult part. They must now somehow make their way to the depths of the dungeons undetected if they were to retrieve Lark and Archangel in this, the fortress of assassins. That was to speak nothing, however, about getting out once they located the Royales and freed them.

Galin and Kael were sweating and leaning on each other. They were drained of strength and focus. The noise of their deep breaths could not be concealed, despite their best efforts. Their shape-changing normally restored them when they were weak, but they had given too much of themselves in summoning the storms. There could be no delays, however; it was too dangerous to linger, so they pushed themselves on.

They were in a stone corridor roughly ten feet wide and ten feet high. It was dark, though every now and then a large torch jutted out from a metal sconce in the wall, giving just enough light to see by until the next was revealed.

Upon meeting, they did not stop for an instant. Each knew the plan. Elenari would lead. Her Elven cloak helped her to blend in with the stone almost completely. Since they knew where to look for her, they could see her frame faintly outlined against the stone. Occasionally, in the half-light of the torch, they could see her whole form shimmering in and out of sight. A cursory glance would never spot her though. She would look as part of the corridor to anyone else.

Their luck continued to hold. Each time they approached an intersection in the corridors, one of the Druids would change into a mouse and scout ahead. This procedure allowed them to avoid several soldiers and even brought them to a staircase going down. Cautiously, they spiraled downward, continuing through dark corridors with hope as their only guide. The castle was quite large and its lower levels ran underground, disguised by the outer appearance of the fortress.

Hawk, Nari, and Algernon would wait in the shadows of the corridors for the Druids to return, sometimes for long, unsettling minutes. On one such occasion, Algernon broke the uncomfortable silence with the two Rangers in a barely audible whisper.

"It's been too long," he said, "and we've come too deep within these walls.

Even if we find them, our chances of escaping are growing less and less. I'm afraid we must consider abandoning the attempt while we can."

Hawk and Nari were silent. They were clearly uncomfortable as well this deep in an unknown structure, but all Nari wondered was, if she were captive in a place like this, would she want those looking for her to give up the search? Or would she want those closest to her risking harm in such an endeavor? Which was the lesser of two evils?

"We've come this far," Hawk answered. "Perhaps . . ."

Before he could finish, the Druids abruptly appeared, and when they felt it was safe, they returned to human form with a green flash. Such a display of light was dangerous. It would be visible in nearby connecting corridors. Though they were still pale and sweating, their shape-changing had renewed their strength somewhat, but their spirits were clearly weak.

"We think we may have found them," whispered Galin urgently as he fell back against the wall of the corridor. Hawk quickly caught him until he steadied himself. "Down four more corridors and one more staircase is the prison level. There's a guarded area with two guards. They have chainmail armor, swords, and crossbows. If we move now we might be able to make it without bumping into anyone else."

"Very well," Algernon said. "I will take care of the guards."

The others looked at him quizzically, but they did not have time to discuss it; they first needed to get down there.

Elenari continued leading them as Kael whispered directions to her. They moved at an agonizingly slow pace, avoiding all contact with patrols or guards until they reached the next staircase.

Stairs were a very dangerous proposition, as they could not conceal noise well. Again, they spiraled down farther and deeper than they wanted to be. The thought of getting out again with wounded, unarmed men was something no one dared bring up at this point, especially since their luck had been exceptional and to think otherwise was getting harder and harder to conceive of.

They continued straight from the stairs until they reached a very dark intersection within the corridor. Around the corner, to the right, was the guarded area in which the men were being held. Straight ahead was unknown to them, and behind them, the staircase.

Algernon reached to the pouches at his waist and produced yet another dust of some sort. After pouring some in his hand, he turned to them in hushed tones, "Wait until you hear me sneeze, then you may come down the corridor."

They all looked at him without fully comprehending, but thought better than to waste time asking questions. The old Sage then disappeared around the corner.

Algernon walked slowly toward the two armored men leaning heavily on his walking staff. As he came into view from out of the shadows, the guards unsheathed their swords and approached him.

"Halt, who are you, old man?" they demanded. "How did you get down here?"

Algernon moved slowly, hanging on to his staff. He made it appear as if it were a great effort for him to speak.

"The Viscount," Algernon stammered, "the Viscount . . ."

"What about the Viscount?" said one of the guards, pointing with his sword. "What's wrong with you? Come on out with it, I'll not ask you again. Drop your staff!"

Algernon immediately complied, dropping his staff, and then doubled over in a fit of coughing. The guards were right on him now, and one of them put his sword under Algernon's chin and forced him to look up at him.

With that, Algernon opened his hand and sneezed a small cloud of dust in their faces. A moment later, both men dropped their swords and collapsed at his feet.

Within seconds, the others arrived from down the hall.

"Quickly, the keys from the guards," Algernon said. Hawk was already searching their bodies. "Bind them," the Sage ordered. "They must not make any noise until we are well away."

Elenari produced rope from her pack and started the task. Hawk was trying the keys in the lock of the great oak door. Suddenly, he met with success; the tumblers gave way and the great door opened.

Within seconds, they were repulsed by the mixed stench of sweat, dung, and urine that hit them from the stale air beyond. Inside, they found a very dark octagonal chamber. Moaning could be heard off to the right. Straight ahead, a man hung shackled by the wrists. Galin and Nari headed right toward the direction of the moaning, while Kael and Algernon went straight to the shackled man.

As Kael drew nearer, he quickly realized the man before him was not Lark Royale, nor was it Archangel. It was, in fact, a large, powerfully built Dwarf in tattered clothes. His body had been besieged with whip marks, cuts, and gashes. He had curly reddish hair, which covered his lips and ended in a long beard shot through with streaks of gray. Blood had pooled in the corner of his mouth, but seemed dried. There was also a discoloration on the side of his head, indicating recent injury from a blunt object. He appeared unconscious. Algernon nudged his arm gently.

Without warning, the Dwarf awoke, bellowing in an uproarious voice. "Didn't I tell you, laddie? Your mother likes it in the backside, she does! Think about her screamin' my name as you snap that wrist, you can be sure I'll be thinkin' about it!"

Algernon quickly covered his mouth. "Good sir, please be silent. We are not your tormentors; look!" He watched the look of the surprised Dwarf as he attempted to make out their appearance in the half-light. He squinted his eyes and when Algernon sensed he was calmer, he removed his hand.

"Who are you?" Kael asked.

"I'll know who the bloody hell all of you are before you'll be gettin' my name," the stocky Dwarf answered.

"I am Algernon of Wrenford," the Sage replied. "These people have been sent here by the King of Wrenford. We are looking for two other prisoners named Lark and Archangel Royale. If you'll excuse me a moment, Master Dwarf. Galin, Nari, who have you got over there?"

"A human, maybe forty, badly beaten," Nari replied. "It's not Lark or Archangel though."

"Royale, you say?" the Dwarf said gruffly as Hawk quickly freed him of his shackles. "He was here, all right, that poor devil over there is here because of your Lark Royale. He was on guard duty the night your friend attempted to escape. Apparently, your Mr. Royale got farther than he should have. They blamed that poor bugger and have been beatin' him night and day. He's only got about a day's worth of life left in 'im."

"Did Lark escape?" Kael asked eagerly.

"I'm sorry, lad; don't know for sure, but I don't think so. Accordin' to that poor soul over there, he was to be moved . . . to where, I've no idea."

"Galin, can you help that man?" Algernon asked with a tone that indicated time was of the essence.

"I can heal much of the physical damage. I don't know if he'll wake up or be able to walk again right away though."

Just then, Kael touched the Dwarf on the arm and a yellow light began to move from his arm through his chest and back, soothing the rawness of his injuries and healing the lacerations.

The Dwarf grabbed Kael's arm suddenly. "Thank you, lad, sincerely, but I'd be obliged if you left a scar or two all the same. A scar helps a warrior remember there's somethin' to pay back to the enemy." He gave a hearty chuckle.

"Can you walk?" Kael asked.

"I'll bloody well walk out of here, you can be sure."

"What is your name, Master Dwarf?" Algernon asked, though his eyes never left the great door through which they had entered.

"My name is Mekko, General of the Armies of Cordilleran."

Algernon looked at him suddenly, astonished. He turned away from the door for a moment and knelt down to help Kael lift the muscular Dwarf to his feet. Algernon then bowed his head.

"I am honored to meet you General; your reputation precedes you. How long have you been here?" the Sage asked.

"Oh . . . little less than a week I'd say," Mekko replied. "Just gettin' started as far as the torturin' goes. The honor is mine. I know your King Thargelion. Long has he been a friend and ally to our King Crylar."

Algernon watched impatiently as the Rangers quickly dragged the bound and gagged guards inside the chamber.

Mekko marched over to Galin and the unconscious human. "I'll take hold of 'im, lad. It's the least I owe 'im for bein' a good cell companion." Mekko threw the man across his shoulders and back as if he were a sack that barely weighed anything.

"We've lingered here too long," Algernon said fiercely. "We must leave now. Is everyone ready?"

No response was needed as everyone took their place. They departed the chamber and closed the great door. Hawk locked it, stowing the keys on his belt. Silently they crept forward through the dark corridor. Elenari took the lead. Kael followed with Algernon between him and Galin. Mekko bore the unconscious man over his shoulders behind them, and Hawk cautiously brought up the rear. Nari nocked an arrow to her bowstring, and Hawk loaded a bolt into his crossbow, ready for what might come. The Druids, though exhausted, were prepared to call upon their magic if need be. It was hard for the others to determine if Algernon had any more tricks up his sleeve should they encounter trouble. Still, they pressed on, silent and swift, like wraiths haunting a tomb.

They moved as fast as their need for silence would allow. They made it to the first set of stairs with no sign or stirring of the castle's inhabitants. They continued through the next two corridors, turning and twisting, until they came to a four-way intersection. It was here where Nari suddenly stopped the party. They each braced themselves against the sides of the stone walls. It was at that moment that their luck finally lost some of its potency.

Simultaneously, down the north corridor ahead of them and the south corridor behind came two squads of armored soldiers, marching directly toward them. How many were coming was unclear, but one thing was certain: in the second they had to react, there would be no hiding. There would be no clever plan to escape detection. They would now be seen, and they had to decide whether to run or stand and fight.

Nari turned and fired over Hawk's shoulder at the group to the south. Simultaneously, Hawk fired his crossbow over Nari's shoulder to the group at the north.

Both weapons found their mark at the same time, and screams of alarm were raised by the soldiers. Nari turned to Hawk and ordered, "Take the others east, I'll go west; they'll have to split up!"

"No, Nari!" Kael yelled. "We must stay together!"

The sound of running soldiers closing in on them from two directions made Nari's decision for her. "Go, keep Algernon safe. Trust me, Father. Go!"

With that, Nari was off like a flash down the west corridor. Hawk burst to the lead, yelling for the rest to follow him down the east.

Elenari ran toward the second staircase, her longbow still in her hand; if she could make it to the top, with luck, she could make a stand there. That is, of course, if she were lucky enough that no soldiers were coming down as she was going up.

She gained a considerable lead on them and found the second staircase empty as she had hoped. She bounded halfway up the stairs and halted. She nocked an arrow to the string, turned, and made ready.

Long seconds passed until finally the company of soldiers stumbled into her sights, encumbered by their chain mail. Before they realized what was occurring, two of them fell at the bottom of the stairs, with feathered shafts buried deep in their chests. A third dropped as he turned to run, a shaft protruding from the middle of his back. The rest of them pulled back out of range of the deadly bow.

After a moment, the soldiers peered out from beyond the stone corridor, and watched in disbelief as Elenari placed her longbow on her back and then drew a curved sword, illuminated by a faint yellow glow, from the scabbard at her hip.

Elenari took a reverse grip on the hilt with her left hand and held the weapon behind her so that the tip of the blade rested comfortably behind her left shoulder. Then she waited. A moment or two passed as she peered down to the far end of the corridor and saw two of the soldiers hastening forward, aiming crossbows at her. They fired in unison.

Faster than their eyes could follow, Elenari swatted the bolts away like gnats buzzing about her head. Again, she waited.

A moment later, a large soldier appeared between the other men and began moving toward her. He was a dark-bearded man, dressed in chain mail and carrying a great two-handed sword. He was well over six feet and extremely broad. He was nearly three times Nari's weight, though not an obese man by any means. *An officer*, thought Nari.

The man's pace quickened as his eyes found those of Nari. She saw the confidence in the man's eyes. The officer had absolutely no fear of her, deeming her a far smaller and lesser opponent.

The soldier climbed the steps and was now little more than five feet away, looking up at Nari. He leaned back, lifting the great sword behind and above his head for the blow that would split Nari in half.

Then, at the last possible second, Elenari swept her sword across with a one-armed, underhand stroke that halted the lumbering officer in mid-stride.

The other soldiers watched, yet heard nothing, and were not entirely certain what they had seen, as it happened so quickly. They did not hear the striking of a sword against armor. Perhaps the little woman had missed completely and had taken a warning swing at their commander. Still, they watched, waiting for him to kill the girl. He stood menacingly, looking down at the intruder, sword poised above his head for the kill, but he did not move for several seconds.

Then, without warning, their commander's torso began quivering and simply . . . fell off at the waist. The lower portion of his body remained erect, legs still standing, but shaking uncontrollably. Blood gushed upward as if from a fountain. Blood splattered in all four directions of the corridor. Elenari stepped back just in time to avoid it.

Carefully skirting the lower half of the commander's body, Nari slowly, mockingly, nudged the commander's torso down the stairs with her boot toward the remaining soldiers. She did not know how many she would be dealing with, but she felt their fear would give her an advantage. She knew this was no rabble, and despite her display, they would not just turn and run. But she wagered they were not fools either and would not recklessly put themselves in her path.

She saw nearly a dozen soldiers now had gathered within the corridor she had just run through. All of them had their swords out, yet all continued backing up as Nari advanced.

Then, suddenly, their retreat stopped. Another had arrived, to the rear of the retreating soldiers. He was different from the others. He wore no armor of metal and appeared to be carrying no weapons. The soldiers cleared the way for him to approach.

Elenari saw him more clearly now. He was tall and lean, covered with a black, cloak-like material from mid chest to his head. He wore what appeared to be soft, black leather armor, as well as long black leather gloves. He crossed his hands in front of his waist and, in a smooth motion, drew forth two long, curved daggers. He held them beneath his wrists and moved them through the air with such speed to indicate he had great skill with them. He approached Nari like a predator stalking its prey.

"A Brother of the Shadow, I take it?" Nari quipped, sweeping her short sword through the air, demonstrating her own fighting skill.

"The shadow of your death," replied a cryptic human voice from beneath the darkness of the black cowl.

Now . . . we shall see, thought Nari, *just how well-trained you assassins really are.*

"Run as fast as you can," Hawk yelled back to the Druids, who now toted Algernon along by each arm. "Stay with me!"

Hawk ran a few feet ahead of them. They had been running for several minutes now. Hawk did not know how many pursued them, but several soldiers could still be heard in the distance.

He also had no idea which way he was going. He knew with certainty that it was not the way they had originally come. All he knew was they must keep going. Their mission, which at first to him was just another job as a hired guide, had become suddenly precious to him. They must keep Algernon safe and protect the Emerald Star.

His legs were beginning to tire. He could hear the others scrambling behind him and knew their situation could be no better. He had no idea if Mekko was even still behind them. Carrying a man on his back after a week of torture at the pace they were going would be a difficult feat indeed. He could not think about it now. He couldn't stop to find out. He must find a way to lead them to safety.

It was then that he looked up and saw the stairs before him. "Quickly, up the stairs and watch your steps!"

He made it to the top without stopping. He looked ahead to see the corridor stretched another thirty feet, only to end at a great wooden door with metal hasps and hinges.

He knew he had no time to guess whether the door was open or not. If the soldiers were still pursuing them, they would be close to the stairs. He must not stop. He increased his speed. Swinging both arms back to his right, he launched his left shoulder followed by all the weight of his upper body into the door, smashing through with terrific force. The others spilled through the open doorway after him . . . and were rendered as immobile as he, staring ahead in shock.

They were in a great chamber, over three hundred feet in length with a vaulted ceiling some thirty feet high. Within they saw a mass of soldiers, perhaps a hundred or so in number, wearing dark armor bearing the crest of the red hydra: the Stygian Knights. In addition, there were at least another two hundred or more armored men with no identifying crest. Outlining the walls of the room were racks of various weapons, shields, and armor. It appeared as if the Shadow Prince's army had already infiltrated the boundaries of Mystaria, establishing a training camp here in Shadowgate.

All activity ceased, and all eyes turned to the intruders. For one long moment, the only sound that could be heard was their breathing as they leaned against one another, gasping for air. Their luck had finally run out.

Elenari watched carefully for movement; a near-countless number of soldiers lay scattered throughout the corridor piled around her. She had a gash across her left cheek and her right shoulder had been sliced, but the majority of the blood covering her person was from her attackers. She had won; she had killed them all.

After she had defeated the Brother of the Shadow, who clearly underestimated her, she had mown through the rest of them as if they were made of straw. *Their fear made them easier to kill,* she thought. She was disgusted that it had come to this, but she knew it was necessary. There was no other way. When she was sure that there were none to pursue her, she doubled back toward the others as fast as she could.

Galin stood, breathing heavily, carefully studying the dimensions of the chamber and ceiling. His mind was racing. Many times before, he had hesitated; this would not be one of those times.

Algernon had fallen to one knee. Kael bent down to support him from falling completely. Mekko, still with them, slowly lowered his unconscious cellmate to the ground and moved nearer to Kael and Algernon.

Hawk dropped his crossbow, raising his hands up just enough to show that they were empty. He looked at Galin, who was steadily inching away from the rest, and wondered what foolishness the Druid was contemplating.

Galin began concentrating. He could barely breathe with any degree of regularity. He was drenched in sweat and completely exhausted. Still, this was his moment of truth. Though not a warrior by trade, he was a student of military tactics and one basic rule of combat was now repeating loudly in his mind: *Always do that which the enemy will least expect.*

Galin stepped forward and shattered the silence. "Drop your weapons, all of you!"

Another second of silence followed while the assembly stared at them in disbelief. Then, roars of laughter broke out among the army. Kael, Algernon, Mekko, and Hawk looked at Galin in sheer astonishment.

Again, Galin commanded, in the loudest voice the others had ever heard him use, "Drop your weapons now!"

The laughter slowly died down as one of the Stygian Knights stepped forward, an officer from the markings on his armor.

"And if we don't?" he answered Galin mockingly, sneering at him.

"Then each and every one of you will die tonight, here in this room," Galin replied with such confidence that even his companions were unsettled.

Hawk noticed that Kael's eyes had been closed since Galin began addressing the soldiers. The Druid was deep in concentration. Hawk's unease grew; he had no idea what to expect.

The knight casually raised his right hand, and several men behind him produced crossbows with bolts already notched.

It suddenly occurred to Hawk that the soldiers who had been pursuing them had not yet entered the chamber. They had been only steps behind, it had seemed.

The Stygian Knight chuckled. "Cut them to pieces, but I want that one's head," he said pointing at Galin.

Hawk, Mekko, and Algernon looked at one another and at Kael, who was still concentrating with his eyes closed.

"So . . ." Algernon uttered softly, "it ends before it begins."

The next thing the old man heard was a whistling hum right beside his left ear. Within the blink of an eye, half a dozen crossbowmen collapsed with arrows in their chests. The old Sage turned and saw Elenari behind them, firing arrows faster than the eye could follow.

Galin pressed the advantage, lifting his arms up high, fingers spread. A reddish-orange fire shot forth from his outstretched hands in a sweeping arc from high to low, striking in the middle of the chamber floor. It erupted into a consumptive blaze that took the shape of a great wall as high as the ceiling and spread out across the length of the entire chamber. The fire ripped and tore through the rows of soldiers that barred its way. Those struck within the heart of it were charred to bits, while many others were forced backward, burnt and screaming.

Mekko quickly found a battle-axe—the weapon of choice among his people—on a nearby rack. Gripping it in his hands, he felt strong and alive again. He looked to see one of the Stygian Knights charging at Galin from the side. Gleefully extending his arms, he let the weapon fly in a wide circular swing. The bewildered soldier's head came off before he even realized the Dwarf was there. The remainder of the lifeless body fell at Galin's feet.

"Beware an axe-wielding Dwarf loose in Mystaria!" Mekko roared cheerfully.

Galin, still releasing the fire from his fingers, looked around until he found Kael's face. When the older Druid saw him, a look of understanding passed between them. Quickly Kael grabbed Algernon by the left arm; Hawk had already been holding the Sage by the right.

"Come this way!" Kael shouted. He steered them directly toward the wall of flames. As they neared it and the heat became almost unbearable, Kael raised his hand, made a quick circular gesture, and an opening appeared in the wall of flames large enough to admit them. The flames shifted and formed a tunnel around them, shielding the party from the soldiers. Once they were through the wall formed again between them and the soldiers.

Kael led them to the doorway and turned toward the rest. "All of you go with Nari; she will lead you out. We have some unfinished business here." He looked to Galin.

With that, Mekko picked up his cellmate and went with Hawk and

Algernon back the way they had come, following Nari, passing several of the soldiers that had been pursuing them earlier and who now lay dead in their wake.

More victims of Nari, thought Hawk, as he saw arrows in their backs and chests.

Satisfied the others were gone, Kael produced a piece of green chalk from a pouch at his waist and began drawing a circle on the floor. As soon as he'd completed the circle, he sat in the center, legs crossed and his head down, speaking a strange incantation.

Galin, standing a few feet away, felt his power continuing to weaken. The flames were getting lower, but he knew he could not falter. Kael would need at least ten minutes to complete the spell. It may as well have been an eternity. He could hear the soldiers moving, shouting orders, and attempting to organize behind the wall of harsh flames.

Kael had begun the summoning the moment he had become aware Galin was going to attempt something. He called to the elemental plane of earth. It was a plane of existence that was not of the physical world, but of the elemental world—a world which both surrounded and coexisted with the physical. In essence, the four basic elements, air, earth, fire, and water comprised the prime material plane. The elemental planes contained sentient beings of varying power and intelligence, which could only reach the material plane through means of magical summoning.

Galin knew Kael was attempting such a summoning. He also knew such a spell was incredibly draining, even to one who was well-rested. He was worried what the strain could do to Kael.

However, he had more immediate concerns of his own. He did not know how much longer he could maintain the wall of fire. Any interruption, no matter how small, would spoil the summoning. *Something of a moot point,* he thought, *since the charging soldiers will kill us instantly anyway.*

Elenari had led them back the way they first came. Racing up stairs and through empty corridors, they made for the southeast tower. They knew they were at least above ground now but fatigue became their new enemy. Algernon had slipped twice, and the third time he lost his footing completely. They stopped as Hawk tried to pull him up.

"No, leave me!" The old Sage's breathing was labored, and he was unable to catch his breath. "Here . . . take the Emerald Star. It must . . . go to Cordilleran. Go . . . I cannot go on."

"Not a chance," Hawk said as he lifted Algernon over his shoulder and turned to Mekko. "After you, General."

The Dwarf smiled through his own breathlessness, and they continued behind Nari as fast as they could manage. Despite the pain and anguish that washed through them, their spirits were renewed at the thought that each step was one step closer to the outside and freedom.

Elenari finally reached the incline in the corridor she had been hoping for. It was another fifty or sixty feet up the sloping gradient to the tower. She freed her short sword and held it in a guarding position before her as she urged the others forward. She knew there would quite probably be several men of the watch to contend with.

Elenari had closed the distance between them and the tower to fifteen feet when she saw them. Ahead, through the tower, by the outer doors, which led to the outer wall and battlements, two crossbowmen had taken position, aiming right at them.

They fired as Nari ordered the party to stop. She dropped to one knee and blocked the bolts with a swift swing of her blade.

Just as the crossbowmen fired, other men came to reinforce their position. Instead of coming in after them, they began to close the great outer door, slamming it shut with terrible force and sealing their means of escape.

"We have to make for another way out," said Mekko.

"No," replied Hawk. "We don't know where we're going in here, and Kael and Galin will be coming this way when they can."

They ran into the circular tower, and Hawk set Algernon down with his back against the wall. The old Sage indicated with his hand that he was unharmed. Hawk turned to Mekko, who had relieved his own back of the human cargo he carried as well.

Pointing toward the outer door with one hand and drawing his sword with the other, Hawk said, "General, through the door and through whatever waits behind it. If you wouldn't mind."

"Aye, let's have at it then," Mekko replied eagerly.

Together, they hacked and slashed at the great wooden door. Elenari could hear the men outside; though it did not sound like there were many, they were calling for aid. Judging by the thickness of the door, it would take Hawk and Mekko some time to force their way out.

Kael had completed the summoning. He pushed himself up from the floor, knowing he had only moments left. He staggered out of the circle he had drawn and then collapsed near the doorway that would lead them out.

A terrible rumbling started. The walls and floors began to vibrate. It sounded like the beginnings of an earthquake coupled with thunder.

Galin used every last force of will he possessed to maintain the flames. He quickly moved to the doorway where Kael had fallen. The flames burned on through the sheer force of his iron will. He put his arms around Kael and held him under the protection of the doorway, as stones started to give way, falling from the ceiling and walls.

Suddenly, just as quickly as it began, the rumbling stopped. Galin looked to the circle. In the next instant, the floor of the chamber within and around the circle exploded upward and out, leaving a great gaping hole in the floor of the stone chamber.

A moment later, there was movement. Something huge and monstrous gripped the edge of the hole, pulling its way upward out of the depths of the earth.

Galin watched as it crawled out. It was huge, nearly twelve feet in height, and vaguely humanoid in appearance in that it had arms, legs, and a head. A collage of dirt, stones, metal, and precious gems comprised its enormous body. Its head was a large round stone, similar to those that had comprised the floor through which it crawled. It bore a cold, expressionless face composed mainly of two sparkling eyes—multifaceted gems that gave off a brilliant energy. Slowly, it stepped out of the hole and looked down to where Galin sat gently cradling a semiconscious Kael in his arms.

Galin let the flames drop so they were just high enough to conceal the elemental from view of the soldiers.

"WHO HAS SUMMONED ME?" It was a question, but the words came through like a command.

Kael looked up, wearily fighting to stay awake. He knew he must be the one to answer; the elemental would only consider obeying the Druid who summoned it, if it chose to obey at all.

"I summoned you . . . Kael Dracksmere . . . Grand Druid and ally to the elementals." Kael let his head fall back against Galin's chest.

"DRUID, WHAT DO YOU WISH OF ME?"

Galin gently slapped Kael to keep him awake.

Kael spoke again, "I ask that . . . you protect us from the soldiers . . . so they cannot follow us. I ask . . . in the name of . . . the four . . . elements . . . that make up our world . . ."

Kael could no longer speak. He was barely alive. The elemental hesitated for a brief moment.

"I WILL DO AS YOU ASK, DRUID."

With that, Galin quickly put Kael's arm around his neck, turned, and made his way down the darkness of the corridor. The last thing he saw before turning away was the elemental slowly turning to face the soldiers just as the wall of fire fell.

Galin smiled bitterly. They would not be able to even hurt the elemental. They had had their chance to surrender.

After hacking the great door for several minutes, Mekko and Hawk had barely made a dent in it.

"This door is much thicker than even the door to General Mekko's cell was," said Hawk, as he put his hand where they had caused several large splinters to chip away. "It was built to withstand siege weaponry."

"Aye," Mekko said, "it's hopeless."

At that moment, Galin burst into the room, half-carrying the inert form of Kael at his side. He gingerly set Kael down by Algernon. Steadying himself and his breath, he moved next to Mekko and placed his hand on the stout Dwarf's shoulder.

"That word, General, does not go over well with this group," Galin said with a mocking smile across his lips.

In the next instant, his hand fell off Mekko's shoulder as his whole body seemed to contort. His shoulders hunched in and he started to fall forward within a green flash of fire. The others' hands flew up to shield their eyes, and when they withdrew them, a huge brown bear filled the tower where Galin had stood a moment before.

Mekko's eyes widened as he shrank back against the wall in fear. "Aye, as I was saying . . . it looks very promising."

The bear that was Galin reared up on his hind legs and came down with tremendous force, smashing through the great door. The sheer mass and power of Galin's bear form were just enough to force the door outward.

Galin walked out to the outer wall and faced the company of watchmen. The nearest men, holding crossbows, were in such shock they did not even aim their weapons. Galin reared up on his hind legs again, standing nearly eight feet. He roared ferociously, causing the nearest soldiers to push into one another and flee in panic.

Suddenly, Elenari launched herself in the air. As Galin's bear form landed on its fore legs, she, in turn, landed right on his shoulders, wrapping her legs around his neck. Instantly, she began firing her bow into the soldiers. One, two, and then three fell, but she did not have enough arrows left for all of them. She whispered into Galin's ear, and the next moment, a green flash of fire momentarily blinded their enemies as they gave the bear-form some distance.

As the soldiers lowered their hands, they heard roars of a different sort as Mekko and Hawk charged them, sword and axe in hand, hailing them with cries of rage. The soldiers, their senses assaulted, could barely strike a blow of defense before the attacking madmen slammed them off the wall.

There were a dozen of them, yet the battle was over within seconds. Hawk and Mekko urged the others forward out of the tower. Nari went back and helped Kael while Galin hefted the unconscious human, and Algernon was back on his own feet again.

Hawk produced some of the rope that they had left from his pack and lowered it down the wall. As he was about to tie it around his waist to anchor, so the others could climb down, Mekko grabbed the rope from his hands.

"Hey, boy, give it to me a second," the General commanded. He secured the rope about his own waist. "No disrespect, but I'll be able to hold nearly the whole lot of you on one line. I'll wager we'd have to go one or two at a time with you anchorin'. Be obliged if you'd carry this axe down for me."

He handed the weapon to Hawk as he braced himself against the battlements. Unable to argue with the General's logic, Hawk stood beside him and helped the others over the edge of the wall on the rope. Hawk marveled that Mekko, even with his bare feet braced against the top of the wall, was strong enough to hold the rope with five of them descending at once. Still, Dwarves had a reputation for heartiness and great endurance.

He saw the powerful Dwarf closely now for the first time. His shirt was torn to bits—the whip had cut it to shreds—and his pants were stained with dirt, blood, and sweat. He was nearly five feet high, a good six inches taller than most Dwarves. His eyes gleamed with a distinct sharpness. The charismatic appeal of his face was obvious; there was strength there, strength of character, which could not be denied.

Hawk, the last to go over the edge of the wall, grabbed the rope and came face-to-face with Mekko. "General, how are you going to get down?"

"You just leave that to me, laddie. Off you go now."

As Mekko watched them descend into the dark, a humming buzz passed his left ear. He turned his head just enough to see that one more crossbowman had taken position on the east wall. The distance of the shot and the darkness of night were Mekko's only protection as he waited until he no longer felt weight on the rope. Finally, he turned just as two more bolts missed near his legs and feet. Quickly his eyes found a dropped long sword, which would be adequate for his needs. He took momentary cover against the battlements and tied the rope to the blade, hoping it would serve to be an adequate anchor. He waited until he was sure the soldier was ready to fire and stuck his head up, waving his hands about.

"Blast it, lad, why bother? I may die of old age waiting for you to hit me."

The Dwarf laughed and rolled to his right, dodging the incoming bolt. He braced the sword in the battlement and jumped over the side of the wall before his frustrated attacker could reload.

Hurriedly, the Dwarf scurried down the rope to Galin, who awaited him at the bottom.

"Come, lad, there's more of 'em up there!" Mekko said excitedly.

"I know, General, go . . . go that way. We have horses waiting." The Druid pointed west. The Dwarf did not hesitate and began running through the open grass.

Galin had one more spell to cast if they were to escape. His lifted his hands above his head and closed his eyes. As he extended his fingers skyward into the night, a dark mist seemed to ooze forth from his hands.

Black as coal, an obscuring smoke poured from the Druid's fingers and permeated the castle, saturating it with darkness. In the passing of a minute, the smoke cloud was so great that it had enveloped the castle entirely.

Moments later, the horses appeared. Nari rode with Kael, holding him tight in front of her. Hawk took Mekko's cellmate with him, and Mekko took Kael's horse.

Galin quickly whispered into each of the horses' ears, then mounted his own steed. The party rode swiftly into what remained of the night and through what remained of Mystaria.

Chapter 13

They rode throughout the night and straight on until morning. The horses were as spent as the passengers they bore. Hawk found a patch of trees for them to shelter beneath. They were near the Mystarian border, and there would have to be some discussion as to which course they should take from here. Still, it would have to wait until they rested. Galin helped Kael, who was fading in and out of consciousness, off his horse and propped him against a tree. Algernon came over to examine him. Elenari quickly moved to Kael's side as well and took hold of his hand.

"How is he?" she asked them urgently. "Is there anything you can do for him?"

"Unfortunately . . . very little," said the Sage, as he looked around at the rest of them. "There is no healing for what he needs—only sleep and complete rest will help. And we have very little time for either."

He pulled Hawk and Elenari away from the others to confer about their traveling plans.

Mekko's cellmate came awake as the general helped him to a resting position. The man was more pathetic in his appearance in the light of day. He was lean with the moderate physique of a warrior, but he had no shirt or pants, only a soiled undergarment. He was clearly embarrassed that he was so scantily clad in the presence of Elenari, though she clearly took no notice or interest. He brushed the dense black hair from his eyes as he addressed them.

"Thank you, General," the man said humbly, "and thank you to all of you, whoever you are, for saving me. My name is Driskel, and if I can repay you for what you've done, I will."

"Perhaps you can. What do you know of Lark or Archangel Royale?" Algernon asked quickly.

"I don't know the names. We never spoke about prisoners in terms of names however there was a high-value prisoner in Shadowgate for a time. Only certain guards were allowed near him and part of the dungeon was cordoned off for a time. However, such prisoners were moved frequently and I was away from my post when this prisoner attempted escape so I never saw him. I wish I could tell you more."

Algernon nodded and gathered them together. "I suggest we save all conversation and questions. Though I do not like the idea of resting in the daylight, we all need sleep. We will rest two hours; Elenari will take watch. Make as much of this as you can; we may not be able to stop again until nightfall."

Though none of them liked the idea of such a short rest followed by another forced trek, they knew there was no other option. There was danger ahead and the possibility of pursuit from behind. They were still some distance away from the border of Bazadoom but their travels might yet take them through that dreaded region. They knew there were dangers there that never slept.

Their rest came and went with the blink of an eye. Elenari was waking them far too soon, but even she was not immune to the fatigue that plagued them. She could only hope their next rest would make up for it. They were in need of supplies as well, which she had reminded Algernon of before they had slept. Hawk had lost his crossbow, and she had only a few arrows left. Their food and water would begin to run low as well, now that they had taken on two new members. They had only a little rope left, and two of them had no decent clothes to speak of. They would have to purchase supplies in the Republic of Averon. However, Averon was still several days away.

"We must discuss our course of travel," Algernon said. "I had originally hoped to go around Bazadoom, but our current situation may dictate otherwise. We can cut several days off the journey to Averon by cutting straight through the Bazadoom, however—"

"Bazadoom!" Mekko interrupted. "Hell, we wouldn't make it one day in that godforsaken wasteland! If the climate doesn't kill us, the monsters that prowl the countryside will."

"Perhaps you could offer us a different route, General," Elenari said, placing her hands on her hips.

"We could try to make it back to Mystaria City to get supplies," posed Hawk.

"Back to Mystaria?" roared Mekko. "I'd sooner take my chances with the carrion-eating slime of Bazadoom."

Kael, finally making it to his feet, leaning heavily on his staff, smiled. "I can see, General that you have a surplus of ideas that we shouldn't try."

Galin came to his side for support while Elenari went to his other side.

"How are you, Kael?" Algernon asked.

"Alive . . . and glad to see all of you are as well," the Druid answered, though his face was flushed and his weakness was painfully apparent. "I will not have the strength . . . to use magic . . . again for some time . . . I fear."

"If we go through Bazadoom, we may well need the magic of the Druids," Hawk said.

"Aye, and the rest of us will need to be fully rested for sure," Mekko added.

Algernon's gaze was distant; he stood deep in thought, considering all that had been said. "How far until we enter Bazadoom?" he asked Hawk.

"I'd say by the end of the day, depending on the weather," Hawk replied, bringing his hand up to shield his eyes as he looked southward.

"So be it," Algernon said confidently. "Our enemies will assume that we will go around, and they will be less likely to follow us into Bazadoom. South it will be. Rangers, lead on."

Kael approached Algernon and led him a few feet away as the others prepared to leave. "Algernon, forgive me, we almost all died and lost the Emerald Star for nothing. They weren't even there. I was selfish. Why did you agree to even try?"

"Let us say that I owe both you and Lark Royale a debt I can never pay and we shall leave it at that." He turned and went to gather his things.

They mounted and made their way south as midday approached. The morning sun gave way to clouds and the green of the day was replaced with dull gray. Without the sun to filter the breeze, the coolness weighed upon them, especially upon Mekko and Driskel who were unprotected against the weather.

The wildlife became less and less populous the further south they went. The grass and trees began to dwindle. The clouds continued their blockade of the sun, and although they threatened rain, still none came.

In the distance ahead, rocky outcroppings and hills came into view. These they knew to be riddled with caves, where various races of monsters made their homes. Orcs, Ogres, Ogrens, Goblins, and a myriad of other cave dwellers resided there somewhere in the darkness.

Galin saw a small flight of birds to the distant east. They were smart; they had the luxury and the good sense to go around Bazadoom. It was at that moment that Algernon rode up beside him.

"You showed an impressive display of power back in the fortress," said the Sage in the familiar, soft tones Galin had become accustomed to. "Your quick actions saved us from certain death. Even I believed it was the end."

"The quickness of Elenari's bow is what saved us," the Druid answered humbly. "I merely took a chance with our lives, and luck smiled upon us."

"True, but your confidence in yourself is what persevered. Learn to trust it. You will need it many more times, I fear, before our journey sees its end."

With that, the Sage smiled and let his horse fall behind to where Mekko and Driskel shared a horse.

"General, how was it that you became a prisoner of that place?" Algernon asked.

The General laughed calmly, but Algernon detected a sense of shame behind the laugh. "Ah, through my own foolhardiness. It happened along the outskirts of Cordilleran. You see we have patrols, just as in your homeland, out in many directions at all times. My King often insisted that I take men with me, but I was too proud for such precaution. I often would go from patrol to patrol on foot to show our men they should never fear to be on the border of our homeland. In truth, I never feared I could be taken, or that anyone would dare attempt something so close to our borders. My entire life, I walked the borders of our lands alone, with pride and without fear. Well . . . pride is no substitute for a dozen axe-wielding Dwarves at your side, now, is it?"

The Dwarf scratched his beard. "Well," he continued, "these men came from nowhere. Fact . . . I didn't see 'em hardly at all. I was on the ground and unconscious 'fore I even knew what hit me. Woke up sometime later in the dark chamber you found me in."

"What type of questions were they asking you?" the Sage inquired.

"They wanted to know mainly about our defense," Mekko responded. "How we would defend the homeland against attack. Did we have any special defenses and how would the army deploy if invaded? Things of that nature."

Algernon nodded and smiled. "We will talk more when we stop, General, and I will share what information Wrenford had on the current state of events outside Cordilleran."

Again, he let his horse fall back until he was at the end of their line beside Elenari.

"Thank you for saving us again, Elenari," the Sage whispered. "Stay close to your father. I will fear for him until he regains his strength."

Elenari felt pride and satisfaction that Algernon had personally acknowledged her helping to save them. She did not need any such recognition, nor would she ever seek it, but she found herself drawing comfort from it all the same. She smiled to herself as she watched him ride up and take his place within the column.

They rode for several hours. A cold breeze seemed to move beneath the clouds and bite into them. They could smell rain in the air throughout the day, yet still it did not come.

Finally, Algernon signaled them to stop for a few minutes of rest.

Hawk stopped them by a rare, deep patch of bushes, which surrounded a single oak tree deep-rooted into the ground. Such features of the landscape were becoming more and more fleeting the closer they crept to Bazadoom. They dismounted and sheltered beneath the tree as best they could. Elenari had given her robe to Driskel, and Hawk had given his green robe to Mekko, but the cold penetrated nonetheless.

Hawk, seated with his legs crossed, turned to Driskel. "So, I've been meaning to ask you what it's like working for assassins and torturing inno-cent people. Perhaps you could enlighten us?"

"I never tortured anyone!" Driskel cried. "I was a guard who worked for the castle. I was a soldier and citizen of Mystaria. Do you know how hard it is to be a non-wizard citizen of Mystaria? And . . . I was paid well. I didn't question my leaders or their politics. I did what I was told, plain and simple. If you'll excuse me, I'll be in the bushes beyond." He rose and stomped away angrily behind the bushes that flanked the tree.

"Nature calls does it, lad?" said Mekko with a chuckle. "Well, when nature calls, we'd best answer, and answer quickly." When he was sure Driskel was out of earshot, he turned to Hawk. "You know, you look as if you may have served a master or two for money yourself in your time. None of my business, but you may consider giving the lad a wee break."

Hawk did not respond, only leaned back and gave thought to the Gen-eral's words.

Algernon came and sat near Mekko. "General, I fear much has happened since the time of your capture," Algernon stated calmly. "King Thargelion had sent an emissary to Cordilleran, bearing grave news to your King Cry-lar. News brought by Wrenford's scouts who indicated many armies were massing and about to march toward Cordilleran."

"What?" the Dwarf gasped, outraged. "Who? Who would dare attack Cordilleran? And to what purpose, sir?"

"That . . . is a somewhat longer story. Suffice to say we have knowledge of a great evil, which threatens all the free people throughout the lands everywhere. Cordilleran has one of the strongest and largest armies, and this evil, known to us as the Shadow Prince, believes in destroying what he perceives as the greatest threat first. Do you understand, General?"

"No, I don't bloody understand. A pox on this Shadow Prince, I never even heard of him; where's he from? Who is he to the Dwarves?"

"The Shadow Prince is a creature that hails from the Pytharian Empire, and you would not have heard of him as he has been a mortal enemy of Wrenford alone in years past. But he has returned more powerful than we could have ever imagined. He is a threat to all lands. We thought him destroyed on more than one occasion, but . . ."

"The Pytharian Empire!" Mekko burst into laughter. "Do you know how far that is from Cordilleran? Everyone knows the Empire has been destroyed and in ruins for decades. You mean to tell me this Shadow Prince means to march his army all the way from there to Cordilleran, of all places? Have you gone daft man?"

Mekko continued laughing until Algernon lost his patience and grabbed Mekko about the shoulders. "General, how and why are not important; the Shadow Prince has rallied an army from Koromundar, Jarathadar, and creatures of the Bazadoom, and marched them toward Cordilleran days ago. Those are just the armies we know about. When they join, they will have three to four times your numbers in Cordilleran. They go to annihilate the Dwarven nation and kill every man, woman, and child they come across!"

Mekko had finally gone silent, seeing that Algernon was in deadly earnest.

"A few days ago," Algernon said somberly, "one-third of this force invaded Wrenford and destroyed the Citadel, killing everyone in the kingdom . . . including Thargelion himself. Wrenford is no more. For all we know, the fighting may have already begun in Cordilleran. We do not know. We have no answers.

"My companions and I are attempting to forge an alliance of nations to go and aid Cordilleran before it is too late. This mission was the dying wish of King Thargelion—the same King who warned your King Crylar of the threat to Cordilleran. Now do you understand? Will you come with us and help us?"

Algernon slowly released his grip on the bewildered Dwarf. Mekko stared at the old Sage in silence for another minute, trying to digest all he had just been told. Suddenly, he jumped to his feet, grabbing his battle-axe and saying, "Cordilleran . . . under attack? I must leave now, at once. I demand you loan me a horse—"

It was at that moment that a shrill, ear-piercing scream, culminating in a high-pitched tone that defied conscious activity, rang out. It was a sound that went well beyond fear and crossed the bounds of normal physical pain.

They all sprang to their feet. The sound had come from beyond the bushes where Driskel had gone. They knew that if he were the origin of that torturous sound, he had done so without ever knowing such screeching was even humanly possible.

Then an unusual *whoosh* through the air forced them to look up. Something had been hurled high up in the air and now came crashing down between the group at Elenari's feet.

She looked down and saw something grotesquely horrible. She suddenly put her hand to her mouth as she recognized the remnants of her cloak mixed with the molten, sludge-like puddle at her feet. What she saw was formless; she could tell there was skin, bone, sinew, and tissue, but it was no longer solid. It was all liquid, melted from some intense heat. It was Driskel.

Nari took a step back, unsheathed *Eros-Arthas*, and turned toward the bushes. The others looked on in sheer horror, unable to comprehend what kind of monstrosity could have done that to him. The horses began to jump back and away, sensing some unseen danger very near; they were clearly afraid. Kael took hold of them and attempted to settle them.

They backed away from the bushes and formed a semicircle. They watched helplessly as it approached. Slowly, the base of the bushes melted away as it burrowed into the ground, moving toward them. It was like a tributary of a river, only it appeared to be composed of molten lava. Moving effortlessly, it melted the ground ahead of it away, facilitating its locomotion. While only a few feet in length on the ground, it was deep, thick, and voluminous. The bushes shriveled away as it moved to the base of the oak under which they had taken refuge.

The group instinctively backed up, not knowing what to make of this crimson substance, which approached them as if it were a living thing. Suddenly, something changed. They felt the heat now as it spread out over the ground and began to coagulate. It gathered itself in one large pool and began changing shape, rising straight up from the ground, forming an almost humanlike frame. Its colors changed as its outline went from bright yellow to orange and finally back to crimson at the head and torso. Thick legs formed as a base for a shifting stomach and torso. Its body never stopped moving, constantly bubbling and shambling from side to side, changing its volume and shape. It rose to nearly ten feet, and a round molten head coalesced at the top. Finally, a barely visible, crimson gemstone seemed to pop out of the lava comprising its head and situated itself in the middle of where its face should have been. Arms revealed themselves slowly with no discernable hands or fingers.

"What is it?" Hawk asked nervously. "Some sort of elemental?"

"This is no elemental," said Algernon in a slow, uneasy tone.

Suddenly, the gemstone in the middle of the creature's head pulsed brightly twice, and the creature turned toward Algernon.

Instinctively, the others scrambled to place themselves between the creature and the Sage. Elenari did not hesitate. She fired two of her remaining arrows. They landed in the creature's torso and melted into its chest.

The creature responded by launching part of its arm toward Nari. It was a molten missile, which struck her directly in the chest with terrific force. She was thrown back several feet, her leather armor ignited into flame on contact with the molten substance. It hit her with such force that she had difficulty breathing, but retained the presence of mind to roll around on the ground to douse the flames.

Hawk unsheathed his great two-handed sword and stood toe-to-toe with the creature. Swinging the blade with all his strength, he drove the weapon down through the creature's right shoulder, burying it in the middle of its chest. It was then the intense heat struck him. He'd gotten too close; the exterior of the skin about his face and hands began to burn. He released his grip on the sword, which still impaled the creature, but before he could back away, the creature responded with a backhanded blow to Hawk's face, sending him flying through the air, screaming.

Mekko then charged the creature from the side. With his battle-axe in both hands, he ran at the fiery beast. At the last possible moment, when it seemed he would run right into the beast, he dove into a forward roll between its legs. His screams from the intense heat were heard by all, but he ended up behind the creature, virtually unscathed. Without hesitation, he swung his weapon in a circular arc through the creature's legs. The blow was just unexpected enough that the beast momentarily toppled forward.

Galin watched in disbelief as the creature reformed itself in seconds and turned to face Mekko, who was now desperately trying to crawl away from the agony of its heat. Galin's eyes widened with terror, fearing the creature would kill the Dwarf any moment. He turned to the others. "Kael, get Algernon out of here, now!" he barked.

Galin spread his arms and hands out before him and pointed them toward the ground. A green glow spread out from his palms. Out of the corner of his eye, he watched as Algernon and Kael mounted their horses and rode south with all speed.

The ground beneath the creature began to come alive, and the recently scorched grass sprang up into strangling thick weeds, massing and rising from the ground. The nearby grass multiplied into vines and grassy overgrowth, which encircled and encapsulated the creature. The vines melted as soon as they formed, but they formed so quickly and in such great numbers as to give the illusion of caging the creature. They served as enough of a distraction for Mekko to get up and flee.

At that moment, the rains, which had been threatening in the skies throughout the day, finally made their appearance. Pouring down, they assaulted the lands and the fiery creature. The rains struck the beast, creating smoke and steam, but seemed to have little effect, as the creature maintained its shape, size, and potency.

Nari was back on her feet now. Short sword in hand, she watched as Galin's spell dissipated and the creature began moving toward Galin. The creature frightened her, but something about it aroused her curiosity as well. She had seen how Hawk's blade had melted, and she had no intention of losing her sacred weapon to such a monster.

She ran at the creature full speed and, while still several feet away, jumped high in the air, executing a forward flip. She came to eye level with the creature and, still in midair, she brought her blade around with a swift, underhand stroke, striking the gem in the beast's head, careful not to let her blade touch the lava. At the point of contact, a dreadful sound was heard, a loud, dull echo as if a church bell had been stuck by a piece of metal. She landed and nimbly rolled away from the creature, allowing her some distance from the heat. She landed in a crouched position just in time to see that the gem had turned a dull brown and the creature had melted into a puddle.

This victory was short-lived, however, as almost instantly the gem returned to its crimson coloration and the lava began to swirl upward, reforming its bipedal shape. She turned to Galin. "Go tend to Hawk," she ordered. "Get the others mounted! I'll hold it."

Galin quickly obeyed her as they could hear Hawk moaning from the time he was struck. He found Mekko suddenly beside him, and they ran to where their guide lay, writhing in pain.

Hawk was turning from side to side, holding the side of his face with both hands. They saw at once that the dreadful burns had eaten the side of his face away, down to the bone.

"General, quickly," Galin commanded. "Take his hands away from his face and hold them back."

Mekko quickly seized the burly Ranger's hands against his will and used the weight of his body to hold him down. "Easy, lad, hold on now; healin' is on the way."

Yellow magic flowed from Galin's right hand, washing over Hawk's face, soothing his burns. Slowly, the magic began repairing the damage and reforming tissue and blood vessels. Nerve endings reattached as skin reformed over the wounds.

Elenari continued her acrobatic attacks, moving too fast for the fiery creature. She would move just within striking distance, only to evade it at the last second. Three more times she struck the gem with her sword, and three more times it had the same effect, producing the awful, unnatural sounds her blows caused when her weapon struck the gem. The rains made the ground muddy, and she started to slip, almost losing her footing twice. She would not be able to keep this up much longer. She turned to see that Galin and Mekko had finally helped Hawk onto Silvermane's back. The Dwarf then mounted and guided Silvermane south and away after Algernon and Kael.

Galin waited until there was an opening in the battle for him to get beside Nari and speak to her. When his chance arrived, he grabbed her arm, "Strike the gem one more time for me, then get on your horse and get out of here. Leave the rest to me."

Holding her sword defensively before her, she waited until the creature advanced again and, faking an attack in one direction, she swiftly spun around, ducked, and plunged her sword forward in a thrusting motion so that only the tip of the blade struck the gem. As before, the gem lost its color and the beast collapsed into a molten puddle. As swiftly as she attacked, Nari was on her steed and riding away as Galin had instructed.

The Druid did not hesitate. He raised both his hands above his head and flung them forward. From his left hand, water shot forth, striking the liquefied form of the creature, causing steam to rise in a massive cloud. He then placed his right hand within the stream of water he aimed at the creature, and suddenly the water became solid. The water that had pooled around the monster solidified into a block of ice. He layered the ice thick and high before he ceased the spell.

Then he watched. While the lava appeared frozen and did not move for a few seconds, he quickly mounted his own horse. As he looked at the creature one last time, to his disbelief, he could see some movement within the ice. At any rate, his spell would hopefully hold it until he could catch up to the others. *The gemstone is the key*, he thought.

He spoke to his steed in a language only horses could understand, urging it to carry him away with all speed. It was a request the animal was all too happy to carry out.

Galin and his horse swiftly caught up with the others. They rode as fast as they could, unhindered by the inclement weather conditions. Fear propelled the horses to carry their masters faster and farther through the rains than they normally would have tolerated. Riding through the fatigue and pain, the group found themselves at the border of Bazadoom by nightfall.

It was here where they would have to stop for the night. Everyone badly needed rest. Physically and emotionally drained, they had barely escaped with their lives. There were many questions that would have to wait until morning, when everyone's nerves would be less frail. The Druids assured the others that the horses would alert them if danger came. They all went to sleep, knowing one thing for certain: it was no coincidence that such a horror found them in the wild outskirts of Mystaria.

Morning came, delivering them from a state of rundown exhaustion to one of cautious fear. They had gotten a full night sleep, despite the cold and dampness of the rain. The clear skies and warm sunlight were a welcome relief from the gray of the previous day. Whey they had caught up with one another the night before, Hawk had led them to a grassy hilltop where they had a clear line of sight around them, should trouble find or try to assail them.

Kael and Elenari woke earlier than the rest and were gone when the others awoke. Algernon assured them there was no reason for alarm, and that father and daughter would return shortly. Algernon sat in a small circle with Hawk, Mekko, and Galin, sharing small portions of bread and cheese. It was Mekko who broke the maudlin silence.

"I want you and the others to know that I'm grateful to you for rescuing me, as it were, from that place. I apologize if I got a little loud with you yesterday. Don't know what that thing was we encountered . . . don't want to know. But I hope you understand . . . I need to get back to Cordilleran as soon as possible. If what you said is true—and I've no reason to doubt you based on how they interrogated me—then my home, my King, and my men are under siege right now." He hesitated for a moment and got to his feet, surveying the surrounding land. "I put it another way. If you and the others from Wrenford had had a chance to be with your King before that invasion came, what would you do?"

Just as Hawk was about to put food to his lips, his hand hesitated, and he looked at Algernon, anticipating his answer.

Algernon looked up to meet the General's gaze. He took a deep breath before he spoke. "I did have a chance to be with him. We all did. Instead of taking that chance, on his order and out of respect for him, we find ourselves here, on what may be a vain mission to form an alliance against a darkness only Thargelion had the foresight to see. So selfless was his act that he sacrificed his life and the lives of his people so that all might have a chance to live."

"So you think I'm behaving selfishly, do you?" Mekko said with a tone of irritation.

"No, General," Algernon replied sincerely. "In fact, quite the contrary. You may take one of our horses and feel free to leave us at any time you wish, of course."

"Well, then, I'll be takin' my leave. Wish to do it with no hard feelings though. Please?" the General extended his hand.

Algernon quickly rose with a smile and took the General's hand, shaking it warmly. Hawk also offered a hearty handshake to Mekko. As the stocky Dwarf turned to Galin, he hesitated a moment. "I owe my life to you, lad," he said. "That's something a Dwarf never forgets. That beastie would've lit a fire under my arse sure as the sun is shining if it wasn't for you. Thank you. If you're ever in Cordilleran . . . and you need a favor . . . you got it, no questions asked."

Galin reached down to grasp the Dwarf's muscular hand, and he guided him away a few steps from the others. "Let's talk about that, General."

It was at that moment that Kael and Elenari returned. They dismounted and quickly joined the others.

"Kael, what have you learned?" Algernon asked.

"Not much." Kael turned toward Hawk, who was at something of a loss as to the nature of their conversation. "I went this morning to commune with nature. Galin will tell you that such interaction is a deeply private thing; a Druid needs complete solitude to effectively communicate and understand Mother Nature's speech. Nari stayed just close enough to watch for danger." He turned back to Algernon. "The creature is not a product of nature, nor is it an 3lemental of any kind. All I could find out is that it dries up streams, eats through the ground, destroys trees, and kills plants and animals. It first appeared approximately the time we departed Wrenford. That is all."

"I may be mistaken, Algernon," Elenari said, "but the creature did seem to look and move toward you."

"Are you suggesting its purpose is to kill Algernon?" Hawk asked.

"From what you told me, Nari," Kael said. "I'd say it means to kill us all."

"Perhaps," Algernon interjected. "However, it may have an alternate agenda aside from our deaths." With that, the old Sage produced the small, metallic box from within his robes, which contained the Emerald Star.

"Do you think it can track us through the Emerald Star?" Hawk asked.

"It is at least a possibility we must consider," the Sage replied.

"Then let us consider it," Galin interrupted, as he and Mekko rejoined them. "I've been talking with General Mekko. Perhaps if this creature is following us, it might be prudent for us to split up. Algernon, if I leave now with the General, we can cross through Bazadoom together until we go our separate ways. I can go to Alluviam, while he goes to Cordilleran. I will be well-received there, as you know, and I can plead our case before the Elven King while the rest of you go to Averon. We can hit three birds with one stone."

Algernon and the others stared at him, pondering his words.

"Do you think it's wise to weaken our party by another member?" Kael inquired skeptically. "We're stronger with you than without you."

"I don't like weakening the group either," Galin replied. "I also don't like seeing the general go through Bazadoom alone. And I like even less that . . . thing that almost killed us. But if it is following us, maybe it will get confused and follow us instead of you." He saw the frown of disbelief on Kael's face and continued, "At any rate, if we split, we can get our message to three nations, probably, in the time it would take to reach one. Algernon, what do you say?"

Algernon hesitated and looked to each of their faces before answering as if trying to judge what was in their minds. "So be it. We will go around Bazadoom to Averon, while you go through it. Wait for us in Alluviam, Galin; luck willing, we will meet you there. Then, my dear General, when next we meet, hopefully it will be while we are marching an alliance army to Cordilleran's aid. Goodbye, my friends . . . and good luck."

As Hawk and Galin exchanged goodbyes, Hawk pulled his old comrade close. "Do you think you can arrange one of these splits where you and I team up again, like old times?"

"I would," Galin replied, "but they need you. They might need you to save them even more than I do, if you can believe that. And I think you might want to keep that girl where you can see her." Galin smiled and looked toward Elenari.

"Save them?" Hawk answered incredulously. "How? No sword, no crossbow, just my hand axe left to protect them with. Oh, and I doubt Nari could care less about me."

"Well, maybe you can chop some wood and throw it at the next enemy you see," Galin said with a laugh.

"I'll do that," Hawk said, patting him on the arm. "Safe journey."

Within moments, they were all mounted and heading their separate ways. Hawk pulled back on Silvermane's reins for a moment and turned to watch Galin and Mekko riding south into the Bazadoom. Try as he might, he was unable to dispel the feeling of dread that caused him to question whether or not he would ever see his friend again.

Chapter 14

The sky was gray, and the feeling of rain was once again in the air as Galin and Mekko made their way south through Bazadoom. Early on, they elected to walk, guiding the horses, trying to spare them. Should they run into trouble later, they might have need of their swiftness. Although Galin was tall and quick-footed, Mekko was able to keep up with him, taking two steps for every one of the Druid's.

They crossed a riverbed, which had almost dried up completely. There was still some trickling water at the bottom as they guided their mounts through it. They stopped on the far side to allow the horses to drink before proceeding any further. The water appeared stale and discolored. Galin bent down and closed his eyes, reaching out his hands so that his fingers barely entered the water. Mekko watched as a blue glow emanated from Galin's palms and seemed to extend outward into the water. Suddenly, the water took on a fresh, clear appearance, reflecting the blue of the skies above.

"You may fill your flask, General," Galin said, smiling. "There are advantages to traveling with a Druid."

"Indeed there is, lad," Mekko said as he bent down and filled his flask and splashed some water on his face and hands. "Not a bad little trick. Not bad at all."

As they continued heading southeast, they noticed several scattered trees about. The trees here were tall and thick, covered with thick, dying vines that seemed to be slowly choking the life out of the trees themselves. Much of the vegetation, though showing signs of overgrowth in a time long past, was now shriveled and had turned to a dull brown. There were few traces of animal activity as well. No natural animals of any kind would be able to adapt to the harsh environment here.

As the Druid and Dwarf made their way through the afternoon, the air became stagnant, and the sun became hidden more and more behind the twisted knotted trees until it was completely blocked from their view.

They had been riding for many hours now well into the wasteland territory of Bazadoom. The land they trod upon had been named so years before anyone could remember it coming to pass. All those living now knew was that this area had become the most feared and loathed stretch of lands within the known world. It was a place full of death and the dregs of the natural environment. Civilized people rarely dared to ever travel here.

Nevertheless, the world's garbage was often sent here to rot. People who were no longer considered worthy to be part of their respective societies had often been banished here over the years as an alternative to death. They were left to die, and it was expected that they did so. Mekko had informed Galin that there was a time in Cordilleran's history—a darker history—when Dwarven criminals had been banished into these lands to pay for their sins. They were sent here, into lands crawling with Goblins, Orcs, Ogres, and other natural enemies to the Dwarves. Most would have preferred a quick death, he had said.

They both knew that stories told of beasts of every kind could be found in these hope-forsaken lands, from dangerous predators to scavengers and carrion eaters. Galin remembered Prince Crichton tell them how he used these lands as his hunting grounds years before. He remembered seeing on Crichton's wall the stuffed heads of myriad vicious-looking creatures that would make the average warrior cringe. And yet, here they were, a Druid and a Dwarf, trotting through one of the most feared places in their world.

Deep in the caves and mountains were said to be thousands of Orcs and Goblins and who knew what other type of tribal monsters, but even they had been warring amongst each other for centuries. In truth, there was little worry that the creatures of Bazadoom would ever band together and invade the outlying lands, as they were incapable of uniting.

Galin and Mekko eventually mounted and rode their horses at a slow pace, conserving their strength as there was still the danger of the lava creature to consider. Though neither would admit to the other openly, they were on edge from the thought of it as well as the hundreds of other unknowns that could assail them at any moment.

Mekko had been humming some sort of barroom tune in an effort to keep his nerves under control. Galin pondered the sad state of nature here as the trees became more rotted the deeper they traveled. The ground itself was cracked and appeared completely infertile. He wondered how long this place had been neglected to cause such decay, for this was clearly a place where the poison in the lands had flourished. He could almost feel it. He thought about attempting to commune with one of the trees, but he soon realized it would be a moot point. These trees would not be able to talk to him, and he was not entirely sure he would be able to pull any useful information out of them if they did.

The broken trees continued to litter the ground of what had been at one time a vibrant forest. Some had fallen after death and were little more than rotted logs, in such decay that they appeared as if they were matchsticks that had fallen from their boxes.

Darkness was coming upon them as the moon's rays made their first appearance upon the trail. Both men were thinking of the prospect of traveling at night and knew it was time to broach the subject.

"Druid," said the Dwarf riding at his side, "the way I see it, we can travel throughout the night and into late morning. By that time, we will be only about two days from the southern edge of Bazadoom, closer to the Averon border. From there, you can turn toward Alluviam, and I'll go my way to Cordilleran. Aye, lad, as long as we keep our heads up and our weapons sharp, they'll be nothin' to worry about." He let out a hearty chuckle.

Galin thought he laughed more to cover his own nervousness at the prospect of traveling throughout the night. *Still,* Galin thought, *if we did travel through the night, it would cut our journey significantly.* They were already saving three days by cutting through Bazadoom. He knew Mekko was impatient to be back in Cordilleran. *There are few things worse,* he thought, *than an impatient Dwarf.* Reluctantly, he agreed with Mekko's plan.

The night was quiet, save for the incessant humming of the General. The usual sounds of nightlife and buzzing insects did not exist in this place. It was as hushed as a graveyard. The ground beneath them was hard and fractured in many places; even a torrential rain could do nothing to enrich it. The footfalls of the horse's hooves echoed loudly throughout. It was impossible to move stealthily, between that and the General's singing.

Three hours of the night had turned into three hours of listening to the General's caterwauling. It was becoming unbearable. Galin was unable to meditate, much less think, and he found himself staring into the darkness, becoming highly agitated at the thought that enemies could be closing in on them due to the noise. The situation had to be addressed.

"General," said Galin finally, struggling to calm his voice, "perhaps you could see fit to find a different tune to hum before we're ambushed on all sides. With all due respect, I think three hours of *Another Round for the Big-Bosomed Maidens* is all I or anyone else should ever have to hear."

Mekko let out a large laugh, shattering the silence around them. "Perhaps I could, laddie! Are you jealous of my singin'?"

"Is that what you call it?" Galin replied.

Mekko obliged, and they traveled onward, talking less and listening harder for anything that might consider them a late-night snack. The trees seemed to moan as an occasional cold wind shot through them, making brittle branches sway and creak against their trunks like old doors in need of hinge grease.

Their horses were becoming increasingly restless and somewhat short of breath. They were becoming harder to direct. Something had spooked them in the darkness. A strange scent had upset them. Galin held his reins tightly and spoke soothing words in his steed's ear. Mekko's horse, however, was jumping back and beginning to buck.

"Whoa there, horse," said Mekko attempting to pull on the reins. "Calm down you stupid mule."

But the horse was jerking from side to side now in what seemed to be a fit of fear. Both horses were bumping into each other. Suddenly, Mekko was thrown from his saddle and fell flat onto his back with a thud. Galin quickly regained control of his mount and grabbed onto the reins of Mekko's horse, holding it steady.

"Damn mule, I'll show you who's boss here! Throw me off, will ya? I ought to skin you alive. Come here!"

Mekko snatched the reins from Galin, and a moment later, the horse took off, running toward a patch of trees to their right. Mekko took off in pursuit. "Aye, you better run, because when I catch you, you'll be lucky to be horse steak when I'm finished!"

"General!" Galin called to him. "General, wait! Let the horse go!"

As Mekko pursued the spooked horse, something appeared from behind the trees directly in front of him. At first, it took him by surprise, and he skidded to a halt on top of dried leaves. Slowly, he pulled his battle-axe off his back, finding himself eye to eye with an Orc.

It stood somewhat taller than the Dwarf. Its snout and sweaty yellow skin hung over its skeletal frame partially covered by animal hide. It held a wooden spear ending in a crudely fashioned blade.

Galin quickly rode up and jumped off his horse to stand behind Mekko.

"Well . . . what do we have ourselves here?" Mekko said as he stroked the blade of his axe. "Are you lost, my pig-faced friend? If so, it's your lucky night. I have a little somethin' here I like to call 'the finder of lost Orcs.'"

Unexpectedly, more Orcs started to appear from behind the surrounding trees. Mekko tightened his grip around his weapon and held his ground. "Druid, I count just six of these filthy animals. I can finish 'em off with just a few swings." Mekko tossed his double-bladed axe from one hand to the other. "Come on, you piles of rat dung; don't have me waitin' here all night!"

"General," spoke Galin calmly, with his hands in the air to show the Orcs he held no weapon, "let's take this slowly. No need to rile them up, especially until we know how many we are dealing with."

"Laddie, I tell you there's only six of these filthy stinkin' pigs; we'll be done with 'em in no time!"

As Mekko spoke, more Orcs dropped from branches high above them to stand beside their comrades. Their numbers had now tripled.

"General, in case you haven't noticed," Galin said, with the urgency increasing in his tone, "the situation is not improving."

"You disgustin' eaters of dung, I'll butcher the lot of you and send your maggot-filled carcasses home to your rat-infested mothers!"

"General, please . . ."

"How can you beasts so much as even stand the smell of each other? You smell worse than a pile of decaying skunks." Mekko continued to swing his axe from side to side, as the Orcs slowly moved inward, encircling the two of them.

"Mekko!" the Druid screamed.

Finally the Dwarf turned to him.

"I think you are angering them," Galin said, pointing at the fifteen-plus Orcs that had just arrived behind the others.

"Them, Druid? They're animals!" The General continued, "They're more stupid than a headless zombie. Hell, I've met Dragon dung smarter than they are! They can barely understand each other in that heathen blathering let alone civilized beings."

One of the lead Orcs took a step forward and pointed its spear, staring at the Dwarf. "Kills zem boths and roast the little onez."

"Well, a diplomat you're in no danger of becoming General," Galin said as he pulled his scimitar from his waist.

Mekko and Galin pressed their backs against each other as the Orcs moved in for the kill.

"All right, laddie, here's the plan: you take half, and I'll take half."

Galin shook his head. "Please tell me there's a plan B."

"Aye . . . there is a plan B, come to think of it," Mekko replied, spying more Orcs in the distance.

At that moment, the fifteen Orcs charged at them, screaming. Mekko's axe met the first three and felled them instantly. Unable to summon his magic, Galin twirled his sword and knocked two of the Orcs to the ground.

Next, Mekko threw all of his weight into an axe swing, cutting madly in a circle so that his leverage cut the Orcs spears in half and turned him completely around. Misjudging his trajectory, Mekko's swing brought his axe too far around, and it cut into Galin's robes, nearly drawing blood. Galin looked down at him in disbelief.

"Oh! Ah . . . sorry about that, laddie!" the Dwarf exclaimed.

Galin quickly dove to the ground in front of three charging Orcs, taking out their legs and toppling them to the ground. Mekko stepped forward and made short work of them with his axe as they struggled to get up.

Galin rose to face the surge of charging Orcs, who came at them from the woods behind. He put his hand before him in an attempt to summon his magic, but an Orc he did not see punched him in the ribs from behind and grabbed him around the neck with the shaft of his spear, choking him.

As Mekko moved in to help, two Orcs grabbed him by his arms and flung him into a tree trunk. Their victory was short-lived, however, as Mekko, still on the ground, spun around with his axe and took their legs off at the knees. They shrieked and howled as they fell to the ground amidst pools of their own dark blood.

Galin stepped back and successfully flipped the Orc who was choking him onto the ground. Having wrestled the spear away, Galin drove it down with all his might through the creature's chest. He picked up his sword and ran toward Mekko.

From the corner of his eye, Mekko saw that the Orcs had killed Galin's horse, and he heard the death throes of his own horse from the woods. They would no doubt use the animals for food. He got to his feet. "Kill my horse, will you, pig-faces?" he bellowed, cutting through two more Orcs. The final impact of his axe on the last Orc's skull forced him back against a large tree. "Well, he may not have been the smartest beast that ever lived, but he was a damn sight preferable to the stinkin' lot of you!"

Galin quickly moved next to him, scratch marks streaked across his face. He was out of breath and holding his side.

Galin panted in short breaths. "Are you all right?"

"Aye, laddie," said the Dwarf as he straightened his battle-axe. "I think they're gettin' tired. We've got the upper hand on 'em now."

Mekko patted Galin on the shoulder. Before the smile could take root upon the Dwarf's face, an arrow struck the tree, having just grazed his temple. They both turned to see at least half a dozen Orcs loading bows and aiming toward them. They leapt behind the tree as six arrows struck the bark where they had just been standing.

"General, what was that plan B?" Galin asked, breathing in short bursts as he peered around the side of the tree. Even in the darkness, there seemed to be Orcs coming from everywhere. "General?"

Having received no reply, he turned back and saw Mekko was no longer beside him. He then looked around and beyond the tree to see the Dwarf running for all he was worth back along their trail.

"RUN, DRUID!" Mekko cried.

With that, Galin pushed himself off the tree and began running behind his companion as sorties of arrows and spears flew all around him.

Mekko, though short and stout, ran vigorously, digging his boots into the ground. Galin quickly caught up to him, with the Orcs hot on their heels. Their only defense now from the archers was the zigzag pattern in which they darted through the trees, which were becoming fewer in number with each passing moment.

The Orcs were not firing arrows quite as much as they were throwing spears, and were coming very close to the targets. At one point, two spears landed right in front of them, causing them to veer their course apart and then back again. They could hear the Orcs snarling and screaming. Their rage had made them hungry for blood now, and they were not going to give up until they had it.

The fleeing pair were beginning to increase the distance a bit, but they would not be able to run much longer. They were tiring fast.

"General!" Galin yelled, nearly breathless. "This . . . isn't . . . working!"

Mekko caught up to him, panting heavily. They could not see the Orcs, but they could hear them in their proximity.

"We can go right or left up ahead, off the trail," Galin suggested. "I think we should go right, there is more brush to cover us, and it will lead us closer to the Averon border."

"Laddie," huffed the General, "We should go left, it will lead us where we need to go . . . *that* is the way to the Averon border."

"Respectfully, General, going right will lead us to Averon, I have a very keen sense of direction."

"Druid," Mekko cut him off, "I outrank you. We're goin' left."

Galin could not argue anymore. The Orcs were in sight now; there was no time. He followed behind the General as they broke off the trail to the left. They continued for several yards until they noticed that the Orcs were no longer behind them, almost as if they had suddenly given up. It was pitch black; they were moving now in complete darkness. Mekko told Galin not to worry, as Dwarves possessed the same infravision as Elves, and he should follow close behind him. Finally, they stopped for a moment.

"What did I tell you, laddie? We lost 'em, and we're as good as home fr—"

Without warning, the ground gave way, and both men plunged into the blackness. Unable to control their rate of descent, they found themselves sliding downward, with rocks, dirt, and dead vines entangling them. They tried to grab on to whatever lay in their path, even digging their hands into the dirt, but to no avail.

Finally, after several minutes, they came to an abrupt stop. They lay there for many long minutes, figuring out they were still alive and trying to determine the extent of their injuries.

Covered in debris, Mekko pushed himself up slowly, spitting out a mouthful of dirt and leaves. Galin moaned slightly as he struggled onto his knees. Their bodies ached, and their heads were throbbing.

Galin stared intently at Mekko with a disgusted look, waiting for the Dwarf to speak. He could tell Mekko was trying to avoid his gaze, as he stood and began brushing away the dirt.

"Druid . . . you followed too close behind; the ground couldn't hold all that weight. I was about to tell you we was on a fragile bit of dirt, but you didn't—"

"*Me!* My weight . . . followed too close behind?! Mister I-can-see-in-the-dark-as-well-as-any-Elf!" Galin stormed up, infuriated, an incredulous look on his face.

"Now, now, lad, let's not harp on it," said Mekko patronizingly. "I understand you're sorry about it. Water under the bridge as far as I'm concerned. The important thing is we're still in one piece. It can't get any worse, that's for sure."

That's when they realized they were standing at the rocky base of a cliff-like hillside, adjacent to a large clearing that was maybe three hundred yards in length. As the light of the moon shone upon the clearing, they saw hundreds of tents crowding the space, with fires burning around the perimeter. Instinctively, they both shrank back against the hillside. As they peered into the clearing, they saw large, dark forms moving in the moonlight. The forms were far larger than men, three to four feet larger on average, and there were hundreds of them—maybe even a thousand. It was an Ogre encampment, and the only way out was straight through the camp.

They quickly scrambled behind a large rock to stay out of sight of any patrols that might have seen their unfortunate tumble.

"Guess what?" Galin whispered in Mekko's ear. "It just got worse."

An Ogre army out in the open in a clearing in the middle of Bazadoom wouldn't be at all unusual, except that they knew the border forts of Averon had to be somewhat close. The Republic of Averon had established a network of fortifications along their northern border decades ago, separating them from the southern border of Bazadoom. As a nation of rich merchants, they had no illusions about being a tempting target for invasion by any nation. They had decided long ago they would take no chances with Bazadoom. The forts were manned by their elite fighting force, the Sentinels of Averon.

The Ogres were no doubt planning to attack one or more of the forts. Mekko told Galin it had been many years since the Ogres had come together in large forces such as this. It was a bad omen to see such a gathering, and it did not bode well for the men who garrisoned the border forts. However, they had to look to themselves before they could think of warning the soldiers of Averon. Daylight had come as the hours passed, and they had to keep very still or risk being seen.

"General, what if we created a distraction over in the north side of the valley? Perhaps it would keep their attention long enough for us to slip across the southern side of the camp."

"Terrible idea," groaned Mekko.

"What do you mean *terrible idea?*" Galin scoffed. "I suppose you would suggest we run at the camp and take them all on just the pair of us."

"No, that wouldn't be my first choice, but I'm startin' to like the way you think, boyo," said Mekko. "You see, lad, you're goin' to use that magic of yours. You Druids can affect nature right?"

"Depending on the conditions, yes," Galin replied.

"Okay, then," Mekko said brightly, "can you make some of them vines and weeds come up from the ground and grab them oversize dung brains, maybe knock 'em on the ground?"

"You're talking about over two hundred and fifty yards worth of land," Galin replied. "That is a very large area I'd need to spread my magic over, and even if I could, I'm not sure the vines here would hold the Ogres for very long."

"That's okay, laddie," said Mekko, smiling. "We don't need much time—just enough that we can run past their camp. See, beyond the clearin', there's a river cross the way; can you hear it? That's the Steel River if I'm not mistaken. It will take us down around the clearin', past the Ogres, right to the Averon border. Ogres don't like water much; they sink like rocks. There ya have it—home free."

"And this is different from my plan how exactly?" Galin asked.

"Your idea lacked refinement and elegance," Mekko responded. The General was all smiles as he watched Galin contemplating his idea.

"I believe I can do as you ask," Galin said skeptically. "However there's no guarantee that all of the Ogres will be entangled, and some may escape quickly."

"Fair enough, lad," replied Mekko.

"I will need to meditate for a few minutes. The scope of the area I need to cover is large and will require me to summon strength from deep within. Additionally, the poison in these lands is accelerated far beyond that in any other place we have seen. My magic will have to dig deep in the soil for such a feat."

"Atta boy," the General said confidently. "Just give me the signal when you're ready."

Mekko peered out from behind the rock to look at the camp. Ogres were going in and out of their large tents. They were huge, muscular beasts, wearing mostly half-furs and broken bits of metal for armor. There were Ogrens as well, only a little smaller than their larger cousins. Their skin was much darker and they were a foot to two feet smaller on average. It was difficult to see them closely from their vantage point, but their size and the size of their weapons could not be mistaken. They carried huge spears, axes, swords, hammers, and clubs.

On his knees, deep in meditation, Galin drew upon the very strength of his soul. He summoned the magic they needed, which worked not only from within him but from the ground below. The Druid and the earth were becoming one in fulfillment of a sacred covenant established centuries past. They were sharing one soul, one mind, and one body. There were no barriers between them any longer. Even the strange poison infecting the land could not prevent such a merging. It was a wonderful feeling, as if the Druid were being cradled within the arms of Mother Nature herself. It was warm and inviting, even here in one of her more depraved and ailing lands.

Magic erupted from within Galin. He could feel it coursing through him and flowing in all directions. His eyes opened and closed briefly as his heart raced. His body was in a semiconscious state, awaiting his soul, which was moving away from the earth now and back into his corporeal form. The warmth disappeared, replaced with an ancient magic. The magic was building at an enormous rate, but due to his knowledge and experience, he was able to control it and wind it within himself, like a ball of twine, to be released as needed. He waited for all the magic to surface.

At that moment, a green light shot forth from the Druid's hands and back into the earth from whence it was drawn. The light encompassed the length of the clearing just below the surface. The valley itself shook slightly as rocks and pebbles fell from above. Druid and Dwarf stood fast, watching the clearing. The Ogres were looking all around, unable to understand what was happening.

Galin's face was strained with the force of the magic. He could no longer moderate it. It was time to let it all out to do what it was meant to do.

The ground within the clearing began rumbling as small fissures opened in the soil. Little leaves started sprouting up from the ground all around the Ogres. The huge beasts looked down as vines grew at unimaginable speeds. They tore out of the soil, shooting five, ten, even fifteen feet into the air, their leaves spreading open almost as rapidly. All around the valley, vines appeared and grappled with the startled Ogres. Some of the Ogres swung swords or axes and cut the vines apart, but for each one they destroyed, many more appeared. The vines wrapped around anything that they could hold on to: tents, barrels, and the Ogres themselves.

It was at that moment that Mekko and Galin decided to make a run for it. Mekko kept a close eye on Galin, who was clearly fatigued from the spell but managed to run as fast as he had the previous night. They ran, looking straight ahead and ignoring the Ogre camp completely, hoping they would go unnoticed. They were more than halfway through when the flabbergasted Ogres started yelling and pointing toward them.

Dwarf and Druid did not have to look to know they had been found out. Galin's spell had been more successful than he had hoped it would be, allowing them to get farther than they'd anticipated. However, three Ogres who had been on the perimeter of the camp, unaffected by the spell, were moving to intercept them. If the companions did not dispatch them quickly enough, others would arrive and their efforts would be for naught.

They could see the beasts clearly now. Their skin was infested with warts, and pus-filled vesicles dotted their misshapen bodies. Two had spears and the third a club. Mekko dove into a forward roll toward the one with the club. The Ogre swung down, just missing the Dwarf with a smashing blow. Mekko came up on one knee behind the beast and, with his fist, hit between the creature's legs with all his might. The blow struck on target, driving the Ogre to his knees.

Galin stopped running, drew his scimitar, and faced the Ogres with the spears. As they closed in on him, flames suddenly shot up the length of his curved sword as if the blade were composed of fire. The magic caused the Ogres to take a fearful step back.

As the other Ogre fell to its knees, Mekko picked up the huge spiked club and swung it around, embedding its spikes in the creature's eyes. It fell to the ground wailing, moaning, and turning from side to side.

Galin reached into a pouch at his belt and threw several acorns into the air toward his two opponents. The acorns stopped in midair and began swirling about their heads. Angered, the monsters swatted at them like insects. Galin tossed his sword between and behind them to Mekko, who caught it and, without hesitating, slashed the flesh behind the left knee of one Ogre, causing it to fall onto its other knee and drop its spear. Galin quickly lifted the spear and ran at the other Ogre who, still distracted by the floating acorns, did not see him, even as the Druid rammed the spear into its face through the back of its head.

Leaving the hobbled Ogre behind them, the two ran for the river with everything they had left. They knew many of the Ogres would be free and upon them in moments. The remainder of the distance vanished quickly, but as they reached the river, Mekko suddenly stopped.

"What's wrong?" Galin asked between inhalations.

"I . . . just remembered. Dwarves don't like the water, either."

"Ah . . . well, in that case, General, allow me to adjust your delicate sensibilities." Galin grabbed Mekko by the collar of his cloak and threw him into the river, leaping in after him as the angry shouts of the Ogres drew nearer.

The fast-paced current swung them southwest, back past the hills and cliffs that separated them from the Ogre encampment. Mekko yelled over to Galin as they attempted to keep their heads above water.

"Druid! If I didn't know better . . . I'd think you enjoyed that!" Mekko managed, spitting water out of his mouth.

"Not . . . at all, General!" Galin yelled over the thrashing water. "It was merely . . . a strategic act . . . necessary to refine . . . your plan!"

They tumbled around and were brought under the water more than once, slamming into the riverbank and each other. At one point, Galin frantically reached up and grabbed the branches of an overhanging tree, only to have them ripped from his grasp as Mekko knocked into him.

It seemed like a long, tiring ordeal, though in truth they had only traversed the river for several minutes at high speeds. The river's strength finally subsided enough that they were able to grab some vines running along the riverbed and arduously pull themselves free.

They rolled onto their backs and decided not to move for many minutes. Sheer physical exhaustion prevented them from doing anything other than attempting to catch their breath.

It took them several more minutes of coughing until they were able to stand up. They were soaking wet and shivering, as the water had been intensely cold. They surmised that one of Averon's border outposts was nearby, and that, if so, Averon must be warned of the Ogre army's presence. They began walking.

A good part of an hour had passed before they saw something in the distance. Judging from the pointed wooden spikes of the walls, they had found one of the forts that guarded the border between Averon and Bazadoom. Mekko recognized the banner—two swords crossed behind a shield, which was the standard of the Sentinels of Averon. They began jogging to get there quickly and to fight off the dank cold in their joints.

As they came closer to the fort, it quickly became apparent that it had recently come under heavy siege. The walls were riddled with holes. The main gates had been splintered and smashed through, though they still held together, but only just barely. The fort itself was basically a great square surrounded by a wooden palisade with the main gates on the north side. Within could be seen two large, rectangular buildings. One was the barracks and the other the mess hall. In addition, there was a third, smaller building, which was the armory. There were archery towers on the corners of the palisade and near the main gates. Mekko estimated the garrison to be anywhere from two to three hundred men.

The Druid and the Dwarf suddenly stopped in their tracks as a mass of bodies became visible before the main gates. They were a combination of men mixed with Orcs. Fear got the better of them, and they hesitated, wondering if the fort had already been taken. However, as if in answer to their questions, they heard the common tongue of men from within and saw armored soldiers on the archery platforms, calling for the main gates to be opened. Apparently, their approach had been spotted and observed for some time.

As they entered the fort, wet and shivering, they saw a handful of soldiers, all of whom were very young men, with the eldest being in their twenties. They approached the newcomers slowly; there couldn't have been more than fifty of them. A small boy emerged from within the group carrying two large white towels. He approached them with a cautious smile. Fear and insecurity exuded from the group, though they wore the chain mail and uniforms of the Sentinels.

"Welcome to Fort Renault," said the boy, who couldn't have been more than twelve years old.

"Thank you," said Galin, as the Druid and Dwarf quickly wrapped themselves in the towels.

The boy bade them to follow him, and he guided them to the mess hall. A fire had been lit near the kitchen, which they eagerly drew close too. As the rest of the young men crowded in the kitchen, Mekko addressed them.

"Where's the officer in charge here, lads?" the Dwarf asked.

"Dead, sir, with the rest of the garrison." The response had come from somewhere within the group.

"Listen, lads," said Mekko, "there's an Ogre encampment to the northeast of here, not far at all. There's an army there; could be a thousand strong. You lads have to leave this place and go to your next closest outpost along the border to warn them."

"We cannot do that, sir," most of the boys replied, almost in unison.

"What do you mean?" Galin demanded. "Why not?"

Again, many of the boys spoke at once.

"No men of the Sentinels have ever abandoned their post!"

"To do so would bring both shame and dishonor to our families."

"We must stay and fight, regardless of the end."

"Lads, listen," Mekko said gently. "I'm a soldier; have been for many years. Even if the Ogres send half their force here, you have no chance of holdin' out. To stay would be suicide. No sense in it, lads."

"You're a soldier? Perhaps you could help us!" said one of the boys.

"All the older more experienced men were killed in previous attacks along with the lieutenant," offered another.

"Can you help us plan to fight?" asked a third.

"This is no mere soldier, men of the Sentinels," said Galin. Mekko turned and gave him a scowl. "This is General Mekko, commander of the armies of Cordilleran. I would heed his advice if I were you."

Much to the intrepid pair's surprise, the boys' jaws dropped at the mention of Mekko's name and rank, as if a leader for their cause had suddenly fallen into their midst. They began firing questions at him.

"General Mekko, sir, can you help us defend the fort?"

"Can you suggest a strategy?"

"Will you lead us?"

"Now wait just a second, lads," Mekko interrupted. "I'm on my way to my own country. We only stopped here to warn you, and I'll say again: you need to pack your flags and leave this place."

When the boys heard him again, their spirits seemed lessened. They looked down and slowly left the room, leaving Galin and Mekko alone with the fire.

"Listen, General," Galin said urgently. "I can change form and fly down to Averon City and get aid for these boys, but you've got to get them out of here."

"Did you see the look in their eyes, Druid?" Mekko replied. "I've seen that look before. Foolish and prideful; those boys won't leave this place. They intend to die behind these walls, I'd say."

Galin was silent for a moment. "Well then, General, I suggest you figure a way to keep them alive. You must help them somehow—at least show how to mount the best defense they can—and then be on your way. I shall make all haste to find help and return as fast as I can for them."

"I suppose I could give 'em a few pointers," Mekko said, holding his hands before the fire. "Damn fools though, these lads."

Galin stood up and faced him. "As much as my body aches, and as tired as I am, I have to leave immediately if I'm to be any good to these boys.

Just show them a few things, General, but make sure you're not here when those Ogres get here. Don't stay here and commit suicide with them."

"You don't have to worry about me, lad," Mekko said, standing up.

"Luck be with you on your road to Cordilleran, General," the Druid said. "May your road be a safe one and may Mother Nature's blessings be with you."

"And with you, my Druid friend. May you fly fast and true, and arrive in time to help these poor, brave lads."

With that, Mekko locked arms with him, and a moment of sincere respect passed between them. Another moment later, the Druid left the room and was gone.

Chapter 15

Hawk led what remained of the party as they moved at the gallop west along the border of Bazadoom. Algernon and Kael rode side by side and, as before, Elenari brought up the rear. They traveled as fast as the animals would allow.

The morning sun rose high overhead. The grass and trees had all but left them. They were on the border of the wasteland. The land became cracked, arid, and even desert-like in patches. If the lands were suffering from a slow poison, it would be here that such poison would flourish, as the land would succumb easily to such malevolence.

Along their trail and deeper to the south, great clumps of rocks massed together as if the giants had hurled them down from the looming Darkstone Sierras, a deep mountain range whose black jagged peaks shadowed them on the western horizon line and whose vastness dwarfed the Andarian Ranges. Algernon had explained to them that few had ventured there and little was known about those mountains or what lay beyond them.

Hawk explained their path would take them on the Bazadoom border west-southwest for two days until they reached the Soubia River. From there, they would follow the river southeast until it connected to the mighty Steel River, which flowed directly south through Averon to the capital, Averon City. The first two days would be the most difficult, as they would somehow have to stretch the meager food and water they possessed. Once they reached the river, they would have a greater chance of hunting or finding food.

There was another factor that weighed heavily on their minds: the molten creature. None of them wished to speak of it, but clearly they were all thinking what they would do if it found them. What could they do? Elenari could distract it with her sword, but she could not stop it. Their only hope would be Kael's magic. Kael, still wrestling with his own inner demons, now had one more to add within the tangled forest of his mind, a forest full of fear and self-doubt.

A latent coolness still lingered within the warmth of the sunlight. It should have been warmer, yet it wasn't. The skies were blue above them, but there were distant clouds rolling in from the east, from within the heart of Bazadoom—dark clouds. They took it as a signal that indicated nature's fury may not yet be done with them. They hoped they could out-run them.

Algernon held his cloak tight about him, fighting off the unnatural chill. He looked down at the infertile, dry land around them. Like the air itself, the poison therein could not be seen, but still it was there. It lingered, masking its presence. Worst of all, it was patient. Through its patience, the poison permeated the lands, right under the noses of Druids and Elves alike. It took its time, manifesting itself with such deliberate slowness that, by the time it became recognizable, it would be like a wound infected beyond all curing. Soon the water would go bad. Next the plants and ani-mals would begin slowly dying off. The crops would wither and starvation would ravage the lands like a plague.

What power, Algernon thought, *is behind the Shadow Prince? What has resurrected him with such far-reaching wisdom, the likes of which he had never possessed before?* So far, he had been ahead of them at every turn. His plans had the cunning and patience of this strange poison that had infected the lands. He knew the answers and he could never let the others know. These thoughts and more gnawed at the old Sage like the cold dry air.

Hawk absentmindedly put his hand to his cheek where Galin had healed his terrible burns. Over the past few days since they left the others, his thoughts had become increasingly centered on Elenari. Though many times he tried to put such thoughts out of his mind, still they kept coming back to her. He thought of the time they shared in Mordovia. He thought of how she saved his life in the Andarian Ranges. Most of all, he remem-bered the look on her face when she thought Crichton had killed him.

Her smile, which she kept so guarded, was easiest to see when he closed his eyes. Perhaps it was better that way, he thought, for now, whenever he saw her smile, he had to fight off the urge to drop to his knees and con-fess his feelings for her. It took everything he had within him not to stare endlessly at her hair, the smoothness of her face, the beauty of her eyes, and the contours of her slender form.

He had never thought to trust another woman again, but he more than trusted her. It was not lust he felt; it was the sound of his heart beating again. He knew she had caught him staring more than once, but she was never embarrassed and sometimes met his gaze with a smile of acknowledgment. If only he had the courage to convey his feelings for her aloud. *Courage on the battlefield pales,* he thought, *compared to courage of the heart.*

Having regained his physical strength, Kael still suffered from insecurity. Oblik had increased his power. He had defeated Talic and was the Grand Druid, but he had certainly not been acting like one. His thoughts drifted to the Druid Council in Arcadia. What were they doing in his absence? Surely they must have felt the poison infecting the lands by now. Perhaps they were already working on a cure.

He knew that was wishful thinking at best. With a man like Talic in charge for so many years, there was no telling how many were like him and had lost their way. Despite the fact that a Druid from the council watched over each nation, the order had always believed the will of Mother Nature alone was their charge, and the problems of others, if unrelated to nature, did not concern them. He could be the one to change them, unite them with the outside world, and teach them that the outsiders and their problems were intrinsic to Mother Nature.

He could do nothing while so far away, though. Perhaps, after they visited Alluviam, he could venture to Arcadia to enlist the aid of the council. Still, he feared he would be inadequate as the Grand Druid as surely as he feared the lava creature and the Shadow Prince himself. *Terrible thing to live in fear,* he thought.

Elenari nudged her horse on with her heels as she thought of her encounter with the creature. There was clearly something about the gem; it was definitely the creature's weak spot, but how they could use that fact to their advantage remained hidden from her.

She found herself wondering what Hawk was thinking. She had never thought to enjoy the company of another human beside Kael. She had never wondered what it would be like to be touched by a man. Years of sword combat training left time for little else. She had never much cared, either, before she met Hawk. She knew he had many secrets and that he hid a dark pain behind them. There was a nobility and compassion in him that she found alluring. She sensed as well that he somehow knew she was a more-skilled warrior than he, and it did not affect his pride. He was very at ease with himself and, like her, had spent many years in the wild, getting to know himself. They had a great deal in common.

All missed the feel of a bed and hot-cooked meal—mundane things for some that could truly be appreciated by those who lived the majority of their lives in the wild. Their morale was beginning to wane, as was any hope they possessed of succeeding. They had been hard-pressed each step of the way. They had failed in Mystaria amid a host of narrow escapes. Now, the molten creature was most likely hunting them.

Without any of them fully realizing it, the clouds had fully chased away the sun, forcing it to take refuge elsewhere. They found themselves below the gray sky of afternoon when the rain began again. This time, the rain fell straight and steady. It was not pouring nor drizzling, but a steady flow that struck the parched ground that hungered for it like a dying man suffering from mirages of an oasis in the deep desert.

Algernon appreciated the sound and steady beat of the rain. It was a sound that blotted out all other ambient noises. It made it easier for him to think. He loved to write in his tome or just lie awake for hours, recalling a myriad of fond memories of people and places to the backdrop of rain against a sturdy roof.

He had been granted a longer life span through magic. But his mortality was becoming all too apparent. He thought of his tome. Within it was information and history that hopefully would one day help guide and teach people not to repeat the mistakes of the past. It was time he found a guardian for his tome, someone to see that it was passed on to the right hands. He had come out of his hermit's life for Thargelion, but age had caught up to him, and he knew his years were numbered. The book contained information equally catastrophic if left to the wrong hands. In fact, if the enemy ever came to possess his book, he would have no need of armies to conquer the world. Within it were secrets so devastating that he may well have to tear them out and burn them before passing it on.

There is one among them, he thought, *who might make a proper guardian.* At any rate, he must live long enough to get the Emerald Star to Cordilleran and use it to ward off the attacking armies of the Shadow Prince. Then, he could give more thought to a guardian for his journal.

The rain continued steadily for hours as they traversed the barren landscape. They stopped twice to rest, but only for brief intervals. There was little shelter from the rain, aside from the occasional rock formations, and they offered no more than something hard to sit and lean against.

They were not looking forward to nightfall. It would be a damp, cold night. The wind became bitter and harsh the later the hour became. There had been no sign of the creature, though they certainly did not fancy a nighttime encounter. They wondered if it had pursued Galin and Mekko. Silently, they prayed that it hadn't.

Night came, and with it, the rains diminished to faint droplets. Though Kael spoke to the horses, Hawk and Nari felt that they should take turns setting a watch. Algernon and Kael readily agreed. They stopped on higher ground, near a large grouping of rocks. They slept, their clothes thoroughly soaked, shivering against the rocks as the night air endowed the stone with such coldness that they felt as if they were blocks of ice.

When Kael's watch came, he entered it lost in thought. He found his mind was so troubled that the cold barely affected him. Years ago, he had possessed the spirit and courage of an adventurer. He had set off to right the wrongs of the world and to protect and serve Mother Nature, which to him meant all that resided within the natural world around him. He had done as he had set out to do, making a name for himself in his own right and through his adventures with Lark Royale. He had acquired a lordship, something unheard of for a Druid, as well as reputation. Druids kept largely to themselves and were mostly unknown to the world at large. Then time had passed, with no adventures for several years, and things began to change in his life. Talic's challenge stirred something in him but, had it not been for Elenari's presence, he wondered if he would have survived such an encounter. She had given him the strength to win and survive more than anything.

As he pulled his robes close about him, a terrible truth began shaping in his mind: He had neither the courage nor desire to do what needed to be done in the here and now. All that was expected of him now as Grand Druid was too much for him to bear. He had known fear in the past, of course, but never like this. It felt as if there were walls closing in around him. He had difficulty breathing. Was it age or had he simply lost his nerve?

Asleep or awake, he continued to have nightmares about the Shadow Prince. He was out there, somewhere in the dark, with the fiery molten creature that was so fearsome and unstoppable. They were waiting for him. It was a terrible death they had planned for him. Had his own life become too precious to him? Perhaps it had become more important to stay alive than to face the possibility of death. He had become a coward, a deserter hiding out in the middle of a battlefield. . . .

No. Never. He looked to Nari. She was his lifeline. He would gladly give up his life, laughingly, to keep her safe . . . to keep them all safe.

As Kael kept watch, Algernon dreamed deeply. Something was there in the dream with him, something so dark it was too terrible to contemplate. It was beyond human evil, beyond lust, avarice, power, and that which corrupts men to the ways of evil. This was evil incarnate, an unadulterated force so devoid of light and compassion that only one thing gave it true pleasure: the thought of extinguishing life. It was not human pleasure it felt, not fleeting moments of joy, but rather a deep satisfaction and utter ecstasy that it could be the cause of pain, misery, and most of all death. It was a force not of this world and far beyond even his comprehension.

Yet, there was something strangely familiar about it as well, as if he had encountered it before. Still, it had entered their world from another dimension, perhaps another time.

The dream was fading. He was losing his focus on this evil, which his consciousness had come into contact with. There was something important coming through but at the same time fading into the short-term memory of the dream world. Something told him it could be the key, and he was losing it. Desperately he fought against his unconscious mind, trying to savor the memory.

In an instant, he was awake. Despite the coolness and remnants of the rain, sweat fell from his brow on to his knuckles as they were clenched tight about his cloak. As he slowly realized he was awake and safe, he released his fingers to see that the nails had dug into his palms almost to the point of drawing blood. He had done it. He had retained the knowledge. He knew he would not remember for long. He did not wish to appear panicked. Slowly, he got up, stretched and went over to Kael to relieve him.

"It's my turn now, Kael," said the Sage. "Get some sleep, it will be morning soon."

For a moment, it did not appear Kael had even heard him or acknowledged his presence. Then slowly he turned his head to see the Sage standing over him. With a faint smile and a nod, Kael allowed his head to fall to the ground fast asleep.

Algernon stealthily went to his horse and quickly removed his journal and writing quill from his saddlebag. Instantly he sat down, hesitating a moment, and turned to a blank page toward the back of the great tome. He could not even be sure of the dream or his feelings and perceptions. Perhaps Thargelion had sent it to him. Beneath the dark, moonless sky, he quickly scratched down, as best he could, what concepts he retained from this horribly intense dream.

What he had struggled to remember was that this force, having entered their world, was now somewhat subject to its magical laws and dictates. In addition, it would inevitably become subject to their frailties and weaknesses. What was most disturbing, however, was he could not discern what context those weaknesses applied to. Were they scientific, magical, emotional, physical? He had no idea.

The dream faded as fast as it had taken hold of him. He put his journal away and summed it up as nervous anxiety from an old man who had lived too many years. By morning, he may well consider it nonsense. He seated himself as comfortably as possible against the rocks and waited for morning.

Morning came to them dark and gray, though the rain had stopped. The air was still frigid, but the wind had subsided, which was at least some comfort.

They quickly consumed a paltry breakfast of bread and water and mounted to continue their journey. It was at that moment that Kael called them into a circle around him.

"Algernon, I'm going to backtrack our trail for a few hours and see if the lava creature is following us."

"Not without me you're not," responded Elenari.

"Nari . . ."

"Kael, to use your own words, we're stronger with you than without you," Algernon said.

"How strong will we be if the creature shows up?" Kael asked. "If I find the creature, I might be able to stop it. If I can't stop it, maybe I can throw it off the trail . . ."

"Or maybe you'll just end up dead like Driskel," added Hawk flatly, suddenly realizing the abruptness of his comment when Nari shot him a sharp look of anguish. "Sorry," he offered, looking toward her. "It's the truth, though."

"Yes, that's a possibility," Kael responded. "However, Druids enjoy special protection from heat and fire. Now, we're by no means invulnerable to it, but I have a better chance of surviving than any of you."

"You don't have to go," said Nari. "There's no need for it. If the creature shows up, we'll deal with it then as a group."

"Excuse us a moment," Kael said as he guided Nari's horse a few feet away from the others. "Nari . . . I have to do this for myself. It's important to me. If I don't find it, no harm has been done. I'll take the form of the falcon and be back with you in no time. Please . . . I need to do this."

Kael held her hand tightly. Nari looked down for a moment, sighed, then lifted her head and faced him. "Fine, I'm coming with you though."

"No," Kael replied firmly. "You have to help Hawk protect Algernon and the Emerald Star, and unless you've learned to shape-change, you'll only slow me down, and you know it. I need to do this myself, alone."

"And if you get killed or don't come back, like Hawk said, how much better off will we be then? How much more prepared will we be for the creature then?"

"Nari, look at me." He waited until her eyes met his. "I will come back, I promise. After all, I'm a hero in these lands, remember?" He gave her a slight smile. "But you have to promise me that you'll stay with Algernon." He looked at her hard.

She could only look down and away, clearly still unhappy with his decision. She faced him with a flat expression. "I promise."

Kael tightened his grip on her hand and then moved to ride back to Algernon and Hawk.

"Father?" Nari called to him.

Kael stopped and turned his head.

"That's the first time I've seen you smile since we started this journey," she said. "I'd like to see more of it when you return."

Kael smiled again and nodded, as he rode back toward Algernon.

"Kael, I'm not happy about this," said the old Sage. "However, I cannot stop you if you wish to do it. I can only urge you to use caution. This is like no creature we have ever seen before; you may be better off to come back and warn us if you see it without confronting it."

Hawk and Nari quickly nodded their agreement.

"Perhaps if the situation calls for it, that's what I'll do. Hawk told me this morning that, by nightfall, you should reach the Soubia River. I'll meet up with you by then, along the riverbank." He nodded to Algernon and Hawk and brought his horse alongside Elenari's, handing her his reins. He took hold of her arm and kissed her on the cheek. "I love you," he said gently.

"And I love you," she replied. "Be careful."

With that he extended his arms out wide and, with a sudden flash of green fire, a brown spotted falcon with a four-foot wingspan appeared in the air above Kael's horse for a moment and, in the next blink of an eye, was skyward bound.

In the form of a falcon, Kael could fly at great speeds and see nearly ten times farther than he could in his human form. In addition, his visual acuity allowed him to discern both color and detail at that distance. He flew just beneath the clouds throughout the remainder of the gray morning.

Hawk led Algernon and Nari southwest, continuing along the border. They rode at a slower pace than the previous day though steady nonetheless. There was an uncomfortable glare in the sky; the type that sometimes resonated in cloudy post-rain skies. It was difficult to look upward, so they rode with their heads down, concentrating on the trail.

Nari rode beside Algernon and decided to break the morning silence. "What will Averon be like, Algernon?"

"The Republic of Averon is the very heart of commerce within our world. Just as the streets of Mystaria are filled with wizards, so the streets of Averon are filled with merchants—merchants of all sorts, dealing in every commodity you can imagine. And unlike so many other places in the world, the merchants in Averon are refreshingly honest. Money makes their country go 'round and their country makes every other nation's economy go 'round. They are not a greedy people, to be sure; it would be more accurate to call them *business people* in every sense of the phrase. Every nation, more or less, depends on Averon for their own economy. As a consequence of this, the nations are very protective of it. I would go so far as to say that they would rally to protect it. The only conflict Averon ever has is border skirmishes with creatures of Bazadoom or those few bandits bold enough to try to attack one of their caravans."

"I imagine they don't have much of an army then," Elenari said.

"It would be more accurate to say they haven't much need for an army," Algernon replied. "On the contrary, they have quite a professional army. However, it has always been a defensive force. They refer to their army as the Sentinels, and they train quite diligently. Their army must protect vast trade routes and supply lines between them and other nations so merchants feel safe traversing great distances on roads where thieves and brigands wait around every corner to raid and steal from them."

"How do they deal with skirmishes from Bazadoom?" Nari asked.

"Many years ago, they established a network of forts along their northern border with Bazadoom. The men of the forts are charged with the task of keeping the borders safe and driving any invading forces back. They have always done an excellent job, though I would venture to say they are some-what undermanned and spread too thin, especially in times such as these."

"Why then would the Shadow Prince and his forces ever attack Averon, if the other nations need it so badly and would join to protect it?" Nari asked.

"Control Averon, and you can bring the other nations to their knees economically," the Sage answered.

"Why did he not attack Averon first?" Hawk asked, interjecting for the first time.

Algernon replied with pronounced conviction, "Precisely for that very reason: Attack Averon first, and the other nations would be highly sym-pathetic to form an alliance. They would mobilize quickly to defend it. I daresay Mystaria and even Koromundar would be on our side had that been the case. No, his planning has been near flawless thus far. Eliminate Wrenford first, since they would be the first to detect him and warn others, then go right to the strongest military force and destroy it to break the others' will. If Cordilleran falls, the other nations will be too preoccupied with looking to their own borders, and they will wait. They will wait until, one at a time, the Shadow Prince invades and conquers them. We cannot allow that to come to pass."

"Algernon, most of us from the lands north and west of Wrenford know something of the stories of the Shadow Prince and his two attempts to destroy Wrenford in the past, both of which met with failure," Hawk said. "What has changed since then that gives him this great strategy and ability to form armies that could challenge the Dwarves? And even the other nations? And all in so little time, it seems."

"That, my dear Hawk, is indeed the most disturbing question that I have yet to answer completely." The Sage suddenly spurred his horse on ahead of them for a moment in a fashion that indicated he no longer wished to discuss what he thought.

They stopped for a brief rest. They reviewed their provisions and would be out of food and water by nightfall. However, if all went well, they would also be at the Soubia River by then. What they had should suffice.

They sat on a bare clearing atop a small hill. The ground was hard and the land barren and infertile. Algernon had his great tome. Lost in thought, he sat and scratched down his private feelings.

Elenari sat wondering about Kael, hoping for his safe return, when her eyes found Hawk's. The rest of the world seemed to fade away. His gaze met hers with wanton relief. He used to look away whenever she caught his eyes on her, but now he kept his gaze steady. She wanted, more than anything, to simply have him hold her at this moment. For a moment, she thought she could convey that thought through her eyes. She hoped he understood. Soon, she would tell him.

Kael had flown for miles with no sign of the creature below. He decided to perch himself atop the highest rock formation he could find and wait. From there, he could see far and wide in every direction.

In fact, it was only a matter of minutes after stopping that he did see something. He detected movement to the east. It was the limit of his vision, but he was able to make out approximately twenty-five men. They carried a large, ornate box in their midst. Two men held handles in the front and two in the back. They were all clad in dark clothes, but the most peculiar thing was they all seemed to have white hair—yet they did not appear to be old. In addition, they had white skin, like ivory. He took off in flight toward them, remaining high overhead.

As he drew nearer, he saw they were heavily armed. They had bows, swords, and dark armor, partially concealed under dark robes. Something else strange became evident to him as well—they had pointed ears. Elven ears.

White Elves, he thought. They fit the description of the people witnessed by the strange hermit Rex Abernackle. But what were they doing here in the middle of nowhere on the outskirts of Bazadoom?

They were on foot and moving deeper in country. He weighed his options. The creature had been nowhere to be seen within hours of the trail. He reasoned it might well be worth it to follow these Elves for a while to see where they led him.

For the remaining hours after noon, he trailed them from high in the clouds. They moved fast with great purpose, never stopping to rest. The men carrying the large box never once put it down. Clearly, it contained something—or perhaps someone—of great importance or value.

They continued traveling northeast, away from his party's trail. The landscape was changing. The earth was becoming brown, or an almost crimson color, like clay or even a layer of ash covering the ground. As he looked in the distance, he saw mountainous formations amid two great volcanoes. One of them leaked smoke into the sky, indicating it was clearly active and alive. The other appeared dormant and inactive from his skyward vantage point. The Elves were on a direct course toward the mountains between the two volcanic formations.

The hour was becoming late and, although he was capable of great speeds, if he did not turn back soon, he would not meet back up with the others until morning, assuming he flew back at top speed. He did not want to cause Nari unnecessary worry, but something about these Elves told him he must at least see what their purpose could be. The box as well fascinated him. Its top curved on the ends, and it was studded on the outside with jewels. There appeared to be a sliding door of some sort on the side of it. It was entirely conceivable that a person dwelled within it, but who could be so important that they would carry by hand such a great distance? He needed to find out.

As they neared the mountains between the volcanoes, the air was dark and the sky became a deep red, a result of the reflection of fiery lava against the heavens. Similar to a blue sky, Kael thought, giving the waters of a lake or ocean a deep-blue appearance.

The opening of a large cave soon became evident within the mountain face. This was their destination. He knew he would have to wait until they cleared the entrance. He also knew that he had to be very careful from this point. All Elves had heightened senses; they may well detect if there was an animal present that did not belong. He thought for a long moment, and then it came to him—the perfect camouflage.

He waited until the party of Elves disappeared from view within the darkness of the cave before he changed shape. In a flash of green fire, unseen by those below, Kael soared toward the cave entrance in the form of a common bat.

He entered the cave, staying as close to the roof as possible. Immediately, he saw torchlight. Only a few yards within, the cave guardians made their presence known: a monstrous creature took him by such surprise that he quickly perched himself upside down on a small stalactite, calming himself so that he could quietly observe them. A giant nearly twenty feet in height, the creature was armored in patches of chain mail and had a nearly ten-foot-long sword at its side. Its muscular skin was a deep brown, while its long, thick hair was flaming red. Beside the giant was a large pile of boulders, no doubt to be used for hurling at enemies. Chained and bolted into the ground were three timber wolves. The wolves were five feet high at the shoulder and snarled savagely, but the giant seemed to be their handler and could quiet them quickly. Guardians such as these were very rare.

When he felt sure of his new form, Kael continued flying farther down the recesses of the cave. Finally, he came to a large circular chamber with many occupants. Fortunately for him, there was a very high ceiling for him to find an acceptable perch, allowing him to observe the entire chamber.

It was here the White Elves finally put down the mysterious box, and then each knelt with their heads low to the ground. One of them opened the sliding door on the side, and from within emerged a woman. *A beautiful woman,* Kael judged from her shape and silhouette.

Kael was limited by the sonar vision of his new form. While it was the perfect form to take to remain concealed, and its acute senses told him where everything and everyone was, he did not have the necessary vision to see details in this form. It would be dangerous to change again; someone would see the flash. He must risk it though. He must know who the woman and the others were. Now would be the time, while they were all standing, and there was a certain degree of chatter among them. He launched himself to a nearby ledge and hid behind a large stalagmite where he transformed in an instant into the form of a small rat.

He crept from behind the sharp formation and cautiously looked down from the ledge. It was a good spot. All appeared to go on as before. His presence apparently unnoticed, he saw the woman now, and his very breath was taken away. He had seen many women in his life, but none like this. Her eyes were a magical emerald green, through which he believed he could see her very soul. Her youthful face conveyed a seriousness, which was validated by the mantle of responsibility that seemed to drape her shoulders like the purple cape she wore. Despite the jewelry that adorned her face, none was needed to highlight the perfect white skin beneath shoulder-length white hair. It was as if nature had taken a dove and given it human form beneath the trappings of clothing and jewelry.

A rounded silver band crossed her forehead through her hair. Obsidian earrings, cylindrical in shape, dangled at her neck to match an ebony necklace. She was a regal beauty who walked without arrogance but with pride as she passed others of her race, who in turn knelt at her feet as she passed. She was perhaps ten years older than Elenari, though he could not be certain. He found himself imagining the hidden feminine curves of her body, though he could not quite see them. If the natural instincts of his animal form had not automatically taken over and dug in with his hind legs, he quite probably would have fallen off the ledge.

It took him a few moments to regain his senses. He was being ridiculous. She was beautiful, yes, but she was in the middle of a dark cave guarded by evil creatures. Though some part of him hoped otherwise, he was sure the purpose of this gathering was not benevolent.

He looked around at the others present. He saw several large, barbaric tribesman, whom he deduced were from Koromundar from the furs they wore and their unkempt manner. In addition, there were dark-robed figures with wrappings about their heads and faces. Next, he saw a group of Orcs, their green pig-like faces giving them away even in the dark. Then he saw an individual that confirmed his worst fears. He was a large soldier with black armor and the symbol of a red Hydra shone on his chest—a Stygian Knight.

Kael watched as they stayed in their respective cliques. They did not speak much with one another; they seemed to be waiting more than anything. There was a large circular stone table within the middle of the cavernous chamber. It seemed to be loosely carved out of the stone from the cave itself. Still, none of them sat, but instead eyed one another curiously and with no great degree of trust, from what Kael could gather from high up on his ledge.

He watched and waited for nearly an hour until suddenly, within the middle of the chamber, there was a great flash of white light. A swirling multicolored vortex appeared, like that of a teleportation spell of some sort. Another dark-robed being appeared through it. His presence clearly caused fear and apprehension throughout those assembled. He seemed to glide as he moved, rather than walk. His head was that of an ivory skull with two red flashes of light for eyes. Atop his head was a shimmering, surreal crown of gold and gems. Kael felt the presence of evil greatly heightened with his arrival. It was at that moment his fears truly seized him, abruptly coming to the surface of his mind with what he saw next.

A second being came through the vortex. Again, he saw a robed, skeletal figure, but this time it was one he knew all too well. The years and time vanished as if he were seeing him for the first time. His robe was brown, trimmed with gold. There was an insignia of the red hydra clearly evident upon his chest. An iron mask covered an unseen face below the hood. He was alive.

It was the Shadow Prince.

Night came as Hawk, Elenari, and Algernon camped along the banks of the Soubia River. Along the river, grasslands and trees flourished again. The sounds of life accompanied them, and the birds of day gave way to the insects of the night.

Hawk found a long, pliable stick and used a bit of string Algernon had given him to fashion a makeshift fishing rod. It was a skill he had developed to near perfection from his many years in the wild. By nightfall, he had caught one fish for each of them.

They reasoned that a fire might be worth a try, since they had traveled another day without incident. Hawk cooked their dinner with the aid of local seasoning he carried in his saddlebags. What would have been a modest meal to most would be a veritable feast for them. The fire, though small, was a welcome comfort against the night air.

Still, Nari was clearly concerned. There had been no sign of Kael. The night was still young, but that did little to ease her worries. While she had hated letting him go, in truth, she was not blind to his daily torment. She knew something had been eating away at him, but now was hardly the time to satisfy his vanity by proving he was still brave and courageous. However, one thing she had learned during her time at the Kenshari Temple was that men have great egos and often felt the need to prove things to themselves or others. Women, while often lacking the ego, suffered from a need to prove they could be equally as skilled warriors as men. She, too, had had her bouts with such feelings, but the Kenshari masters had taught her how to overcome such handicaps. Kael was, however, the Grand Druid, and she accepted that there were certain things he needed to do, whether she agreed or not.

Algernon could see Elenari was clearly worried, as she walked about their little camp, looking in all directions. Hawk had drifted to sleep early after dinner, so Algernon took it upon himself to console her.

"Sit down, my dear, please," he said soothingly. "You mustn't worry about your father. In his day, he defeated a dragon and vanquished the Shadow Prince himself. And that was before the powers of the Grand Druid were bestowed upon him."

Nari smiled and nodded. "I know all that, but he hasn't been himself in some time. He has had frequent nightmares, and I think sometimes he has them in the day as well."

"Indeed. We all have our own inner demons, Nari. At various stages of our lives, we give them more power than we would at other times. Your father is no different from the rest of us in that regard. He is subject to the same weaknesses and fragilities as . . ." Algernon hesitated a moment, as if the words he spoke contained some hidden meaning.

"Algernon . . . are you all right?"

"Yes, child, forgive me; I lost my thoughts for a moment. Suffice to say I have every confidence in your father, despite his problems, as should you. He will come back to us safely. You must believe it; you must have faith." Algernon placed a reassuring hand on her shoulder.

Nari smiled. "Thank you."

She sat cross-legged against a tree to take the first watch. Long after Algernon had fallen asleep, she continued looking out into the blackness of night for any signs of Kael.

Morning greeted them with sunshine and hope; however, the night had come and gone with no sign of Kael. Nari was clearly distraught, though she did her best to conceal it. Algernon and Hawk saw it on her face and thought it best not to dwell on the issue.

Hawk hated seeing her so worried and thought how he might distract her from her concern, even if for a short time. "Well, it appears as if I must catch our breakfast," he said loudly, "since no one else here is capable of doing so."

"What did you just say?" Nari demanded.

"I said it looks like *I'm* going to have to catch our breakfast since *you* obviously don't know how!"

"How dare you?" she said, her tone becoming louder with each passing moment. "I can do anything you can do in the wild, quite probably faster and better."

"We'll bet on that," said Hawk as he walked toward her, pointing his finger at her. "I will wager you . . ." He hesitated and looked at Algernon.

"I'll wager you the finest meal in Averon City that I catch a fish before you do."

"Done."

Nari took her bow and produced additional string from her saddlebag and began to fashion her own fishing pole. Algernon smiled as he sat and began to write in his journal. Except for the absence of Kael, it was a relaxing morning by the river. He found himself feeling at ease, more so than he had been previous days. He was glad Hawk was having success taking Nari's mind off Kael. He felt confident the Druid would appear at any time.

Just as he was about to write in his journal, he caught a glimpse of Hawk casually attaching a fish, which he must have caught before they awoke, to his hook. Nari appeared to be too preoccupied with her own pole to notice. Algernon smiled. *They will make an excellent couple soon,* he thought.

"Are you ready?" Hawk asked, watching her tying a hook to her line.

"Ready when you are."

"Begin," Hawk said as they both cast their lines into the water. At the last moment, Nari spied the fish already hooked on Hawk's line.

"You cheated! I can't believe you cheated like that!"

She dropped her pole and slapped him on the arm. He could do nothing but break out into laughter, as he tried to evade her. She jumped on his back and put her arms around his neck, and although she tried to seem angry, she could not help but join in his laughter. Hawk was thrilled that he had eased her mind, and equally pleased to be so close to her with her arms around him.

The smiles fell from their faces at the sight of the lava creature standing not more than ten feet away, observing them. The gem embedded in its head apparently granted it some sort of sense perception they could not understand.

Nari slid down Hawk's back slowly, staying close to him.

Hawk never took his eyes off the creature as he spoke, "Algernon . . . get on your horse, slowly, and bring our horses toward us as quickly as you can." He held out his arm and backed Nari up toward their campsite.

Nari immediately thought the worst. If the creature was here, then Kael must be dead. Tears fell from her eyes as she drew her short sword and started to step toward the creature.

"No!" Hawk exclaimed. "You cannot; he would not have wanted this, would he?" He grabbed her tightly about the arm, and they continued their backward retreat. "What was the last thing he said to you? To protect the Emerald Star, yes?"

The creature started moving toward them. The gem in its head pulsed brightly twice and its face turned toward Algernon. With that, Hawk grabbed his silver hand axe, slowly arched his arm behind his ear, took aim, and threw it at the creature's head, directly striking the gem with a loud clamor like that of metal against metal. For a moment, the creature fell into itself and dissipated.

They did not hesitate. Hawk and Nari ran for their mounts and, in moments, were away with Algernon. They rode as fast as the animals could travel, following the river southeast, staying close and keeping the river-bank on their right side.

As they raced on, wind in their faces, they saw an incredible sight to their right. It was the creature, in liquid form, traveling through the ground as easily and as fast as their horses, keeping pace with them. It was almost surreal, unimaginable, yet they all saw it. It burned through the ground as easily as they moved through the air. It suddenly had them corralled. They could not break right, and if they broke left, they would be in the river, which would slow the horses but not necessarily the creature. Hawk urged them on, trying to get more speed out of the animals, but it was no use. It was toying with them.

Suddenly the creature overtook them and cut in front of their horses, causing them to stop sharply, rearing up on their hind legs as the riders, out of instinct, abruptly pulled back on their reins. Algernon lost his grip and fell back off his mount, striking the ground with terrible force. Despite the fact that the winds had been knocked out of him, he valiantly attempted to scramble to his feet.

The creature quickly started to form itself. Nari did not hesitate. In almost one motion, she was off her horse and helping Algernon back on to his. Just as the creature completed its manlike form, Nari nimbly leapt back to her steed with inhuman quickness and agility.

Once again, the creature stood only a few feet in front of them. At that moment, to Nari's surprise, Hawk grabbed her hand.

"Nari, listen to me. I want you and Algernon to ride straight ahead, past the creature. Follow the Soubia until you come to the Steel River. It's much larger and has a powerful current. Leap into it if you have to; it will carry you all the way to Averon City," Hawk told her.

"What are you saying? What are you going to do?" In an instant of looking into his eyes, she knew what he had planned. "No! I won't lose both of you to this thing!" Tears streaming down her face, as hopelessness seemed to bring the world crashing down around her. She suddenly felt alone in the world.

"You can protect Algernon better than I can, and you know it." He took her hand and kissed it, as if he could convey all his deep-rooted feelings for her in that one simple show of affection. "Algernon, give me the Emerald Star, quickly, just for a moment!"

Just then, the creature started moving toward Algernon, who quickly passed Hawk the small metal box. In that instant, Hawk freed the green emerald from its box and held it high in the air. He waited until the creature's head turned toward him and pulsed twice with energy. With that, he subtly placed the gem in Nari's hand, looking at her one final time as the creature changed direction toward him. Time seemed to stand still as he looked in her eyes, and despite the tears, he found love, acceptance, and contentment staring back at him.

"By all the gods, you are beautiful. I've always been in love with you. Tell Galin I'll miss him." The creature was almost upon him when he spryly directed Silvermane away and took off, racing in the opposite direction. "Nari, go now!"

Tears blinding her, she spurred her horse and Algernon's forward as Hawk had instructed. They raced to the left with all the strength animals had, while Hawk drew the creature away from them. Nari knew pain and sorrow, like diseased parasites come to ravage her. She wished she had the strength to die.

Hawk urged Silvermane west along the Soubia, skillfully dodging the creature at every turn. Though he could not outrun it, the creature had made several attempts to burn him or slow him, but each time the animal was somehow faster. Silvermane seemed to realize, whether by instinct or the way Hawk guided him, that this was the ride of their lives. If ever Hawk needed his speed, strength, and agility, it was now.

Hawk had to get them as much time and distance as possible. The image of Nari's grief burned into his mind and weighed heavily upon him. He had to focus if he was to be of service to her now. He sensed even Silvermane's dazzling physical prowess was beginning to falter. The animal was tiring and would soon be unable to dodge the creature. Just ahead, Hawk saw his chance. He pulled his legs up so that he was standing on the saddle. His timing would have to be perfect or it would be for naught.

Silvermane approached a large oak tree and, sensing his master's plan, aimed himself at an appropriate branch. At the last second, Hawk jumped from the horse's back onto the oak tree. Immediately he began climbing. He was glad Silvermane would be free and no harm would come to him. He had been an excellent companion, and no man could want more in a horse or friend.

He found himself looking down as he climbed; he saw the creature had formed at the base of the tree and seemed to hesitate, deciding on a course of action. The Ranger continued climbing until he found a spot wherein he was able to wrap himself around the tree tightly. He looked down and saw the creature moving to engulf the trunk of the tree. It took only seconds before he felt it begin to sway. As the tree started to fall, he quickly maneuvered himself to be opposite the point of impact. The tree came crashing down to the earth with horrendous force. As tightly as he held on, the cruel impact bounced him off the tree, forcing him to roll beneath the branches. He tried desperately to get up, but had difficulty breathing and moving for a moment.

Suddenly, the creature was upon him. He was on his back as the leaves crinkled and the branches fell, melting off the body of the tree, exposing him to the creature. There was no escape. Just as the creature was about to touch him, something beyond his comprehension occurred.

From out of nowhere, Silvermane launched himself directly into the creature with such great force that he actually toppled the fiery beast. Hawk sat, catching his breath, watching in utter awe and disbelief at the animal's courage and power. He knew how fearful the horses were of the creature, yet Silvermane willfully sacrificed himself to save him, his master . . . his friend. In seconds, the creature expanded and covered Silvermane, burning him alive. One high-pitched whine was all the horse could manage before a swift death in the molten form of the creature took him.

In shock and anguish, Hawk stood with a renewed anger. A large, thick branch had broken off during the tree's collapse. Instantly, he grabbed for it. Like a man possessed with fury, he charged the creature as it attempted to reform into a standing position. Lashing out, he struck at the gemstone as it rose within the lava causing a terrible sound, turning it a dull brown for a matter of seconds as it collapsed into a puddle.

Two more times, it attempted to rise and form, and Hawk batted it down with all his strength by striking at the gemstone. It was then the puddle that comprised the creature formed around Hawk's feet and legs. It did not matter. He barely felt the intense heat. His wrath shielded him from the pain as he continued striking, even down at the molten puddle where the gem could no longer be seen. He screamed aloud, splashing the lava from side to side with each blow. Still, the lava slowly crept up his legs, consuming him. The extreme heat became excruciatingly painful.

In his mind's eye, he saw Nari's face. This time, there were no tears. There was no sadness or grief. There was only her beautiful smile. Her eyes found his, and he knew she loved him as much as he loved her. At last, he had found peace.

Chapter 16

Kael gaped. Here in the middle of this vast wasteland, he had stumbled upon an unholy gathering headed by his mortal enemy, the Shadow Prince, Wolfgar Stranexx, whom they were all fighting so hard to unite against. Part of him wanted to destroy him now before he could do any more harm, but he did not know if he possessed the necessary power. He could not afford to try and fail.

If he were lucky enough to hear their plans, he knew it may give them the ammunition they would need to stop the Shadow Prince's assault upon Cordilleran, or at the very least help to ally the other nations. Whatever information he could learn here would be invaluable, so he waited and listened.

The dark gathering sat around the circular stone table. Kael wondered who and what the creature sitting next to the Shadow Prince was. Its mere presence caused more fear and apprehension than anyone else present. It appeared almost to be some sort of undead creature, animated by an evil power. When they were all seated and assured of their security, the being Kael had once known as Wolfgar Stranexx spoke. His voice was unchanged from years ago, his tone raspy and hollow as it fought to escape his mask of iron. Kael had always felt his nemesis had struggled to place a human quality to his voice to hide the resonance of death that lingered when he spoke.

"I would like to welcome High Priestess Mya and General Turnia to this table as friends," the Shadow Prince said.

Kael saw he was referring to the beautiful woman he had seen earlier, as well as one of the albino-skinned Elves of her procession next to her.

"They come to us from the underground nation of Rezat'lan," the Shadow Prince continued, *"ancestral home of the White Elves, as allies in our struggle. Like many at this table, they have been wronged for many years. Mistreated,*

267

cast out, and banished to a realm of darkness, devoid of light and warmth. It is the Elves of Alluviam who committed this atrocity, and it is they who will soon be punished for what they have done. It is they who will be cast out and imprisoned in an underground cold darkness. Those who survive—" He paused, allowing the implication of his words to hang in the air.

Mya began to speak. Kael heard a soft beauty in her speech, masked in righteousness. There was a strange, sincere quality to her voice. "Lord Stranexx, we thank you for your welcome and your gracious offer to assist our people. However, we do not wish—"

"Allow me to introduce the Khan of Koromundar, Antar Helan," the Shadow Prince interrupted. "He also rules a great nation, which throughout history has had to wage war just to earn the respect of nations on its borders. He rules a people that too often have been chastised as mindless barbarians, bent on nothing but death and destruction. Each year their borders become smaller, because 'civilized nations' will not negotiate with them due to their appearance, manner of speech, and living habits. No more will they be cast aside or laughed at. Now they will take what has always been theirs. Let the others laugh now."

The Shadow Prince looked to Helan's left, gesturing with his outstretched gloved hand. "There is my ally, the Grand Emir, Aman Rasil, ruler of the desert nation of Jarathadar." He looked at Mya as he continued, "Jarathadar, a desert nation of nomads whom the Dwarves and Elves call bandits and thieves. They choose to live in a harsh land with an inhospitable climate, and because of this, they are labeled as less than other nations, less than other people."

Now the Shadow Prince pointed to Mya's right. "There you see the Mighty Orc Chieftain, Rad Fang. He is not someone you will ever see at any negotiating table, nor will you see his signature on any treaty. Labeled as monsters, animals, and savage brutes by—once again—the 'civilized' races, the Orcs are a proud, noble, and brave people. For centuries, they have been feared, warred upon, and hunted almost to extinction. But now, there is good reason to fear them; they have stopped fighting amongst themselves, replenished their numbers, and united against the common enemy . . . our common enemy. We have all united against your enemy, High Priestess. Any enemy of anyone at this table is an enemy to us all." He placed great emphasis on the last of these words.

Kael was amazed. His reasoning, though twisted, was almost eloquent. His voice, unappealing as it was, became almost hypnotic as he spoke. He could see he was drawing them all in deeper. He could see the woman, Mya, was starting to fall under his sway. The White Elf General seemed whole-heartedly convinced already. Still, he sensed a struggle taking place within the woman.

Much of what the Shadow Prince said was, in fact, correct. Much of it seemed true and even made sense.

"Lord Stranexx, why have you chosen to help all of us?" Mya asked with cunning slyness. "Who are you in all of this, and what do you hope to benefit from it?"

"I am merely a humble prince whose empire is long since dead, the last remnant of a once-great house long bereft of nobility and honor. My nation was destroyed long ago due to its own shortsightedness. I, like my trusted general, Prince Voltan, was a misunderstood soul from the start. Because I was different from others, I became hated and feared and branded a creature, the Shadow Prince, a creature men sought to destroy. And, on more than one occasion, they very nearly succeeded. Now, those who tried have paid the price for their sins."

The Shadow Prince was unable to hide his bitterness in his odd voice, as he continued, *"Prince Voltan, who must hide his true appearance among his people, sits here now, in the open, among you. The righteous would call him a Lich, a creature of evil power to be hated and feared. But what does the word mean, except 'power'? Like myself, he was a great wizard in search of a greater magic and knowledge. However, as both he and I could tell you, such pursuits are not always very forgiving of those who thirst for such knowledge. Hence, our appearances have been forever altered. Power, my friends, is not to be feared. It is neither good nor evil; it simply exits. It just is. I choose to call Voltan friend and ally, as should all here."*

Wrenford, thought Kael, *Voltan destroyed Wrenford.*

The thought of Wrenford and Thargelion snapped him out of the trance-like state that listening to the Shadow Prince's words had placed him in. *He must be using some form of mass charm or hypnosis,* Kael deduced.

The Shadow Prince's evil knew no earthly bounds. He had murdered Thargelion and all the people of Wrenford, and none of his elegant speech would make Kael forget that again. Also, it was Prince Voltan, from Mystaria, in his true form, seated next to him. A lich . . . he had not thought to ever see such a creature in his lifetime. They were undead creatures that existed only in legend. Such creatures existed on the life force of others and wielded terrible powers. They were an affront to Mother Nature and everything Druids stood for. He was as evil as he appeared, and it seemed so even to the others at the table.

His trusted General, the Shadow Prince had said. Things were starting to make sense. If his words were somehow charmed, however, the woman Mya was resistant and clearly not yet convinced of his benevolence. However, with this gathering, he would not need to charm them. Fear would do the convincing for him.

"Where, then, Lord Stranexx, will you be once we've won?" Mya asked, surprisingly without sarcasm. "Once everyone at this table has achieved what they hope to, where will you be? On a throne where we will all come to kneel before you to pay homage?"

General Turnia whispered abruptly into her ear, but she raised her hand to silence him.

"There are some who kneel before me now as a sign of respect and reverence. I do not ask for such deference; however, if that is how some wish to show their thanks and allegiance, then so be it. It was I who brought this table together. It was I who created the plans to give aid to your respective countries. It is I . . . who brings order to chaos."

The Shadow Prince hesitated a moment, realizing he was speaking his thoughts aloud.

"I . . ?" Mya said. "I thought . . . we were all here for our mutual benefit," she said, looking to the others.

The Shadow Prince stared at her for a long moment, and Kael, even in his animal form, sensed he must have been furious behind his mask of iron.

"Excellent," the Shadow Prince said. *"However, you will see that I do not sit on a high chair or at the head of this table. Instead, I sit among equals. I sit among friends. There is a new order coming to the world as you know it. All of us will prosper from it together. Yes, there must be a ruler in every new order. I put it to all of you: who would you have it be? I will stand by your decision."*

Almost in a unanimous voice, their response came immediately: "Lord Stranexx should rule!"

Unassumingly, the Shadow Prince held his hands in the air as if accepting a burden he did not wish to bear. He faced Mya, who had not yet responded.

"In some new orders, there is a council that rules," she said slowly. She was playing a very dangerous game, challenging him before the others.

The Shadow Prince folded his gloved hands on the table before him. When he spoke, his voice was almost sad. *"You shall be my council. All of you present here. I will merely assist you when and where I can as you rule your own nations, which will become larger and have a voice that will be heard. This is what I offer: friendship and cooperation. For the White Elves, I offer an existence on the surface, above the subterranean darkness in which your children will be born. What would your people give for that, I wonder? Treasures? Gold? Their lives? I instead ask only for your friendship and cooperation with the others here. If we stay true to one another, then all can achieve what they wish for. Is that so high a price to pay for what you wish?"*

"No . . . it is not," Mya replied reluctantly.

"Then do the White Elves join our alliance in cooperation with all the nations represented here?" the Shadow Prince asked.

"General Turnia speaks for the warrior caste, and I speak for the religious caste," Mya replied, bowing her head, "and we would be honored to join with those assembled in the new order with you as its leader, Lord Stranexx."

"My friends, please join me in welcoming new friends and new allies to our table."

The Shadow Prince clapped his hands, and soon the remainder of the table followed suit. As the applause ceased, Lord Stranexx seemed to shift to a new order of business. *"Now, Prince Voltan, the commanding general of all my armies, will report our current status."*

Voltan as well had a voice that sounded strained when he spoke in the common tongue. He, however, unlike the Shadow Prince, made no attempt to sound human; he sounded sinister as he appeared, his tone eerie and hollow. *"The invasion of Cordilleran has begun. We have four times their number. They will fall quickly. Their lands will be divided among Koromundar, Jarathadar, and the Orcs. The treasures as well will be equally divided. Any Dwarves taken as prisoners will be sent to Mystaria, as per our previous arrangement with Mystaria and Koromundar.*

"In a separate matter, there is somewhat disturbing news: The Sage, Algernon, escaped the Kingdom of Wrenford with a band of men, two Druids, and two Rangers. They made it to Mystaria, where they attempted to convince the ruling council to join an alliance against us. He knows of Lord Stranexx's return. The council voted them down; however, it is likely they will go to Averon and Alluviam next. It is also likely that they carry the mystical Emerald Star with them."

"What is the Emerald Star?" Emir Rasil asked.

"And who is this Algernon?" the Orc chieftain grunted.

"The Emerald Star is an enchanted emerald gemstone of enormous power," the Shadow Prince replied. "Any nation that possesses it will be invulnerable to invasion. Any army that attacks a nation so equipped will be annihilated. Algernon is the former High Councilor of Wrenford. He is a Sage of great renown. He had retired to live the life of a hermit in the hills of Renarn. However, it appears he has chosen once again to meddle in affairs that don't concern him. He is an old man, with no magic powers, who should have died many years ago."

"We must send a force out to find these men and kill them, quickly, before they can get this Emerald Star to Alluviam," General Turnia burst out in panic. "Before we can carry out any plans, we must know—"

"Calm yourself, General," the Shadow Prince commanded. "There is no need to be alarmed or concerned about a pitiful little band of five alone in the wilderness. Do you truly think one old man and his little group of adventurers can stand against the might assembled here? They have already failed in Mystaria, thanks to Prince Voltan, and they will not live long enough to attempt to rally any more support to their misguided cause. I have sent something, more powerful and deadly than any force of arms you can think of, to dispatch them and bring the Emerald Star to me. Soon its powers and mysteries will be unlocked to serve us."

Mya spoke up, again in such a fashion as to conceal any hint of sarcasm. "Interesting how the Emerald Star is to be brought to *you*, but yet its powers will serve *us*. How do we know you won't use this Emerald Star to make yourself invincible to attack, and thereby free to impose your will upon all—even us, your friends?"

Kael was beginning to like this woman more and more, and noticed that even Prince Voltan took notice of this particular question, and looked at the Shadow Prince, anticipating his answer.

"*High Priestess, when you come to this council, you come with an open heart. You come ready to trust those who are seated on both sides of you. They must come to trust you. I trust each of you unconditionally, and I ask the same of you. Can you give me this trust?*" the Shadow Prince asked.

Kael noticed there were distinct differences in the Shadow Prince's voice. This was not the Wolfgar Stranexx of old; he had tremendous patience now. He spoke with a calm and cautious demeanor, which seemed to make the listeners want to trust him. There were familiar moments where his ego became apparent, but there were other forces at work here. Perhaps something was influencing him. He was almost charming, which he had never been before.

"Yes," Mya replied, "I will trust you and the others here . . . unconditionally, and I will have an open heart. But, as friends, we can still question one another to insure understanding, yes?"

"*How well you phrase it, High Priestess,*" the Shadow Prince replied. "*Of course . . . questions are always welcome so that we all clearly understand one another.*"

"Then you have my trust and that of the White Elves," Mya replied. "Please continue."

The Shadow Prince bowed his head forward in response, then continued to address the assembly as a whole. "*Cordilleran will soon fall. Next we will deal with Averon and Alluviam. With the help of our new White Elf allies and the spies we already have in place, we shall create a trade war between these two nations. We shall then escalate the situation so that open hostilities break out between them. Then, while they are both weakened, we shall strike them hard and fast. Once we have Averon, we will control the merchant guilds and all trade routes. We will sign new trade pacts with the nations assembled here and then we shall cut off trade to the nations south before we advance toward them.*"

"My Lord," Voltan interjected, "*there is talk of a new Great Southern Trade Route from Averon City, which will extend via waterways to the Kingdom of Arcadia and the Kingdom of Bastlandia. It is said that it will be a self-sufficient trade route and, while Averon will profit greatly from it, control will* rest with southern nations as far south as the islands of the Trade Federation. It will be a source of incalculable wealth for those involved. Such wealth could be used to challenge us. The mighty fleets of Arcadia will protect it. The only way we can attack south of Averon is by water."

"Ah, yes," the Shadow Prince replied. "I believe King Zarian of Bastlandia conceived this new trade route, hoping it would insure peace between all the island kingdoms. Then so shall we have mighty fleets to engage them, my friend."

"My lord," Voltan said, "even if we began construction today, it would take months or even years before we had vessels that were battle ready. In addition, we would have to recruit experienced seamen to crew them."

"We began construction, my lord prince, over a year ago. Fear not; we shall have quite a surprise in store for the fleets of Arcadia. For security reasons, the location of our ships shall remain secret for now. You must all forgive me; I look too far ahead into our future. We have much to do yet in the here and now."

The Shadow Prince paused and looked toward the White Elves. "General Turnia, we will need you to form two patrols disguised as Elves from Alluviam. These patrols must block the overland trade routes north and east from Averon. They must be well armed. All merchant caravans will be stopped and their cargo confiscated in the name of King Aeldorath of Alluviam. They will only attack if the merchants resist . . . for now. This will prompt a diplomatic response and that will take time.

"We have already made arrangements for an army of Ogres to attack and destroy some of Averon's border forts. You have told me High Priestess, that you hold surface Elves in your dungeons. We shall need their dead bodies and weapons to be scattered among the ruins of the fort. Simultaneously, we shall arrange for one of the villages outside Alluviar to be destroyed. It shall appear as if the Sentinels of Averon were responsible in retaliation for their forts being attacked. We will let them attack each other, and when the time is right, we shall invade them."

The assembly responded to this with enthusiastic nods of approval.

"High Priestess Mya, General Turnia, I would like the honor of addressing your people personally before the invasion of Alluviam," the Shadow Prince continued. "Our armies will join with yours, and we shall defeat the Elves together. Gather your forces within the caves on the outskirts of the Elven village *of Dragontree. Once our plans have taken root, it shall be there that next we meet. Until then, please coordinate your forces with General Lord Voltan. Success to us all, my most valued friends."*

The Shadow Prince rose and bowed to his right and left. In turn, those assembled stood and bowed to him. As before, the Shadow Prince and Voltan quickly made their way to the back of the chamber and disappeared as before in a flash of light. The others departed the table without further conversation and headed toward the mouth of the cave with their respective guards. Kael waited until the chamber was completely empty before crawling down.

He looked once more to ensure that he was alone. He wanted to study the chamber to see if there was anything he was missing. He would have to be quick; he needed to get back to the others. Nari would be quite worried by now, and he would feel better once he knew they were well and safe. This was the fortune they had been waiting for—just the turn of luck they needed to convince the other nations to join them. He was curious if this dark confederacy moved around to meet, or if this was a place they used frequently. When he felt sure he was alone, he changed to his human form in a flash of green fire.

He moved around the chamber, looking for anything that could be useful. There did not appear to be any secret entrances. He studied the stone table and bent down to look beneath it.

Something hard and heavy came crashing down on the back of his neck. It was the last thing he felt before darkness took him.

Elenari and Algernon rode like the wind. For Nari, the travel was purely mechanical. Tears continued rolling down her face. She was numb. The only thing that still drove her was the last request of the two men she had loved most in the world. She had lost them both in one day. All the physical and mental disciplines she learned among the Kenshari had not prepared her for this. Part of her hoped the creature would catch up to them before they reached the river.

The horses had been well-rested and were prepared to sustain a prolonged run. The sun was shining through fair skies troubled by only a slight breeze, but the animals knew what it was that hunted them, and they would run until death took them before they would quit.

They rode alongside the Soubia River throughout the remainder of the morning and straight into the afternoon before they stopped for a break. They stopped the horses, allowed them to drink, but they did not dismount. So far, there had been no sign of the creature in pursuit, but they stayed ready in case they had to move quickly.

Algernon broke the uncomfortable silence, "Elenari . . . I am sorry. Never have I known two finer or braver men. We do not know for sure about your father, but we mustn't lose hope. If we lose faith—"

"Do not speak to me about faith or hope again, Algernon!" Elenari spat. "I'm sick of it! I had faith and hope in one man throughout most of my life. I never thought to fall in love; I never thought to have faith and hope in a second man. They're dead now! They're both dead! You cling to your faith and hope if you wish; mine has died with them." She looked down at the ground and pulled her reins to move her horse away from Algernon's. "We need to go."

Algernon decided not to reply; any further discussion at this point would no doubt be fruitless. Elenari needed time to grieve, but he would cling to his hope—his hope that their quest was not in vain and those who had died did so trying to achieve something greater than themselves. So many had died now as a result of his and Thargelion's plan that he had begun to question it himself.

He thought of the Shadow Prince as they continued along at the gallop. This darkness was ahead of them at every turn. The enemy's plan was so complete and so perfect that there seemed no limits to its cunning and ingenuity. This was a master strategist they faced. He remembered, ages ago it seemed, when last he had faced such a master. All he could do was hope that what had happened then would not come to pass now, that somehow they could stop it.

He laughed to himself. How dare he give himself such credit, or perhaps he gave the enemy too much credit. Why did he see the enemy's plan as so masterful? Because he could not figure out its nuances? Was it because he, an old retired hermit and Thargelion, an old King of a small kingdom, could not outwit its implementation?

As they continued under the refuge of the trees near the river, he began to formulate a new plan for dealing with the Shadow Prince. The noon sun was scorching, and he began perspiring considerably, but it didn't bother him—in fact, it helped fuel his thought process. Until now, they had been trying to play it safe, fighting only on the defensive, struggling to stay alive. They had accepted defeat in Mystaria, as the Shadow Prince must have known they would. They needed a strategy that would take him by surprise. The time for running and escaping would soon be at an end.

Nari rode in silence; her tears had dried and had been replaced with sweat. How could a day that had begun with such possibility have deteriorated into despair and loss even before noon? She had never felt so alone before, even in those years growing up in the temple or throughout the long stretches of time that had passed between visits from Kael. Now she felt a burning emptiness that she had never known.

Why do men and women hide their feelings from one another? She thought to herself. *Was it some sick game they played so each could save face? Did they behave this way so one of them could say they were not the first to admit their feelings for the other?*

She had allowed herself to play this game of love with Hawk. She had lived most of her life alone in the wilderness with the trees and animals, but this morning, she had envisioned what her life would be like if shared with another. She had wondered what it would feel like to walk hand in hand with Hawk or to sit by a fire being held by him. She had dreamed about building a house with him and what it would be like to be loved so unconditionally.

This was the kind of love she had seen in his eyes when he had looked at her. Each time his eyes had met hers, the look therein had made it seem like it was the first time he was seeing her. It had been almost intoxicating, but she had kept her defenses up and pretended not to notice so many times. In the tradition of the foolish game, she had played her part, never showing too much emotion, never allowing him to get closer. What a foolish, stupid game it was. If she saw him now, she would gladly throw her arms around him and kiss him passionately for all to see and proclaim her love for him from here to the highest mountain peak.

As ready as she was now, he would never hear it. Never would she play this game of love again.

She remembered with crystal clarity the night Kael had first found her. Her Elven half gave her the capacity to remember events from as far back as her childhood with an unclouded certainty that humans did not possess. It had been very cold that night in the forest. The raven had led him to her under the light of the full moon. She could almost feel the warmth of his body, as she remembered it. She heard the soothing tone of his voice, assuring her that everything would be all right now.

He had become the only father she would ever know. She had had teachers at the Kenshari Temple she had greatly respected and even revered, but she loved Kael like a daughter loved a father. She had spent her whole life training to live alone despite Kael, and now she so desperately needed him. If only she could tell him how grateful she was for all he had done, for he had loved her, unconditionally, as a father should.

She could feel herself slipping deeper into a barren darkness that would soon overwhelm her. She barely sensed Algernon's presence beside her.

It was midafternoon when they first saw the rapids of the mighty Steel River ahead in the short distance. It was at least fifty yards wide, and its current was extremely powerful, as Hawk had said. Its waters ran due south, emptying straight into Averon City, their destination and sanctuary. The horses were completely spent; even their stalwart determination and enduring courage could not move them any further without endangering their lives.

They dismounted, and Elenari collapsed to a sitting position with her legs crossed and head down. Algernon quickly examined the outlying branches of several nearby trees, excitedly looking for a width of branch that met his approval. When he was satisfied that he had found some branches that would be adequate for their needs, he moved near Elenari.

"Nari," he said gently, "you must get up. The animals can do no more for us. They'll die if we ride them any further. We must make a raft . . . something to keep us afloat down the river to Averon City. I think I found some branches we can tie together to support us on the river."

"Good, a raft," Nari replied, but she neither rose nor lifted her head.

"Nari," Algernon cried, "I need you to help me cut the branches and tie the raft together! Quickly; we don't know how much time we have! We must work fast! Come, get up!"

Reluctantly, she rose and slowly followed him. He pointed out the branches of a nearby tree that he thought would serve their needs and asked her to cut them down. She used her short sword and easily cut three branches, approximately five feet in length apiece. Algernon produced a last strand of rope from his saddlebags he had been saving for just such an emergency. Nari sat back down again as soon as her task was complete. Algernon tied the branches together as best he could.

When the makeshift raft was complete, he went to the horses, patted them, and gave them the last of the sugar cubes he had been sparingly rewarding them with.

"Thank you my friends. May you fare well in your journeys for you have made ours safer."

Finally, he took his great tome and with a few arcane gestures he conjured a small spell of protection over the book. Once he was sure it was airtight, he motioned to Elenari. Again, in a zombie-like fashion, she got up and walked with him. He lifted her chin abruptly with his hand, forcing her to look at him.

"Nari, we have to hold on very tight to the branches and try to stay in the middle of the current. Do you understand?"

"I understand," she said, as if answering involuntarily.

He shook his head; he knew they did not have time to argue. She helped him lift the branches, and they walked to the river's edge and jumped in as carefully as possible.

Immediately the current took them. It was difficult at first, but they both managed to hang on to the branches while keeping their heads above water. The current tugged and pulled at them, and the water dashed into their faces and mouths.

Algernon slipped once, but Nari quickly grabbed him by the arm before he was lost to the current and guided his hands back to the branches. He looked at her in gratitude but saw only barren blankness in her expression. She was reacting as if her reflexes had a mind of their own. He was an old man, too old for this kind of thing, but he was greatly concerned for her. He was losing her to the unconscious world. She was retreating to some dark place within herself, and soon no one would be able to reach her.

Finally, the initial violence of the current subsided, and they found an ideal spot within the middle of the river where they maintained a calm but swift pace. If they continued at this speed, by nightfall, they would be in Averon City.

Kael awoke suddenly. As he brought himself up, he was just as quickly forced back down. His vision was blurry, but he knew he was in a cramped position. His arms were tied behind his back and a gag had been fitted tightly around his mouth. He found himself within a very narrow enclosed space.

His eyes focused to find a silver boot pressed up against his neck. His eyes followed the line of the leg upward, and seated before him was the beautiful, albino-skinned Elven High Priestess, Mya. He sensed they were moving, though not by their own power. There was an oil lamp lit by her head, illuminating the inside of a boxy space. It was the large box that he had seen from the air. Mya was seated in short chair with large pillows, and he lay at her feet.

He watched as she brought her finger to her lips. In a whisper, she spoke. "I do not think you would want my men to know that you are awake. I suggest that you move as little as possible. If you keep your voice to a slight whisper, I shall remove your gag; however, if you attempt any spell, you will be killed—and rather quickly, I should think. Do I have your word you will attempt no action of any kind?"

He now began to feel a throbbing pain at the base of his skull. He tried ever so slightly to change his position so that he was more upright. Mya relaxed her leg just enough for him to straighten himself, but she kept her boot against his neck. He nodded a promise to keep his voice down, so she leaned forward and removed the gag from his mouth. He immediately attempted to speak, but was quickly stopped by the pressure of her boot as she pressed it hard against his neck, barely allowing him to breathe.

"Remember," she chastened, "light whispering. I ask the questions, not you. You give any answers I don't like, the gag goes right back on. Do you understand?"

He nodded slowly.

"Now . . . I know *what* you are, but I need to know *who* you are. What is your name?"

"How do you know—?" The pressure of her boot against his neck choked him before he could complete the question.

"I will tell you for the last time: I ask the questions. Who are you?"

"A . . . Druid . . . who . . . wandered into the wrong place at the wrong time."

"I hardly believe that," Mya replied. "What is your name? I will not ask again."

He hesitated, but as uncomfortable as he was, he found her breathtaking to look at. He did not realize he was staring at her.

"What are you looking at?" she demanded, nudging his throat with her boot.

"Forgive me . . . I have never seen an Elf like you before, my lady. My name is Kael Dracksmere."

The words seemed to roll off his tongue, but a moment later, he could not believe he had just told her his real name. He feared that he quite probably signed his own death warrant, but somehow lying to her felt wrong. Telling her the truth, however, was surely idiotic at best.

"I am a White Elf," Mya said. "Our skin may be different, but do not think us less deadly than our surface-dwelling cousins."

"Quite . . . the contrary . . . my lady," he gasped. "I've no doubt."

"Do not mock me, Druid." She pressed her boot hard against his neck, threatening to choke him fully. Then suddenly, a moment later, she removed her boot from his throat.

"We will talk more later," she said as she put the gag back around his mouth. "Rest while you can."

He sensed something distinctly about her in that moment. He sensed she was sorry for her behavior. She seemed visibly disturbed. His suspicions were confirmed beyond doubt a moment later when she leaned forward and placed a pillow on the floor of the box and eased his head down onto it with her hand.

This is not an evil woman, he thought.

Instantly, his rational mind rebelled. She was in league with the Shadow Prince! He wrestled with his thoughts, wondering where they were going. Perhaps her beauty had forced him to superimpose positive characteristics in her that he wanted to see, rather than what was truly present. He could not be sure.

Chapter 17

Mekko found himself encircled by fifty war-weary soldiers, mostly young men, some even boys, with fear plastered on their faces. He could see their lips quivering with uncertainty. They refused to run or retreat, which did them great credit, but he had not come here to lead Averon's soldiers to die against impossible odds.

Yet Galin, for good or ill, had introduced him as the General of the armies of Cordilleran. Though he was dressed little better than a peasant, some of the older ones had heard of him and they treated him with awe and great respect. They looked to him, a battle-hardened soldier and a man of great experience to lead and inspire them.

He desperately wanted to leave for Cordilleran. He did not have time for this. Still, they had asked him to assist, these fellow soldiers who were either too proud or too dumb to abandon their posts. How could he turn his back on them? How could he leave them alone to face the overwhelming force coming for them? He owed them at least as much respect as they had given him.

They stared at him, pleading with their eyes and hoping he could give them some type of plan that would forestall their deaths until help could arrive to save them.

"Have you ever had occasion to observe the beasts of nature, lads?" he asked them in his gruff manner.

They looked at one another strangely and then back at him in silence. Not one of them fully comprehended what he was asking, and most of them were too afraid to guess.

"Specifically, have you ever watched a bear in the wild?" Mekko asked.

Again, they looked at one another wordlessly and then back at him.

"Now, the bear, one of the largest predators of the forest, has a soft spot for honey, you see. Even the largest bear, lads, will walk right up and stick his snout, without fear, into a nest of bees to get that taste of honey. The bees start flyin' like all hell around his big head and start stingin' him for all their worth. The bear, he just keeps stickin' his snout in the nest, pullin' out the honeycombs, happy as a clam because the stings don't penetrate his thick skin and fur. But when one of those bees stings 'em square on the nose, you'll see that bear pull out and run away from those little bees.

"That's what we're gonna do to those Ogres, lads,—sting 'em bad enough on the nose that they run away. Now, then, we have a hell of a lot to do lads and very little time to do it . . . are you ready to go to work?"

They nodded, smiling. "Yes, General."

"Well, let's get to it, then," Mekko declared. "First damn thing, someone get me a shirt, some chain mail, and a battle-axe." One of the young men hurried away to do, as he asked, "Who's the ranking officer here?"

He watched as a young man, probably in his early twenties, walked forward. He was tall and lean but had a sullen expression and hunched a bit. He brushed the chestnut hair from his face, but his dark eyes remained on the ground when he addressed Mekko. "That would be me, sir," the young man said softly. "Roland Denataunt, Corporal of the Watch, sir."

"All right, lads, gather 'round and listen up," Mekko barked, placing his hands behind his back in a posture of authority. "Effective immediately Corporal Denataunt is receiving a field promotion to acting Lieutenant."

A thin, dark-haired young man spoke up in a broken, scared voice, "Ah, excuse me, General? This is the army of Averon, the Sentinels of Averon, sir. Do you . . . have authority to grant promotions?"

Mekko gave the young man a look of disgust and marched briskly right up to him. "So, this is the army of Averon, is it? Stand at attention, man, when I address you!" He watched as the man immediately straightened up. Without looking away, he spoke to the now-Lieutenant. "Acting Lieutenant Denataunt, do you surrender command of the fort to me?"

Denataunt hesitated a moment, looking at the men, and then replied, "Yes, General, I . . . surrender command of the fort to you."

Mekko glared into the face of the dark-haired young man, raising his voice to a bellow. "Good! I accept command. This just became a Dwarven fort under my command. That means every one of you just became, for the time bein', members of the Dwarven army. Do you understand that, sir?"

The young man nodded vigorously. "What's your name, lad? Come on, out with it!"

"Ranoulf, sir," he said, looking straight and trying his best to stand at attention and not to appear as afraid as he clearly was.

"Well then, Mr. Ranoulf, if myself or Lieutenant Denataunt says 'jump,' you bloody well better ask 'how high?' Do I make myself clear?"

"Yes, sir," Ranoulf answered, trying his best not to anger him any further. "Crystal clear sir."

"I said," Mekko shouted, glaring at all of them, "do I make myself clear?"

The ragged army snapped to attention. "Yes sir, General!" they answered in unison.

"That's bloody well better," Mekko said. "Very well, then. Lieutenant, form four companies! I want two details outside the fort, two details inside. Understood?"

"Yes, sir," came the reply.

Denataunt divided the men into four groups as Mekko had asked. Once the men had taken their places, he quickly reported back to Mekko, whom he found dressing for battle in a white shirt and a coat of chain mail. Mekko motioned for Denataunt to come close to him so he could whisper in his ear.

"Listen, son, you know this promotion is not goin' to mean a good tinker's damn to the Sentinels when they arrive, but these men need one of their own to lead them and give them courage. That's you. Now stop slouchin', stand up straight, and for god's sake, look the men in the eyes when you address them! That includes me, understood?"

The young man quickly straightened and looked Mekko in the eye. "Yes, sir. Thank you, sir."

"Very good," replied Mekko, impressed. "Then carry on, Lieutenant."

Mekko pulled a few soldiers from each of the four companies and immediately sectioned them off in groups with different tasks. He instructed one group to chop wood and make two-foot long spikes and another group to dig ditches of about five feet by five feet in strategic locations in the ground around the palisade. He explained to the men and boys that these were called killing pits. They would secure a few of spikes, points upward, in the bottom of each of the pits and cover the holes up with scalps of dirt and grass.

He assigned a third group to repair the perimeter walls and construct new walls inside the fort. He explained that if the Ogres could be driven or corralled, much like horses, where they wanted them to go, they could attack them on their terms. The fourth group he enlisted was assigned to widen the existing archers' platforms against the perimeter fence and to build additional ones as well.

Mekko passed one of the young men sharpening spikes for the pits and saw that he was putting all of his strength into trying to make the edges as sharp as possible. *Hard workers, these boys,* he thought. They impressed him greatly. They were young but surprisingly well trained and refreshingly disciplined; there was not a lazy one in the lot. All of them worked hard and were fast learners. Mekko bent beside the boy.

"Hey, boy, easy does it now. The spikes just need a little bit of an edge, lad. See, the Ogre's weight is what makes the pits work." Mekko used his hands to help illustrate. "The monster falls, and his own weight will push the spike through his body, no matter how dull the tip, from the fall alone. You follow, lad?"

The boy nodded.

"Good; you'll get twice as many done, now that you know you don't have to make 'em so sharp. That's good work, lad. Just a little overkill for the job is all." He smiled and gave the young man a strong pat on the back and continued on.

Mekko had found the largest cooking pot they had and rigged it over a fire. He had then ordered the men to pour all the cooking oil, lantern oil, and any other oil they had in their stores into the pot. He lit a fire beneath the pot, and when he was satisfied with the size and depth of the flames, he went out to find the boy he had seen when they first arrived.

The boy had appeared especially young—no doubt a visitor or one of the older men's children never meant to be there. He found him out in the field, helping the others dig the ditches. The boy couldn't have been much past puberty, but he pulled his weight and worked as hard as the rest.

"You there!" Mekko called to him. "Young lad! What's your name?"

"Josh Animar, sir," the boy answered as he dropped his shovel to salute Mekko.

"You come with me, laddie. I've a very important job for you."

Mekko walked the boy back to the kitchen area of the dining hall where he had kept the great pot filled with oil.

"Now then, lad, this fire must never go out, no matter what happens. I need this fire to keep going twenty-four hours a day, son. The men could need hot oil at any moment to drive back the monsters from the wall. Also, I want you to find any type of pot or container you can find and have 'em ready and standin' by. Should you go to sleep, do it with one eye open."

"Am I not to fight, sir, with the others?" the boy asked, a hint of wounded pride in his voice. "I can fight, sir, as good as any man in the fort, I can."

Mekko took a moment and looked at the boy. He wore a child-sized suit of chain mail; some of the men must have crafted it for him. He had a hunting knife at his side, which he wore in a scabbard like a sword. He was a fine-looking boy, fair haired and fair skinned. He was small, even for his age, but he had a stout heart and character, not unlike many of the Dwarf children he so reminded Mekko of.

"Now you listen, laddie," the General replied gently, "this is the fort's defenses we're talking about. If that fire goes out and an attack comes, the fort will bloody well fall without oil to pour down on those Ogres. This is much more important than just fightin'. All the men are going to be countin' on you and so am I. Are you fit for such a responsibility, lad, or should I find someone better suited, you think?"

The boy stood straight at attention and promptly saluted. "Absolutely not, sir. You can count on me, General."

"I know I can, lad. I know I can. Carry on, boy, keep a close eye on that fire and do whatever you have need to . . . and keep it lit."

"Yes, sir," Josh replied, as he dutifully carried out his task. "Thank you, sir."

Next, Mekko found Denataunt, and they went out in the field several yards past where the men were digging the killing pits. Mekko stopped when he felt the distance and ground were right.

"Right here, Lieutenant," Mekko said, pointing to the surrounding ground. "I want the men to dig five holes. I want them to dig five holes, the same distance from the perimeter wall in all four directions. These are going to be different than the killing pits. These are going to be about two feet deep and as long as the men who will lie in them."

"Sir?"

"We're going to bury five men approximately this distance from the wall in each direction. We're gonna leave 'em just enough space to breathe. Each man will have a sword and no armor. The men will be concealed in the dirt. Once the Ogres attack and pass the buried men; that will be when they rise up—outta their graves, as it were—and attack the Ogres from behind. Not just attack, mind you; I want these men to strike them precisely at the back of the Ogre's knees, as many as they can. Ogres are anywhere from eight to ten feet tall; take out the back of their knees, and they'll drop like stones. May even be able to take a few heads while they're at it."

Mekko slapped Denataunt on the back. "Now the key to this, son, is the men in these holes have to be stomach down. On the chance the Ogres march over 'em, it will only likely impact 'em into the ground a bit. If they're stomach up and get stepped on by an Ogre, it could kill 'em or seriously injure them. These beasts are upward of three hundred fifty pounds, and that's on the light end. You follow me, Lieutenant?"

He watched as the young man nodded enthusiastically. From there, they walked back to the fort to check on the progress of the archers' platforms up against the inside of the perimeter wall.

"Lieutenant, I want two archers on each platform—that's twelve plat-forms, twenty-four men. Now, if the Ogres were smart, they'd attack the fort from all four directions; however, I'm bettin' they're dumb as a stump on a rock and will probably attack from only one, maybe two, directions. When that happens, lad, I want the archers on the other platforms to con-verge on the platforms on the two walls being attacked. That will give us at least five archers on those platforms we're extendin', and leave extra men to go and get hot oil to pour over the wall—and to assist me, should the wall be breached."

"Yes sir, I understand." The boy replied excitedly.

"All right, then. Last points of business, lad. Come with me." Mekko beckoned him to follow outside the fort. "Now, Roland, we need an alarm system—a silent alarm system. I want you to find the five fastest men we have. They need to leave their armor and carry only a short sword. We're goin' to spread 'em out a hundred yards from the fort about twenty-five yards apart, with the very fastest lad bein' closest to the fort. So if one spots something, he runs to the next closest lad, you see, and so on, 'til the fastest boy runs to the fort and warns us. You follow me, son?"

"Yes, General," Denataunt answered.

"Then hop to it, lad," Mekko ordered. "Get that warning system in place, then report back to me when it's done."

Mekko could see the confidence building in the boy's eyes as he saluted and rushed to carry out his orders.

These young men work fast, he thought. There was little else he could do to prepare them or the fort in the time they had left. He hoped it would be enough to keep them alive until Galin arrived with reinforcements. He looked south into the distance.

Algernon awoke as someone pulled him onto the riverbank. His arms were wrapped around his tome like a vise. He coughed suddenly, as the taste of river water remained in the back of his throat. With another free hand he grabbed the Emerald Star unseen just to make sure it had stayed with him.

It was nighttime. There were several men pulling him. Immediately he looked for Nari. She was there, next to him, unconscious. He started for her to make sure she was all right. The men quickly restrained him. One of them spoke then, and his voice was strong and honest.

"Easy, old man; she's all right. She swallowed a lot of water, but she's breathing. She should be fine with some rest. You are safe now. My name is Arthur. I'm Captain of the Watch. These men are with the Sentinels of the Republic of Averon. You're in Averon City."

"My name is Algernon," the Sage replied weakly, barely able to speak. "This woman and I . . . are here on the business of the King of Wrenford. We must see . . . the Merchant Guild Council."

"Well," the Captain replied. "We're going to get you to some quarters with some warm clothes and a fire. Your business is going to have to wait until you're in better condition, sir."

Algernon allowed himself to collapse. They had made it to Averon City. That much, at least, he was thankful for.

Kael awoke in complete darkness. The air was dank and stale. He could see absolutely nothing. There was not even a hint of illumination. His hands were still tied behind his back, but he felt they had been retied, as they were extremely tight and all he could feel of his hands and fingers was a prickly numbness. The gag remained around his mouth. He tried to move his legs and they, too, were bound at the ankles. His captors were taking no chances with him.

There had been no further communication between him and the High Priestess. He did, however, vaguely recall that, at some point, she had sprinkled a powder over his face, which had no doubt put him to sleep. He listened, and strangely enough found that he could not hear anything either, besides the scraping of his boots against what was probably the stone floor he was lying on and the sound of his breathing and heartbeat. Unfortunately, his pillow, as well, was gone.

He had no concept of how much time had gone by. He thought of Elenari. By now, she probably thought him dead or worse. The unpleasant thought of whether she was still safe, as well as the others, entered his mind. Here, in the darkness, he could not allow himself to contemplate such things. With any luck, she was in Averon City by now, with Algernon and Hawk. Hopefully Galin had reached Alluviam, and Mekko was back in Cordilleran.

Well, he thought, *what a brilliant idea this turned out to be.* It was almost laughable. In fact, were he not gagged, he felt sure he *would* be laughing at the perfect stupidity of it. He had overheard all this wonderful information, had actually seen their greatest enemy, and had heard his deepest plans, and yet he felt certain he would not live long enough to tell the tale. At this very moment, the Shadow Prince was no doubt plotting his demise. Mya had surely informed him by now of Kael's capture, since he had been fool enough to tell her his name.

Mya . . . the beautiful woman who so enamored him. He wondered if he had indeed made a connection with her. What motives could such a woman possibly have for joining with such evil as the likes of the Shadow Prince and his Lich General, Voltan? She clearly sensed their evil; Kael had seen it in her eyes. She was not deceived by their compelling lies.

Kael had not seen any sign of wickedness when he had looked into her eyes. She was his only hope, his only chance of survival and escape. He had to try to reach her. She knew he was as Druid; he had to find out what else she knew. He had to tell her what the Shadow Prince was doing and what he would do to her people after he was finished using them. If only he could see her again before his death.

Algernon awoke this time in the comfort of a bed. It was a comfort he seemed to have almost forgotten and sorely missed. He found himself alone in small but more-than-adequate quarters with a small fireplace near the bed. The cold of the river still lingered in his bones.

He thought of Elenari. He hoped that she would wake in a better state than last he'd seen her in. She was becoming lost in a depression that could consume her if nothing was done. He had to think of something to stir her out of it. It was a task he considered with no great fondness or anticipation, nor was it one that could be easily shirked.

He looked to the small chest of drawers near his bed where a dry black cloak and robe had been provided for him. Atop the chest were his tome and the metal box containing the Emerald Star. He quickly sat up and examined both items to insure they had withstood the river with no damage.

He quickly dressed. He had to check on Nari. As he opened the doors to his quarters, a young man in chain mail was standing guard. He turned quickly to address Algernon.

"Good evening, sir," he said. "How are you feeling?"

"Much better, thanks to your hospitality," Algernon replied. "I'd very much like to see the young woman who was with me, if I may."

The young soldier opened the door to the adjacent quarters and motioned for Algernon to look inside.

He saw Elenari sleeping soundly. The young man whispered to Algernon, "She moaned a few times in her sleep, but has yet to wake, sir."

Algernon saw no reason to wake her prematurely. "Thank you."

"I've instructions to bring you downstairs to have you fed. After such time, the Captain of the Guard will come to see you. After me, sir, if you will."

The young soldier led him down nearby stairs to a mess hall of sorts, where Algernon was served generous portions of a hot meal and wine. He found that he possessed a voracious appetite. There was chicken and deer meat, tender, well-seasoned, and falling off the bone. The wine helped to chase away the latent chill he still felt.

He thought of the Merchant Guild Council. There was a ruling council in Averon, of course; however, they were merely there to handle small domestic issues. The Merchant Guild handled any serious issues involving diplomacy with other nations. Any requests for protection from the Sentinels of Averon could only be approved by the Guild. This would indeed be a difficult discussion. The merchants were honest and fair, but extremely rich as well. They fully believed that the use of force was the very last alternative to solving any diplomatic affair. They would rather talk about their problems with others than get involved in costly fights over them. Their motto was "a peaceful business is a profitable business."

There were positive factors to be considered as well. There would be no ruthless dealings, backroom scheming, or base deceit in talks with the Merchant Guild. They were well renowned for their candor and honest intentions. However, they had much to protect, and they would not be easily swayed to weaken their defenses. He considered these things and more as he enjoyed his wine.

At that moment, a tall, armored man entered the dining area where Algernon sat and came over to him. He removed his silver helmet and placed his gloves within it and placed the helmet on the table. He was a smooth-skinned young man though clearly older and more experienced than most of the men Algernon had seen until this point. A serious frown was evident upon his face beneath dark hair parted on the side. He was not a very broad man, but seemed extremely fit nonetheless.

Algernon rose to greet him, and as the man took hold of him in a firm handshake, he recognized something vaguely familiar about him. He had never met him, but something about the features of his face, especially around the eyes and nose, was not foreign to him.

"Good evening," the young man said flatly. "I am Captain Etienne Gaston. At your service, sir."

"A pleasure to meet you, Captain," Algernon replied. "Are you ... are you by chance the son of Edward Gaston?"

The man's serious frown changed to a quizzical one. "I am, sir. You know my father? Even this far south, some of us have heard the name Algernon before, and yet I do not recall seeing you before."

"I do know him, young man, and I am glad to say I know him as a friend, although the last time I visited here you were probably very young indeed. How is your father? Is he still on the Merchant Guild Council?"

"He is well, I thank you for asking. Please sit down, sir. My men have told me your name and that you were with a young woman." He watched Algernon nod in agreement. "They also informed me of the rather unusual way you came to be with us."

Algernon smiled and nodded again.

"I am told you have asked to see the Merchant Guild Council," the Captain continued. "I regret to inform you they will not be able to see you, at least not for some time, due to more immediate matters of a very serious nature."

"I assure you, Captain," Algernon said earnestly, "that what I have come to speak to them about is more serious than anything they can possibly be dealing with at the moment. And I no doubt possess invaluable counsel that they will need to hear before they pass judgment on the matters of which you speak."

"I do not doubt you, sir," Gaston answered. "However, they are not seeing anyone for the time being. Perhaps ... I could arrange a visit with my father, should he agree to it, after I inform him you are here. For now, that is the best I can do."

"Very well, Captain," Algernon conceded. "Can I inquire as to what has them so occupied?"

"Perhaps my father will tell you when you meet. I am sorry." He shook Algernon's hand again. "Please ask if you need anything in the meantime. I hope you and your companion do not mind the barracks for the time being, until you are better rested and we can provide you with alternative quarters."

"No, your hospitality has been most agreeable; thank you, Captain."

Algernon watched as he turned and exited the room.

Though his young face was unusually hard to read, Algernon saw a pronounced concern when he asked him about the matters the Guild was preoccupied with. He sensed a definite fear of the immediate future as well. He hoped he could see Gaston's father soon. He did not have time to waste here. Every second brought the Shadowlord closer. He had a final glass of wine and retired for the night.

Kael heard a door opening and saw it was only a few feet from his head. Light came streaming in, forcing him to abruptly shut his eyes. An unknown amount of time had passed since last he'd seen the light. It was only torchlight, but it was too much for his eyes to handle until they could adjust. He heard at least two pairs of booted feet enter the chamber, possibly a third.

The next thing he felt was a sharp kick to the center of his back, followed by another to the middle of his stomach. Both blows put him in intense pain, and he coughed in between gagging.

"Open your eyes, surface-dwelling scum!" It was a voice he had not yet heard.

"What's the matter, you can't see in the dark?" Again, it was a different voice, unfamiliar, and one of them loosened his gag so he could speak.

Next he felt them dragging him along the floor by the collar of his cloak until he was propped upright against a wall.

"So, Kael Dracksmere, are you enjoying our hospitality?" It was finally her. He recognized Mya's voice.

"Your hospitality . . . lacks a certain subtle quality I can't quite . . . place, my lady," Kael replied.

Kael's response was answered by a swift kick across the face from what he perceived was one of the other men who entered his chamber.

"Enough!" Mya commanded. "Leave us."

"Yes, High Priestess."

She waited until they were gone before she spoke again. "We are not in the habit of treating spies with open arms. Now I urge you to think before you speak. Who were you spying for in the cave?"

He could not see her. The light from without was still too much for his eyes. He sensed from her voice that she was somewhere in front of him.

"You are having difficulty seeing?" she asked dryly. "The darkness you endured is exactly what the first White Elves experienced when they were banished beneath the earth. We make sure all surface-dwelling prisoners are exposed to those same conditions during their stay with us."

"An effective technique . . . to be sure . . . my lady. Now . . . to your question. I was not spying. I told you . . . I got caught . . . in the wrong place . . . at the wrong time," Kael said, still trying to catch his breath.

He heard her walk quickly toward him, and suddenly felt a slap across his face.

"That's the last time you take me for a fool. I'm calling my men back in here." He heard her footsteps moving away, presumably toward the door.

"All right!" Kael gasped. "All right. Why . . . are you helping them? You know he's evil; you sensed it . . . I saw it in your face the whole time. You know the Shadow Prince—your good Prince Stranexx—and Voltan are evil incarnate. Why are you helping them?"

There was a long silence. He heard her near the opening, and then he finally heard her reply in a whisper, "I do not know."

With that, the door slammed shut, and she was gone. He looked in the direction of the sound. It could not have been a conventional door, as not even a crack of light came through. Its movement across the floor, though smooth, had sounded heavy. Whatever it was, it apparently served to re-create the darkness in which they lived. He licked his lips, his cheek still stinging from her slap. He had hope. Once again, he had heard sadness and reluctance in her voice. Perhaps it was not too late.

Night had descended upon Fort Renault like a bird of prey. It was late when the men finished all the preparations Mekko had tasked them to. Mekko and Lieutenant Denataunt gathered the men in a circle around a fire in the center of the fort. All the men who were not on watch attended.

Mekko saw the nervous anxiety within their eyes. It was something he had seen many times in his life before battle. It was the type of feeling that played tricks on soldiers and allowed them to second-guess themselves during the fighting. They were tired, but he wagered few if any would get any sleep. The attack could come at any moment. He needed to get them mentally prepared now.

"Now you listen to me, lads, and you listen well" he said. "When the attack comes, it will be hard and fast. The Ogres will plan on it bein' fairly easy. You're fewer than they are, and smaller and weaker in their eyes. You lads have to keep your heads and stay focused on your jobs. You have to decide, right now, that you're goin' to survive. That means you fight to kill and do whatever you have to in order to stay alive and keep the man beside you alive, you follow?"

They looked intently at him and nodded.

"Make your peace with it now, lads. You have to fight with everything you have inside you to make it through this. It's all right to be afraid; you'd all be damn fools if you weren't. But you can fight through the fear. You have to harness all your love, all your fear, all your hate to give you that edge that can make you survive anything. There's no mistakes in war, lads. There's no 'I tried my best'; it's kill or be killed, plain and simple."

He gave them a few moments to digest what he had told them.

"You archers, you need to make every shot count," he continued. "Ogres don't fall from one arrow, especially in the chest or stomach. You aim strictly for the head and eyes, see, and if you miss, don't panic; just keep firing and aim better next time. Any fightin' to be done close quarters, you aim your weapons low. You go for the knees and between the legs, parry, slash, and thrust like we went over. Anyone dumpin' hot oil over the wall on them, same goes for you; aim for the head and eyes. We don't need to kill them all, lads; we just need to give 'em a good sting so they think twice about comin' back. Now, you all go and get what rest you can."

As they began to walk away, Mekko suddenly stood. "And lads . . . I'm damn proud to be fightin' alongside you men of the Sentinels."

With that, they smiled to the last man and wished him and one another a good night.

Mekko sat alone and thought about Cordilleran. He prayed all was well. He knew they had the finest army in the lands and that his presence alone would not be the difference between victory and defeat if they were, in fact, being invaded at all, as the old man had said. It was his shame that gnawed at him. King Crylar needed him now, and he had been fool enough to allow himself to be captured and so find himself here, fighting a battle for another country when his own appeared in dire need of him. He prayed his country would still be there if he survived this one-sided battle and made it home. He needed to apologize to the King, his friend, in person. He needed his forgiveness, and then his spirit would be healed.

Algernon awoke this time to the crashing sound of his door being kicked open. He arose suddenly to find Elenari in his room, holding her short sword to his throat. A look of hate and disdain had overtaken her face; she was in a furious rage.

A moment later, two of the Sentinel's guards entered the chamber. Elenari spun around faster than words and, with two swift strokes of her sword, disarmed the first man and then kicked him in the chest, sending him crashing into the doorframe with such force that he fell to the floor unconscious. As the second man lunged at her with his sword, she side-stepped the blow, grabbed his arm, and flipped him onto the floor on his back. Swiftly, she kicked him across the face, knocking him out, and then bent down and took his sword in her free hand.

It was in that moment that Captain Gaston arrived with five more men. When Algernon saw him, he put both his hands up to caution him. "Captain, please! Take your men outside and close the door. Captain, I assure you, whether you believe it or not, this woman is capable of killing every man in the barracks. Please do not test her!"

"I do not take kindly to guests of our hospitality dictating terms in our own barracks, sir," said Gaston as he began to draw his sword.

Like lightning, Elenari cut his belt, causing his weapon to fall to the floor. Her stolen sword she leveled at Algernon, and her own sword was poised at the Captain's throat.

"You heard the old man," she snarled. "If you value your life, Captain, and the lives of your men, get out!"

Gaston stared back at Elenari, a look of iron on his face; he did not move.

"You're a brave man, Captain, with your own life," she said venomously. "Let's see how brave you are with someone else's." Still clutching the second sword, she quickly grabbed the soldier at her feet by the hair and pulled him up to his knees, pointing her sword at his throat.

"Elenari, no!" Algernon cried. "What are you doing?"

"Shut up! Don't you say one more word! How about it, Captain?" Elenari taunted.

"All right . . . everyone outside," Captain Gaston ordered reluctantly.

"Good choice."

She threw the unconscious man at the Captain and kicked the door shut, leaving herself alone in the room with Algernon. She turned and pointed both swords toward the Sage.

"You killed them!" she screamed. "You killed them as sure as that thing out there killed them! You and your mission. What *was* your mission? To go places where no one wants us or even believes us? Places where they try to kill us? For what? 'Protect Algernon . . . protect the Emerald Star.' It's *you* who should be dead, but instead everyone else is dying so *you* can live."

Tears ran down her cheeks, but hatred and bitterness were still plain on her face. Algernon calmly raised his hands and pulled apart his cloak, exposing his bare chest.

"If it will make you whole and bring you peace of mind," he said, "then drive your weapon home and take my life, for I have lived far longer than I ever should have. But . . . let all your anger and hate die with me, and grant me one small request aside."

"What is it?" Nari demanded as she placed her blade under his chin.

Algernon could tell her hands were beginning to shake, but her eyes were still filled with hate. "My journal is more than my memoirs," he said, pointing to it. "The book contains knowledge that could turn the tide catastrophically against us should it fall into evil hands. Swear to me that you will be its guardian after I am dead and will not allow that to happen. That much, at least, will give my death meaning."

Elenari looked at him strangely, tears still spilling uncontrollably out of the corners of her eyes. She felt as if she were outside herself, watching, or as if she were dreaming a horrible dream from which she could not awake. She looked at him, as he stood there, calm, with peace and forgiveness in his eyes. He was ready to die and even seemed somewhat relieved at the prospect.

An eternity passed in a matter of moments. Suddenly, the door to the room was forced open and a robed figure entered. He was perspiring terribly with a look of shock and sheer disbelief across his face. It was Galin.

Kael heard the strange door to his chamber open again followed by the footfalls of one set of boots. Judging from the softness of the steps, he deduced that it was Mya. She walked toward him, and he could sense she was very close; he could smell her scented perfume. He felt something cold touch his lips and he flinched.

"Drink," Mya said.

He sipped the liquid—water—and found it most welcome. He had been very thirsty. She allowed him to drink and then walked a few feet away.

"Your name is Kael Dracksmere," she said, matter-of-factly. "You are one of the two Druids who travel with the Sage Algernon. There can be no other explanation."

"Well, my lady, you know who and what I am and now you know what I'm fighting for. I, on the other hand, know who and what you are, but my question remains. What are you and your people fighting for?" Kael asked.

"How utterly naive you are, Druid," Mya replied. "My people have been living underground for ages. Did you know that the first of us were banished here, thinking they would die in the harsh subterranean climate? No good, fertile ground to grow anything, no wood or supplies, no warmth—just an abundance of darkness and strange monsters and a host of underground dangers it would take hours for me to describe to you. Those surface-dwelling Elves of ages ago figured my ancestors would die below the earth. Instead, those first few spawned an entire race. We've built cities and established an entire culture. Rumors and legend speak about us as being evil monsters. We are people, Druid. We cry, we laugh . . . and we love. We live in families. We . . ." Her voice trailed off.

"And you sit at a table and call the most powerful evil I have ever known your friend and benefactor. Why?"

"Our society exists in three castes: religious, warrior, and worker. We have no King, and we have no ruling council. It is the religious caste that rules; the warrior caste acts as our advisors. The warrior caste carries a large voice among the people. Lord Stranexx has convinced the warrior caste that it is possible for us to be vindicated and restored to our former glory. Alluviam will become our land; we shall inherit our surface homeland and take our revenge on those who banished us," Mya said.

"What vindication?" Kael demanded. "Why must this all end in revenge? The Elves who banished your people don't even exist anymore. Your people who were first banished don't exist anymore. Their fight is neither yours nor that of your people."

"Our children are born in the cold and darkness and never know the warmth of the sun because their eyes become too sensitive to look upon it," she exclaimed. "You think we should just accept that and go happily about our lives forgiving and forgetting our surface-dwelling cousins?"

"No," Kael replied gently. "I think if you are as civilized as you claim to be, then you should go to Alluviam proudly and negotiate the terms of your coexistence. Rejoin your surface cousins in peace. Whatever reason there may have been for revenge and vindication has died on both sides. Surely you know this?"

There was a long silence as he waited for a reply.

"I once thought it could be so," she answered, sounding almost unwilling to reply. "I have spoken of going to them in peace, of rejoining our surface kin together as one people. There are some who agree, but too many in the warrior caste do not, and those who were considering it have been swayed by the promises of Prince Wolfgar to deliver Alluviam to us by force."

"Well, then, there is clearly something your people haven't considered," Kael said shrewdly.

"What is that, Druid?" Mya asked.

"They haven't considered what the Shadow Prince will do to the White Elves after he's finished using you for his own purposes. I know you don't trust him; a fool could have seen it. I know you believe he's evil. How can you—?"

"Enough!" she snapped. "The Shadow Prince as you call him will be coming to address my people before the invasion of Alluviam. At that time . . . you will be presented to him as a token of our good faith."

Kael heard her walking away from him, but she stopped by the door. In a flash, a torch was lit inside his chamber on the wall. In the next moment, she exited, and the door was closed.

It would take some time for his eyes to adjust to the light, but it would take longer for him to adjust to what she had said. He wondered if his only hope had gone out the door as well.

Galin couldn't believe what he was seeing before him. "What the hell is going on in here?"

Elenari turned and saw him. A well of emotions stirred within her. She looked back at Algernon, then at Galin again. She was suddenly dazed, unsure of herself. Abruptly, she dropped both swords and stumbled toward Galin.

Galin caught her, and she collapsed to her knees, sobbing and clutching the front of his robe. "Oh, Galin," she choked, "he said . . . he would miss you."

Galin looked at Algernon. "Algernon what's going on? What is she talking about?"

Algernon slowly came forward and placed his hand on Elenari's head. Then he lifted his head and looked Galin in the eyes. "Hawk . . . risked his life to save us from the creature. He's dead . . . and Kael is quite possibly dead as well."

Galin winced and closed his eyes. After a moment, he opened them, bent down, pulled Elenari close, and held her for a moment as tightly as he could. Gently, he let her go, and she turned to Algernon and held on to him.

Algernon consoled her in a whisper, "There, there, child, it's all right. It's just a bad time for us all. Let it out, child. Let it all out."

Galin left the room, his eyes red and water, and found Captain Gaston waiting for him.

"Captain, I have come from Fort Renault," Galin explained. "More than half its number has been routed; all that's left is about fifty young men. There's an Ogre army camped nearby with more than enough numbers to take the fort. The boys refused to leave, however, afraid to embarrass their families by abandoning their posts. General Mekko, from Cordilleran, is there, preparing what defenses he can, but the fort will not hold. They need immediate reinforcements."

With a look of shock he tried to contain, Captain Gaston turned and headed downstairs, his men following him in a rush.

Galin followed him and, upon reaching the lower level, quickly bolted out the nearest door. His breathing came rapidly, and tears fell down his face as he thought of Hawk and Kael. Out in the courtyard, he looked toward the sky and, shaking his fists in rage, cried out, "I will destroy you! Wherever you are, wherever you go, I will destroy you!"

He had cried out with such power that many of the men came outside to see what the commotion was. Algernon was among them, and Galin turned to face him. His will was set; his eyes were red, but his look was ice.

"We have to go help Mekko, and then that creature dies." He looked up to the second level of the barracks where Elenari was. "For her. . . . for me, and for Hawk and Kael, the creature dies by my hand. I swear it by the Sacred Mother!"

With that, he turned back toward the barracks.

The Ogres charged the fort on the north and east side just before daybreak. The boys had alerted the fort in plenty of time. There was no movement within the walls. Mekko had ordered all the archers to converge on the platforms on the north and east walls. They stayed low, with their heads below the spikes of the walls. The Ogres slowed their initial charge as they came closer, no doubt thinking the fort deserted.

Mekko peered through a hole in the wall, Denataunt standing beside him.

"Well, they're only half as dumb as I would have hoped, attackin' from two directions," he whispered. "No one moves until I give the order, Lieutenant. Take your position, lad. Good luck."

"Yes, sir, and to you," Denataunt replied.

The extra men at each platform had collected hot oil in various pots and containers, ready to pour over the walls upon the killing pits they had constructed on those two sides of the fort. Mekko stood ready near one part of the wall, while Denataunt moved to the other wall with his sword drawn.

The Ogres were huge. Most of the young men had never seen an Ogre up close before, much less hundreds of them marching on their fort. They were like Mekko had described, some as tall as ten feet. His description was no substitute for seeing them up close; they were unsightly creatures. Their skin, though tough and leathery, appeared covered with bumps and suppurating lesions. Though some had the skin tone of humans, others had hides ranging in color from yellow to dark brown. Some were smaller than the rest, Ogrens, they could be spotted by their dark bluish skin. They had dark, coarse, unkempt hair, which often covered their faces. Some wore the large furs of animals, while still others wore old, cracked, and dented metals for armor. They seemed to be carrying spears for the most part, although clubs and axes were seen as well. Many were muscular about the arms and chest while particularly dense in the stomach region.

They had slowed to a leisurely walk, still approaching from both directions. Mekko watched them through cracks in the wooden fence. "Just a few more yards, you big dumb oafs," he whispered.

Just as they closed on the walls, Mekko heard what he'd been waiting for: the death shrieks of Ogres as they started falling into the killing pits.

"Archers, north wall!" Mekko ordered.

Instantly the archers on the three platforms inside the north wall popped up and began firing their arrows at the stunned Ogres.

"Archers, east wall!" Mekko snapped at them.

Immediately they appeared, and began firing at the heads of the approaching Ogres.

The sight of the fort coming alive infuriated the Ogres. They charged at the main gate and along the north and east wall, quickly filling the two indented corrals created along each wall. When both square formations had filled with Ogres throwing themselves up against the wooden walls, Mekko gave the signal to Denataunt.

Both Mekko and Denataunt cut their respective lines, which released sliding wooden fences that slammed shut, enclosing the two corals, trapping dozens of Ogres.

"Hot oil, now!" Mekko yelled.

All the men began pouring the boiling hot oil on the captive Ogres, causing howls of pain to fill the fort. Some of the archers followed by firing down on the trapped Ogres who made easy targets in their wooden corrals.

The remaining Ogres continued ramming the wooden fence and main gate on the north wall, smashing it into large pieces with their huge axes and clubs. Many continued to lose their footing near the main gate and ended up impaled at the bottom of the deadly killing pits.

Mekko yelled to the boy, Josh, who still kept the fire going under the great oil pot. "Now, lad! Ring that bell nice and loud!"

With that, Josh rang the alarm bell of the fort, signaling the next phase of the attack. They had established a system of rings that would indicate to their buried men which directions the Ogres were attacking from so they could converge behind them.

At the sound of the bell, the twenty buried men rose from the earth and converged behind the attacking Ogres. They approached them by stealth and mercilessly attacked as Mekko had taught them, slashing at the backs of their knees cutting through flesh, bone, and tendons. The creatures went down by the dozens, many suffering ancillary blows to their heads.

Within the fort, the wooden wall had started to splinter and weaken in several places. Mekko and Denataunt were there; before the wall could be completely breached, they would strike a well-aimed blow at an Ogre arm or hand as it came through the fence. The men joined them by splashing hot oil through the large holes the Ogres had made in their attempt to smash through the walls.

The archers continued firing incessantly. Arrows stuck in the heads of all the trapped Ogres as they began to pile in the corrals in which they'd been trapped.

Outside the fort, the Ogres began to turn in number to face their rear attackers. Suddenly, the men of the Sentinels found themselves surrounded in great numbers. There was no chance for escape. They focused on parry, slash, and thrust as Mekko had shown them. They blocked attacks, crouched low, slashed the Ogre weapons aside, and thrust between their legs. The men broke off in pairs, back to back, and faced their attackers with courage and fortitude.

The archers, seeing their predicament, concentrated their fire to aid their encircled comrades. However, this left room for several Ogres to assault the walls. The howls of Ogres burnt by the oil dumped over the walls could be heard over and amidst the fighting and missile fire.

Denataunt was running from platform to platform, urging the archers on, and telling them to keep firing no matter what occurred. He barked orders at the others, telling them to go fill their containers with oil and where to go with them. He ordered the archers to constrict their fire to those Ogres closest to the fort who posed the greatest threat to breaching the walls.

Mekko ran up to the center platform, closest to the main gate. Looking outward, he saw there were only five men left alive still fighting outside the fort in a circle still heavily outnumbered. Looking down, he saw a cluster of Ogres beneath him.

The archers watched in disbelief as Mekko launched himself over the wall and into a group of five Ogres. He knocked one to the ground with the sheer force of his impact. Still on his knees, he swung his axe wildly, chopping off their legs just above the knee. He spun his body around in a sweeping circle, using the momentum of his axe to carry him, chopping off feet above the ankles all around him and following up with killing blows to the monster's heads. Then he was up and running out and away from the fort, barreling through the Ogres like a juggernaut. The enemy weapons seemed to glance off of him as if they could not penetrate him. In moments, he burst through to join the circle of the fort's men.

"Follow me, lads!" he shouted. "Stay low, don't stop, and don't look back!"

Instantly they took off behind him. As the Ogres formed up to block his way, his swung his axe through the air like a giant cleaver, swatting weapons aside and taking arms and hands with them. Any who got in his axe's way felt its sting and shrank back from him. Fear of him alone caused the Ogres to give ground.

Mekko did not hesitate and led the men as close to the killing pits as possible. Some of the Ogres who pursued them were not agile enough to dodge even the already exposed pits, and slipped and fell down atop their brethren. The archers discouraged any further pursuit as they filled the air behind them with a deadly hail of arrows. Denataunt opened the main gate just long enough to admit them and quickly closed it again behind them.

"Grab some oil, lads," Mekko ordered between gasps. "Pour it, splash it, whatever you can do!"

Denataunt and the men Mekko had rescued used oil to clear the wall of Ogres as the archers focused their fire further from the fort to those creatures that still approached from a distance. Finally, the wall had been cleared, and those Ogres who were burnt and still lived retreated from the walls of the fort and urged those still approaching to do the same.

The men were all utterly exhausted. The archer's slumped to the floor with their backs against the walls, their supply of arrows nearly depleted.

"Lieutenant, when the Ogres are out of sight, deploy skirmish parties and salvage every weapon and arrow that can be used back inside the fort," Mekko instructed breathlessly. "Only strip those bodies that are close, and make damn sure they're dead first before you get in arm's length of them. Then, get me a casualty count as soon as possible."

Mekko let himself fall against a platform. Covered in thick Ogre blood, his armor had been pierced in many places. He had several gashes on his shoulders, back, and face. He had no serious injuries however.

Several minutes later, Denataunt, returned carrying a small body in his arms. It was the little boy Josh.

Slowly Mekko rose with a look of disbelief on his face.

"He must have slipped out the west wall door," Denataunt said miserably. "His hunting knife was beside him near his hand. He wanted to fight so badly."

Grief-stricken, Mekko covered his mouth with his hand. He saw the boy's head had been smashed, no doubt by an Ogre club. Gently, he touched the boy's cheek and then watched as Denataunt carried him away.

Mekko removed his helmet and threw it at the wall. "Damn it all to hell!" He thought he had given the boy a job to keep him out of harm's way. Josh's death was a grim reminder to him that there was no such thing as a safe place on the battlefield.

They had lost sixteen men, leaving them with thirty-four. It was a miracle that even that many had survived until now. They had little oil and only a few arrows left. The wall was broken and nearly breached in several places. He hoped Galin would be on the way with reinforcements by now, but even on horseback, they would not arrive until morning, if they were coming. They could do nothing but wait now and hope. Mekko had given them hope; now he would wait with them, or die with them.

Chapter 18

Kael had finally drifted to sleep for a few hours, his torch had died leaving him in darkness. He awoke, startled, as at least two men picked him up off the floor. They moved him toward the opening of his cell and he closed his eyes, as the light was still a little too much for him to bear. He saw as he entered the corridor that the door to his chamber was not a door at all, but a stone device carved into the subterranean structure they were in. As he squinted, he could make out enough to know that he was clearly in an underground dungeon of some sort as everything was carved out of a mineral-rich rock.

There seemed to be other cells like his. They had removed the bonds around his legs so that he could walk under his own power; however, his hands were still tied tightly behind him. They quickly moved past the last cell, which was different from the others. It had bars, and he could see inside a bit. He could not make anything out clearly, but he determined a man was inside being beaten by more than one other man. From what he could hear, they seemed to be enjoying beating him as well.

He thought about Lark Royale for a moment. If he was still alive, he was in a place very like, or perhaps worse, than this. Perhaps it was Lark back in that cage. He felt the excitement of the thought only for a moment before surrendering to himself how unlikely that would be. He hoped Lark and Archangel were still alive somewhere, but it was becoming a desperate hope, just as his survival was becoming. Perhaps he was being taken to the Shadow Prince even now. He knew there was no chance of surviving long if that were the case.

He thought of Elenari. He worried for her safety and prayed she was well, along with the others. She would not understand his death and would most probably be angry with him for it. And she would be right, he surmised. He knew she had Hawk to watch over her. She certainly did not need a protector of any kind, but he had seen the unspoken attraction between them growing stronger. Hawk was a man of honor, a friend of Galin's, and had helped save them within the tower of Mordovia. He was glad she would have such a man to lean on when the time came, and he was happy to see her finally taking an interest in companionship. He pondered Elenari's future as he was marched through the strange, dimly lit, cold corridors.

He continued thinking about his own personal fears. He was afraid no longer, not of the Shadow Prince, not of the lava creature, not even of dying. At long last, he had found his old courage. It had been renewed within him through the eyes of Mya. He was a middle-aged man who had never married, but was lucky enough to enjoy the love of a child.

From the first moment he saw Mya, he realized for the first time what it meant to be in love. There was strength in her as well; he could see it. Without realizing it, she had helped him find it within himself. He must do the same for her.

Finally, they took him to an open chamber. A raised dais and altar stood in the very center of the room. Beyond the altar, sitting on a high chair, was Mya, still clad in dark robes. The chamber was lit by torchlight, and there appeared to be no one else present, although there were openings on the east and west. The two White Elven guards suddenly forced him to his knees as they bowed their heads low. One of them grabbed his head and forced it down.

"Bow your head, surface scum," the guard snapped.

"Sit him down," Mya ordered.

They moved Kael around the altar to a chair that stood about a dozen feet from Mya's seat.

"You may leave us," Mya instructed. "Stand guard outside."

They bowed low and complied.

"My lady," Kael began cautiously, "I am gratified to have the pleasure of your company once more."

With that, Mya rose and slowly walked toward him. When she was only a few inches away, she drew a shining dagger from her belt and held it, gleaming, before his eyes.

"My lady, I assure you," Kael stammered, uncertain of her intentions, "that was not meant to offend, I genuinely am pleased to see you."

She suddenly brought her finger to his lips, quieting him. A moment later, she walked behind him so that she was no longer in his view.

The next moment he felt her breath close to his ear and heard her whisper, "Do I have your word that you will not attempt anything foolish? That you will not move from this chair, that you will not attempt any spells? Swear it by Mother Nature herself."

"I swear to you, my lady, by Mother Nature herself. I will neither attempt to move nor try any spells."

The next moment, he felt her cutting his bonds and freeing his hands. Then she returned to her chair and sat down.

"Thank you, my lady," said Kael, rubbing his wrists, relieved to have the movement of his hands again. He could feel the blood rushing back into his hands and fingers finally.

"I'm glad you gave your word, Druid, because there are guards close by you cannot see who would kill you sooner than I could stop them if you *did* attempt something. I know your hands have been tied behind your back for quite some time."

"I appreciate your kindness, High Priestess," Kael replied. "I wonder if I could impose upon you a small request." Mya's eyebrow rose in suspicious curiosity. "Could I ask you to call me Kael, as opposed to Druid? And may I call you by your name, or would you prefer that I not?"

"When we speak in private," she replied, "you may call me by my name. However, if you dare to do so in front of another White Elf, you will certainly be sorry for it. Does that answer your question . . . Kael?" Her mouth twitched in a hint of a smile.

"Yes, my lady, thank you," said Kael, inclining his head respectfully. "I will, of course, obey your restrictions."

"So you have traveled with this man Algernon," she said plainly. "Tell me, what are his plans?"

"Algernon keeps his own counsel, my lady, even around those closest to him."

"You must know something of his intentions," she replied shrewdly.

"His intentions, my lady," Kael answered, "are to stop the Shadow

Prince at all costs. That is as succinctly as I can put it. Algernon and I have an extensive history with your Prince Wolfgar."

"What is your history with him . . . Kael?"

"When last he walked in the world of men, I destroyed him—or I thought him destroyed, at any rate. I watched him kill and terrorize. I saw him create famine and pestilence in the small Kingdom of Wrenford. Now, his hand reaches far indeed. He has destroyed the Elves of the Great Forest of Hilderan. He has destroyed the Kingdom of Wrenford. He will continue to kill and destroy until eventually he turns on you and your people."

"Silence!" she snapped. "My people—the warrior caste—have embraced him as an ally, and so I must for the sake of my people."

Kael shook his head in disgust. "What else would you ask of me, my lady?"

"Tell me about your magic?" she asked suddenly.

He looked at her quizzically. "My magic?"

"Your powers are based on the surface world environment, are they not? Ours are based on the subterranean environment. I would think our magic is very similar to your own. The members of the religious caste and I could be called Druids in another reality, a surface-life reality," she ended bitterly.

"Must everything come down to your people's grudge against surface dwellers?" Kael asked impatiently.

"Yes!" she shouted. "You have no idea what life underground is like, raising a family, just the daily struggle to survive . . . you have no idea, Druid!"

"I have the idea that because the Elves banished your people ages ago, your people now hate all surface-dwelling races. You despise them, and you blame all of them not just the Elves."

She hesitated. "That's not true . . . we don't—"

"Don't you dare say it's not true when minutes ago your own guard called me surface scum," he interjected. He perched on the edge of the chair, barely able to contain himself. "Did you not say to me yourself that all prisoners in your dungeons are put in those chambers devoid of light so they can get a taste of how your people live? The non-Elves as well, my lady, do they get punished extra just for living on the surface? Punish them for their crimes, yes, but don't punish them for your crimes."

Mya's face held a bitter scowl, but it seemed to dissolve as she found herself looking at the floor. "You speak of things you do not know, Kael," she said finally.

"Oh no, my lady," he replied softly. "Blaming everyone else for my troubles I do know something about, and that's what you and your people are doing."

"Silence! We will not speak of this any further." She took a deep breath and dropped her head.

Kael allowed a few moments to pass before he spoke again. "My lady, who is the prisoner in the open cell?"

"Someone of no consequence to you, Druid," Mya said flatly. "Just another surface dweller."

"Is his name Lark Royale?" Kael asked in a whisper.

"I do not know his name," she shouted, losing patience with him, "and do not ask me these things; I will answer no further!"

"Please forgive me, my lady," he said quietly. "I have a friend—a very close friend—who was taken prisoner some time ago. My lady . . . Mya?" He hesitated to call her by her name, but he smiled, in spite of himself, hearing it pass through his lips. His smile quickly dissipated into a serious glance. "My lady, why is it that your men seem to enjoy beating your prisoners?"

"Everyone has their jobs, Kael, even here under the earth. Some are less pleasant than others, and some require less civilized behavior than others like anywhere else." She heaved a sigh. "Kael . . . I do apologize for losing my temper with you. I live in a society where it is not always wise to disagree openly. Despite how it may seem, we are not an evil, vengeful people. We seek to live in peace. Even the warrior caste would be content to preserve the peace, but . . . you must understand that ages of resentment are not an easy thing to overcome. We could have moved to the surface to live hundreds of years ago, but we chose not to. We chose to no longer be part of a world that would cast us out."

"Then why do your people wish to fight a war over Alluviam?"

"We will not move to the surface to carve a niche for ourselves," she said firmly, "but we will take back what should have been rightly provided for us."

"My lady . . . if someone strong, like you, stood up and showed your people the way to peace, they'd follow you to it. If you gave the right reasons and made them stick, they'd listen." Kael made his hand into a fist.

"No, Kael; I forbid you to speak of it any further." She rose, crossed to his chair, and retied his hands behind his back. "I will have food brought to you soon." She clapped her hands and instantly the two guards appeared again.

He smiled. "Last meal for the condemned man. My thanks, lady, but the honor of your company and being in your presence has meant much more to me." He bowed his head. He saw she was visibly uncomfortable and unable to bring herself to look him in the eye even as he was being taken away.

Mekko awoke just before dawn. He had fallen asleep sometime after midnight. The remainder of the day and night around Fort Renault had been quiet. Today, if luck was with them, Galin would arrive with rein-forcements from Averon.

It had been too quiet up until now. They had survived the attack yes-terday, but Mekko knew there were more than enough Ogres left to finish them. He had no more war tricks left; their supplies were too low, and there was too much damage to the walls. If there were another attack, there would be no escape for any of them. Still, he had given the men a day, and in that day, they had found a pride and courage they had never known.

Denataunt came and sat next to him. When he was sure no one could hear, he whispered, "General, what do we do if they attack again?"

"Well, we pulled off a wee bit o' magic yesterday, lad," he whispered in reply, "but if they attack again before help arrives, we stand a better chance runnin' away."

"You know the men won't leave, sir," the young officer replied.

"Aye. Pride, bravery, honor . . . they are often thought to be the same, but I assure you, lad, they are not. Any one of these boys' families couldn't give a damn about anything except seein' 'em alive again," Mekko answered.

A young man standing watch on a northern platform shouted down to him. "General! The Ogres are marching toward us, sir. This time they're coming from all four directions!"

"Damn that fool of a Druid!" Mekko shouted as he stood up and put his helmet back on. "What, was he flyin' backward to Averon, I wonder?"

"Should the archers take to the platforms, sir?" Denataunt asked.

"No, Lieutenant, every lad grab your swords and make a wide circle. You want to make your families proud? Now's your chance, lads." As the men scrambled to follow his orders, Mekko put the top of his axe to the ground and bent to one knee, and spoke in a whisper so they wouldn't hear. "Crylar, Cordilleran, forgive me. May you fight and endure long after I'm gone."

Mekko rose, surveying the remaining men gathered around him.

"Now," he said loudly, "let those big dumb bastards in here. Don't let them break the circle, lads; we fight for our lives."

The men stood side by side. They could feel the ground tremble as the Ogres approached from all directions, and yet, as Mekko looked to each one, they had the look of iron determination on their faces. The fear was gone to the last man.

"Men of the Sentinels, for Averon we fight!" Denataunt cried suddenly.

The men answered his cry and rallied together.

The Ogres began hacking through the wooden walls of the fort, turning the loose pieces of the palisade into matchsticks. Within moments, the walls were breached, and they were surrounded on all four sides.

At the last possible moment, the sound of war horns rang out from the south—first one, then many. The Ogres looking toward the sound, angered and confused, hesitated in their advance.

"It's the horns of the Sentinels cavalry! Our troops have come to save us, men!" It was Denataunt yelling to the men, who responded in a rousing cheer, raising their swords to the air.

"I knew the Druid would come through for us, lads!" said Mekko as he ran forward and, in two swings of his axe, smashed the nearest Ogre's spear out of his hand and buried his axe deep in the monster's stomach. "Didn't I tell you he would?"

Denataunt came to his side and motioned with his sword arm. "Forward, men!"

Mekko looked at him in awe, recalling the shy young man he had chosen to lead them.

At that moment, mounted horsemen began streaming in through and over parts of the fort's broken walls. Mounted crossbowmen began firing on the Ogres as they fell back, scattering outside the fort.

Mekko made his way through a gaping hole in the north wall and watched with a smile as the Ogres retreated north with at least two hundred horsemen of the Sentinels in pursuit. Shielding his eyes with his hands, he looked further into the distance and saw a second force coming into view—another group of cavalry, which rode around the Ogres' flank. *Excellent strategy*, Mekko thought.

Suddenly, he recognized one of the horsemen pursuing the Ogres. It was the half-Elven girl, Elenari. She rode hands-free, firing arrows at them with her longbow.

Mekko spun around, startled, as a horse nearly rode over him as it pulled right up to where he stood. The horse reared up on its hind legs and came down to reveal Galin as its rider. The Druid quickly dismounted.

"We rode nonstop as fast as we could to get here," Galin said with a smile. "Sorry if we cut it a little close there. Glad to see you are still in one piece, General."

"Ha, nonsense, lad!" he answered, slapping Galin vigorously on the arm and shaking his hand. "I never doubted you, not even for a moment."

"Did you suffer many losses?" Galin asked.

The wide smile left Mekko's face, and he looked to the ground. "Aye . . . sixteen dead, including the wee boy, Josh. Never saw a more able group of brave young lads though. I tell ya, I was damn proud to fight alongside them."

Elenari rode ahead of the others until she was right behind a group of fleeing Ogres. She brought her right leg over the animal so that all her weight was in her left stirrup as she rode, literally standing in the saddle, on the left side of the animal. She waited until she was behind a group of them and then let herself fly into them. None of them fell, but nor did she. The moment she was on the ground, her short sword was free. She threw herself into the fight with unbridled passion. A frenzy overcame her as she sliced through them. Her blade moved faster than the eye could follow, cutting into their flesh and bones as if through butter.

The two forces of cavalry pinned the Ogres down and, as crossbow-men fired from the southern force, the northern force hacked at them with swords from horseback.

Eros-Arthas moved through the Ogre's bodies and their weapons effort-lessly. Their blood splattered in all directions as Elenari felled them faster even than the missile fire could. She was taking her vengeance out on them in defiance of every oath she had ever taken. She was making them pay for her loss.

Mekko and Galin looked on from a distance.

"Crylar save us," uttered Mekko. He watched Elenari kill the Ogres indiscriminately with such speed and ferocity that he almost pitied them.

Galin placed an arm on his shoulder and bowed his head. "The Druid, Kael, Elenari's father, and Hawk, the Ranger, are both apparently dead, killed by the lava creature. I do not know . . ." Galin voice faltered, and he brought his hand to the corners of his eyes, wiping away tears. "I do not know how much death will be enough to satisfy the evil powers in this world."

Mekko placed a strong hand on his arm. "I'm deeply sorry, lad, for the loss of your friends and . . . I'm sorrier to say that I think this is only the beginnin' of the death yet to come."

When it was over, they had killed every Ogre down to the last—over four hundred of them—and still several hundred bodies of those killed the previous day lay strewn about the fort.

In the middle of the field stood Elenari, her face, hair, and clothes sat-urated with their dark, thick blood as if she had bathed in it. A fearsome expression came over her face as she looked for any sign of life among them so she could cut it out from them. Ogre carcasses, limbs, and heads were piled at her feet.

The men of the Sentinels looked at her in sheer disbelief unable to comprehend that a woman was capable of such battle prowess. Never had they seen anything remotely like it. Even Captain Gaston, a battle-hardened officer, looked at her with awe. Time seemed to stand still, and no one seemed able to move from the field between the fort and the borderlands of Bazadoom.

Abruptly, Elenari turned and walked carelessly on the bodies over the carnage, making her way to the forest, and disappearing from view.

An hour later Captain Gaston and six of his men entered the fort with a large wagon in tow. Mekko and Galin met him as he entered.

"What have you got there, lad?" Mekko asked.

"Strange," the captain replied. "My men went to the Ogre encampment as you directed us and found this wagon. Its contents are somewhat puzzling."

With that, he removed the tarp they had draped over the wagon, revealing a pile of bodies. There were over a dozen Elven bodies in addition to Elven weapons.

"This was meant to be a massacre, Captain," Galin said as he turned away. "And, from what Algernon tells me, it was meant to look like the Elves did it."

"Where's the old man?" Mekko asked.

"He's in Averon City," Galin answered, "negotiating with Captain Gaston's father to enlist the aid of the Sentinels to go to Cordilleran."

"General Mekko," said Gaston as he removed his helmet and lifted his hand in salute, "Corporal Denataunt and the men of the fort have told me what you have done here. On behalf of the Republic of Averon, I would like to humbly thank you, and, as a Captain of the men of the Sentinels, I would like you to know that, whether our council sends my army to your homeland or not, I will go there and stand and fight with you as you stood with our men here." Gaston then placed his right fist over his heart, which was the Dwarven salute signifying commitment, loyalty, and honor.

The fort suddenly went silent. Already overwhelmed, Mekko looked around and saw Denataunt, the men of the fort, and all the rest of the Sentinels present, mounted or otherwise, place their right fists over their hearts. Visibly touched by their gesture, Mekko returned the salute and bowed his head.

"Damn, you men of Averon are a noble breed," said Mekko as he sniffed and rubbed his nose. He took Gaston by the arm and pulled him so he had to lean over to listen to him. "You should thank the lads, Captain, not me, and give every one of 'em a medal if you can. I'll adopt every one of 'em and take 'em to Cordilleran with me if you don't. I've seen battle-hardened men drop their weapons and run at the sight of what these young lads fought off."

Captain Gaston smiled and nodded.

Mekko continued, "Oh, and laddie?" Captain Gaston nodded attentively again. "Whatever damn-fool jackass filled these boys' minds with the idea that they can't retreat from their posts needs to have his mouth washed out with Orc dung. I advised 'em from the beginning to leave the fort, but the lads wouldn't hear of it; said no Sentinels troops ever abandoned their post before, said they'd dishonor their families. I beg you to send word to your other outposts, lad: there's no honor in unnecessary slaughter, and I've seen enough of it to last a lifetime."

The captain took the Dwarf's hand and shook it solemnly. "I will send the word, General."

Suddenly, Elenari reappeared and entered the battered main gates of the fort, walking slowly toward them. Her leather armor and clothes were still stained with blood, though she seemed to have washed her face and hair clean. Her face was blank, almost expressionless, as she approached them.

Mekko removed his helmet and bowed. "My lady."

"General," she spoke flatly but politely in return. She turned and looked at Galin. "Now . . . it's the creature's turn to die."

Galin, seeing the fierce look of determination on her face, grabbed her outstretched hand and nodded.

Mekko reached out and put his hand on theirs. "After all you've sacrificed to help save my people, I'd like to help you do this."

Captain Gaston stepped forward. "I, too, owe all of you a debt of gratitude, and I would be greatly honored if you allow me to come with you to whatever end it is you seek. At the very least, let us provide you with an escort back to Averon to rejoin with your friend."

They nodded to him as he placed his hand on theirs.

Their course was set, and not even death had the power to alter it.

Kael sat in his chamber under the torchlight, eating from the plate of food recently provided for him. His hands were freed so that he might eat again, with the proviso that if he attempted any spells or escape, he would be immediately killed with no warning. It was a hot meal, to his surprise. It was an unusual type of meat, no doubt some subterranean creature. However, it was pleasantly palatable, though somewhat on the spicy side, and still he was voraciously hungry. A goblet of wine was even provided for him, which further convinced him this would indeed be his last meal.

Just as he finished the wine, the door to his chamber slowly opened. He had become accustomed to the sound of the stone scratching the floor as the door slid open.

Mya entered the chamber alone. Kael immediately stood and bowed his head.

"Please, Kael, sit down. Did you enjoy the food?"

"Very much, my lady, thank you. May I ask what type of meat it was?"

Mya smiled and looked down. "It is . . . probably better if I do not tell you," she said as she raised her hand to cover soft laughter. "Would you like more?"

The simple gesture and the elegance of how she moved captivated him. He had begun to appreciate the sheer beauty of everything about her—the warmth in the smile she tried to hide, the strength behind her eyes, the wavy layers of her hair, and the smallness of her feet. She had a statuesque quality, which Kael likened to regal beauty. "No, thank you," he replied, "the portions were more than generous. I am, however, still curious about the meat."

"The meat is from a creature you would consider to be a . . . scavenger, shall we say," she replied. "However, we consider it to be a delicacy nonetheless."

"Ah . . . I see. Is it a carrion eater?"

"One could describe it that way I suppose."

They smiled at each other. Mya saw an implicit honesty in Kael's face. He had a genuine quality about him that she could not ignore, no matter how she tried. He looked at her like a woman, not a religious leader. She felt a caring in his glance she had not felt for many years. Her face became serious again.

"Kael, I am sorry for how you have been treated and that you are a prisoner here. I sense you are not my enemy nor an enemy of my people. I have known it since our first conversation. I wish there was another way out of this for you, for us both . . ." Her voice trailed off.

"There is a way out, my lady." He stepped forward and held her arms. "I am not just any Druid; I am the Grand Druid and head of the Druid Council. I give you my solemn pledge that if you free me, I will do everything in my power to negotiate a peace between the Elves and your people. You can be one great nation under the sun with no bloodshed, no death, and no vengeance."

She started to tremble and shake her head. "You lie . . . do not think us uninformed of surface matters. A man named Talic is the Grand Druid." She tried to pull away from him.

He held her strongly. "I defeated Talic in single combat. If my eyes cannot convince you of the truth, have your spies confirm it. I am the Grand Druid."

Again she shook her head, and her voice was shaking. "You would say anything to get away . . ."

He suddenly released her and faced her, eye to eye. "I swear what I have told you is true. I pledge my life that I will help you and your people. I trust the strength I see in you to know the truth." He dropped to his knees, bent his head, took her hand and softly kissed it.

Gently, she placed her forefinger under his chin and tilted his head so his eyes would meet hers. Within his brown eyes she saw only one thing: love. It was the only word she could think of to define it.

Slowly he rose, never taking his eyes off hers. He saw within her eyes a life he had never known. He saw a world of feelings he had never explored or knew existed. She, in turn, saw a freedom in his eyes and possibilities for a future she had only dreamed about. She opened her hand, slowly placing it on his cheek, letting her fingers run over his ear and into the softness of his hair.

He placed his hands gently on her shoulders, as if he were touching something so fragile that the slightest pressure would shatter it.

They became lost in each other in that instant; the harsh realities of the worlds they lived in faded away. It was as if they they created a new world for each other devoid of evil and hopelessness. It was full of light, warmth, and happiness.

Suddenly Kael felt a vicious blow to the back of his neck that sent him crumbling to the stone floor. Before he knew it, the guards were kicking him from both sides in his back and stomach.

"How dare you touch the High Priestess, filth!" one of them spat. "You will pay with your life." The guard suddenly drew his sword and rushed forward to thrust it into Kael.

"Enough!" Mya screamed, coming forward quickly and placing her boot on Kael's back. "Do you think this surface dweller could ever harm me?" She turned Kael's body over with her boot. "Put away your weapons and leave me, I've not finished questioning him. See that you do not interrupt me again!"

"Yes, High Priestess."

Both guards bowed low and left the chamber quickly. Mya bent down and placed her hand to the back of Kael's neck. Yellow energy came from her hand and washed over his bruise, soothing it.

Kael, coming back to consciousness, suddenly grabbed her hand and locked eyes with her.

She returned his glance, a tear forming in her eye. Something unspoken passed between them. She quickly got up and exited the chamber.

This time many hours had passed—perhaps even a day, Kael was unsure —until his chamber opened again. In the torchlight, he recognized the two guards he had become familiar with. They were dragging a third person between them, whom they violently threw to the ground before exiting.

The man rolled over twice before he stopped moving. It was the human Kael had caught a glimpse of in the open cell. He was completely naked, filthy, and beaten to a pulp.

Kael checked him over. His breathing was labored, partially due, perhaps, to internal injuries. One of the man's eyes was swollen shut from abuse; the other eye was missing, and the skin about the socket appeared black and burnt. His body was covered in lacerations, bruises, and purple discolorations. He smelled like a combination of vomit and dung; Kael could barely tolerate it at first. The man was a swollen bloody mess. It was a miracle he was still alive.

Suddenly, Kael began to recognize familiar features in the man's disfigured face. He quickly dragged him close into the torchlight. A gasp of dismay escaped his lips. He knew this man; it was Archangel Royale.

An inestimable amount of time passed. To Kael it seemed like days, though he had lost all concept of time here under the ground in the half-light of his chamber's torch. It could have been only hours for all he knew.

He used the time to gradually use his healing powers on Archangel. His injuries were so extensive that if he healed him too quickly, the shock to his system might be enough to kill him. Even in his darkest nightmare, he could not imagine the pain Archangel must have endured since his capture. It would be some time before he would be conscious, and even then, there was no guarantee his mind would not be damaged. Kael did manage to get him to swallow some water now and then.

He had healed the burnt skin about the socket of Archangel's missing eye, though there was scarring present that even magic could not completely heal. He feared for Lark. If Archangel had been disfigured so, he did not even want to think what manner of torture Lark had to withstand.

Kael was unsure why Archangel had been placed in the chamber with him. His only conclusion was that Mya knew he would be able to help him. He had not seen her in what seemed like an eternity. He felt a burning longing for her, and it was a sensation he had never experienced, a feeling both terrible and wonderful.

Without even meaning for it to happen, his love for her had been revealed. Even from the beginning, he had found it difficult to hide anything from her. Beyond all his hopes, he had felt her love for him in return. He began to despair again as he dwelt on his life. To have knowledge of what happiness could possibly be and, at the same time, to know that it could never be was a miserable wisdom he wished he had never learned.

He thought of Elenari. He thought how wonderful it would be to have Mya meet her and have them laugh and become good friends. It was a fantasy, an empty hope he harbored. At that moment, he recalled something Algernon had said long ago: "*As long as hope exists in some part of the world, evil could never truly be victorious.*" He hoped Algernon was right.

Kael awoke to Archangel moaning. He seemed to be having a nightmare.

As he went to comfort him, suddenly Archangel opened his eye and frantically scrambled to the back of the chamber away from him. Kael cautiously approached him, slowly, with his hands out and open.

"Archangel, it's Kael Dracksmere. I'm not going to hurt you. Do you understand who I am?"

Kael watched as he squinted and seemed to recognize him, even in the torchlight. "K-Kael . . . Dracksmere?" he intoned, clearly confused. "It can't be; I've seen so many friendly faces in my dreams and nightmares. Are you just another apparition?"

"No, my friend," Kael said gently. "I am the real thing. Come forward and touch my hand."

Archangel crawled forward and touched Kael on the hand and then grabbed his robes.

"Watch," said Kael as he used his magic to heal a blotchy discoloration on Archangel's chest. "I do not dare to think I know what you've been through my friend, but I've been looking for you and Lark for some time now."

"Lark . . ." Archangel muttered. Suddenly he grabbed onto Kael's robes again as if still trying to convince himself of Kael's tangibility. "Where's Lark? Where's my brother?"

Kael relayed to him everything he and the others had been through since his and Lark's disappearance. As he told the story, Archangel became more and more lucid and actually started to eat some bread and drink water. At the mention of the destruction of Wrenford and the death of all its inhabitants and the King, Archangel's face fell in disbelief. Tears for the many friends he had had, now dead and gone, streamed down one side of his face.

When Kael finally finished, he asked. "What's the last thing you remember?"

"My last memory is seeing Lark . . . right before they took my eye. He was alive then. That's all I know, Kael. How could the Shadow Prince be alive? You and Lark destroyed him. It's not possible."

"So I thought as well," Kael replied, "but I've actually seen him, and Thargelion and Algernon were convinced of it before even that. I do not know. I do not know why or how any of this is happening. I have no answers, unfortunately."

Kael did not speak to him of his feelings for Mya, except for his beliefs that she was not evil and more a victim of circumstance. Archangel made it clear he had no tender feelings for the White Elves in any capacity because of the pain and suffering he'd endured at their hands. Kael was grateful that Archangel's mental faculties seemed relatively undamaged, and they were able to carry on meaningful conversation.

As they continued to speak of events in the outside world, they suddenly noticed the door to their chamber was open. Neither of them had heard the characteristic scraping, and no one had entered; the door was simply open.

Cautiously they stood and approached it. As they peered out into the hallway, beyond all believability, Mya was there to greet them. She had a great sense of urgency about her as she quickly threw Archangel a cloak and handed him a long sword. She raised her hand to her lips to indicate they should be silent.

"Do not speak," she cautioned. "Follow me—quickly!"

They turned left, opposite the direction Kael remembered being dragged before. They passed the other stone cells and went down a narrow corridor, which seemed to end in a wall of stone. Mya touched the stone in three places and the wall opened much like the stone door of their cell. Without hesitation, they followed her through.

They found themselves in an extremely dark passage on a steep upward slope. Sensing their inability to see, Mya lit a torch and handed it to Archangel. As they moved, they could hear water dripping, and various jagged rock formations jutted out above and below where they walked. The rocks seemed purple or even pink in hue in places, though they could not be sure in the torchlight. They continued on an upward slope for several feet until they found themselves in an enormous cave. It was many times larger than the cave in which Kael had first seen Mya.

It was here Mya stopped them. "Now go that way," she said, pointing. "Go until you come to the cave opening. You will see two horses saddled and waiting for you at the cave entrance. Ride west. We are close to the Elven village of Dragontree, but do not go there; you would not be safe. They will be following you. Continue westward until you reach Alluviam; you will be safer there."

"Mya, why are you doing this?" Kael asked.

"You must go *now*," she urged, looking back the way they had come. "You do not have much time."

Suddenly Kael grabbed her hand, forcing her to face him. "Come with me."

She met his intense gaze and saw deep affection there. Reaching her hand up to touch the side of his face, she smiled and shook her head regretfully. "I cannot, Kael. I must stay with my people. They need me. You know it must be this way."

For the first time, Kael ran his fingers through her cloud-white hair and tried to imagine never being able to touch her again. He closed his eyes, wincing, then opened them and looked at her solemnly. "I will come back and help you unite your people. I will keep my vow."

"No! You must never come back," she said. "They'll kill you."

"Kael, we must go now," said Archangel, looking around for signs of anyone following them.

"This is where the Shadow Prince will address your people, is it not?" he asked her quickly.

She looked to the ground and nodded, guilt reflecting in her expression.

"I am coming back," he whispered softly, letting his hands slide away from hers. With a last look at her face, he turned away, and then they were off.

Chapter 19

Captain Gaston left the heart of his forces to bolster the forts along the Bazadoom border. Riders reported back that, fortunately, none of the other forts had been attacked. He took an escort of twenty men on horseback to guide Galin, Mekko, and Elenari safely back to Averon City.

They rode south, leaving the carnage at Fort Renault behind. Captain Gaston advised the trio of the most recent events, which were just as troubling as the attacks from the creatures of Bazadoom.

"The Elves of Alluviam have, for reasons unknown to us, blockaded several of the main trade routes leading out from Averon. Many merchant caravans have had their wagons and cargoes confiscated in the name of Aeldorath, the King of Alluviam. The merchants are crying out for armed protection, which we would normally be more than happy to provide. However, the Merchant Council fears that, if any hostilities break out, Averon will be at war with Alluviam. The Elves have ever been our friends and allies, and we do not understand what has triggered these events. The Republic of Averon has never fought a war in its collective history. The men of the Sentinels were assembled and trained as a defensive force. We could not hope to win a war against the Elves, much less any of the other major countries."

"I think your forces are much stronger than you give them credit for, Captain," Mekko reassured him. "They're a damn disciplined bunch and damn well-trained. They've provide protection for all the merchants comin' in and out of Averon for decades. Now I know why no bandits would dare attack a caravan under the protection of the Sentinels."

Galin spoke up then. "I think what your people need to concern themselves with, Captain, is who wants you to be at war with the Elves. I know

King Aeldorath well, and I can assure you he desires no wars for his people. A war with Averon serves no purpose for the Elves; they already enjoy a free and prosperous trade with your country.

"However, I agree with General Mekko in that I believe your army could make a very effective offensive force against the true enemy at work here. We must go to Alluviam and make peace between your two nations so that you both may unite together under one banner against the Shadow Prince, for it is he who is your common enemy. War is coming, Captain, make no mistake—coming to Dwarves, Elves, and men on all fronts and from all sides. If we do not unite as one people—as free people—putting aside our differences, then we will fall to the ruin of innocent lives everywhere."

Galin's statements weighed heavily on Gaston as they traveled for the remainder of the day until nightfall settled upon the land. The men made a simple camp on the grassy plains beneath the night sky. The moon fought its way through the dark clouds to illuminate the landscape below. The night was clear, the air fresh, and the moonlight painted enough to show them their place in the world. To the west lay the Kingdom of Alluviam, concealed deep within the forests of green, while to the east lay the Kingdom of Cordilleran amid the eastern mountain peaks.

Mekko stood apart from the camp, staring at the distant mountains of his homeland. They were still so far away, but it felt as if they were at arm's length. *Galin was right*, he thought, *war is coming, and Cordilleran may already be its first casualty*. They would need allies though. Prior to his capture he wouldn't have thought so but now he was sure.

Elenari also camped separately from the others. She had not spoken a word since they had left the fort. Her distance from the camp clearly indicated she did not wish to be approached.

The captain carried a small bowl of stew to where Elenari sat, her legs crossed and her horse nearby. He could see she was aware of his presence from a distance. He put the bowl beside her and raised his hand as if meaning no offense. "I just thought you might be hungry."

Backing away slowly, he turned and began to walk away.

"Captain," said Elenari softly, almost in a humble whisper.

Her voice was so low that Gaston barely heard her, and he turned back to ensure he hadn't misheard her.

"Thank you," Elenari said flatly with less emotion this time.

"Milady." Gaston bowed his head, and then continued back toward his men.

It was late when Mekko finally returned to lie down near where Galin was camped. He was trying to be as quiet as possible, knowing most of the other men were asleep and that the Druid appeared to be as well.

"That was a brave thing you did, General," Galin whispered, "staying and fighting with those boys against those odds."

"It was a brave thing *they* did, Druid," Mekko whispered back. "I just . . . couldn't bring myself to leave 'em alone. You see pure bravery like that maybe . . . once or twice in a lifetime. I've been blessed to have seen courage such as that many times, of course, but it's the type of thing, lad, no matter how many times you see it, it stirs somethin' deep inside you. It's a rare feelin', Druid, one that you never get tired of, and it's just as meaningful and even more special every time you feel it. Do you know what I'm sayin'?"

Galin's response was a light snore. The sound brought a smile to the general's lips. *Aye,* he thought, *the Druid and his companions know what I mean all too well.*

Algernon left the main audience chamber of the Merchant Guild Council of Averon and was escorted to a nearby, ornately decorated ante-chamber. He had finally been granted an audience as a courtesy, but the council was clearly preoccupied with the dilemma of the Elves.

Having argued with the council for two days with the same sour result, he grew even more disgusted and angry as he looked about the gaudy chamber. Satin cushions adorned the furniture, and handmade imported rugs of intricate designs covered the floors. Priceless paintings surrounded him on each wall, and long, flowing, amber drapes of silk covered the small balcony behind double doors of glass. And this was just a small waiting room. It reminded him that the merchants' love of money and the protection of their income had become more paramount to them than the safety of their people.

Even his old friend, Edward Gaston, had told him their forces were too strung out and they dare not risk pulling any forces from Averon City. They had all become so rich that protecting their businesses was all that mattered to them now. The council had told him they did not believe they were in any danger, as the surrounding countries would rally to protect them against any threat, and they needed proof more convincing than his word before they would even consider lending their armies to an alliance.

And so, he had failed once again to enlist aid against the looming threat of the Shadow Prince. It was at that moment, when he was feeling overwhelmed by despair, that the door to the chamber swung open to admit Captain Gaston and his comrades.

"My friends!" he exclaimed. "You are all safe? For that much, at least, we are blessed."

"My Lord Algernon," the Captain replied, "how go your talks with the council?"

Algernon sighed deeply and shook his head.

"Aye, that bad eh?" Mekko said. "Well just let me in there; I'll tell those potbellied rich fools something to get them off their fat merchant arses."

Captain Gaston immediately moved to block Mekko. "Excuse me, General," he said. "Perhaps it's better if I speak to them. In light of what I've seen, I believe I can change their minds."

"Anything you can do, Etienne, will be in the best interest of your people, I assure you." Algernon said.

Gaston nodded and left them to wait in the chamber.

Algernon greeted the rest of them warmly—all save Elenari, who moved away and opened the glass doors to stand out on the balcony. After a few moments with the others, Algernon followed her outside.

"I see you are still troubled, child," the Sage said.

Elenari looked below to the crowded streets of Averon City. They were reminiscent of those of Mystaria, except here the streets were lined with merchants instead of wizards. They were in the very hub of the Merchant District, the largest part of the city, which consisted of many heavily guarded, large warehouses that stockpiled goods from throughout the known world to be shipped out in trade.

"Algernon," Elenari began, staring blankly into the distance, "what makes any one of us different from our enemies? I know we are not inherently evil . . . but do we not commit evil acts in the name of goodness?"

Algernon walked close to her, putting himself between her and the view beyond. Gently, he brought his hand to the side of her face, directing it so that her eyes met his. Immediately, she attempted to look down, but he brought her chin up so she could not look away.

She saw a strange blue fire within his aged eyes.

"Now hear me, child, and hear me well. There is one thing above all others that makes you different from the Shadow Prince, his minions, and his allies: hope. Hope is the thing they do not have, nor will they ever have it again. Yes, they desire; they lust for wealth and power. They have . . . a longing, a need, for more power to dominate and conquer, but they can never kill enough or pillage enough or destroy enough to ever fulfill this need. The reason that is so, child, is because they can never hope for anything better. The Shadow Prince himself was born a man, and at one time, long ago, he too had hope, but the evil to which he succumbed replaced that hope with a desire to dominate living things. Now, he jealously hates those of us who still have what he has utterly lost, and he wishes to show us he has the power to take it away from us before we die. Do you understand?"

Elenari nodded as a tear formed in her eye, and she felt ashamed.

"No more tears, child," Algernon said gently. "Come; even now as the shadow of evil grows, we have it within ourselves to stay its course and drive it back."

Elenari embraced him and held him tight, glad to have his counsel.

Nearly an hour had passed before Captain Gaston returned to the chamber. They quickly rose as he entered the room. He looked first to Algernon, then to the rest of them.

"The council has decreed that I and two diplomats are to accompany you to the Kingdom of Alluviam to try to negotiate a settlement to these blockades and further assess the situation before any further aid is considered," Gaston explained. "They wished to extend their thanks to you,

General, for all of your assistance. In the meantime, they will continue deliberations on whether to send troops to aid Cordilleran."

"Bah! They can keep their thanks," said Mekko. He turned and attempted to storm out of the chamber, only to be held fast by the strong hand of Gaston on his shoulder. Startled and somewhat taken aback, the Dwarf looked up at the Averon officer, and the solemnity of his eyes and face calmed him instantly.

"I told them, General, that regardless of what they decide, I am going to Cordilleran to stand with you," the tall soldier said calmly.

Mekko brought his hand up to rest on the Captain's arm. "I know you will, lad . . . I know you will."

"Well, Captain," said Algernon cheerfully, "in an hour you have made more progress than I after two days of arguing. There is hope after all." As he spoke, he winked at Elenari, who looked down at the floor and smiled.

"Please, come with me," Gaston instructed. "Any and all supplies you wish will be made available to us before we leave."

"Let us make haste then, Captain," Algernon replied, "for lives from both countries depend on our ability to resolve this dispute, which should have never been."

They set out west for Alluviam just before noon. The two Averon diplomats had joined the party. The first, Lord Louis Devon, was their Chief Arbitrator in matters of business disputes with other nations. He was well known and well-liked by many of the surrounding countries. The second diplomat, Minister Jacques Fornier, was their Minister of Foreign Affairs. They had settled on an escort of five soldiers in addition to Captain Gaston and the others. Though Lord Devon had pushed for a larger number, Minister Fornier, Algernon and Galin insisted any more than that could be misinterpreted as non-diplomatic.

The day's weather was fair, and they rode at a brisk pace toward the Vineland Woods, a dense forest that served as a buffer zone between Alluviam and the rest of the world. The Elven village of Dragontree was near the outskirts of the Vineland Woods, though it was farther south than where they would be traveling. Once they passed through the Vinelands, they would enter the Sylvanwood Forest, which immediately surrounded the Kingdom of Alluviam. Galin had assured them the Elven sentries would intercept them shortly after they entered the Sylvanwood.

Galin was glad to be finally headed back to Alluviam. Too long had he been away, and it was the closest thing to a real home he had ever known. It was the first place he had ever been where the serenity of life was revealed to him as a powerful thing, the place where first he'd found people in the world who chose to have a symbiotic relationship with the environment around them. The Elves were a magical, yet subtle, people who revered the harmony and majesty Mother Nature had to offer them.

King Aeldorath had provided Galin with his own cottage upon his appointment as Druid of Alluviam and often took long walks with him in the Sylvanwood. There would always be one or two of the King's personal guard, the Emerald Watch, with them, but they would walk and talk for hours on end of rare wildlife, their childhood, their families, and the simple love of life they shared. The Elves were not quick to trust outsiders, but once they had learned to trust him, they embraced him as a brother.

The Elven language had become as natural to him as the common tongue, yet still the Elves were sometimes a mystery to him. Their culture was thousands of years old, and as simply as they lived their lives, they could be very complex in the most mundane matters. They had broken down every facet of everyday living to a near perfection. Everything—the way they moved, the way they gardened, the way they built, the way they spoke, the way they fought—was done with the utmost attention to detail. The simplest occupation was carried out with painstaking precision and focus. Yet, for all their dedication to form and perfection, he had never seen a people so quick to laugh or to celebrate joy with one another. That, he supposed, they did perfectly as well. As unique as their culture was, still they were not above strong emotional outbursts, nor were they quick to forget those who had slighted them in the past. All these thoughts passed through Galin's mind as they approached the Vineland Woods.

Elenari guided them with Galin at her side providing direction. Algernon rode with the two diplomats in the middle, and Captain Gaston and their escort brought up the rear.

Elenari let her thoughts dwell on the lava creature. It was still somewhere out there in the wild, pursuing them. Soon enough, they would face it again, and this time there would be an end to it, one way or another. It would be destroyed, or they would all be dead; she would not allow any other possible outcome. She did not fear, however, for she knew Galin and the others were as committed as she. Even Mekko and Captain Gaston, who had no real stake in the matter, had committed to help destroy a beast that would quite probably kill them. *They are both honorable and brave men,* she thought. *Exceptional friends.*

The prospect of traveling to Alluviam held unpleasant consequences for Elenari. At odds with herself, she both desired and dreaded to visit the Kenshari Temple and speak with her old mentor, High Master Reyblade. She so desperately wanted his counsel, yet the shame she would endure from confessing her many failures to him held no allure. She had failed him in every way, gone against all his teachings. Still, she had to speak with him. At the very least, she needed to solicit the help of the Kenshari Masters to fight against the forces of the Shadow Prince.

They made camp that night, still half a day's journey from the Vineland Woods. Elenari disappeared into the darkness shortly after they settled down to scout ahead, as she routinely did. Galin and Mekko sat and talked before they went to sleep, having become close traveling companions. Lord Devon and Minister Fornier, men who did not routinely travel or exercise for great periods of time, found that sleep came quickly to them. Captain Gaston slept near his men, the soldiers of their escort.

Algernon sat awake for some time, lost in thought. If they could settle the dispute between Averon and Alluviam, he was confident they would unite to help Cordilleran. Still, with the absence of Thargelion, he felt somewhat alone in the world. He and these few brave companions who had sacrificed and lost so much to follow him knew and believed in the evil that was becoming stronger each day, threatening their world, but those who led nations capable of stopping it could not see what was clearly before their eyes. The Emerald Star, properly employed, could stop even the vast armies the Shadow Prince was amassing. But its powers could not reach everywhere at once; if they did not succeed in finally forming an alliance, soon there would be nothing left to defend.

He opened the metal box containing the Emerald Star and looked at the gem. It did not shine with quite the same luster as it had before they had left Wrenford. It was weakening; as the festering malignancy which drained life from the land increased, the power of the Emerald Star waned as if the two were connected. He dared not tell the others. He alone would have to bear the burden of this knowledge. He placed the gem back in its metal container, which he concealed as usual deep in his robes, and curled himself into a position of sleep.

Their next day began early, just after sunrise. There was a sense of urgency in all of them; even the two diplomats, whose purpose was not as global in scope, projected the same seriousness as the others.

As they rode in the same order as the previous day, the Vineland Woods began to take shape before them. These were not great thick oak trees; instead, they were smaller in size and width, but were far greener throughout. The bark of these trees was layered with vines that resembled veins, which spread from the base of the trunks to their leafy crowns. The trees were dense and numerous, growing very near to one another. As they entered the woods, the air became close and the space more confined.

Captain Gaston thought these woods served as a most effective natural defense to Alluviam. A large invading force could conceivably enter and travel through, but not without tightening their formation considerably. They would also be severely slowed regardless of the numbers in their ranks. It was a dark forest as well, though not in an evil or foreboding manner, but the sunlight had difficulty penetrating to the ground. The vines and moss were thick even on the ground, so much so that the animals themselves sometimes had slight difficulties negotiating the trail.

After a few hours of slow travel, Galin indicated they were more than halfway through the Vineland Woods. He said the elven sentries would show themselves shortly after they passed through a small elven village, Leafshaven, and transitioned into Sylvanwood Forest. Shortly thereafter they would enter Alluviar, capital of the elven kingdom and home of King Aeldorath. Yet, as close as he made their destination sound, they were still more than a day away.

Elenari suddenly brought them to a halt. They looked around, but heard and saw nothing. She stood up in her saddle and tilted her head in such a way that indicated she could hear something they could not. Several

334 | Farrell & de Weever

seconds went by, and then she turned and waved Captain Gaston to join her. As the captain trotted up to her, she maneuvered her horse so they were facing opposite directions, side by side. She whispered in his ear, and immediately he called his men to the front of their line.

The captain and the five men took out their crossbows, nocked bolts at the ready, and fanned out in a semicircle. Elenari advised Galin to take Algernon and the diplomats far away into the cover of the trees. She maneuvered her horse to within the center of the circle of Averon soldiers and nocked an arrow to her bowstring. Then they waited.

Only seconds later, Gaston saw two figures approaching their position on horseback. They both appeared to be clothed in black.

"Be prepared to fire," said Gaston to his men. "They could be scouts in the service of the enemy." He faced the oncoming riders and raised his voice to a shout. "That's far enough, riders! Stop and we will know your business, if you wish to remain unharmed!"

Rather than slowing, the riders seemed to increase their speed, riding directly toward them.

"Prepare to fire on my command!" Gaston ordered his men.

"It cannot be . . ." whispered Elenari. "Put down your weapons, Captain."

Gaston watched as she dismounted, slinging her bow across her back, and slowly walked toward the approaching riders, moving as if she were no longer concerned about any potential threat.

Galin rode up behind the soldiers to see what was happening. Instantly, his eyes widened and his mouth fell open. "Kael!" he exclaimed. "Kael, is that you?"

Hearing this, Algernon hurriedly rode forward out of the cover of the woods, a sudden wide smile on his aged face and a sigh of relief escaping his throat. "The fates have been kind to us at last," he whispered to himself.

Elenari's steps had slowed. In that moment, she was once again the small child scrounging for cover in the woods, afraid and unsure of the tall stranger who had found her that night in the moonlight, led by the raven perched on the branch of the tree over her head. He had come to find her once again. Tears filled her eyes as she watched the two riders come to a halt and dismount. She put both hands to her face, covering her mouth, as her father approached her.

"I told you I'd be back, my darling daughter," said Kael as he took her hands away from her face and held them in his own. "A little later than I planned, I grant you," he chuckled, "but back nonetheless."

Tears streaming down her cheeks, she smiled and jumped into his arms. "We thought you were dead," Elenari breathed, holding him tightly.

"Well, I confess I thought the same for a moment or two," he whispered to her with a smile, "but we'll keep that between us."

As Elenari released him, she took a good look at the man with him and rubbed the tears from her eyes, gaping in disbelief. "Archangel?"

"I thought never to see your beautiful face again, young lady," Archangel replied.

She saw that his eye had been lost and could not help but gasp in sympathy, placing her hand on his cheek. Algernon and Galin had dismounted and now came to join them. Warmly, they clasped hands, first with Kael and then Archangel.

"Life is good this day, is it not, Elenari?" Algernon said.

Elenari grasped his hand tightly for a moment in reply and smiled, still with tears of joy in her eyes.

Galin retrieved a strip of black cloth from his saddlebag and tied it around Archangel's head so that it covered his missing eye. They elected to stop and made an impromptu meal; both Kael and Archangel were thirsty and starving. They shared the provisions as much as possible. As they sat and ate, Algernon briefly introduced Captain Gaston and the Averon diplomats to the newcomers.

"There is much to tell, Algernon," said Kael. "I have seen and heard much to our purpose in the time I've been away from you."

Algernon interjected and quickly explained their situation at Averon, and how and why they were bound for Alluviam.

"I've seen the Shadow Prince and what's more I've heard what he plans from his own mouth," Kael revealed. The others looked wide-eyed at him.

"Where is Hawk?" Kael asked suddenly.

There was a hushed silence as Galin and Elenari bowed their heads. As Algernon started to answer, Elenari raised her hand to silence him.

"He gave his life . . . to save us from the lava creature," she answered, managing to maintain her composure.

"I'm so sorry," Kael replied, wrapping his arm around Elenari and holding her close. "Galin . . . I'm so very sorry. He has saved us all. A brave and honorable man . . . I too shall miss him."

"What news of Lark?" the Sage asked.

Both Kael and Archangel shook their heads. "When last Archangel saw him, he was alive in Shadowgate," Kael replied, "but that was some time ago. That is all we know."

"Let us be on our way, then, to the safety of Alluviam," Algernon said. "We dare not linger. Come, Kael; ride with me and tell me everything there is to tell."

The captain and Elenari made haste to conceal any sign of their passing and stopping there. As they rode, Kael relayed to Algernon all that had befallen him since the time they had parted. He told him everything, from what he had overheard in the cave in the Broken Lands to all he had learned from Mya.

During the time they spoke, the group entered Sylvanwood Forest. Here the trees had changed again. They were tall and thick, and nearly devoid of vines and moss. The air opened up, as the trees were not so close to one another. Here, instead of green, the leaves were amber. Even as they fell to the ground, they reflected the sun's rays, filling the forest bed with a glorious light that chased away any hint of darkness.

This forest was full of life. All manner of woodland creatures, which had been so conspicuously absent from view of late, were strong in number here, as if they had merely been hiding in this place all along. Birds were singing and chirping their songs of joy amid the foraging squirrels and chipmunks busily gathering all sorts of food on the ground. Here, the poison infecting the living things of the lands was least evident, having yet to rear its ugly head. It was as if nothing could touch this pristine place. It was as if poison and evil never existed at all and were only bad dreams in a place of such beauteous grandeur as this. Elenari, too, having reunited with her father, felt as if she were slowly waking from a bad nightmare.

Yet, as they rode on, Galin became increasingly nervous. He advised Elenari that the Elven sentries should have intercepted them some time ago. It was then that they saw something ahead in the distance that did not fit—fire, smoke, and blackness.

"Leafshaven . . ." Galin said in a horrified whisper.

They rode ahead at a faster pace and saw the forest was burnt and blackened in the distance. It was the village of Leafshaven, burnt to the ground. Many of the wooden homes were still aflame, and Elven bodies or their remains lay scattered throughout the forest floor. Slowly they trotted through, horrified by the condition of the bodies. Some were mangled, melted, and even charred. There were women and children as well; none had been spared.

"If you hadn't survived at the fort, General," Kael said, "Averon would have blamed the Elves for that attack just as the Elves might blame Averon for this tragedy."

"No force of arms committed this atrocity," said Elenari bitterly, holding her hand up to indicate they should halt.

There, across the field, where the last remnants of the village ended, stood the lava creature. Heat spread outward from the beast as it stood dripping lava, like a bear just emerged from splashing in a stream. The crystal moved back and forth within its head, as if surveying the death and destruction that it had left in its wake. The trees and bushes surrounding it were shriveling and dying from the radiating heat.

"What manner of creature is this?" Minister Fornier asked, shock and disbelief on his face. He looked at Lord Devon, who viewed the monster with similar horror.

"It is a creature born of an evil magic," Algernon replied, "more powerful than you can possibly conceive. Pray you never have to see it closer than this. Come with me now, gentlemen. Ride!"

He directed the diplomats back in the direction they had come.

The creature's gem pulsed brightly, sensitive to the presence of the Emerald Star. That was its main purpose: to retrieve the magical gemstone by whatever means were necessary, killing and destroying any and all that came in its path. It had been searching for many days now. The waning power of the mystical emerald had made it more difficult to detect, but still the creature had always known the general direction in which to travel to find it. It had come close a few times, killing some who barred its way. Still, its reason to exist remained unfulfilled. It must get the Emerald Star and place it in the hands of its master and creator. Here, once again, it faced those who would hinder its goal.

Elenari quickly instructed the captain and his men to dismount, as she knew from previous encounters that the horses feared the creature immensely and would soon be beyond control. They obeyed quickly, fanning out in a circle again, weapons drawn and crossbows at the ready.

The heat was unbearable, almost scorching, and they had no choice but to back away as the creature headed toward them. The heat came through the air in waves so intense that even some of the soldiers felt faint from it. General Mekko tried to step closer to it, swinging his axe in a wide arc, but did not even come close to striking it.

Elenari circled the beast, closer than all the rest, tossing her sword from one hand to the other. This was what she had been waiting for: to destroy this abomination that had killed Hawk. She kept just enough distance from it to make the heat bearable. Anger burned within her, swelling into hate, and, for a moment, she lost herself to it. It was a feeling she had become used to; indeed, a moment wherein she did not feel some sort or hate or anger had recently become a rare thing.

Then she realized her feelings were woefully misdirected. She had so much hatred for this creature, which was itself nothing more than a magical construct, devoid of thought and conscious morality. It had a programmed purpose, nothing more. She relaxed her breathing and tried to calm herself.

Kael and Galin came forward. They felt the heat to a far lesser degree than the others, but they knew the creature was quite capable of killing them as easily as the others.

Kael did not like how close Nari was to the creature, and he called to her. "Nari! Nari, pull back! It's too powerful!"

She could not hear him; all her thought was bent on how to destroy the creature. Though she tried to calm herself, still her mind raced and her heart pounded.

Gaston signaled his men, and they all fired their crossbows, but their attack was futile, as the bolts struck and melted like ice deep within their target's molten body.

At that moment, Algernon reappeared, riding up to where Kael and Galin stood.

"The diplomats are safe," the Sage said, holding fast to his reins and trying to steady his frightened steed. "My friends, I fear this creature is unbeatable. Its strength is far too much for us. Our only hope is to run."

"Algernon," said Galin, his breath coming in short gasps, "we cannot run forever. This thing will follow us, killing innocents along the way, until we are dead or it is destroyed. The line must be drawn here. How many more would you see it kill?" As he spoke, he gestured toward the dead of Leafshaven.

"My young Druid," Algernon said as gently as was possible, "this thing has been created from such a dark magic that the only chance we have left is to run. I know that I would not see any more killed in my defense. We do not have the magic or the weapons necessary to defeat it."

The magic, thought Galin. His mind raced over Algernon's words again. *The magic . . . of the creature's gemstone.*

"We canna just stand here and let this thing kill us!" Mekko exclaimed. "I won't go down without a fight. By Crylar's beard, I won't!"

With that, the general held his axe high and charged at the monster. He remembered from the last encounter the heat was not quite as severe behind it, so he circled around behind it and swung high into the creature. The axe cut through the molten lava but became lodged in the creature's back. The blade melted almost instantly as lava trickled out from its back down along the hilt of the axe. Mekko released his weapon and watched as the beast absorbed it completely.

"Get away from it!" Galin screamed.

But it was too late. The general was barely able to turn and run before a ball of lava shot forth from the monster, striking him in the back and sending him to the ground face first. His chain mail armor started melting immediately into his skin and body, causing him to scream in terrible agony. Gaston rushed to his aid and started pulling the armor away, but it was so hot to the touch that his hands were burnt even through his gloves. Galin rushed forward then, quickly summoning his healing powers. Gaston continued to pull off the armor, which had now become a sheet of melted metal. Together, he and Galin dragged Mekko several feet away from the creature. Gaston peeled off the rest of the mess that was Mekko's armor despite his burnt hands, and Galin held the Dwarf's head as he slipped out of consciousness.

Galin looked on, helpless, as the creature made its way toward Kael and Algernon. He watched as Kael made several gestures with his hands and suddenly a swirling bolt of snow and ice shot forth from Kael's palms and struck the creature with tremendous force, knocking it over. Yet the beast reformed itself almost instantly and seemed to be increasing the heat it was generating, enabling itself to engulf the ice so that its only effect was to create a cloud of fog and steam. Still, Kael's distraction gave Algernon sufficient opportunity to circle around the monster to where Mekko lay.

The creature shrugged Kael's ice spell off and launched a spray of lava at him in retaliation. The Druid threw himself to the left, rolling across the ground, and the attack seemed to only graze him. Kael sprang immediately back to his feet, not realizing that the back of his robe was on fire until Nari shouted to him. Quickly, he pulled it off and threw it aside.

Galin watched Kael's struggle with the creature. All the while, the words "created from magic" raced through his mind.

Suddenly, it clicked. The answer was there right in front of him all along.

Galin stood and threw his arms out wide, fingers extended toward the beast and head bowed in concentration, and began to chant in an ancient language.

The lava creature had turned again toward Algernon, but found Galin standing between it and the Sage. Elenari, having rushed to Kael's side, watched in disbelief as Galin stood his ground while the creature approached.

"What's he doing?" Kael muttered.

Etienne Gaston had been in battles before, but never against anything like this. Fear raced through his body, but fear or no, he would stand or fall, honored to die with courageous companions such as these. He picked up his sword and motioned for his men to form a living barrier before Algernon and the still-unconscious Dwarf.

A hot wind swirled around them, cutting at their skin like razors. The creature was less than ten feet from Galin now, waves of heat generating from it and scorching the very air. Even the men of Averon and Algernon, who were several steps behind Galin, had to move back in order to breathe.

At the last possible moment, Galin's fingers sprang out and a green bolt of energy shot forth and struck the gemstone in the creature's head. Nari and Kael were caught by surprise and sprang back. The others looked on, bewildered.

The creature began to sway back and forth, lava dripping off its body and bubbling to the ground. It seemed to lose its equilibrium for just a moment, then, without warning, it imploded, falling to the ground into a puddle with the gemstone floating in the middle. The heat dissipated, and the group looked in amazement at Galin.

Kael rushed to Galin's side and placed a hand on his shoulder. "What did you do?" he asked incredulously.

"I used a dispel magic incantation on the gemstone," Galin replied. "*That* was the source of the creature's power, not the Shadow Prince's will."

"What does that mean?" Gaston asked.

"It means that to defeat such a creature, you must dispel the magic upon the object that controls it," Kael replied, "which our friend here appears to have done."

Algernon walked toward them, concern evident on his face. He looked at the gem; though it no longer had the same brilliant, red glow it once did, he was still wary.

"That was too easy," the Sage mumbled as he walked toward them. "There must be more—"

But before Algernon could finish his thoughts, the hot wind picked up again, and suddenly the molten lava began reforming itself again. The heat became increasingly uncomfortable as spatters of lava rose from the ground and started pushing the gem back upward toward the top of the creature's now-reforming head.

"It did not work!" Gaston screamed, tightening the grip on his sword. He ordered his men to circle the beast, giving it multiple targets to focus on.

Kael grabbed Galin's wrist. "Perform the spell again, with our combined power this time!"

Algernon wrapped his arm around Elenari. "Come with me now, child! Quickly!"

As Algernon and Elenari scrambled in the opposite direction, the Sage immediately began fumbling about one of the pouches at his belt, spilling a strange blue powder into his hand.

The creature had completely reformed now, its heat exciting the air around it as before. Kael and Galin were too close.

Nari watched as Algernon brought the handful of powder to his lips and blew on it. The powder transformed into half a dozen hovering arrows of blue energy. With a gesture, he guided the arrows toward the lava creature.

They struck furiously, punching large holes in the creature. This made for barely a momentary setback, however, as the lava quickly redistributed to fill in the holes.

The creature moved toward Nari and Algernon.

"Algernon, stay behind me now and do as I say." Nari spun around to face the beast, screaming in rage. "Your evil will die this day, one way or the other!"

Before Algernon could stop her, she took a running jump toward the creature. With acrobatic skill, she jumped over it, spinning sideways in midair as she attacked with her sword, striking the gem. She pulled her legs toward her chest and rolled backward on the ground, coming immediately to her feet right in front of Algernon.

It was then that the Captain noticed a crack in the gem where Nari's sword had struck. Galin's spell had worked to some degree; it had weakened the gem that held the monster together.

At that moment, Kael raised his staff and a second charge of green lightning sprang forth from the two Druids' hands, enveloping the creature's head for a moment. When the electrical discharge faded, the gemstone had turned a dull brown color, no longer red at all.

"Now!" Kael shouted. "Attack it with all your might!"

Elenari rushed forward. Without warning, her foot landed in a small puddle of lava, causing her to cry out and lose her balance. She fell short of the creature and it towered over her, ready for the kill.

"Averon free forever!"

Elenari, startled, looked in the direction from which the cry had come. Suddenly Captain Gaston was there, lifting her up and shoving her away just in time to spin his sword around. It connected with the creature's gemstone with such force that his blade shattered on impact, sending the captain reeling backward.

The creature became frenzied, as if it had been blinded, stumbling about, launching globs of lava in every direction. Kael and Galin dove out of the way as lava splattered the trees and the ground all around them.

Nari took a deep breath and rose to one knee. She was covered in sweat, her blonde hair matted down to her head and cheeks. Dirt and burn marks covered her clothes and legs, and black smears even covered the fair skin of her face. She held her sword reverently in her hands before her, and her eyes locked on the shining blade.

"*Eros-Arthas*," she whispered, "I call upon your sacred power . . . for Hawk." With that, she grasped her sword tightly, raised it above her head, leaned back, and launched it at the creature.

The sword tumbled through the air, blade over hilt, gleaming like a shooting star, and struck the gemstone with an explosive force. A tremendous flash of bright light and violent waves of energy shot out in all directions. Leaves and dirt were blown all about as the companions were all thrown to the ground, shielding their eyes against the debris.

As soon as the blast subsided, it was silent.

When they uncovered their eyes, they saw that although the creature was standing where it had been, it was now a headless statue of soot and ash. The gemstone had split in two and had fallen at the feet of General Mekko, who still lay on the ground.

Protruding from the trunk of a tree behind the creature's remains, Nari's sword swayed and shimmered in the sun.

Mekko began to awaken, pushing himself up and wiping the dirt from his face. At his feet, he saw the shattered gem. He raised his gaze to the creature's standing remnants, and his eyes widened. "Bless my soul, I didn't know I had it in me!" the general said with a toothy grin.

Chapter 20

The group helped one another to their feet, dusting themselves clean of the debris that clung to their clothes.

Elenari went first to Galin. They faced each other solemnly for a moment, and then Galin drew her into a strong embrace. The others gathered round as well, Mekko placing his hand on Galin's shoulder and nodding to the Druid.

"You know, Hawk and the others are not truly avenged until the Shadow Prince is defeated," Galin whispered in Elenari's ear.

"All I know, Galin," she replied softly, "is that vengeance is a dangerous path. But still, the creature will never hurt anyone." Her eyes filled with tears for a moment, and she pulled back and looked him in the eye. He met her gaze and nodded.

Algernon admired the pair with pride in his eyes. He and Thargelion had indeed chosen well; they had accomplished what even he had thought was impossible. For the first time since they had begun, he allowed himself to believe they could actually succeed entirely in their quest. "Remember this moment, always," he said, "for you are all bound by it. You have come together from different lands to defeat evil, fighting as one. Indeed, this is a great day."

Slowly, Elenari walked to her father and embraced him. After a moment, she released him and headed to the tree where her sword remained stuck, monument to their victory. As she slid her fingers over the pommel, suddenly she sensed it. Her head snapped around, a look of fear etched upon her face.

"Oh, no."

She looked at Kael, whose smile melted away as he saw the expression on her face and the fear in her eyes. Elenari looked past him and saw the shadows of dark forms moving in the forest, preparing to fire their bows.

"You were followed!" She had barely gotten the words out before they were under attack. Dark arrows filled the air. In moments, three of Gaston's men fell with arrows buried in their chests. Like lightning, in one motion, Nari dislodged her sword from the tree and swatted down an incoming arrow, which would have otherwise struck Kael in the chest. Without hesitation, she shoved him to the ground and yelled to the others, "Get down! All of you get down, and take cover!"

She stood protectively over Kael, shielding him even as the thought that their efforts might not matter crossed her mind. They were vulnerable in the open and their attackers were well back within the shelter of trees. *They must be Elves,* she thought; otherwise, she would have sensed them sooner. But why were they attacking?

In the same moment, she sensed the presence of many others approaching from behind and heard the whistling of arrows flying in the opposite direction—toward their attackers. Help had come.

The fighting was over quickly; their enemies were vastly outnumbered. Fortune had smiled on them yet again.

Galin raised his head and saw a pair of brown boots. As he gazed upward, he saw the sparkling green vestment of the king's Emerald Watch.

"My Lord Calindir?"

Galin recognized the voice instantly as that of Layla Anorien, Princess of Alluviam, Captain of the Emerald Watch, and youngest daughter of King Aeldorath.

Nari helped Kael to his feet, as many green-clad Elves moved about the clearing.

"Is everyone all right?" Nari called. Her eyes found Galin, Captain Gaston, Mekko, the two Averon soldiers who had remained alive, and Algernon.

Algernon . . . there was something not quite right about him.

"Algernon!" Elenari screamed.

All heads turned to look upon Algernon. He was standing very still, with a strange look in his eyes that could only be described as relief mixed with regret. They did not see it at first—the dark-feathered shaft that protruded from his chest—as he still wore the dark cloak and robes he had acquired in Averon.

No one moved; time had stopped in what was left of Leafshaven. His eyes seemed to gaze back into each of theirs, every look different and distinct, carrying a secret message for each of them and seeming to last for eternity. He did not speak aloud, but still they could hear his voice in their minds. In his eyes, they saw friendship, respect, love, and most of all hope. These were the things they had always seen in him, things that he projected so strongly at one time or another. In his eyes, they saw his thoughts: at least they had a chance now, and he was glad he had lived long enough to believe it.

His hands resting comfortably at his sides and his eyes glazed over, he fell. Robes swirling in slow motion through the air, he surrendered to the pull of the earth and the sleep that had finally claimed him.

Amid cries of disbelief, Galin and Kael raced to the Sage's side, yellow magic bursting from their hands. As fast as they reached him, it was too late; cries of disbelief gave way to cries of grief. There was nothing they could do. The arrow had pierced his heart. Algernon, the great Sage of Wrenford, was dead.

"No Algernon, no!" Kael cried. "Not like this!"

"Not now!" Nari sobbed. She tugged helplessly at her father's robes. "It cannot be! Bring him back, father!"

Elenari collapsed, sobbing, with her head on Algernon's shoulder. Kael sat, holding the Sage's wrinkled hand, looking lost. Galin knelt beside him, expecting at any moment to see the resourceful old man he'd come to know and respect spring back to life, having used some trick to dismiss the arrow. He fully expected to hear one of the Sage's light-hearted jokes meant to ease their grief-laden minds. Mekko, too, looked at the Sage with remorse. Even the death of the little boy at the fort had not affected him like this.

Algernon had led them this far, kept them true to their course, and never let them give up hope. He was the keeper of the Emerald Star and, more than that, had been meant to be the one to wield it when the time came. All was lost. Hope was lost. Their sense of despair was so profound that it affected all present.

The Princess of Alluviam, Layla, looked at Galin, whom her people knew well, and the others, weeping almost like children over the body of the old man, a man with whom she was familiar only through stories she'd heard in her youth. Layla knelt, followed in turn by each of the Elves, bowing their heads in respect. When she rose, her face was as grief-stricken as theirs.

She followed her men as they raced into the woods. By the time she reached them, she saw they had collected the bodies of the attackers, and that the look of them was not unfamiliar to her.

"There are five of them, my lady," said Findel, one of her advance scouts.

"Dark-clad Elves with albino skin, my lady?" one of her men asked.

"White Elves," Layla replied bitterly. "Bring their bodies."

Gently, Kael pulled Nari away from Algernon's body, holding her tightly as she wept. "He helped me so much, Father," she sobbed. "When I thought you were dead . . . he helped me so much."

"I know he did," Kael said sadly. "He helped us all . . . more than he knew, I suspect. Now go, child. Go with the captain and gather the horses. Please, Nari."

Reluctantly, she walked away, leaving Kael, Galin, Mekko, and Archangel with Algernon's body.

Kael bent down, closed his eyes, and, swallowing hard, reached deep within Algernon's robes and removed the metal box that contained the Emerald Star. He looked up at Galin and Mekko. When Algernon had looked at him, he had heard in his mind, "*You must lead them now, Kael; you must safeguard the Emerald Star. You must provide hope in the face of darkness. Do not grieve, for this was a long time coming, and you no longer need me. You are ready . . . all of you. Farewell.*"

"He wanted me to take this for the time being," Kael said, bowing his head. "At least that's what I think."

Galin and Mekko nodded.

"His was the first voice I heard when you freed me from that damn stinkin' cell of mine," Mekko said.

As Elenari gathered their horses, she suddenly felt something nudging her arm. It was Algernon's horse. The animal continued to nudge her with its nose. Algernon's dying instructions to her rang in her mind: "*You must take my journal, Nari. Protect it with your life; it must never fall into evil hands. Destroy it before you allow it to fall into the wrong hands. Learn what you will from it. Swear you will do this; you are its guardian now.*"

"I swear it," she said aloud, fighting through her tears as she recalled how it had felt to hold his hand in the moment that she had been reunited with Kael.

The next moment, Layla reappeared and stood before them. She, like the rest of the Elves present, was clad in a green vestment that sparkled in the sunlight, though these they kept mostly hidden beneath their brown cloaks.

She greeted them officially by bowing low, placing her hand over her heart, and then reaching out her open hand as if to invite a stranger in. Her hair was raven-black, long and flowing, unique for an Elf. The beauty of her indigo eyes could not be fully realized because of the sorrow reflected in them.

"My Lord Calindir," she said, bowing to Galin. Then she turned and bowed to Kael. "My Lord Dracksmere, the Grand Druid, you are known to us. We know Algernon, the Sage of Wrenford, as well. He was the apprentice of the great Corinthian, and he was old even when some of my people were young." Her tone was full of remorse. "My father called him a friend to all Elves. He was extremely well versed in our lore and magic. Now, all that he was—everything he knew—is lost." She bowed her head toward Algernon and then knelt before them. "We beg your forgiveness; my father dispatched us here when he saw smoke in the forest coming from Leaf-shaven. Had we been swifter . . ."

Kael raised his hand, stopping her speech. "There is no need, my lady. Your aid is most welcome. Please rise. What has been done here cannot be undone by any of us . . . and there is blame enough for many, not least of all myself."

"Please . . . allow us to tend to the great Sage," Layla asked. "It will be our honor."

Kael nodded his consent. Layla gestured for her men to come forward, and they gently lifted the body of Algernon from the ground and bore him in their arms. As they did so, several others of their company appeared, leading the Averon diplomats in their midst.

"We thank you for killing the creature that destroyed our village," Layla said. "Those two gentlemen told us you were fighting a fiery creature when we came upon them in the forest. My father—Alluviam itself—is in your debt. My father will be anxious to see you; I'm sure there is much to discuss. Please, take your steeds and follow us."

She bowed again and turned away, walking ahead into the woods. Elenari, Captain Gaston, and Archangel brought their horses. They mounted in silence and followed the company of Elves onward through the Sylvanwood Forest. Their grief blinded them to the beauty of the forest. Amberleaved trees gave way to trees of golden blades the closer they came to Alluviam.

Galin knew they were close, as the leaves were falling all around them. They did not fall in only one season here; they fell year round, but they did not wither and die upon the ground; instead, the leaves were broken down and absorbed immediately by the earth in an age-old seamless process, and their nutrients were continually reabsorbed by the roots of the trees in the ongoing cycle of life.

Galin recalled how he had disagreed with Algernon about their quest. He had even thoroughly disliked the plan Thargelion and the Sage had conceived of in the beginning. At every turn, he had doubted the old Sage's physical ability to undertake such a journey, and at every turn Algernon proved him wrong. Try as he might to escape them, he could still hear the Sage's last words in his head: "If you lose hope, then evil will triumph. Never lose hope! There will come a time when it will abandon you, but you must remember that, with hope, all things are possible for you."

As they moved deeper into the forest, Elenari saw many well-camouflaged Elves situated in the trees above, no doubt going unseen by the others. The way was indeed well-protected.

So many times, when she was deep in the throes of despair, Algernon had come to her aid with words of wisdom and encouragement. It was inconceivable to think that she would never see him alive again. She felt terribly ashamed for causing him so much trouble, and for even going so far as to put her sword to his throat. None of that mattered much anymore.

Mekko regretted not having a chance to know Algernon better. Still, something of the old man's voice stirred in his mind: "The time will come when you will have to ally with your enemy, take command, and give them all the strength to fight." The words were distant, in the back of his mind, but he heard them all the same. He rode through the lush forest, able to appreciate its beauty but still longing for the mountains of home.

Etienne Gaston had lost three of his men. Their bodies were slumped over their horses, which the Elves were leading by the reins. He would have the unfortunate duty of taking them home and reporting to their families. He had never been to Alluviam before, though they were neighbors, and he had never traveled through the Sylvanwood. The Elves were magnificent creatures, as was the forest through which they traveled. Though he felt remorse for his lost men, he sympathized with his new comrades. It was as if they had lost a member of their family.

He shook his head, as his ears were ringing. Then, he heard these words in his mind: "*You must bring the Sentinels to Alluviam and then to Cordilleran. No matter what, you must bring them.*" It sounded like Algernon, and he wondered if his mind was playing tricks with him.

Archangel had never thought to breathe free air again. He thought of Lark. If he were alive, the news of Thargelion's and Algernon's deaths would strike him grievously indeed. At that moment, he heard whispering. He looked around quickly and realized none of the others had seemed to hear it. He was the only one who could sense it. It was the Sage's voice, saying, "*If you truly love your brother, you must fight him and keep him distracted from the others; he is your responsibility and no others.*"

Suddenly, without their having realized it, they had passed into a valley that seemed to have simply appeared in the middle of the forest.

"Behold, Alluviar, capital city of the Kingdom of Alluviam. Welcome friends of Algernon and men of Averon," Layla said.

There before them were several smoothly polished white marble structures. Between the buildings, a series of intertwining canals of sky-blue water connected them to each other, upon which many Elves were gliding in silver skiffs.

Many of the structures had multicolored stained-glass windows that were curiously shaped, being both oblique and oblong. The buildings were slanted, with one dimension, either width or length typically longer than the other. Despite this, they appeared to maintain a certain inexplicable symmetry. The buildings centered on a huge water fountain that stood within the heart of the city. A large obelisk of white stone stood within the heart of the fountain. Its base appeared to run deep under the ground. The water shot up high in the air, encircling the stone and creating a light mist as it fell.

As they entered the city, they noticed that it was, in fact, built on a very large lake. They could not tell if the canals had been carved out between the buildings or if the city had been built around them. The city itself did not seem overly large. As they entered the main thoroughfare, the grass gave way to a path of gravel. Layla led them immediately to a large stable where they could billet the animals, then down to the waterside, where they boarded one of the silver, canoe-like boats.

One of the Elves rowed, giving the newcomers a chance to survey the marble city. Mekko found himself gazing into the water; much to his surprise, he saw fish of various shapes and colors sharing the waterways with them.

Galin found himself looking at Layla, who in the past had usually made him feel very uncomfortable for a variety of reasons. Her ebony hair was rare among her kind, but it made her that much more enchanting and elegant to behold. In addition, she had a mischievous streak, which often enabled her to convince her father, albeit begrudgingly, to send her on missions of great danger and importance. Her skill as a warrior was beyond question, and she had a cunning wit that often tried Galin's patience, not to mention her own father's. However, to her great credit, she had wholeheartedly and solemnly deduced the magnitude of their loss, and her empathy was comforting.

"Hark, the Great Fountain of Life," Layla said, pointing to the central edifice. "A mere sip of its primordial waters is capable of quenching even the deepest thirst."

Instantly, Kael saw a vision of the fountain in his mind. The great white rock was shattered, and blood shot forth from it instead of water. Blood filled the canals and waterways. The bodies of dead Elves littered the city, floating face up in the crimson water by the hundreds.

"Kael!" It was Archangel, whose grip steadied him from behind, and Elenari, who grabbed his arm from the side.

"I'm all right," he said. "I'm quite well . . . just tired. Forgive me."

Why he had had such a bizarre vision was a mystery to him, but he hoped never see anything so horrible again in vision, dream, or anywhere else. The loss of Algernon weighed heavily on him; no doubt the vision was a side effect of his stress.

In a short space of time, they had traveled to the far side of the city, leaving their craft at a small dock. Again, a polished-marble trail led from the dock, leading for about twenty yards to an unbelievable sight. Here, where the forest met the mountains and from a height beyond imagination, fell the longest most breathtaking waterfall any of them had ever seen.

To their amazement, the great waterfall actually fell right through where the marble trail ended. There was a narrow chasm between the forest and the mountainside. Layla guided them down the trail, heading directly toward the waterfall.

Mekko came stubbornly to a halt. "Oh no, you're not getting me to fall over the edge to my death! Thank you, no!"

Layla smiled softly. "Come with me, then, Master Dwarf, and take my hand. Keep your thoughts as pure as the water, and I promise no harm shall come to you."

Mekko looked into the beauty of her blue eyes and the truth behind them, and was so charmed by her that he took her hand and walked with her despite his fears. She bade the others to follow.

They watched as Layla and Mekko walked right through the sheet of falling water and disappeared entirely from view. Galin assured the rest that all would be well, then followed fearlessly after Layla and the general, passing through the water as they had. The men of Averon were particularly skeptical, yet they dutifully followed the others.

They emerged on the other side, dry and in one piece. Mekko had only just now opened his eyes when the last of them emerged, and they all gaped at what lay before them.

"Behold the true realm of Alluviam," said Layla.

There, before their very eyes, stood a great palace of ivory-colored marble, and beyond, miles and miles of green pastures filled with hundreds, even thousands, of dwellings and homes, in every design and material imaginable. They were spaced out in a row, with green hills and fields beyond for children to play and others to ride upon. These lands were filled with Elves on horseback, and children running and laughing. It was a paradise, kept hidden by a powerful illusion.

"None with evil thoughts or intent can pass through the waterfall," Layla said. "It is the perfect protection for us."

The palace before them was accessible by a great arched gate that opened like a door. The standard of King Aeldorath—an emerald green flag with the veined outline of a single gold leaf within—hung above the gate. The flag displayed the same brilliant sparkle that the vestments of the Elves who had rescued them possessed. On the right and left end of the palace stood two granite guard towers with many archers stationed on top. Two guards, armed with great pikes and clad in shining silver armor, met them at the gate and guided them beyond into the foyer.

From there, Layla guided them through a large set of double doors, past two more guards, and beyond into the throne room. It was not as grandiose as they had expected. The floor of the small chamber was a beautiful turquoise marble decorated with a green carpet that led to a large stone chair with burgundy cushions. A great circular stained-glass window dominated the wall behind this chair and looked out over the entire view of the Elven homes and pastures beyond.

A tall, lean figure stood looking out the window, surveying the lands of his kingdom. The only indication of nobility about this figure was the small gold circlet about his head atop shoulder-length, silver hair. There were no jewels or gems upon the crown. He wore robes of forest green. He turned suddenly to greet them, and they saw the gentleness of his hazel eyes, yet something noble and stern seemed hidden behind them. Layla bowed and approached him, whispering softly. After a brief discussion, she bowed again and left them in the room, alone, with King Aeldorath.

"Greetings, Galin," the King said, opening his hand to him. "It gladdens my heart to see you once again." He turned to Kael. "Greetings to you, Grand Druid, and to all of you. Welcome to Alluviam. The death of the Sage Algernon comes as ill tidings to my people. We are less rich and devoid of wisdom in our journey through this life without him. It is an ill omen in this time of growing darkness. We ask that you permit us to honor him with a ceremony on the morrow. It will be a ceremony for him and the others who have lost their lives in defense of our borders and in the fight against evil.

"Now, men of Averon, my ministers await you. I fear there has been much confusion and misunderstanding between our people." The king motioned, and one of his soldiers bade the captain and two diplomats to follow him. "Forgive me now, but I must speak to the Grand Druid in private. My daughter will arrange for food and rest for you in the meantime."

Galin, Mekko, and Archangel followed Layla out of the chamber. Elenari turned to Kael. "Father, there is an errand I must undertake while we are here. I will return shortly."

"I understand," Kael said as he embraced her and allowed her to leave.

"Kael," the king said as soon as they were alone, "it was foretold to me that you and your companions would be coming here."

"My lord?" Kael asked.

"The last of the Elven seers, Corinthian, lies waiting to see you. He wishes to speak to you most urgently. There is little time. If you will follow me."

The king directed him toward a side door within the chamber.

"My lord, I don't understand," Kael said. "I don't even know—"

"He is near death," the king interjected. "He slips in and out of dreams at the gate that leads from this world to the next. He was . . . he *is* my friend and has been my advisor for many years, just as he was to my father before me. His last wish is to speak with you; it is all that keeps him alive now. I will see his will is carried out. Much as Algernon was to you, so Corinthian is to me."

Kael followed the King through a short hallway and up a flight of spiraling stairs, which took them to a long corridor on the second level of the palace. They came to a door near the end of the corridor, which the king gently opened. He did not enter, but instead looked at Kael.

"He will see you alone," Aeldorath said.

As Kael entered, a young blond-haired Elf maiden stood up from her seat beside the bed, bowed politely, and exited the room. As Kael moved toward the bed, he saw the ancient frail figure of an Elf lying there. Withered and bent, he was far older than even Thargelion had been. His skin seemed to have more of a gray hue to it, yet despite his wrinkles and aged appearance, still, Kael thought, Elves aged much more gracefully than humans did. His hair was thin and white, and he opened his dark blue eyes to meet Kael's.

"Kael of Wrenford. Long have I waited to see you."

"You have asked to see me, Corinthian," Kael said, bowing his head slightly. "How may I be of service?"

"Kael Dracksmere, the Grand Druid," Corinthian said thoughtfully. "I have the gift of foresight, as did my greatest pupil, Algernon, and as do you."

Kael looked into the old man's eyes. "You are mistaken."

"You sometimes see things that later come to pass," the old seer wheezed. "Your increased powers have enhanced this ability, yes?"

Kael hesitated, gazing down; he could no longer deny what he had known since before the quest began. Several moments passed in silence until he spoke again. "These visions . . . are they destined to occur? I saw Alluviar; there was blood and death everywhere."

"Nonsense!" the old Elf broke out into a coughing fit. When finally his condition eased, he spoke again. "There is no destiny, Kael of Wrenford, save that which we make for ourselves. I have counseled kings and dignitaries for centuries. I've warned them of visions of death and war, and they, in their infinite wisdom or foolishness, steered their destinies accordingly. Sometimes they worked to prevent them, sometimes to aid them. Now fate . . . ah, that is a different subject altogether. Alas . . . we do not have time to discuss it. The one you call . . . the Shadow Prince . . . comes three days hence with an army to ally . . . with our kin beneath the surface." Corinthian took a moment to catch his breath. "You must not let the armies join forces. They will destroy Alluviam if that happens. You know the place where they will meet."

The Elf reached over to touch Kael's hand. "Kael . . . beware the Shadow Prince. He is not . . . what you think; he is . . . much more."

The elf's hand fell limp from Kael's arm. Those were the last words spoken by the aged seer.

Kael sat beside the bed for a long time before he left the room.

Elenari rode to the northwest tip of the Sylvanwood. It was here, where few would know to look, that the Kenshari Temple would be waiting for her. She saw the huge, dark wooden fence that enclosed the training grounds. The fence was nearly twenty feet high and several inches thick, built of oak wood. However, there were no guard towers; in fact, there were no guards at all. Many outside of Alluviam believed the Kenshari to be legend, and those within knew better than to attempt to enter uninvited.

As she entered through the main gate, she saw disciples and students practicing their craft within the courtyard, some with their masters and others on their own. Students practiced in the archery range, while others, weaponless, practiced bare-handed martial disciplines. The temple itself was a tall, thin structure, angular at the top and constructed of beautiful blue marble. The building imparted serenity to those who beheld it. Beyond the temple walls were the gardens where all students were taught the importance of caring for living things and the illogic of waste. As she gazed upon the grounds, Elenari was overcome with nostalgia.

High Master Quentil Reyblade sat in a kneeling position, meditating within his chambers. There were few comforts within save for a crackling fire; however, the eyes of any student who entered would immediately be drawn to the two gem-studded scabbards resting on a mahogany display. *Hunir* and *Munir*, chaos and order, the two constantly opposing forces always meant to be kept in balance, were the given names of his swords.

The one other object in his chamber that always interested students was a painting of a coat of arms. It consisted of a silver shield with a coiled gold dragon flying through it. Legend said that it was the coat of arms of a warrior who had defeated Master Reyblade in battle centuries ago. However, when asked, he would often say it served as a reminder to him of humility and mercy, two traits every warrior must exemplify and demonstrate.

Silently, Elenari knelt behind him, placed her head on her hands, and then bent forward until her hands touched the ground. "Greetings to you, my master."

"Ah, child, I heard your steps from as far as the main gate," Master Reyblade replied. "My favorite student returns with a great burden upon her shoulders, so much so that your step has become heavy."

Elenari's voice was solemn. "I have brought dishonor upon both you and this temple. I have failed your teachings in every way since I left here. I have drawn my weapon in rage; I have threatened the lives of innocents . . . and I have failed you miserably." She straightened up and bowed her head.

"Child," Master Reyblade said, "you came to me with physical abilities I'd not seen in a pupil for centuries, yet do you remember what I told you before you left?"

Elenari nodded.

"For all of your vaunted abilities," the master continued, "you were still so young, and with such ability comes greater responsibility, a burden for which you were neither mentally nor emotionally prepared. You've mastered all of our tests, yet there is so much more to life than fighting and so much more to fighting than life."

Elenari rose and moved to stand before her master. Holding her sword out with both hands, she placed it on the ground before him. "You advised me not to leave, but I did not listen. I am not worthy of this sword you have gifted to me."

The master laughed heartily. "Nari, the purpose of learning would not exist without failure. I have lived longer than a hundred lives of men. I have done things beyond your comprehension. I have learned through some of these heinous acts that I desired to live and act a certain way, a way to which I have committed my life. If you feel you are no longer worthy of your blade, I say pick it up and make yourself worthy."

She smiled for a moment and bowed low. "I am grateful, Master, for your wisdom." Straightening slowly, she lifted her blade, looked upon it, and proudly strapped it to her waist.

Reyblade rose without a sound and moved to where he had been brewing tea in a small pot near the fire. He knelt, and Nari knelt by his side. As he handed Nari a cup, he spoke again. "Now, child, tell me what else you have come here to say, for there is more that weighs upon your mind."

Nervously, Elenari circled the rim of her cup with her finger, trying to find the right words to begin.

"Speak, child," said the master. "Your silence is as deafening as leaves rustling in the wind."

"War is coming," she said, "under the looming darkness, at the hands of a being known as the Shadow Prince. Unless the free nations unite with one another, his armies will rain fire down upon those who stand in his way."

"You have come to ask us to join in a war," Master Reyblade replied. "You know our code. We are teachers. We are not mercenaries. Many have tried to find us in the past, to solicit our services in battles and wars. If we agree to join any war and use our abilities, we will be sought after, constantly offered money and other worldly treasures for our service. A Kenshari does not sell himself for a bag of coins or a loaf of bread. We have not even joined our own kind in wars that have plagued our race in the past."

"Master, this is no war of political agenda; this is an invasion of evil seeking to destroy and subjugate all life that is not willing to bow to him in utter submission. His armies have destroyed the Wood Elves of the forest of Hilderan—and the nation of Wrenford, down to the last child. Even as we speak, they have no doubt laid siege to Cordilleran. How long do you think it will take these evil forces to find this place, Master?"

"He is already aware of it," Master Reyblade replied simply. "I have seen the great seer concerning this matter; I have heard what may come to pass. If the Kenshari Masters join this war, then you must make a promise to me, child."

"What is it, Master?"

"Promise me that you will take the disciples and students from here and find a safe place where they can stay, apart and away from what is to come."

"As you wish," Elenari replied.

Again the ancient sword master rose and walked to look out a small window. He watched the students practicing the Kenshari's time-tested methods of fighting, older than those of any other race. "There is one other thing I must ask of you: If we are destroyed, promise me that you will continue the teachings and the legacy of Kenshari way."

Elenari was shocked. "Master, I cannot . . . I don't possess such knowledge." Turning to Elenari, he said, "Then you must find it within yourself. You must be the last to be the first."

Elenari jumped to her feet. "The Masters are too strong. They could never all be killed."

"Do you promise me, child?"

She looked deep into her teacher's eyes, and though only seconds passed, it felt like an eternity. She did not answer at once, but finally, she nodded. "I will do as you ask, of course, Master."

Reyblade smiled. "Then we shall join the king's forces. Go, child, and tell him. We shall need time to prepare."

She bowed low and left him.

He returned to gazing out the window, sipping the last of his tea. His gaze went far beyond the field below where the students trained. Perhaps this is what they had always trained for—for this moment in history when they could no longer remain apart from the world around them. They were needed now, and even he could no longer deny it. This would be their time.

Galin walked alone in an open field just before dawn. Alluviam was still sleeping. He closed his eyes and reached his arms to the skies. Then he listened. The breeze strengthened where he stood. It was nature's way of responding to the Druid. He let his mind ask questions. The somewhat puzzling answers came in a combination of images and sounds. The breeze disappeared as he lowered his arms and stood in silence, contemplating nature's response to his commune. As the sun began to rise, he made his way toward the palace.

One of the palace guards took Galin to the throne room, explaining to the Druid that the King had not slept. As he was admitted to the throne room, Galin saw the King staring out his large circular window. He was attended by both his daughters; his oldest daughter and heir, Princess Trinia, a tall blonde-haired beauty who had been blessed with her father's nobility. Beside her stood Layla. Though also a Princess, Layla much preferred to think of herself as a captain in the Elven army.

"My lord, my ladies, I bid you good morning," Galin said bowing low. "I am told you have not slept, my lord."

"Ah, Galin, sleep does not come easily to me as it once did. There is much to do and still much to discuss," the King replied.

"Allow me to express my sorrow at the loss of the great seer. I know you were very close." Galin bowed again.

"When we need their counsel most," the King replied somberly, "both men and Elves have lost the greatest Sages of their history. We shall have to endure without their wisdom. In truth, how much did either race ever heed them, I wonder? Forgive me; that is a selfish thing to say." The King turned back toward his window.

"My lord, forgive this intrusion," Galin said, "but I went out alone before dawn to commune with nature. I fear, in the coming battle, that the power this evil commands will be far greater than the combined magic of Kael and myself. The Shadowlord and his second-in-command, the Lich Voltan, will be there. I asked the earth if there were any weapons we could possibly acquire to aid us against such powerful evil. The answers I continually received led me to believe I should see you, my lord."

The King's daughters looked at their father, dread evident on their faces. Layla stepped forward. "Father, perhaps there is another way . . ."

The King silenced her with a raised hand. "Leave us, my daughters."

Both Trinia and Layla bowed to the King and exited the chamber.

The King turned to face the Druid. "I know why you have come, Galin. Strange; we both fear the future."

Galin watched quizzically as the King went to the side of his throne, bent down, and waved his hand quickly past it. Suddenly, a hidden compartment in the side of the throne opened. The King removed a metal box from within and placed it on his table. He bade Galin to come forward.

"My lord, do you have in your possession a weapon that can aid us?" Galin asked, forgetting his formal tone in his surprise. "If so, why would you keep it secret?"

"It is not as simple as that, Galin," the King replied, opening the box.

Galin saw within a black weapon, immaculate, comprised of a shaft a full two feet in length and a round ball beset with protruding bumps at one end.

"Behold *Livinilos*, the mace of many blessings," the King said reverently. "In ancient times—ancient even by the reckoning of Elves—our legends tell of a necromancer who threatened Alluviam. He raised an army of the undead and lay siege to Alluviam in a time before the kingdom was hidden by magic. It is said that the Elven Cleric, Dorthonian, used this mace in a time when such creatures walked the earth in mass numbers. Armed with *Livinilos*, he vanquished them.

"Its time has come again. It is a sturdy enough weapon in normal combat, but in the presence of the undead, its true power comes to life. It will glow as bright as the sun. The undead will shrink back in fear of it. If it strikes any lesser of the undead, it will blast them out of existence. If it strikes those that are more powerful, it will damage them permanently and ultimately destroy them. However, you must now be warned, Galin. There is a price one must pay to command such power. Unlike other weapons, this one chooses its wielder, and if you do not pass the test . . ." The King hesitated. "If you do not pass the test, then you die where you stand. I love my daughters, Galin, more than my life, but were I ever to have a son, I imagined he would be much like you. Do what you must."

Galin returned his stare, realizing what was at stake. He felt ashamed for having raised his voice moments earlier. He looked down at the mace, then back at the King. He took Aeldorath's hand in his and kissed it. He bowed low to the King, then turned and knelt before the box containing the mace. He pulled a small branch of mistletoe, the ancestral holy symbol of all Druids, from a pouch at his waist.

"Blessed Mother, long have I strived to serve you as best as I could. I ask you now to give me the strength to serve you best. If my death serves you best, then so be it."

He bowed his head for another moment, then stood, took a deep breath, and lifted the mace from the box. It rested in his hand for a moment with no change, and then, a tremendous shock overwhelmed him. A flash of light and electrical energy seemed to consume his entire being. He screamed in pain. He could not move. His hands, arms, and legs shook violently. He felt certain that death was coming to take him.

Then, it was over. He fell to his knees and found, strangely and to his surprise, that the mace was still in his hand. He was alive, though the shock of the test had left him weakened.

"Corinthian told me you would come seeking a weapon," the King said as he lifted the Druid to his feet and sat him down, "but even he could not see if you would pass the test of the mace. It is yours to wield now, my friend. May it serve you well."

Later that morning, all of Alluviam—thousands of Elves—gathered in the green pastures where a great ceremony was held to honor those who had died in Leafshaven, the dead of Averon, the Seer Corinthian, Hawk, and the Sage Algernon.

It was a beautiful day. Here, in this land hidden from the rest of the world and untouched by the growing poison of the surrounding lands, the skies were blue and saturated with the warmth of the sun's rays. The King conducted the ceremony in both the Elvish and the common tongue.

The bodies of many were placed atop funeral pyres of wood. Kael had told the King he intended to take Algernon's ashes and bury them in Wrenford. The dead of Averon were wrapped in burial shrouds and prepared for the journey home, but still the King honored them and gave thanks for their deaths in service of the Elven cause.

Each time the King said a blessing for the dead, all the Elves in Alluviam knelt and bowed their heads in homage.

When the time came, the King nodded, and Galin, Kael, Elenari, Mekko, Archangel, and Captain Gaston stepped forward, bearing torches, and lit the wood beneath Algernon's pyre. They watched in silence as the smoke reached far into the clear sky, each remembering privately what the old Sage had meant to them.

Mekko started out just after the ceremony. He took a lone skiff back through the city of Alluviar to where the stable was located. As the Dwarf packed his horse, he was startled by the sudden presence of his companions behind him.

"Thought you would sneak off without saying goodbye, did you?" Galin said with his arms folded. "Fortunately, Elenari spotted you."

"Well . . . no, of course not," Mekko replied. "Just thought I'd leave without a lot of fuss is all, Druid. After what everyone's been through, last thing anyone needs is a long, drawn-out goodbye. You know I need to get home."

"We know," Kael said, shaking the sturdy Dwarf's hand. "We thank you for helping us, and we wish you and your people well. We will see you soon, General."

Etienne Gaston came forward next and joined hands with him. "My army and I will march to Cordilleran. I swear it."

Mekko returned the handshake, and the two soldiers saluted each other.

Elenari came forward and hugged the Dwarf, much to his surprise. "Be careful, Mekko. Have a safe journey."

The Dwarf blushed. "I might have left sooner if it meant gettin' a hug from you, lady," he said gruffly.

Finally, Galin came and joined hands with the Dwarf. "I think I will miss your singing most, my friend," the Druid said, smiling.

Mekko grinned. "Hah! There'll be plenty more when I can treat you to the hospitality of my home. May you always fly swift and true, my Druid friend."

"May Mother Nature watch and protect you," Galin said as he helped the Dwarf up on his horse. "We will see you soon, with allies."

They all stood together and watched as Mekko disappeared into the Sylvanwood.

Captain Gaston and his remaining men, along with the two diplomats, then mounted their horses. Their dead had been loaded into a wagon to be transported home. "It is time for us to leave as well, my friends," the captain said as he waved to them.

At that moment, Layla passed the stable, leading five men behind her.

"Please tell your father for me, my lady," the Captain called, "that I shall return on time with an army from Averon, and my men and I humbly thank him for his kind words in honor of our dead."

"I shall, Captain Gaston," she replied. "I hear iron in your words. No signed document can hold the iron. We will trust you and await your return. My men and I will escort you through the forest."

The companions watched as another of their friends departed, escorted by Layla's Elves. They contemplated what lie ahead. There was still much to discuss and much to plan. The greatest battle of their lives was yet to come.

Chapter 21

He walked swiftly through the palace. These days, it was rare indeed for a man in his position to receive an urgent summons to see the King. Though he and his unit were sometimes thought obsolete, the respect they garnered from the other Dwarves was unsurpassed. Any soldiers he passed, especially within the capital, would stop to salute him. Aside from the Generals and the King himself, no one was treated with more reverence.

He was Raybeck, Commander of the Corps of Engineers. His high forehead and arched eyebrows seemed to indicate a man who was always thinking. True to form, he found himself playing out several different scenarios in his head that might explain why King Crylar would need to see him so urgently. None of them, however, had a pleasant conclusion.

The Corps, known as wizards without magic among the Dwarves, was the most elite unit of the army. Throughout history, their special abilities had turned the tide of more than one battle for the Dwarves. Only five hundred strong, long tales often accompanied by ale and song spoke of them as miracle workers with rock and stone. The craft of engineering had been passed from father to son for generations within the Corps.

The patch of the golden hammer, the insignia of his unit, adorned the shoulder of Raybeck's uniform. His broad, even shoulders provided support for a modestly burly frame, and his bulging forearms gave way to massive hands. Aside from these, the rather short curls of his brown beard made him physically unremarkable.

A lone figure sat waiting outside the throne room. It was Tyran, Raybeck's second-in-command. Tyran had been at his side for years. Raybeck, though generally cautious, ever keeping his counsel for himself for the most part, Raybeck had still come to rely more and more upon Tyran as the years passed. One day, Tyran would lead the Corps, but at the moment, Raybeck could not concern himself with such thoughts. The King was waiting.

Tyran rose to stand with him, his deep-set black eyes greeting his commander with concern. He brought his hand up to the thick black hair the covered his head and chin and then lowered his fist over his heart in salute. Raybeck stopped to return the gesture and greet him momentarily.

"You must wait here, Tyran," said the commander with a nod. "He asked to see me alone."

Tyran nodded in understanding and resumed his seat; Raybeck knew he would be there waiting when the meeting ended. Raybeck took a deep breath and beckoned for the guards to admit him to the throne room.

As he entered the throne room, he saw only two people. The first was King Crylar, who stood with his back facing him, looking outward from his balcony to the north. Though he did not appear at first glance to be the most vivacious Dwarf, there was a rugged luster about him. While clearly overweight, even for a Dwarf, there was a stately nobility about his brow and stature. His stance was exceptionally well-balanced, which made him appear taller. The rosiness of his cheeks suggested a certain heartiness. His elongated beard flowed out like a swath of pure snow beneath his chin. The hair atop his head had receded all the way down the back of his head between his ears. He was a cautious man, but knew well when to employ boldness. He had an unadulterated affection for his people. They, in turn, considered him one of the greatest Dwarven Kings in the history of their race.

The second individual he saw was Cormayer, the King's personal aide. He was a robust, young Dwarf, fiercely loyal to Crylar. He was somewhat shorter than average for his race, but the honesty and sincerity of his face made up for the lack in his physique. It was his job to arrange the King's schedule from the moment he awoke until the moment he bedded down for the night. He attended all manner of tasks and errands for Crylar, and his trust and loyalty were beyond reproach. In fact, he was one of only two Dwarves in Cordilleran who had such unrestricted access to the King. The only other Dwarf who was known to have such access was General Mekko.

"Commander Raybeck is here, Sire," said Cormayer.

The King turned to see Raybeck bring his fist over his heart and drop to one knee.

"Rise, Commander," the King commanded. "Come over here, please. Thank you, Cormayer. You may leave us."

Cormayer saluted, bowed, and quickly left the throne room. As the door closed behind him, King Crylar spoke again, "A rider arrived from Wrenford this morning, bearing dispatches from King Thargelion. The information contained within was so disturbing and unbelievable, I sent out several long-range scouts to attempt to verify it." The king's gaze was distant as he hesitated for a moment. "Put your unit on full alert, Commander."

"Sire, what—?"

"The information, Commander," the King interrupted, "was that a mass invasion of Cordilleran is imminent and that we should take all precautions, as the invading army will far outnumber our own." The King looked at him, and Raybeck saw he could not hide his dismay. "Share this with no one; just mobilize your unit and have them ready."

"Sire." Raybeck brought his hand over his heart, bowed, and started to exit the chamber. As he was about to leave, he turned. "Sire, about the contingency plans we've discussed in the past, should I—?"

"No!" the King said sharply. "As I told you, I will never sanction those plans unless I'm convinced there is no other way. You have your orders, Commander."

As Raybeck silently exited, Cormayer entered and bowed. "Sire, General Valin is here as you instructed."

"Very good," the King replied. "Send him in."

General Valin, the remaining senior officer in the Dwarven army and one of the oldest still serving, entered the throne room as Cormayer exited again. Valin had a lengthy gray beard, which comprised the extent of the hair he had left. While somewhat short in stature, his broad shoulders indicated a once-mighty frame, which suffered from age and lack of exercise. He was an honest man, though never known for excessive cunning or daring on the battlefield. However, he did follow orders and was well-liked by the other officers and men. He bowed and saluted the King.

"General Valin," said Crylar flatly. "I am appointing you Commander of the Dwarven army."

"Sire," Valin began, "you do me a great honor but I do not think—"

Outraged, the King swatted two goblets off a serving table near the throne. "I'm not asking what you think, General! The time has come, and we both may as well get used to the fact that the army needs a new Commander. The sooner you and I make the adjustment, the sooner the rest will as well!"

The King took a deep breath, clearly upset with himself for losing his temper. Valin bowed his head, his hands folded before him.

"I am worried about him as well, Sire," the general said gently. "We all are."

"I told him, Valin, countless times. I told him to travel with guards. Now we may well stand on the brink of the greatest threat our nation has ever known, and we may have to face it without our greatest soldier." Crylar walked to his throne and collapsed into it. "Gods, let it be a lie. Let it be a mistake. I want the report immediately when our scouts return, no matter the hour, no matter whether it be good tidings or bad. You understand, General?"

Valin saluted and exited the throne room, leaving the King alone with his troubling thoughts.

Two days passed until finally, at midday of the third day, Valin burst into the throne room unannounced.

"Our scouts have reported in, Sire" he began. "They bear grave news . . ."

"As bad as Wrenford's reports indicated?" asked the King, leaning forward in his seat.

"As bad, and worse, Sire," the old Dwarf replied. "Three armies approach us as we speak. The barbarians of Koromundar approach from the northwest, the desert dwellers approach from the north, and an army of Orcs approach from the west. When the three armies meet, Sire . . ." The old Dwarf hesitated.

The King nearly leapt out of his throne. "Out with it, General!"

"They will have more than twice our number," Valin said grimly.

"Men fighting alongside Orcs?" said Crylar, as he sank back in the throne. "I never thought even the barbarians of Koromundar would sink so low."

"Sire," Valin continued, "the reports also indicate the beasts of

Koromundar are heavily armored. Where could the barbarians have obtained such quantities of armor?"

"Need you ask such a question?" Crylar replied wearily. "Only the wizards of Mystaria hate and fear us enough to aid the wolves of Koromundar. How it has come to this . . . even the wisest cannot say. How soon until the armies reach us?"

"Two, maybe three days. Sire . . . without help from the other nations, we cannot stand."

"We can!" The King suddenly rose. "And we will! Summon Raybeck to me at once! I will meet him alone, and then summon all the generals and commanders. In two hours, I want the entire army in formation outside my balcony, as well as everyone from the city that can be gathered within the *Barrick Cropaal*. We will have a war council meeting one hour after I address our people. Go at once and give the order, my friend. Tell the others . . . I want nothing but courage displayed in front of the men. If I even hear of an officer despairing in front of his troops, so help me, I'll take his head off with my own axe!"

Raybeck came again before the King, saluted, and dropped to one knee.

King Crylar rose from his throne and approached him. "Rise, my friend." The King waited until they stood eye to eye, and he placed his hand on Raybeck's shoulder and faced him solemnly. "Do whatever you must to save our people. No matter what the cost. Prepare for all contingencies."

Raybeck's hand came up and locked upon the King's elbow. He nodded with complete understanding. No further words needed to be spoken between them.

By afternoon, Crylar looked down from his balcony and observed the great procession that was the whole of the Dwarven army. The bellow of war horns sounded vibrantly through the air. The columns of Dwarves filled the space outside the palace, from the inner wall, across the moat, and all the way to the *Barrick Cropaal*—"the Great Barrier Wall" in the tongues of men.

The army was divided into columns and separated by division. Each division proudly displayed its banner behind its respective commander. In the front were the pikemen with their great spears. Behind them were the infantry, with axes, swords, and shields. Next, came the crossbow division with short swords and shields on their backs, then the heavy artillery division comprised of soldiers who operated all of the heavy siege equipment. Beyond them was a reserve division clad in lighter splint-mail armor and armed with two-handed axes. Finally, against the *Barrick Cropaal*, was the Corps of Engineers, who had only leather armor and swords, as they needed to stay mobile at all times.

The King walked out onto his balcony and instantly the horns stopped. All talking and activity ceased at once.

"My friends, soldiers, and citizens of Cordilleran," he boomed, "I come before you today, not as your King, but as one of you, your native kin. I come before you like this because there is no command I can give to prepare for what is needed and what is to come; I can only ask you.

"A dark power, which has nothing to do with Dwarves or our nation, has risen in the north. Its goal, as far as can be determined, is to extinguish or subjugate all life that threatens it. It sees any free nation with its own force of arms as a threat. Our allies from the friendly nation of Wrenford have warned us of this threat, and our own scouts have confirmed their warnings. This darkness, for reasons of its own, and through no offense given, has turned its attention here to Cordilleran."

His voice took on a somber tone. "I am saddened to tell you the nation of Wrenford no longer exists. It has been destroyed, down to the last child, by one of the armies that march toward us. The Wood Elves of Hilderan, too, have been slaughtered to the last."

He watched the crowd shuffling as gasps and whispers rose up from below. He gave them a moment and continued, "This threat is not of our doing or making, yet it comes to our front door from foreign lands. It comes to us where we live and breed to wipe us from the face of the world. As I speak, there is a brave attempt to ally other nations of Men and Elves to our aid. However, we must be prepared to stand alone. We have never relied on others for help, and we cannot assume that others will come to fight in our stead. This enemy has amassed huge numbers for its purpose. Even our great army will be heavily outnumbered."

He hesitated, giving them time to digest what he had said. "I put the alternatives before you, my people. We have just enough time to abandon our lands and our city and flee to the mountain caves where any force that follows would be hard-pressed to attack." Again, he hesitated and looked all throughout the procession. Nothing, not even a whisper, could be heard. "Or ... we can make our stand here and fight for our survival."

A roar, the likes of which the King had never thought to hear during his lifetime, erupted from his people and army. The pride he felt brought tears unexpectedly to his eyes. He raised his fist high. "The people have spoken! So be it!"

Again, cheers and roars filled the nation of Cordilleran as the King stepped in from his balcony. Even as he returned to the council chamber and faced his senior officers and commanders, the people below continued to cheer, "Cordilleran, Cordilleran!"

Crylar faced his war council, a look of fierce determination on his face. "Listen to the crowd out there. That is our army and our people out there. Listen, and never forget it. Days from now, if the tide of battle should turn against us, remember what you heard here today. Make sure your men remember."

They all placed their fist to their hearts in unison.

The King knew that he and Cordilleran could not have stood in better company or had their fates in better hands than the men assembled before him. "Gentlemen, I am appointing General Valin to be the Commander of the army in General Mekko's absence. I would ask you to understand that it is as difficult a transition for him as it is for the rest of us. Out of respect for General Mekko, I ask that you give Valin the same loyalty and allegiance that you have always given Mekko. Now, Commander Raybeck will begin by outlining what the Corps of Engineers has planned. Let us begin."

They remained within the council chamber, adjacent to the throne room until the sun rose the next morning. Cormayer had heard many heated arguments throughout the night beyond those doors. He did not like the events of the past few days, mainly because of the toll they had taken upon the King.

The King had gone the past two days with no rest and barely anything to eat. He knew what was at stake, but if the King collapsed of fatigue on the field, where would they be then? It was a dangerous chance he was about to take, but he could withstand no more. His patience at an end, he threw open the double doors to the council chamber to the shock and dismay of all assembled inside.

"My lords, forgive the intrusion, but the King needs his sleep," said Cormayer, staring at the shocked faces of the war council. "I think you will agree if he is to lead us through this crisis, he needs to be alert and well-rested. That is something he cannot possibly be without sleep or food for two days. I must insist that the council take a recess until such time that the King has rested."

Though dreadfully tired, the King smiled, deciding to yield to the logic of his young aide. "Well, gentlemen, I think we can adjourn for now before my aide decides to take over the palace. Commence with the plans; every man works. See that each of you take this time after giving orders to your units to get some rest yourselves. Valin, I want our scouts out as far as possible, but I want to be able to recall them quickly if need be. Thank you, gentlemen."

The officers of the war council saluted in turn and left the King alone with Cormayer.

"Sire, your bed awaits you as does a full meal when you awake," Cormayer said sternly.

"Yes Papa, no Papa," Crylar joked wearily as he allowed the young Dwarf to guide him by the arm. "I wonder that I never made you a General in the army, my young friend. I believe you liked asserting your authority back there." His voice became grave. "Cormayer . . . I want all women and children and noncombatants evacuated. I want them to make for the sanctuary caves to the east. See to it first thing today. See that the order is given to all our surrounding towns and villages. And don't let me sleep for more than four hours."

"Yes, Sire, as you wish."

Cormayer had no intention of failing his King in the upcoming days, or ever.

When Cormayer woke Crylar as commanded, the King reluctantly ate a full meal and then insisted on going into the city to see how the evacuation was proceeding. At Cormayer's insistence, two of the royal guard accompanied them.

The King walked briskly through the cavernous city, occasionally stopping to lend a hand or to grasp a hand in farewell. The impending crisis seemed to have added some vigor to his step. He watched as shopkeepers, innkeepers, and merchants packed up their livelihoods to make for the eastern slopes. Time was becoming precious, however, and Cormayer began insisting that they return to the palace, but still the King walked the city, helping where he could and giving a word of encouragement where it was needed.

Finally, Crylar agreed to turn back toward the palace. As they made their way back through the city, Crylar turned to an open doorway on the left and was caught by a scene in progress. Cormayer shook his head and began to protest, but the king's hand came up suddenly to silence him. Cormayer peered around the king's broad frame to see what had caught his eye and stopped him in his tracks this time.

A soldier, unknown to them, stood in a doorway with a woman—his wife. He gently held her arms in his, brought his hand to her face, and caressed her cheek. It was at that moment that two young children—a boy and a girl, close in age—appeared and ran to cling to their father's legs. He lifted them and held them in his arms. His wife held his face in her hands and kissed it. He handed the children to her and kissed her in turn and, for a moment, held all three of them in his embrace. Then, axe and sword in hand, he was away up the street. His wife and children watched him, unmoving, until he was well out of sight.

"That," King Crylar said softly, "is what we are fighting for, Cormayer, that . . . simple feeling, that simple freedom. Do you understand?"

"I do, Sire," the young Dwarf said, ashamed at having tried to rush the King moments earlier. The King stared at the forlorn family for a long moment and then walked over to them. Immediately, the woman bowed low still holding her children, shocked by the King's presence.

"Oh no, my lady, please rise," said Crylar, touching her arm. "And who was that brave lad of the infantry who just left you?"

"Our father, Sire, Telgar, the bravest man in the Kingdom," answered the young boy.

"Yes," laughed the King. He looked down at the children with a warm smile. "I've no doubt that he is. And who might you two be?"

"I am Valgar, Sire," said the boy. "This is my sister, Elina."

"I am Latonia, Sire, their mother," said the woman trying to perform a curtsey, but the King held her by the elbow and would not allow it.

"A beautiful family you have, my lady," spoke Crylar softly. He turned again to the children. "Now, for you two loyal subjects of the crown. You are brave and loyal subjects of the crown like your father, yes?"

"Oh, yes, Sire," the children answered as one.

"And you will follow what I, Crylar, King of all Cordilleran, command, just like your father. Correct?" the King asked proudly.

Again the children answered together. "Oh, yes, Sire."

Now Crylar's voice was soft and sincere, and he spoke slowly and deliberately. "Then I, the King, command both of you to watch over your mother on this journey, and to go find a new Cordilleran . . . and to live free and love and grow old. Do you understand?" He asked this last question knowing full well they did not.

The children looked at him oddly, but they nodded their heads.

"Good . . . then go and do as I, the King, command."

"Thank you, Sire," said the woman, a tear streaking down her cheek.

Crylar grabbed her hand and held it tightly. "No, my lady, thank you." He released her, turned, and quickly made his way up the street. "Come along, Cormayer. I believe you were telling me we have much to do."

Cormayer smiled, and he and the guards ran to keep up with their ruler.

Raybeck and Tyran walked the length of the *Barrick Cropaal*, then turned toward the castle and the palace. Raybeck looked to the eastern mountains beyond the castle and allowed his gaze to roll back toward where they stood. He thought about the remarkable geography and beauty that was Cordilleran.

Thousands of years ago, the first Dwarven Engineering Corps had carved the niche where the castle now stood into the base of the mountains. The blue mountains to the east beyond the castle seemed to disappear into the clouds. The mountains came down in a reverse C shape around the small valley, with the castle at its base. The *Barrick Cropaal* joined the two sides of the mountains, completely sealing off Cordilleran from the outside world. One hundred yards from the foot of the great wall, across a clear plain of green, was an *embreck*, or moat, some twenty-five feet in length, which led, via drawbridge, to the inner wall and beyond the castle. Going through the castle was the only way to enter the city of Cordilleran, which was completely within the mountains, safe from the elements and outsiders.

Raybeck's gaze encompassed the great wall, some hundred and fifty feet high throughout the valley and fifty yards in width, and traveled down to the inner wall, which was fifty feet high. Below, the valley was buzzing with activity. His men were scattered throughout, digging, building, measuring, and working feverishly on multiple tasks. There was much to do, and they had only a day, maybe two, to do it all.

Raybeck and Tyran turned to face the opposite direction and watched the horizon from where the enemy would come. Ahead, almost as far as the eye could see, were grassy plains—no trees, few hills, just open space. Still, they had many advantages. They knew, essentially, when the enemy would arrive. The enemy would have to attack from the west toward the *Barrick Cropaal* and would not be able to attack from three fronts, as they may have hoped. The mountains on each side of the castle, though small, were too jagged to lead men through. These armies had never worked together before, and that in itself would cause the enemy problems. And the Dwarves had the tunnels, which the enemy did not know about. Indeed, the element of surprise was on the side of the Dwarves. They hoped it would be enough.

Raybeck and Tyran now turned to view the castle. It was like no other castle in all the lands. Though the realms of Alluviam and Arcadia were renowned as the most beautiful kingdoms, Cordilleran was a magnificent splendor to behold, a remarkable feat of craftsmanship with no equal.

Much of the inner keep was constructed of silver- and gold-plated stone. The keep was largely built of silver while the outlying towers sparkled of gold. The castle rose in three ascending levels like a pyramid. At present, engineering crews were hard at work installing siege artillery, which had never before been used to defend the realm itself, along the rim of the inner wall and the west side of the second level.

Raybeck was unsure whether the enemy would attempt to use siege artillery against Cordilleran. The Orcs had been around long enough to know it would be futile, as the rock of the *Barrick Cropaal* and the inner wall was rich in an alloy known as adamantite. Adamantite was one of two precious metals found only in the mountains of Cordilleran and a heavy, indestructible alloy. It was so rare that many believed it was only legend and that only legendary weapons and armor were forged from it. Thought not legend, it was nearly impossible to come by. The deepest Dwarven miners came upon it in quantities so small as to barely be of use.

While their walls could likely not be breached, Raybeck knew the enemy would attempt to go over them. They would use siege towers constructed by the Orcs. When the clans of Orcs united, he thought, the Orcs could be quite formidable, and their skill at forging was not to be taken lightly. Yes, they would use great siege towers, long in the making within the bowels of the Orc forges in Bazadoom, to circumvent the walls.

Crylar's plan of defense would work. It *must* work.

Crylar and Cormayer returned to the throne room to find General Valin patiently waiting for them. The General saluted as the King removed his robe and quickly poured himself and the General a goblet of wine. Crylar then climbed the steps and relaxed into his throne.

"What is our status, General? Have our scouts reported in?" Crylar asked.

"They have, Sire," Valin answered. "The armies will arrive by nightfall tomorrow. Our guess is they will need some time to consolidate so we can expect the attack to begin anytime from tomorrow night till dawn the next day."

"And the evacuation?" the King pressed.

"Everything is proceeding as planned, Sire. However, the men and I cannot object strongly enough to this plan of—"

"The matter is closed, General," the King interjected calmly. "The decision has been made, and there will be no more discussion about it. If that is clear, please see to your duties. I want you visible to the men and encouraging them at every turn. And I expect you to support my decisions even outside this room."

"Always, Sire."

The old Dwarf saluted and bowed before he left.

Crylar knew Valin only objected out of affection and loyalty, like the rest of the commanders, but he would not be moved to reconsider. He could only hope what he was doing was best for his people. The King called for his aide, and instantly, the young Dwarf sprang into view, coming from behind him.

"Cormayer," Crylar said, "I want all the men with families relieved of work early tonight. Tell them they can start again at first light. I want them to be able to say goodbye to their loved ones, if at all possible. Please spread the word to the commanders, and inform General Valin."

"As you wish, Sire."

Instantly, the young Dwarf was off. Two guards, who would now be with Crylar at all times, replaced Cormayer. It was wartime, and the King would be guarded twenty-four hours a day. Even when he slept, he would not be alone. This was procedure for the royal guard, and, though he did not like it, Crylar understood the importance of it and did derive some peace of mind from it.

The next morning came far too quickly for Crylar. Though he had gone to bed early, his sleep had been plagued by bad dreams, and he found himself awake most of the night.

Cormayer was there to greet him with a large breakfast. Just having the young Dwarf around him always lightened Crylar's spirit. He could hear the sounds of work below in the valley even before the sun had risen. If the day before had been a busy day, this day would be three times so. He found himself rushing to finish the food on his plate. He was anxious to be out amongst the men. On the prior day, he had given himself to the city; now he would spend this one with the men of his army.

Cormayer helped him dress, as he did each day. The young man fastened the King's robe and placed his golden circlet atop his head. Today, Cormayer and the guards could barely keep up with the King as he rushed through the palace.

The King was a marvel to watch as he stopped to greet each of his men individually. Much to Cormayer's surprise, the King knew many by name. Occasionally, Cormayer or an officer would whisper a soldier's name in Crylar's ear, and even then he would exchange heartfelt greetings and solemn exchanges with each of them. He came to each of them like a long-lost father, come home at last to his grateful sons. He was not a King; he was more like a man at a family reunion, that guest or family member everyone had come to see. He was all this and much more.

By all rights, it should have been a day of great anxiety. A nervous edginess mixed with fear was the tone of the morning, but by midday, Crylar had conquered those feelings in his people and replaced them with hope, pride, courage, and love. Even Cormayer, who worried constantly for the King, found himself at ease, unable to show anything but admiration and love for this great man he served.

Lastly, Crylar visited the members of his own royal guard, thanking them for every moment of their service and telling each of them how much their dedication meant to him and the people.

By the afternoon, Crylar was back in the throne room for a meeting with General Valin to discuss the final preparations. Valin assured him they would be ready ahead of schedule. Crylar had given various dispatches to Cormayer to take to several of the commanders, containing last-minute orders, which kept him busy until nightfall.

The King looked down into the valley and out beyond the great wall. All they could do now was wait. Even he, the King, was prisoner to the dreadful waiting.

The valley below was quiet. All the men were inside the inner wall, save for those few who waited in the mountains.

Everyone should be at their post by now, he thought.

Two hours passed, and at approximately nine o'clock, General Valin entered the throne room with his personal guards. He quickly saluted, bowed, and spoke. "The armies have arrived, Sire. They joined some three miles west of us. They appear to be forming camp for the night. I suspect they will attack at first light."

At that moment, Cormayer entered the throne room and rushed to General Valin's side, a slip of paper in his hand. Valin studied it, took a deep breath, and sighed despondently.

"What is it, General?" the King demanded. "Good or bad, I wish to know immediately."

"A cavalry command has arrived, Sire," Valin answered. "They are darkly robed, some five thousand strong, and carrying dark lances."

"Five thousand?" The King could not keep a look of dismay from his face. "This is a separate force in addition to the three armies?"

"It is, Sire," the general replied with a weary nod of his head.

"Cormayer, find Raybeck," the King ordered. "Bring him to me at once."

The Dwarf was gone almost before the sentence ended. Crylar and Valin looked out the window to the west and saw in the distance, upon the Fields of Aramoor, the sparkles of light that were the fires of the enemy camp. Minutes later, Cormayer returned with Commander Raybeck at his side. The Commander saluted as he entered.

"Commander," the King said, "a cavalry of this Shadow Prince's dreaded Stygian Knights has arrived. I think I would like them to meet with some mischief before the morning, Commander. Do you think you can arrange that?"

"I believe I can, Sire," Raybeck answered confidently.

"Then, gentlemen, proceed," Crylar commanded. "I wish to be informed of the results immediately."

"Yes, Sire," Valin said. He bowed, and he and Raybeck exited the throne room together.

Crylar knew there would be no sleeping tonight. He asked Cormayer to help him put on his armor. Cormayer meticulously fitted the King with his suit of mithril armor. Mithril was the second precious metal found within the mountains of Cordilleran. It was lighter than any other type of armor, but stronger than the hide of a dragon. Mithril was almost as rare as adamantite and worth more than gold, diamonds, or any precious gems. Miners did not have to go quite as deep in the earth to obtain it, and it existed in greater quantities than adamantite.

Crylar's mithril armor was of a ring mail design in silver with gold trim, just like his castle. A golden helmet replaced his circlet, and a great crimson cape was fastened to the shoulder plates of his armor. The King kept a shield with a golden hammer on it to the left of his throne, and a great double-bladed axe to the right of it. Once the King had been fully dressed, he signaled to the two royal guards who nodded and left the throne room. Cormayer turned his head and looked at the King with a familiar look of concern.

"Sire, the royal guards are not to leave you alone, especially during—"

The King did not allow him to finish. "They are just outside the door, Cormayer. It will only be for a few moments."

Crylar went to his serving table and poured two goblets of wine. He handed one to Cormayer and bade him to sit next to him by the throne.

Cormayer accepted the goblet, not understanding why the King had offered it to him. "Sire, I don't understand," he said as he took his seat.

"I wanted to have this quiet moment with you, my young friend, before any of the fighting started," the King said. "I want to tell you how much you have meant to me these past few years. You are the best of the best. You've earned your money each day, ten times over. Without you, I could no more find my crown than my own bed. I have enjoyed our time together, and I feel I am a better Dwarf for having known you." He got to his feet. "Stand up, Cormayer."

"I thank you, Sire," the young Dwarf began, "but I don't understand . . ."

He fell silent as Crylar faced him, extending his arm. Cormayer hesitated, then grabbed the King's arm, locking his arm around it.

The King pulled him into an embrace and held him tightly for a moment. "You are all that I could ever have wanted in a son if I had been so blessed with one," the King whispered. "But since I cannot make you my son, I have instead appointed you to the High Council." Crylar released him and handed him a scrolled parchment. "This confirms your appointment. I have already sent word to the other members of the council."

Cormayer was dumbfounded. "My Lord, I do not know what to say . . . other than I am not worthy of this great honor. What about the older members?"

"What about them, indeed?" the King scoffed cheerfully. "They need to hear a fresh young voice that speaks the truth, plainly and honestly, to power. They need to hear it as I have heard it these past years."

"But, Sire, the council members have all left for the mountains—"

"And so the royal guard waits to escort you to catch up to them," the King interrupted with a nod.

Cormayer backed away, a horrified expression on his face. "Oh no! I'll not leave your side when you need me most! No Sire, I won't!"

"Cormayer, listen to me now, lad. I need you to go to the east with our people and find a new Cordilleran, or come back here and rebuild this one. I want your vote to be heard when it is time to elect a new King."

Cormayer held his place, facing him. "New King? You speak as if you will not live through this . . ."

"Surely you, who watches all so closely, must have realized the bulk of our army is no longer present here?" the King replied.

"Of course, but I thought it was part of the battle plan," answered the youth with growing concern in his shaking voice.

"It is, my young friend—the plan for our people to live on. As proud as I was to hear the people say in one voice that they wished to stay and fight, Cormayer, I will not commit genocide. Our people must live on. The family we saw in the streets yesterday convinced me of the rightness of it."

The King eased himself back into his throne.

Cormayer sounded desperate as the reality of the situation closed in about him. "But you will commit suicide instead?" the young Dwarf cried. "How can it possibly be wise for you to stay here and die needlessly? What will become of our people without you?"

"My dear friend," the King replied gently, "I don't expect you to fully understand my reasons. Naturally, all the officers and men wanted to stay and fight; I, the king, had to order them to leave here. I had to give them direct orders to leave their castle, country, and King to face a ruthless enemy. Can you imagine how difficult it was for them? I, the King, had to order those who would stay here—outnumbered, facing almost certain death, knowing they will not see their families again—to try and buy time for our people. Every second we hold the enemy at bay here is another second for the future of our people. If I were to leave here and go east, I would have to live with the order I have made to those who would stay. That is something I cannot do." Crylar rose again from the throne and stood before his young aide. "No . . . I choose life for you, Cormayer, even though I know you would gladly stay here and die by my side. Now go, my boy, and make a new life for our people—a better life."

He embraced Cormayer one last time before he called the guards. "Though I am doubtful of an alliance," said the King with a proud smile, "if there is to be one, the Dwarves must be part of it. See to it, Councilor Cormayer."

With tears streaming down his face, Cormayer looked at the King one last time. "I shall never forget you. Our people . . . shall never forget you."

"No Dwarf or King can ask for more than that, can they, my lad?" the King said, loudly and proudly, with a smile that belied his warring emotions.

Cormayer smiled and brought his right fist over his heart, bowed his head, turned, and was gone.

The King walked to his balcony and, when he was sure his royal guards had their backs to him, wiped the tears from his eyes.

Chapter 22

Tyran crawled with his chin low to the ground with four men of the Corps behind him. They had covered themselves from head to toe with a black salve, allowing them to blend in with the shadows of the night.

They entered the enemy camp easily. It consisted of a great host of tents and fires, which covered the countryside like sparks. Their sheer number was staggering; there were tens of thousands of them. Men shrouded in robes, men in armor, men in animal skins, and the foul stench of Orcs were all around them as they crept like worms in the earth among the enemy. Tyran and his men were on the west side of the encampment, while five of their counterparts were on the east side. Each of them had a light crossbow strapped to his back as well as backpacks full of sulfur bombs. The bombs were small, spherical, and highly incendiary.

The horses of the enemy cavalry were gathered at the far western end of the camp, though they were not the real targets of Tyran's mission. Raybeck had given him another objective, in which the horses would prove to be an excellent distraction. They had detected the foul stench of the Orcs and could hear bits of Orcish speech coming mainly from the center of the camp. Though it was night and they were among armies that would barely recognize each other, the size and appearance of Dwarves would stand out instantly. While it was fairly easy to enter the camp, they had to struggle for every inch they progressed without being detected.

Tyran knew that which he sought would be somewhere in the middle of the Orcs' encampment. He would have to stay on foot while the others would be on horseback. If he found it quickly enough, he would be able to get back to where one of the others could pick him up. Whatever was to happen, he could not fail in his task.

It was time. The five Dwarves made their way near the horses and lined up side by side, kneeling on one knee each. Carefully, they each notched a bolt to their crossbows. Tyran struck a match and lit the tips of all five bolts. They took high aim and fired into the middle of the camp. Three of the bolts struck tents, quickly setting them ablaze. On the eastern side of the camp, their five counterparts saw the signal and fired their bolts on the other side of the camp. Heads started to turn, voices began to rise, and men and Orcs alike began to stir, unsure of what was occurring.

Without hesitation, Tyran helped each member of his group up on a horse and swatted the backsides of the horses, driving them on and away. Two of the Dwarven riders yelled, spurring and scaring the other horses into a sporadic charge. Instantly, the thousands of horses broke formation and began running in various directions. The other two riders shot directly through the encampment, barely visible as they launched sulfur bombs at tents and men alike, setting them ablaze and causing chaos to spread faster and farther.

All five Dwarves on the eastern side of the camp, pitch-black shapes appearing as little more than animals, bolted amid and around the enemy men, tossing sulfur bombs as they ran, setting men and canvas afire.

Screams and confusion amid the men and Orcs became rabid. All grabbed for their weapons, and many scattered in different directions, some chasing after the horses and some not knowing who or what they were chasing.

Tyran was free now, running through the chaos. He was moving fast and deep into the Orc camp now. The Orcs were running about with no clue what was occurring.

They always did spook easily at night, Tyran thought.

He was a dark specter among them, little more than a blur to their shocked eyes. Tyran did not carry any sulfur bombs; his backpack and the ammunition therein had a much different purpose.

Though it had only been several seconds, it seemed like an eternity before he came upon it: the true object of his mission, the enemy's battering ram. It was an imposing structure, as black in color as Tyran had painted himself. It consisted of many painted oak trees tied together as if to form one. The ends had been sharpened just enough to allow for maximum impact. It was nearly a hundred feet in length. Shields of metal and wood protected its top and sides. There were many handles from one end to the other on each side and it was set upon a set of great carts at the ends and the middle. Such a device, while unable to break through the *Barrick Cropaal*, could be used to force the city gates open, as well as penetrate the drawbridge of the inner wall. Cordilleran stood prepared to deal with the enemy coming over the walls, but not through *and* over.

Tyran quickly went to the middle of the ram, removed his backpack, and placed it under the center of the device. He pulled a powder horn from the pack, broke the end of it, and immediately scampered away with a trail of powder following behind him. When he was just a few feet from it, he turned and smashed the one sulfur bomb he had down onto the trail of powder. The powder lit on impact, and just before it reached the battering ram, Tyran dove to the ground and covered his head.

The battering ram exploded up and out with such concussive force that it took some twenty Orcs with it. It shattered into a wave of splintering wood that flew through the air, impaling several other Orcs who had not even been caught in the blast.

As the explosion subsided, Tyran was up and running back to where he had started. They would be looking for him by now. He found all he could think about was the ram, surrounded by thousands of enemies; he hoped the King had seen the blast from his balcony. He heard them now, a handful of horses galloping behind him. His timing would have to be perfect on the run and in the dark.

"Tyran, now!"

He heard it and, without looking, launched himself at the first horse to come up alongside him. He grabbed the leg of the rider and held on for dear life as they sped onward.

Amidst the chaotic disorder of a war camp in disarray, five lone mounts managed to escape. Each was double mounted with riders who appeared black as pitch as they steered toward the *Barrick Cropaal*.

Dawn came to Cordilleran like an unwelcome guest. The remainder of the night had been spent celebrating the success of Tyran and his men. The King had been there to greet them and congratulate them upon their return, and the soldiers within the castle had greeted them with cheers and praise. Their first encounter with the enemy had been a victory, but a victory that had incited the enemy into a wild bloodthirsty rage before they launched their first attack. It had worked both for and against them.

The King watched from his balcony as the enemy approached, still distant, at a slow march. There were no horns or banners within the enemy force to announce their pride and presence. They had been made fools of the night before, and they were hungry for vengeance. Men and Orcs alike could not hide the hatred and anxiety for blood, which fueled their anger. They would assault the castle like a raging storm. Their victims would come to know their fury firsthand; they would kill every Dwarf they came upon. They would never stop until the Dwarves were wiped from the face of the land.

Gray clouds hung over Cordilleran, accompanied by a low-lying haze on the ground, pierced in many places by a cool breeze. There was no sun present to bear witness to the awesome spectacle below. Thousands upon thousands of men and Orcs mingled and became one force, drawing ever closer to their prey.

The walls of the *Barrick Cropaal* shook as the ground beneath it responded to the marching feet of the enemy. Atop the great barrier wall stood a lone company of one hundred Dwarves from the crossbow division. They stood in the gaps in the battlements, weapons ready, aimed and poised downward, awaiting targets to strike at. These Dwarves saw the several large dark structures within the enemy body being drawn forward on wheels—the great stone siege towers. Incredibly long, they would be able to scale up the great wall if they got close enough. There were dozens of them scattered throughout the enemy army. They were composed of light stone enclosures, designed to protect their inner wooden ladders and those who would climb them. The outer stone of the towers would protect against missile fire from crossbows and artillery from siege weapons.

When the front line of the enemy army closed to within one hundred yards of the great wall, it started. The enemy began a full-out sprint, charging forward with the siege towers in tow. The Dwarves atop the wall had set up in four lines. Each row, consisting of twenty-five men, stood directly behind the one in front of it. The Dwarves had distanced themselves so that they were an arm's length away from one another within their respective rows.

The King, resplendent in his armor, his crimson cape flying in the wind, stood on the balcony of the palace with General Valin and Commander Raybeck. Crylar lifted his right arm and brought it down swiftly, signaling the crossbowmen on the wall that they could fire when ready. When the enemy was nearly twenty-five yards away, the first line fired a volley of bolts through the air, striking the attackers and throwing them back in mid-stride.

The Dwarves had arranged themselves so they fit between one another like the pin and tumblers of a locking mechanism. The first row fired and stepped back, then the second row fired and stepped back, and so on. By the time the fourth row had stepped forward and fired, the first row behind them was reloaded and ready. Within seconds, nearly a hundred Orcs had fallen dead as a result of their synchronized accuracy. Still, these hundred were nothing, trodden into the ground instantly by the thousands charging.

The Orcs, who made up the bulk of the first wave, hungered to reach the wall. Their red eyes burned like flame in contrast to their grayish-green skin. Faces covered with bristly black hair were highlighted by short snouts guzzling air and exhaling rage. The weather was perfect for them, as they hated direct sunlight. The Orcs were an old race, harboring ancient rivalries with both the Dwarves and the Elves; many Orc clans killed them on sight. Once their siege towers hit, and the spiked wheel locks dug into the ground, the Dwarves would not be able to knock the towers away. They would put up a fight, of course, but in the end, they would be helplessly overrun and slaughtered.

Any Orcs who were felled by crossbow fire were mercilessly trampled underfoot. The injured and the dead were only hindrances to the living and would only serve to weaken them and slow them down. There would be no quarter given to the Dwarves, and no pity for their own fallen brethren.

The Orcs expected to be assaulted by siege artillery, yet none came; perhaps the Dwarves would wait until they got over the first wall. It mattered not. The Orcs had joined with enough man-creatures to kill every Dwarf in the world four times over. Then they would divide their lands and plunder their riches.

The crossbow fire had taken down hundreds of Orcs, and still they raced to within feet of the great wall. Just before they would reach the wall, the missile fire stopped. The Dwarves turned and frantically made for the side stairwells of the *Barrick Cropaal*.

The first of the siege towers struck the wall. The wheel locks dug into place and ground crews pulled up the towers. The Orcs and men scrambled up the towers like ants being smoked out of their earthen homes. As they reached the top of the great wall, they looked to the valley below to see the Dwarves fleeing toward their castle.

Filthy little creatures, they thought, *running in fear as they should.*

The Orcs howled in excitement as they spilled onto the wall and pushed one another toward and down the stairwells along the sides of the mountains. Some Orcs were indiscriminately pushed off the *Barrick Cropaal* by their comrades, falling to their deaths. Seeing an enemy flee before them made them insane with bloodlust.

The Dwarves were halfway through the valley, running for the open drawbridge of the castle. They could see the King on his balcony waving them on, encouraging them. Many slipped and fell along the way, bumping into and grabbing one another. Always, several would stop to help the men around them. No one would be left behind. Despite the fact many of them had fallen several times, it appeared they would all be within the safety of the drawbridge well ahead of their pursuers.

The Orcs spilled onto the valley bed, their rust-colored armor and helmets clanking against one another as they fell and pushed one another on. Dozens were trampled as they ran and tripped, longing for the blood that was rightfully theirs to shed. The thought of feasting on Dwarven flesh drove them on like starving wolves. The image of the Dwarven King's severed head held high above them in victory was a rapturous vision they would soon make into reality.

Above, Crylar sighed deeply as the last of the crossbowmen made it safely over the drawbridge. The order was given to close the bridge. Now, all they could do was wait.

Siege towers continued to line up against the outside of the great barrier wall. Barbarians of Koromundar and nomads from the Jarathadar deserts were joining the Orcs clambering up the ladders.

Within the great wall, the valley was becoming dark, filled with the shapes of Orcs slipping on the grass as they closed the distance to the inner wall that protected the castle.

They reached the moat and flung themselves into it without hesitation. They only fell down a few feet as the water was only knee deep now, having been drained down from the top. They waded their way across, easily climbing and jumping up the other side. The first of them hit the inner wall and immediately used their own bodies as ladders for those behind them. They scaled the walls on the backs of their brethren, madly trying to ascend to the top. As the valley filled up with thousands of Orcs behind them, it began.

The King brought his arm down in an abrupt motion. In that instant, great horns sounded from the towers and all three levels of the castle. The enclosure of the mountains around the valley created an echoing effect within, carrying and amplifying the sound so greatly that even the bloodthirsty Orcs hesitated and stopped running and climbing just for a moment.

The Orcs held their ears and found themselves looking up and all around them, wondering just for a moment what the uproarious sounds of the horns could mean. The Dwarves blew them proudly as if to signal some great event. All their activities ceased on the wall and below in the valley just for the few seconds it took them to raise their heads.

The Orcs looked up toward the layers of the castle, seeing that they had become filled with hundreds of Dwarves who stepped forward with crossbows. Then they saw many catapults moving forward on the corners.

Lastly, they saw something that, in one horrific moment not only removed their bloodlust, but bulged their eyes replacing all the lust, rage, and hate with fear. It was a fear that snapped them out of their euphoric state and caused them to look closely at their hands, feet, and the ground beneath them. They were—all of them—standing in oil. They watched helplessly as all the crossbow tips were lit and flaming pitch was loaded into the catapults.

Before they could move or utter a scream, the Dwarves fired flaming bolts and pitch into every section of the valley and moat. They fired, and kept firing—not at the Orcs, just at the ground and water—just enough to light the oil.

Fire sprang up everywhere, blazing and zigzagging across the valley like a living, breathing thing. The flames moved like a serpent through a garden, but faster than the eye could follow. The fire became as an army unto itself. It was a separate force on its own side, there with its own intent. But like the Orcs, its wrath was terrible, it hated, and it showed no mercy; nothing could escape its path.

Within minutes, nearly every living thing in the valley was on fire. The thousands of Orcs screamed and howled inhumanly. The fires burned high and hot enough that even the flames of hell would be envious. They could not run fast enough to escape, and there were too many of them crowded together so they had no choice but to stand and be burned alive until death freed them. Some, rather than wait, unable to move, to be singed alive, used their blades to take their own lives. Death was the only escape.

The Engineering Corps had spent the last three days soaking every inch of the valley with oil. Mixed within was an ancient herbal ingredient, which masked the pungent scent of the oil. The moat had been drained and oil had been mixed in, diluted by the water so as to be unrecognizable. It had been planned very carefully. The King knew the Orcs would go into a blood-frenzy if a handful of Dwarves snuck into their camp and destroyed their battering ram on the eve of their attack. The Orcs would be so maddened that they would not notice the oil, even as they slid and fell into it. The King had been betting—and rightly so—that the two armies of men would gladly let the Orcs rush the castle first.

The King watched the valley of flames from his balcony as the stench of charred flesh began to dominate the air. The men and Orcs who had been on the great wall, once the fires began, had hurriedly climbed back down the siege towers. It would be hours before the fires burned out or even burned low enough for the enemy to begin another attack. They had taken out thousands of the enemy without losing a single Dwarf. They were still gravely outnumbered, but it was an important victory. It sent a clear message that the Dwarves would not go quietly into the night, and all who entered Cordilleran to attack it did so at their gravest peril.

Several hours passed, and the fires still burned, but not as brightly. The valley had become an Orc graveyard, lined with blackened bodies burnt beyond recognition. The smoke rose high into the skies, a dark billowing smoke that reeked of death. The smell of burnt, rotting flesh became so overpowering that the Dwarves had to tie scarves around their mouths and noses to keep the stench at bay.

The drawbridge opened and the men of the Engineering Corps emerged with wheelbarrows. The intense heat of the air made it impossible to breathe and drove them backward until they developed a tolerance. They had the unpleasant task of clearing the Orc bodies away so they could stage the next phase of their defense.

The Orc bodies had been burnt so deeply that many of the limbs had become brittle. Arms and legs would break off at the handling. They dumped as many bodies as they could into the moat and then cleared a path halfway through the valley. It was then that they wheeled out their two largest catapults and brought them to mid-valley. There, they stopped with three-man loading crews and two large boulders primed and ready to fire in each. Twenty men of the infantry stood to guard them. Again, they could do nothing but wait now.

On a small hill several hundred yards west of the *Barrick Cropaal* stood a large, dark tent. This tent was far away from any other and looked down on the others. None in the enemy camp went near it; none wanted to. A large, pitch-colored stallion could be seen outside the tent. It was a dark beast with red eyes that exhaled smoke from its nostrils. It was not tied to any post or tree; such bonds were unnecessary. It was bound eternally to its master, Prince Broderick Voltan.

Within the tent, Voltan dwelt alone in his true form, which would soon be his only form at all times. In the new order, he would have no more reason to masquerade in his human form. The Council of Princes would be dissolved; they would all be killed, and he alone would be King of Mystaria, as well as Lord of the entire world. The Shadow Prince would rule, but he would be the Shadow Prince's Chancellor, and in time, he was confident he would find a way to dispatch the Shadow Prince, as well. However, he would use his power to bury those thoughts deep within, undetected, until the time was right. The matter at hand was Cordilleran. He had heard of his army's nighttime defeat, and he was thoroughly displeased.

He called for his familiar. In the next instant, the creature appeared. It was a small creature, only three feet high, with leathery, bat-like wings. It had a segmented tail, which ended in a large stinger, like that of a scorpion. The twisted horns on its head gleamed white, matching its jagged teeth. Crimson skin covered its elongated fingers and clawed feet.

It was an imp. Much like a magician's black cat, imps were attracted to magic and often served evil wizards and lords of great power. They possessed certain small types of magic as well, including the power to polymorph.

As it materialized beside Voltan, the imp's green, slit-like eyes looked up at him. "What is thy bidding, Master?" it hissed.

"*The accursed Dwarves should never have been allowed to dig themselves up from the earth,*" Voltan said in hollowed tones. "*Their famed ingenuity could cause more losses than we planned on. Nonetheless, they should know when they are conquered. It is time, Kempec, that I had my own eye and ears within those walls. See to it at once.*"

"Yes, Master," the imp hissed with a bow of its head and dematerialized as quickly as it appeared.

Night had come and the fires had died, the smoke had gone away, and all that still lingered was the smell of death. Two Dwarves stood watch atop the great barrier wall. The enemy waited in their camp nearly one hundred yards away. It was nearly nine o'clock when the enemy began marching again.

The two Dwarves raced down, yelling to the catapult crews, "To arms, to arms, they march!"

The King and Raybeck stood on the royal balcony, watching and hoping all would proceed as planned. Once again, timing would be the key element.

Tyran, concealed in the tunnels below the *Barrick Cropaal*, awaited the signal. At the proper time, he would light a powder fuse that would cause a chain reaction.

This time, the shrouded nomads and the barbarians of Koromundar joined the Orcs in equal numbers as they marched toward the siege towers. The desert dwellers were swathed in hooded robes from head to toe. Many had turbans upon their heads, and their boots curled up at the toes. They favored the curved scimitar as their sword of choice. Living and fighting in desert terrain all their lives, they were out of their element here. Many were not entirely sure why they were even in this foreign land, fighting so far from home. They knew there was a new political climate within their country. There was a new leadership. This leadership called for war and insisted that the Dwarves were threatening to attack, but the reasons were unclear. Still, they were a fiercely loyal people, and they would go where their leaders took them.

The barbarians of Koromundar were born warriors and had always been a warlike people, favoring expansion and strength over peace and supposed weakness. They had been fighting expansionist wars against every country on their borders for years. However, never before had they allied themselves with other countries until now. Their new Golden Khan, Antar Helan, had made them see the similarities between their beliefs and those of the Orcs. He had made them see the advantages of siding with others, assuring them that it could only make them a stronger people. They had easily conquered Wrenford, and they would conquer Cordilleran and many other nations that were too weak and needed to be swept away.

Once again, the enemy forced themselves up the long, narrow siege towers with renewed fury. The Dwarves had already lit their oil trap; now they would have no choice but to face them in direct combat.

This time, the attacking forces lined up on the top of the great barrier wall and watched before they took action. They saw the valley below; aside from the smell of burnt Orc flesh, their only opposition was two catapults, guarded by twenty Dwarves some fifty yards away. They continued to gather on top of the great wall, forming lines, watching, looking for any sign of deception. Slowly, they descended the two side stairs. They moved cautiously; even the Orcs, who sometimes had to be restrained by the men, managed to keep from proceeding too quickly.

Crylar saw the enemy's caution and realized he would need to act quickly to keep the enemy from advancing. He turned to Valin. "Quickly," he ordered, "tell the pikemen, crossbowmen, and infantry to make formation lines in the courtyard."

Instantly, the General was off.

All the enemy siege towers, over twenty of them, were in use against the great wall. The top of the wall was filling with men and Orcs. Only a few of them descended the stairs, while the rest waited.

The drawbridge of the castle opened, and the Dwarven army marched out, proudly carrying their banners. Again, horns blew from the castle to announce the army's temperament. First, the pikemen came out, forming two rows of five hundred. Next came the crossbowmen in a single line of five hundred. Finally, the infantry came, in two rows of five hundred. They marched up and formed behind the catapults.

The enemy watched and waited, many of them still on the stairs. They had not advanced toward the valley yet, but the whole of the battlements of the great wall were teeming with men and Orcs, itching to descend and meet their enemies.

As the Dwarves completed their formation, the horns stopped. They were ready.

The enemy advanced now, unafraid. They were prepared to fight the war that they had come to Cordilleran to make. They filled the stairways now and spilled onto the valley floor. Hundreds more climbed into the siege towers. Anger, hatred, and vengeance were the incentives that moved them.

As the enemy started forming at the base of the Dwarven side of the great wall, Raybeck gave the signal. The two catapults fired their huge boulders. The enormous rocks struck the *Barrick Cropaal* at two points equidistant from the center. They impacted with a terrible smash and then fell down to crush several Orcs and men below.

A few moments after the boulders struck, a tremendous blast was heard and felt underground. The ground of the valley shook, and small rocks started slowly falling from the mountains that were connected to the great barrier wall. The enemy suddenly stopped moving as the wall itself began to shake.

The Orcs and men below looked up to see large vein-like cracks spreading from within the great wall itself. The wall was now visibly shaking and the enemy at its top found themselves clinging to the battlements for dear life.

A great rumbling began now as fear and panic set in among them. Men and Orcs began throwing themselves off the wall, back toward the enemy side. In the next instant, the entire middle of the wall collapsed straight down, followed by the two ends collapsing inward on top of the center. Screams filled the air.

The whole of the *Barrick Cropaal* collapsed with such force that rocks and debris shot out, both forward and behind their points of impact. All the enemy siege towers were destroyed in a single moment, as well as all those within. Hundreds below the wall on both sides were crushed as the wall broke into several heavy pieces. Smoke and debris filled the air, pushed out from the impact.

A few dozen enemies on the Dwarven side who had outrun the impact were quickly skewered by the pikemen. The Dwarves then quickly retreated to the castle.

The King watched the gray, stone-colored cloud of debris that rose where the *Barrick Cropaal* had once stood. He leaned against the wall of the balcony and lowered his head.

"For centuries that wall has protected us," Crylar said sadly. "It would have stood intact until the ending of all things. Now, it lies in ruin by our own hands. What have we done, Commander?"

"We have created a pile of stone that may take the enemy days to remove before they can march any kind of army through," Raybeck answered him. "We have bought precious time for our people to escape safely, Sire."

"How many did they lose on and below the wall?" the King asked, still looking despondent.

"I would say two thousand at least, Sire, perhaps more," replied the Commander.

"Perhaps more . . . and all we had to do was destroy a little more of our homeland to do it." The King turned and walked inside, away from the sight of the carnage. "Go down with General Valin," the King said as he took his place on his throne, staring blankly in the distance. "The men will wish to celebrate our victory. I shall be down in a moment."

Raybeck looked at him and was about to say something, but he could not find the words to help the King understand that what they had done was in the best interest of the people. Instead, he saluted and did as the King ordered.

Sunlight did not come to Cordilleran. The next morning greeted them again with gray clouds and a drizzling, harassing rain.

The enemy had wasted no time, using what wagons they still had to form an assembly line to haul the stone and debris away. Despite the fact that there were thousands of them, they made slow progress, as the stones were piled high and some were extremely heavy. There would be no attack this day, at the very least.

The Dwarves took advantage of the day. The men slept in shifts, catching up on their rest. By afternoon, the rains came in earnest. A tumultuous downpour soaked the lands. However, the Dwarves slept, at ease, to the rhythm of the pouring rain.

Within the throne room, the King, Valin, Raybeck, and Tyran mapped out the next phase of their defense. The King had ordered double rations throughout the day. Although their luck had been incredible to this point and their planning near perfect, the next battle would come to the foot of the palace, and there would be losses, whether their plan succeeded or failed.

Nightfall soon covered the land again, and the rains came down even harder. Just as the intensity of the rains increased, they brought with them yet another enemy. The Dwarven scouts in the valley saw a new force entering the enemy camp and quickly made way to the palace to inform General Valin and the King.

Finally, they finished discussing their plans and the contingency plans for different scenarios, as they had done since the beginning. Before the King dismissed them, he addressed them on a different matter.

"If the next battle is successful, Valin, I want you and Tyran to leave the palace and make all haste east to reach our people in the sanctuary caves. It is not a request, gentlemen; it is an order, and we are all too tired to argue. The army must have a commander; the Engineering Corps must have a commander. Raybeck will stay, as his skills will be paramount in the final phase. That is all. You may retire, my friends. Sleep well."

They each saluted the King as they left his table.

At that moment, a Dwarven scout was admitted, dripping water across the floor. He saluted and knelt. "Sire, a new force has arrived in the enemy camp . . . it is a force of Ogres fifteen hundred strong. They have already begun clearing the rocks. We estimate that, with the help of the Ogres, the enemy will clear a path to attack by the day after tomorrow, near midday."

"Very well," the King said, turning and walking toward his balcony. "You may return to your post." Through the pouring rain, he could only see the distant torches of the enemy camps. "Deploy our men tonight under cover of darkness. We will continue as planned. The Ogres are an ill omen. We must hope they are held back in reserve when the fighting begins. In any event, we fight to the death. Good night, my friends."

With that, the King turned his back to his officers, and they exited in silence.

The morning came, bringing with it a respite from the rains. A fog hung low to the ground, present throughout the valley and the plains beyond.

It was not thick enough to conceal the Ogres from view, however. They were large, ugly, ill-tempered monsters that had great fondness for the eating of Dwarven flesh, among other grotesque delicacies. Hungry for a fight and eagerly anticipating the chance to taste Dwarf again, the Ogres threw themselves into the work of clearing the stone with relish. However, they would have to wait their turn, as the enemy was lining up the cavalry of the

Stygian Knights. They would charge in and cut the Dwarven infantry to pieces once the way was clear.

The Stygian Knights, the elite forces of the Shadow Prince, were some of the finest mercenaries in the lands. They had training camps now in the deserts of Jarathadar, in the plains of Koromundar, and in secret places in Mystaria. Their numbers had grown and expanded from their power base in the northern realm of the ruined Pytharian Empire, the Shadow Prince's former seat of power. Their power was rising again in Branix Major, the Shadow Prince's capital within the Pytharian Empire, and would soon expand to the city of Gereth Minor, which the Stygian Knights had held many times throughout history. They had often been held at bay by the Wood Elves from the Great Forest of Haloreth, the same Wood Elves who had been freed years ago during the exploits of Lark Royale and Kael Dracksmere. The same Wood Elves who no longer existed.

The dreaded, dark knights were dressed in black plated mail of the finest quality. All of them wore black hooded robes. The crest on their chests and shields was that of the red Hydra, the symbol of the Shadow Prince. They rode upon great horses, bred for war and wearing plate barding. The barding was a black, heavy armor, which protected the animal's face, fore, and hindquarters. Their legs were still somewhat exposed to injury during battle. Such animals were designed for endurance more than speed. In addition, the knights carried long black lances to strike from horseback and long swords to fight with on the ground.

Following the embarrassing defeat a few nights prior, they had chased their horses down and gathered them back together and began forming five columns, each a thousand men across. As soon as the Ogres cleared the way, they would charge into the valley. There was no pretense, no secret strategy; they made it very clear how they intended to attack.

Dwarven horns sounded, announcing the first display of a large force. As the drawbridge opened, the Dwarven infantry emerged, armed with battle-axes. They had swords at their belts and shields on their backs. They marched out of the castle and made their own formation of four columns, each five hundred strong. Atop the first tier of the castle, Dwarven crossbowmen formed up in two lines, each consisting of two hundred and fifty men.

Still, the Dwarves would stand little chance, as the cavalry had the strategic height advantage as well as the numerical advantage. The Dwarven infantry would most likely be annihilated, yet they stoically stood just far enough from the castle to keep the approaching enemy within crossbow range.

The morning had come and gone and taken with it the rain and the apprehensiveness that came with the anxiety of awaiting the next battle. The Dwarves, like any other people, were not immune to the dreadful feeling that came with waiting, but they were stalwartly committed. It had come sooner than they had expected. The Ogres worked like maddened animals, as if they were being whipped by a thousand men. Some evil, unseen power was clearly at work on them. The stones would be cleared enough for the cavalry to ride through in a matter of hours. The Dwarves were ready nonetheless.

The King and Valin watched from the palace balcony. The mild cloud cover would make for a decisive battle; there would be no glare from the sun to hinder the combat. There was only a delicate breeze, which would be insignificant to the fighting conditions. The valley floor, however, would be mostly slippery mud as a result of the extended rains. Much of the valley ground was still littered with the carcasses of Orcs, more so near the ruins of the great barrier wall. Now, the bodies would be waterlogged and the horses of the Stygian Knights would trample them deep into the earth.

Today could make or break the Dwarves. In any event, they had lasted much longer than they could have ever hoped with so small a garrison.

When the last great stone was moved, it began without delay. The dark Knights charged. They had to shorten their ranks to two hundred men per column, as the clearing through the debris was only large enough to accommodate that many horses. As they charged into the valley, their ranks expanded. As the first wave of riders reached the midpoint of the valley, the counterassault began. Dwarven horns blew once again to signal the men who had been waiting for such a signal since the previous night.

To the charging knights' bewilderment, they heard the Dwarves' battle cry, as the stout warriors spilled out from their hiding places among the jagged stones of the mountains on two fronts. Scores and scores of pikemen charged the horsemen from both sides of the valley, all bearing razor-edged pikes. The Stygian Knights realized the nature of the trap while still some twenty yards from the infantry. Surprised, they pulled back on their horses' reins. Those in the rear of their ranks hastened back toward the enemy camp.

At that instant, the Dwarven horns sounded yet another signal. As the last of the charging horsemen tried to make it back to the debris of the great wall, to their astonishment, the way was unexpectedly blocked. At the sound of the horns, Raybeck and Tyran had pulled the ropes, connected by a system of pulleys, that hoisted a huge metal net from the ground. This device—composed of pure adamantite in interlocking mesh—when raised to its full height, stood as high as the *Barrick Cropaal* once had. Its width, while pulled tight, also consumed the space of the once-great wall.

The mesh had holes in it that were large enough to stick a pike or shoot a bolt through. The Engineering Corps had been forging the net for hundreds of years, never knowing for certain but assuming it may have great value one day. This day, it served to once again separate the Dwarves from the outside world, and, in addition, it trapped the enemy cavalry on the Dwarven side.

Raybeck and Tyran quickly used great hammers to drive adamantite spikes through the holes of the net into the mountains themselves, securing the net in place.

The Dwarven pikemen used their great spears to force the dark horsemen into the middle of the valley, holding them at bay, impaling the horses and, in some cases, the riders themselves. Unseen to the black Knights, the Dwarves on the second tier of the castle had rolled out several great ballistae on the west wall. They fired into the middle of the dark horde, carving through them, forcing many riders to the ground. With the pikemen holding the riders at bay and the great wooden bolts of the siege ballistae throwing riders to the ground, the infantry advanced forward. More infantry emerged from the castle, racing out to confront the threat. While the metal net had served to trap the enemy and separate them from reinforcements, it had also trapped the Dwarves. The Stygian Knights, who would never surrender, had to be dealt with now, down to the last man.

Within minutes, the scene below the King's balcony was mass chaos. Five thousand Stygian Knights fought nearly five thousand Dwarves.

Though the Dwarves had the element of surprise and were able to render the knights' lances useless, the ground battle was fiercely savage nonetheless. The dark knights would not die easily, and their skills on foot matched—and in many cases, exceeded—their horsemanship skills.

The fighting was furious; axe versus sword, sword versus sword, or sword versus pike, it did not matter. Crossbowmen were quickly dispatched out into the valley. They came forward quickly and made a semicircle around the battle, firing measured shots at the enemy still mounted or on the ground as soon as they presented clear targets.

After hours of fighting, the tide had turned decisively in favor of the Dwarves. However, had they not had the surprise and the aid of siege artillery and the crossbowmen, the struggle would have gone the other way.

Finally, the lot of the Stygian Knights had been unhorsed and lay dead or dying. The Dwarven pikemen had turned their attention toward the adamantite net, charging the many Ogres who pulled on it from the bottom. They skewered the great beasts, killing dozens, until they relented and retreated. Dwarven crossbows fired through the holes of the net, giving their enemies more than enough incentive to keep running in the other direction.

When the day's battle had finally ended, the King watched from above as his infantry moved about the valley, finishing off whatever enemies still lived. The anguished wailing lessened and lessened as the dying were put out of their misery by Dwarven swords. Once again, the valley had become a graveyard, only this time, several hundred of his own people lay dead below. Crylar watched for several minutes, wincing at the sound of each death. He watched and waited for the inevitable battle report from Valin.

Soon, the old Dwarf General entered. Crylar turned to him reluctantly. "How many did we lose?"

Valin tried to put a positive justification on the loss of life. "Over a thousand my lord; the count is not yet complete. These Stygian Knights sold their lives dearly. Still, Sire . . . it could have been much worse."

"Worse?" the King intoned miserably. "I fear next time *will* be worse . . . *much* worse. Leave me, my friend. Order double rations again and break open all the wine and ale. Let the men eat and drink to their hearts' desire."

The King turned and walked slowly toward the balcony to continue watching the grizzly carnage below.

Later that night, two Knights and a large armored Orc reluctantly entered the tent of Prince Voltan. Upon entering, they fell to their knees, heads lowered. The mere sight of Voltan in his Lich form inspired fear. He seemed filled with a dark, black and gray haze that animated his robes. The only color came from his shimmering, surreal crown of gold and jewels, and they were little more than a momentary distraction as they hovered above a shimmering skull, housing crimson eyes filled with hate.

"You fools!" Voltan spat venomously. "These little meaningless creatures outwit you at every turn. Tell me again how your countries and armies are meant for greatness and cannot be defeated? These midget animals defeat you battle after battle! How do you expect to fare against the armies of other men and Elves?"

The Orc chieftain, Grondhammer, rose at that point. "My Lord, we told you we should have sent out more scouts to watch them and judge their strength before we moved against them, but you said—"

Grondhammer never finished the sentence as green fire erupted from Voltan's eyes, swallowing the Orc whole and leaving nothing but ash behind.

"Perhaps one of you has something to add to the chieftain's opinion?" Voltan asked with false good humor.

The response came in unison. "No, my Lord." The knights dared not lift their heads.

"Then go," Voltan hissed. "Prepare all your men for one final assault tomorrow at midday. Look to the skies for me, and you will see your signal. Now get out of my sight, and pray to your gods that you never fail me again."

Voltan then departed his tent, a dark wraith gliding through the night to his dark steed. His eyes glared and pulsed, his facial features seeming to fade in and out of the here and now like the rest of his barely corporeal form.

The great black stallion released a distinctive whine as Voltan silently mounted the animal, then pulled back on the reins and kicked the animal forward. Instantly, the beast bore him up and away from the enemy camp into the currents of the night sky.

The form of General Valin walked the subterranean corridors below Cordilleran. It was a vast, cavernous complex of tunnels that burrowed beneath the city, beneath the valley beyond the *Barrick Cropaal*, and even into the fields where the enemy camp now lay. Some parts of it were so ancient and so complex that no Dwarf knew where and for how far they went. It was down here, below the palace, where the Dwarves could potentially be vulnerable. Torchlight burned, giving no indication of day or night, reflecting in the General's eyes—or rather, in truth, in the imp's green eye slits.

The night fell away and the morning arrived over Cordilleran. The sunlight hinted its presence through the clouds, releasing its light for the first time since the fighting had begun.

Crylar sat on his throne; he was alone save for the royal guards. He had slept there awkwardly, on and off. He had not removed his armor nor slept in his bed since before Cormayer had left. He was haggard; his skin felt drawn and taught as that of a sick, dying man.

It would end soon. They had no more war tricks with which to stave off the enemy. Though he had resigned himself to this fate days ago, the closer it came, the harder it was to accept. He thought of his people; he had given them as much time as possible and more to go deep in the eastern mountains where no army could easily follow. All the merchants, towns, and families had made it safely away. The High Council was safe, as well as some fifteen thousand men of the Dwarven army, sent away to live and fight this evil another day. Cormayer was safe, as were Valin and Tyran, who would soon be leaving. All these things he took great comfort in.

The nations must ally, he thought. *Averon, Alluviam, Arcadia, and the Dwarves . . . perhaps even others. If they could put aside their petty squabbles and unite, they could beat this darkness back to the abyss it so richly deserves.*

Crylar wished he could live to see that campaign, to be part of it. He resolved to himself that it was enough that the Dwarves would be there. He thought of Mekko. How proud Mekko would have been of their efforts here; had he still been alive, who knows what would have occurred. *Goodbye, my friend*, he thought, pondering what could have been.

Crylar was so lost in thought, he barely noticed the guards admit General Valin. He sat up quickly.

"Come, sit, my friend," he said solemnly. "Let us have a quiet drink together before you depart. Where is Tyran?"

"He went with Raybeck down to the tunnels, Sire, to check that all is in readiness," the old Dwarf said, as he poured two goblets of wine.

"Good . . . good. I am glad they will have time alone as well." The King took the goblet and raised it to Valin, who returned the gesture. "You have fought many battles, my old friend. I look to you to set the example that will keep the army united and motivated. Cordilleran thanks you for your dedicated service, General . . . and I thank you for being a good friend." Again, the King raised his glass, and they both drank.

Valin watched as the King rose and headed toward his balcony. His eyes were on the King's retreating back.

Raybeck and Tyran inspected the tunnels beneath the palace, checking the powder trails and fuses of what would be their last act of defense. It would only be executed if and when the enemy overran the castle, as only then would it have the greatest impact.

Finally, they approached a large lever set into the ground, which they had rigged some time ago. If the lever were pushed, it would create sparks that would light the fuses, which, in seconds, would unleash a series of explosions, forever sealing off the city of Cordilleran from its enemies.

When they were content all was ready, they walked back through the many corridors, making their way back up to the castle. It was then that the alarms suddenly sounded throughout the castle. The Dwarves were scrambling to the battlements, arming themselves.

Crylar rushed to the balcony, and what little hope he still possessed was driven out of him as he watched a new enemy approaching in the distance. The men on the wall, at the battlements, began shouting, "Dragons! Dragons are attacking!"

They were, in fact, not dragons but hydras—distant cousins to the dragons. The huge, flying lizards, some thirty-five feet long with an incredible, fifty-foot wingspan, traveled in a flock nearing two dozen toward the castle. What inspired the most fear was their slender-necked, six-headed bodies. With leathery skin ranging from grayish to dark brown, the creatures were nearly half tail, and those tails were deadly strong and accurate whips. Unlike dragons, these creatures had no arms, only great hind legs with protruding talons. Their great mouths housed row upon row of razor-sharp teeth. In combat, they dove at incredible speeds despite their bloated stomachs and cumbersome appearance, snatching their prey. Unlike their larger, more powerful cousins, their breath was neither fiery nor poisonous. Still, they were the creatures whose form and symbol signified the Shadow Prince. He had had dragon servants in the past and had now cast his favor on these, their smaller cousins.

Several curved their wings inward and dove down at great speeds, smashing into the siege weapons on the castle and tearing them to shreds with their sword-like talons. Five of the beasts broke off and aimed themselves toward the adamantite net. Diving down, they grabbed hold of the great metal net and began flapping their great wings furiously, pulling at the net in an attempt to dislodge it.

Dwarven crossbowmen formed up and began firing into the skies. However, their bolts only served to enrage the beasts, stinging them like bees attacking the head of a great bear. The Hydras responded by diving down and snatching up several Dwarves, only to bring their jaws down to snap off their heads in mid-flight.

Below, in the valley, the Ogres had rushed forward and began pulling on the bottom of the net with all their might as the rest of the enemy army stood ready behind them to charge the valley the moment the net was breached. Dwarven pikemen began running toward them as the crossbows continued firing up at the Hydras.

Below, in the tunnels, Raybeck clearly heard the alarms from above. He turned his head immediately to speak with Tyran.

"Tyran, we must hurry, you must get out of here quickly; the castle is under att—"

His words died on his lips as Tyran thrust his short sword, hilt deep, into his stomach.

Raybeck looked up as he slowly fell to his knees. He saw a smiling Tyran before him, holding the sword that had just run him through and pushing on it until it would go no further into him. There was a strange lust and an evil grin upon Tyran's face. Raybeck was astonished, still on his knees. He felt his hands fall to his sides.

"Tyran . . . why?" He choked and stammered out the words. "Why?"

Raybeck watched as, suddenly, Tyran's eyes became green slits and his form dematerialized and shrank into the diminutive form of Kempec, the imp.

"*Fool!*" the imp hissed at him, smiling. "*Your precious Tyran looked infinitely better with his throat slit, just as you do with a sword in your gullet.*" He then raised one of his clawed feet and, placing it against Raybeck's face, violently kicked him off the impaling sword and into the side of the corridor. The imp sauntered over to Raybeck, who lay face down but still vaguely stirring with life. His scorpion-like tail swiftly struck Raybeck in the back, imbedding its deadly stinger. Raybeck convulsed with a terrible cry and then moved no more.

In the next moment, the creature moved to the center of the corridor and gave an echoing whistle. Kempec watched as, within seconds, the Orcs started coming through the tunnel, as he had shown them. Running toward them, he took the lead on their ascent into the castle.

As the Dwarves started taking cover within the towers of the castle, the entire flock of Hydras, having successfully destroyed all the siege artillery, turned their collective attention toward the adamantite net. Nearly all of the winged creatures had grasped the net and now pulled on it from above with mighty force. It would only be a matter of moments before the spikes holding it in place were wrenched free under the combined effort of the Hydras and Ogres.

Within the castle, the remaining infantry and royal guard in the foyer had been taken by surprise by the Orcs, as they emerged from the tunnels.

The foyer was in pandemonium as the Dwarves bravely formed a defensive line and, each time it faltered, they found the will to regroup and drive the savage Orcs back.

Raybeck stirred and turned his head to see scores of Orcs running and shoving their way through the tunnel toward the stairs that would bring them up into the castle. He knew he was losing blood rapidly. The sting he received from the imp, while it caused him great pain, had not killed him, as it would have if he had been a man. In addition to their resistance to magic, Dwarves had great natural immunities to most poisons that would kill men or most other races. He knew he had little life left in him, but he could not allow himself to die before he completed his final sacred task.

Silently, he managed to push himself to his hands and knees. He turned around and began to crawl back toward the lever. The Orcs were too preoccupied by the battle sounds from up ahead to even notice him. He only had to go a few feet, and he could turn a corner. Slowly, agonizingly, he pulled his knees forward with the great strength of his massive hands and bulging forearms. Each breath was agony beyond reason; blood fell from his mouth every inch of the way.

Crylar decided he had waited long enough. Taking his great double-bladed axe in his hands and smiling, he bade his two loyal guards to open the doors of the throne room. He could hear the sounds of combat distantly down the corridors within the palace.

"Draw your swords, lads! For Cordilleran . . . follow me!"

They followed on the king's heels as they hurried to meet their fate.

At that moment, from without, a great roar rose up from the enemy army as, finally, the adamantite net was torn out of the mountainside and hoisted away by the hydras. Without hesitation, the Ogres, the barbarians of Koromundar, and the desert nomads of Jarathadar charged into the valley toward the castle.

Two hundred Dwarven pikemen were there to greet them and a great crunching sound rent the air as the forces collided. Within seconds, however, the enemy overcame the long spears, and the spiked clubs of the Ogres made short work of the Dwarven force, batting them down like flies. Undaunted, the enemy continued toward the castle.

Raybeck had crawled all the way back down to the point where he could see the lever down the tunnel. The lever would be his salvation. He raised his head enough to see that someone else was in the corridor. He watched, unseen, as Kempec quizzically looked first at the lever, then down at the many trails of powder leading away from it.

Kempec should have asked Raybeck about this lever before he had killed him, but he had not wanted to give away his masquerade. *No doubt,* he thought, *another one of their engineering tricks.* The powder trails seemed to lead off in many directions and for great distances into the rock. For now, he decided not to tamper with the device; he would show it to his master when the slaughter was over.

He had barely turned around to start back before Raybeck was on him.

The attacking force hit the inner wall, and much in the manner of the Orcs, the men climbed on the backs of Ogres and one another up and over into the foyer.

The remainder of the Dwarven garrison—twenty plus the King—had been driven back into the King's throne room. They used long axes to bar the doors.

The enemy threw themselves into the double doors. Crylar knew that, as soon as the Ogres came to reinforce them, it would not be long before they breached the doors. So far, all had been going to plan, but Raybeck had not thrown the switch. When the King had heard that the Orcs were coming up through the tunnels, he despaired that Raybeck and Tyran had been killed. Now, they were boxed in with no way to get to the lever. Soon, they would all be dead, and Cordilleran would be naked for the plundering. The thought of it turned his stomach and brought a tear to his eye.

Just one of Raybeck's massive hands would have been sufficient to completely encircle the creature's small throat, but he used both hands. His forearms rippled and contorted as he used all his strength to squeeze the imp's neck.

Kempec's green eye slits knew only bewilderment and fear as he tried in vain to incapacitate Raybeck, using his tail to sting the Dwarf in several places. Though the injured Raybeck was on his knees, he was still tall enough to hold the creature where it stood.

Finally, Raybeck grabbed the imp's chin with one hand and, swiftly releasing its throat, grabbed the side of its head with his other, turning the creature's head with such sudden and terrific force that its neck snapped loud and cleanly. The imp collapsed in a pile on the ground.

Raybeck fell on his stomach. He lifted his head and looked ahead, his chin resting in the dirt. He had expended great energy killing the imp. He had been losing blood from his stomach, back, and mouth. He was dizzy; he had difficulty feeling any sensation in his feet and his hands were becoming numb as well. Darkness was closing in all around him, but he had only five or six feet to go to reach the lever.

He crawled on his belly, no longer able to feel his extremities. His vision blurred; he tried to focus, unable to see, reaching what he hoped were his arms out in front of him. He must be only inches from it now. Death came for him as he threw himself forward.

In the palace above, the Ogres quickly broke through the throne room doors and they, along with Orcs and men, spilled inside. The remaining Dwarves valiantly formed a buffer between the enemy and the King, but Crylar was quickly exposed to several attackers.

With one hand, the King swung his axe above his head in a circle, taking off the heads of two Ogres. He then drew his weapon down into a spinning, two-handed grip, chopping through two Orcs as if they were small trees.

It was then that he felt it.

Suddenly, there was a rumbling and shaking throughout the palace and castle that dwarfed the noise and sound that proceeded the fall of the *Barrick Cropaal*. The palace seemed to be sinking downward, and the invaders began to lose their footing. Several huge impacts sounded from above as if the mountainside was collapsing on the castle.

Raybeck had done it. Crylar's hope restored, he let out a menacing cry. "Scum of Koromundar! Filth of the desert! Pigs of Bazadoom! Let the last word you hear in this life be: *CORDILLERAN!*"

Outside, the thousands of the enemy who had not yet even made it halfway into the valley watched in awe as the great mountainside collapsed into the basin where the Dwarven castle stood. The castle itself sunk, swallowed whole by the earth. The mountainside collapsed in chunks so huge they could never be moved, not only destroying and burying the castle but also forever sealing off the underground mountain city of Cordilleran from the world.

Chapter 23

The White Elves filtered up into the cavernous chamber from deep inside the earth. The dark-blue plated mail armor of the warrior caste shone resplendently in the half-light produced by the mineral-rich rock formations that lined both the roof and floor of the cave they had gathered in. Stalactites and stalagmites of all sizes adorned the cave's interior. The cave was well concealed from the outside world, and appeared from the outside as nothing more than a giant mound of ruinous rocks overgrown with moss and tenuous weeds from the surrounding Vineland Woods.

The warriors carried bows and long swords. The White Elves of the religious caste, men and women alike, wore hooded robes of black. Some carried staves, while others walked with their fingers crossed and heads bowed hidden within their cowls.

They gathered at the base of a large plateau, the top of which overlooked the entire cavern surrounding it. Four warriors carried High Priestess Mya on a chair to the ledge, setting her down between two robed members of the religious caste who waited to attend her. A tall, armored warrior soon joined them. His helmet, dark blue to match his armor, was shaped like the head of a dragon. This was General Turnia. Like his men, he carried a bow, a quiver of arrows, and a long sword. He and Mya watched as their people massed below them. Thousands upon thousands of them formed up, a terrifying invasion force prepared to attack and take over the Elven Kingdom of Alluviam.

They waited for Prince Stranexx and General Prince Voltan, who would soon be arriving with an additional force from Mystaria, including a Stygian Knight cavalry trained within Mystaria. The armies would then merge and march on Alluviam, intent on killing all who resisted.

Mya found herself wondering what would become of those who did not resist. She had never wished it would come to this. This was the day Mya had dreaded for years, and it had finally arrived. Her people would join with the Shadow Prince and take Alluviam by force. The surface-dwelling Elves would never expect there to be so many of them; they would be unprepared. Small teams of White Elf infiltrators would take out the Elven sentry posts in advance. Many of their cousins would die, in a vain but valiant attempt to defend their homeland and their King. They would be slain in cold blood, for they had never had anything to do with the fate of the White Elves; most of them did not even believe Mya's people existed. To them, they would be fighting an outside invader, and yet in truth, these seemingly separate races were one and the same, though those above the earth lived under the sun while the White Elves lived below the earth, separated by deeds done thousands of years ago that none now living remembered.

Kael was right, Mya thought, *about everything*. Though she had done her best to deny it, he had seen through her posturing and into her soul from the beginning. Before the day was over, she felt she would be sorry that she had not gone with him. She hoped he was safe.

A large procession rode silently through the edge of the Vineland Woods, a great dark host led by the standard of the red hydra. Despite the vastness of their numbers, they walked and rode in tight columns. All wore the black plated mail that bore the red hydra insignia of the Stygian Knights.

At the head of the procession rode a dark figure, clad in a gold-trimmed brown robe. A golden helmet fronted by a metal mesh mask of iron concealed his features from the world of men. He carried a pike in his right hand, and atop this weapon was another symbol of a more gruesome nature, meant to instill fear, anger, and hopelessness against all who dared stand against him—the rotting head of King Thargelion of Wrenford. Until now, the Shadow Prince had taken great precaution to conceal his movements, traveling only through means of teleportation spells, but now he rode out in the open, unafraid, personally commanding his forces.

Next in the procession came the undead Prince Voltan, the Shadow Prince's commanding general, in his true form, his head an ivory skull with two red circles of energy for eyes and topped by a shimmering crown of gold and gems. His robes were as pitch black as the stallion he rode upon, whose animated red eyes matched his own. He was glad to be marching on Alluviam. The Elves' very presence was disturbing to him. Though their army was not as large as the Dwarves', they were just as dangerous as a fighting force, perhaps more so. There was no telling what magic they still possessed or what cursed weapons they had to hinder an attack. He would be gladder still when they were all dead. Without the Elves and Dwarves, the human nations would fall easily.

Riding close to Voltan was Viscount Navarre. It was a position of honor for him to be riding so close to his lord on such an important day. He had arranged for the Stygian Knight training camps' establishment throughout Mystaria, and so he had been put in command of the Stygian Knight infantry. He, too, had looked forward to this day, but he had taken precautions to ensure that he would survive it. Riding alongside him was his vaunted bodyguard, a tall, black-cloaked, hooded figure, wearing a black-leather vestment from his chest to his shoulders. Long black leather gloves covered his hands and forearms, and twin short swords hung at his waist. He was the deadliest member of Navarre's secret cult of assassins, the Brothers of the Shadow.

Finally, there rode Lark Royale, encased in his brilliant, full-body suit of silver-plated mail. His two-handed sword was strapped to his back, the frost-white diamond etched into the hilt of the great blade clearly visible. He was the one bright light among a sea of black forms. However, his eyes were glazed over with a glossy, unnatural look. His expressionless stare gave him more the look of a zombie than a man.

The Stygian Knights consisted of two thousand infantry, who marched in front of a cavalry of three thousand. They moved in tight columns, hundreds strong. They had traveled a great distance, some from as far as the Pytharian Empire, though most had come from Mystaria. They were professional soldiers, battle-hardened, well-trained, and even better equipped. If there was to be a new order, these men wanted to ensure that they would be on the side of the victors. Their force alone would prove to be a daunting problem for any enemy to face on its own, but once allied with ten thousand White Elves, they would be unbeatable.

Mya could sense they were close. The hour was drawing near; before the day ended, they would visit death and destruction upon the Kingdom of Alluviam, the likes of which had not been seen in an age. They would take their place in the new order alongside their allies. Mya felt as if she might be sick, though she could not show signs of weakness before her people. They would not understand. Kael had told her that he had seen strength within her. Now she suspected he had seen only what he wanted to, something that was not really there. If she possessed true strength and courage, she would have put a stop to this day's arrival and prevented the impending carnage that would result from the alliance of her people with the forces of darkness. But she had been weak; events were now in motion, which she could not alter. All she could do was hope for forgiveness, and that was a desperate hope, for there would be none left to seek it from after today.

She continued to watch as General Turnia spoke to the warriors, sharing words of encouragement for the battle ahead. She could not hear the words; they had no meaning for her. All she could hear were the roars of enthusiasm from the warrior caste. She was helpless, a prisoner among her own people.

How has it come to this? she wondered.

It was at that moment that one of the warriors approached her. Apparently he'd been speaking for some time, but she had been so lost in thought she hadn't heard him.

"High Priestess, Prince Stranexx and Prince Voltan have arrived with a large army, as they'd promised," the young warrior said, bowing to her.

"Excellent," she replied mechanically. "Show them in."

Mya and her attendants stepped back to make way for the Shadow Prince and his party, which consisted of Voltan, Navarre, and his bodyguard, and finally Lark Royale.

The Shadow Prince bowed low to Mya as he passed her, as did the others. She returned the gesture with no expression, trying to conceal the awful loathing she felt.

General Turnia quieted his people, as the Shadow Prince came to stand with him.

"Behold, my warriors," he thundered, "our friend and ally who will join us in battle this day, who has seen the righteousness of our just cause and has pledged to aid us: Prince Wolfgar Stranexx."

With that, cheers rose from all assembled. General Turnia was able to quiet the immense gathering with but a small hand gesture.

The Shadow Prince's voice was deep and raspy as it escaped through the iron lips of his mask. "*My friends . . . I am proud and honored to be among you this day. I see the size and eminence of your army, and it is a powerful sight indeed. I am told the Elves of the surface world refer to your people as Shadow Elves, and they both hate and fear you. They cast you out of your kingdom and consigned you to a subterranean prison, hoping you would despair and succumb to death. But you have overcome your adversities, despite their hopes to the contrary, and survived to build cities and a mighty society. Not only are you deserving of praise and respect, but I say the Elves and their King should kneel before you and beg your forgiveness!*"

The warriors nodded their agreement and raised their fists in support.

"*And . . . if they do not beg your forgiveness and give you what is rightly yours, there is a fitting punishment for such creatures.*"

With that, the Shadow Prince reached behind him, grabbed the pike that bore the decaying head of Thargelion, and shoved the end of it deep within the ground so that it stood erect of its own accord.

For a moment, there were mixed reactions, but very quickly a rousing approval came forth from the warriors. When they had quieted down, the Shadow Prince continued, "*Like you, my friends, I was cast out of the world by my people, shunned, feared, and hated. Why? Because I was different. Because I chose to fight for my country. Because, just as your skin is different from the Elves of the surface, so my skin is different from that of other men. Small, weak-minded men who hated and feared what they could not under-stand called me Shadow Prince—small men such as this.*" He pointed to the head of Thargelion. "*But no more shall we be shunned and cast out; we shall take what is ours by force, and let those who oppose us reap the consequences of our wrath, and despair!*"

Roars of approval came from the thousands of White Elves assembled. Just as they began to settle down and the Shadow Prince turned and began to walk back toward the cave entrance, a lone, powerful voice rang out above the receding rumblings.

"Prince Wolfgar! Prince Wolfgar! Since when do you have the right to lay claim to Alluviam?"

The voice came from within the crowd somewhere close to the plateau. The Shadow Prince halted and turned back toward the crowd. General Turnia, visibly upset by the outburst, shouted down into the crowd. "Who dares ask such a question?"

"I dare!"

A robed figure stepped forward and removed his hood to reveal the face of Kael Dracksmere.

Mya stepped forward, a mix of fear and exhilaration overcoming her as she tried to determine if she were dreaming or not.

Without warning, the top of the wooden staff Kael held began to glow with an increasingly bright yellow light, causing the warriors around him to cover their eyes and back away.

"Stand back, White Elves, and hearken to me!" Kael roared. "I am Kael Dracksmere, Grand Druid of the lands and Baron of the Kingdom of Wrenford, and I say beware, lest you ally yourselves with a demon that would convince you that murder and lies are virtues and that war is the solution to all problems!"

Voltan stepped forward. "*I shall teach this Druid the price of his impudence.*"

"Druid . . ." the Shadow Prince hissed. "*Good . . . the time for reckoning is at hand. Let the fool prattle for now, Voltan; I have a better way to deal with him.*"

"Hear me now those who would not be pawns," Kael continued. As he spoke, he turned in a circle, allowing the light from his staff to diminish enough so that they could look upon him. "Those of you with families, with husbands and wives and children. Did you raise them to believe that war is the one and only means to solve their differences? Did you teach them that to kill every man, woman, and child of your enemy is an honorable act and worthy of praise? Will you go to your children after today and tell them how it was just and righteous that you murdered thousands of Elves who had not yet even come into existence when the first of your people were banished underground?"

Many of the warriors shook their heads and looked at Kael with contempt and disdain, but some others looked down, almost ashamed.

At that moment, a new voice was heard; one of Mya's attendants stepped forward and threw back his hood, revealing himself to be Galin. He spoke in Elvish to the assembly.

"Many of you can trace your lineage to families among the Elves of Alluviam," he said. "Those of you who can and have chosen to forget know that I speak the truth. They are your brothers, your sisters, and your cousins; do you truly wish to kill them, hatred burning in your hearts, without even trying to negotiate with them? They are your race. Your peoples are one and the same!"

Galin watched and saw even more faces were reflecting upon this. He gestured to the dark council that stood on the ledge. "Take a good look at your ally, Prince Stranexx, and his general, Prince Voltan. You ally yourselves with undead monsters such as this, truly believing their cause to be good, because they have stirred up old feelings of bitterness within you from a time long passed."

"If you destroy the Elves of Alluviam," Kael cried, "you will be destroying yourselves. Who else, then, will your allies have you believe looks down on you or is in some way responsible for your lot in life? Will it be men next? Dwarves? It was men who cast them aside and shunned them. Why then are they so anxious to help you kill other Elves?"

He could see many more now were considering his words. The Druids were starting to reach those assembled. He raised his eyes to the ledge above. Mya met his gaze and found solace and renewed courage in his eyes and the warmth of his smile. She rose from her seat and stepped forward to the lip of the ledge.

"My people," she said, "you must listen to these words! We have been led astray. We have been manipulated, and may the gods forgive me for having allowed it. May you find it in your hearts to forgive me. We will not—we *must* not—visit war and death upon our brethren. The old rivalries and grudges are dead, and we must find the strength and courage to bury them. Instead, we should go to them with our heads held high and find a way to bring the Elves together, united as one race as we were meant to be!"

General Turnia was astonished. "High Priestess! What are your saying?"

"What should have been said long ago, General," said Mya firmly, placing a hand upon his shoulder. "What I've always known and felt in my heart and have been too afraid to say. The Shadow Prince and his allies are using us for their own ends, whatever they may be, but they care nothing for the future of our people. They are deceitful monsters that seek power and possess only the will to dominate others. I will not allow our people to come under their sway anymore. You must order our warriors to stand down."

General Turnia batted her hand away. "No, High Priestess! We have labored too long to reach this moment, and I will not throw it away in the hour of our triumph. You agreed and so did the religious caste. We must strike now! By joining with Prince Stranexx's army, our victory is assured. I cannot follow your order, High Priestess. For the good of our people, I will not."

Some of the soldiers held their swords high, "We follow General Turnia. Death to Alluviam!"

By now, Kael had managed to slip past the crowd and stand a few yards from the cave opening. "Forgive me, General," he shouted, "but you will not be joining with the Shadow Prince's army this day!"

Kael raised his staff with both hands and smashed it to the ground with all of his might. Green fire exploded outward from where it struck, creating a shockwave that shook the entire cave. The very rocks and mineral formations protruding downward from the roof broke away and collapsed in a massive cave-in, completely sealing off the entrance from the outside world.

Outside the cave, the Stygian Knights staggered in the throes of the earth-shattering force. They found the entrance to the cave utterly blocked by a wall of rocks and debris. The officers of the cavalry and infantry hurriedly conferred with one another and, after a brief discussion, assigned men to attempt to clear the blockage as best they could.

As the men began to remove their armor to set upon the task, the surrounding woods echoed with a strange whistling noise. Many found themselves peering uneasily into the shadows of the leaves and branches of the forest, and several of the horses shifted nervously. The moment passed quickly, however, and several hundred men began the process of clearing the entrance. As they toiled, many of the cavalry dismounted and took seats upon the ground, while the men of the infantry began to spread out around the perimeter.

Then, without further warning, the woods began to move all at once. Shadows and shapes moved faster than human eyes could follow. Some of the men stood up, nervously reaching for their weapons. Others moved toward their horses, unsure what was happening. It was if the entire forest had come alive in response to and in defiance of their very presence.

"My warriors, we will fight this day, we will take back what is ours, kill these intruders, they are our enemies and—"

The broad end of Galin's staff interrupted General Turnia's orders, cracking him across his jaw. A second blow to his stomach doubled him over, and a third blow, this time to his back, knocked him clear off the ledge, sending him flying into a grouping of his warriors below.

Navarre drew his jeweled dagger from the middle of his belt and hurled it at Galin.

Like lightning, Mya's other robed attendant, pushing the High Priestess behind her, sprang forward, revealing a silver short sword from beneath her robes. In an upward slicing movement of amazing quickness, the sword batted the dagger up and away at the last second as it came within mere inches of Galin's head.

"I think not, coward." It was Elenari speaking. The cowl over her head fell, revealing her golden hair. "Perhaps you do not have the stomach for face-to-face combat?"

Navarre quickly moved behind his black-clad bodyguard. The dark figure quickly drew two short swords from his waist and held them out before him in a guarding stance.

Galin, unfazed by the failed attempt on his life, leapt off the ledge to a clearing amid the crowd on the cave floor below. Immediately, he snatched a staff from one of the nearby members of the religious caste and, in the same motion, turned and drove both staves down into the ground. He then took a step back, put his hands out in front of him, and exclaimed the words, *"Laves-Tral!"*

The staves instantly started to grow and expand. The wood became thick and rooted at the bottom while jutting out in several directions at the top. Branch-like arms sprang out midway up the shafts. The wood sprouted bark, and dark slits appeared on each of them to signify eyes and a mouth. The staves had disappeared, and in their place, stood two living trees nearly twelve feet high each and two feet in diameter. They began to move, their branch-like arms batting away nearby White Elves with terrific force, creating a clearing. The White Elves' archers fired many arrows at them to no avail; the shafts merely imbedded themselves harmlessly in the trees.

Kael approached the ledge, his gaze locked solely on the figure of the Shadow Prince. Kael's time to confront him had finally arrived; he must be stopped now before his evil could spread any further. With his free hand, Kael removed a pair of items—the two ruby halves of the gem from the head of the lava creature—from a pouch at his belt and tossed them up on the ledge, where they landed at the Shadow Prince's feet.

"Fear not, demon," Kael snarled, looking up at his nemesis. "Your foul monster was responsible for more than its share of death and destruction before we vanquished it." He looked at the head of Thargelion, closing his eyes and swallowing hard; it pained him to see such desecration. "But, like you, it shall never harm another living thing again. Come now . . . let us finish what we started years ago."

In response, the dark figure beckoned with his hand, but it was not toward Kael. A moment later, another figure jumped down from the ledge, landing only a few feet from Kael. It was Lark Royale. He drew his glowing, two-handed sword from its scabbard. Kael immediately recognized the frost-white diamond in the hilt, and he took a step back, lowering his staff.

"Lark . . . it's me . . . Kael. I'm your friend, do you understand? We've searched long and hard for you; we just missed freeing you from Shadowgate."

The look of confidence drained from Kael's face at the sight of the look on Lark's face; there was a strange distance in his eyes, something was not right in their color.

"Yes, Kael," Lark replied calmly. "I know who you are and I understand you. What you're doing is wrong. We were wrong all those years ago; Prince Stranexx is not our enemy—he never was. He wants what we want: peace and harmony throughout the lands. I will not let you and your friends harm him or stand in the way."

"Does that include me as well, brother?" It was Archangel; he had appeared at Kael's side amidst the swirling chaos in the background of White Elves fighting the trees.

"If you stand with them," said Lark, unmoved by the presence of his brother, who stared at him sadly with his one remaining eye, "I'm sorry to say it does, brother."

"Go, Kael!" Archangel said reluctantly, drawing his long sword and facing his brother whom he loved above all. "This is my task."

In the midst of the chaos, Prince Voltan had moved, unnoticed, toward the blocked cave entrance. He would use his power to blast the entrance open so the Stygian Knights waiting beyond could join them and quell this little uprising.

"Prince Voltan!" It was Galin; he had come up behind Voltan, and now the two of them stood alone near the entrance. "Your appearance has changed somewhat since the council chambers of Mystaria, but the evil that permeates from you cannot be concealed by any magic."

Voltan turned slowly, his red eyes gleaming within his ivory skull. "*Puny human,*" the prince said in an eerie tone, "*do you have any idea who or what I am?*"

"Yes," Galin replied as he removed his sacred mace from his belt with his right hand and drew his scimitar with his left. "You are an unholy abomination, who, like your master, will soon vanish into the oblivion that awaits both you and all your kind." The moment the mace appeared from beneath his robes, it began to glow a brilliant yellow, illuminating the part of the cave in which they stood.

Voltan raised a skeletal hand and took a step back, as if in fear. "*What is that accursed Elven relic you hold, human?*" he hissed, trying to block the light.

"It is the sacred mace of the Elven High Priest Dorthonian," Galin replied, "who used it centuries ago to eliminate your kind from the earth. It has been blessed by kings, wizards, and priests. It is *Livinilos*, the Mace of Many Blessings, and it has returned to vanquish you."

"*Elven magic? Sacrilege!*" Voltan hissed in anger. "*It will not save you, Priest. Do you not know death when it looks you in the eye? Have you never wondered what its final gaze would be like? See it now, Priest, and despair!*"

Green fire burst forth from Voltan's eyes. Galin dropped his scimitar and pulled his robes up to block the fire. However, the robes caught fire and were being consumed as if touched by acid. He quickly shed the robes.

The Lich attempted to step forward, but Galin raised the mace and the light from it intensified so much that Voltan shrank back from it.

Swords joined and clashed with one another, flashing reflections as both Elenari and Navarre's bodyguard fought with lethal spinning strokes, countering one another perfectly. They attacked and defended with a speed and tenacity that was unmatched by any of the thousands of combatants below them. The dark Brother of the Shadow's twin blades crossed in the air making an X where they locked with Elenari's single blade. The two moved, shifting their weight, each trying to gain the leverage that would give them the advantage.

"You are far better trained than the assassin I killed in Shadowgate," said Elenari, trying to provoke a response in the dark-garbed warrior whose face remained hidden from her within the blackness of his hood.

Instead of words, his answer came in the form of his twin short swords pushing her weapon up and away. One of them came down across the top of her right thigh, slicing deep into it. They spun around and away from each other.

Elenari looked down at the deep gash in her leg; blood gushed from the wound and ran down the length of her thigh and calf. She smiled bitterly; the dark warrior had drawn first blood.

Outside the cave, a member of the Stygian Knight infantry nervously reached for his sword and, as his hand grazed the hilt, it began.

Simultaneously, from all directions, volleys of arrows fired from unseen bows whistled into the knights' midst from behind the tree-lined perimeter of the clearing. Those working to clear the cave entrance were the first to die. The men who had been seated on the ground went down before they could rise. Volley upon volley of arrows filled the close, heavy air like a swarm of insects.

The Stygian Knight infantry quickly fell by the hundreds. Many of them had been pierced in several places before they fell dead. The men of the cavalry mounted as swiftly as possible and turned, making a break for the forest in an attempt to escape back the way they had entered. Fear overcame them as they watched the men on foot being cut down after only a few steps. The arrows came from everywhere by the hundreds, perhaps even thousands.

The White Elves were in sheer pandemonium. The thousands present in the cave had taken to fighting each other. Many had been rallied by the words of Kael and Mya, though there were still those with war and rage in their hearts who were not so easily convinced and who were willing to fight their brothers and sisters to the death.

Mya could see that many were preparing to target the intruders with their bows. She had been concentrating, uttering words of arcane origin, and suddenly her robes flew open wide, revealing her arms and outstretched fingers. The cave appeared to tremble for a moment, and then, in response to her magic, many of the stalagmites on the cave floor widened and joined with one another, forming a great high wall of stone, protecting and separating Kael and his allies from the masses. She skillfully arranged the wall so the two trees Galin created remained outside of it and continued to fight with those who would approach.

Without warning, the Shadow Prince was there, alone, before her. He raised his hand as a black ball of energy formed in his palm.

"Thank you for blocking the view of your precious people so that I am free to deal with you as you deserve. You have betrayed me for the last time, High Priestess. Now die in exquisite pain, and know that I will enslave your race and then destroy them."

Mya cringed backward, raising her hands defensively. At the last possible second, she stood straight, her eyes widening as her gaze shifted to the space behind the Shadow Prince.

Seeing the shift in her gaze, the Shadow Prince hesitated and slowly turned to see the standing form of a huge brown bear, over seven feet high on its hind legs, just as its claws came crashing down into his chest, launching him from the stone ledge to the cave floor below.

In a flash of brilliant green energy, the bear, now on all fours, shrank and changed. A tail sprouted out as its body, arms, and legs appeared to get longer and stripes appeared on its now bright orange hide. In the matter of a few moments, a tiger had appeared in place of the bear. The tiger sprang from the ledge and landed on top of the Shadow Prince, who lay sprawled on the ground below.

Galin and Voltan slowly circled each other. Galin knew he was about to enter the fight of his life against one of the most powerful forces of evil ever to walk the lands. Voltan was both Lich and wizard, as well as Prince of Mystaria and general of the Shadow Prince's armies. The others were embroiled in their own fights, and there would be no help for him. He would win or he would die; there would be no middle ground in this battle.

Voltan stopped. The red balls of energy that were his eyes locked upon those of Galin. Suddenly, Galin felt as if they were back in the council chamber of Mystaria where he had first sensed the evil from Voltan, only this was different. The power that animated the Lich and gave him life had grabbed on to Galin's soul.

His body began to feel the effects. Fear seized his being and his limbs became numb. He could hear Voltan's voice in his mind, and it was terrible. A dreadful, abject fear forced him back many steps until his back was against the cave wall. His hands fell to his sides and the light that emanated from the sacred mace began to subside. In his mind, he watched as if from outside his body as he died horribly at Voltan's hand. Even such a death was infinitely preferable to the fear that had overwhelmed him. He would have run away if he could, but his limbs were completely immobile.

"Priest, in the past centuries, many such as you have come up against me," Voltan said conversationally. *"They have all died, as you shall. Come here, priest . . . come to me for your death."*

The skeletal hand of Voltan beckoned Galin forward to him.

Galin, fighting with all his being, could not stop his legs from stiffly stepping forward. Ever so slowly, one step after another, he walked to Voltan, a combination of panic, anxiety, and dread battling with his true spirit. An inner war raged within him as evil fought for the possession of his soul and body. Savagely, he fought back with his courage, righteousness, and hope.

His hope. He had nearly forgotten it, almost entirely. He clung to his hope that goodness would prevail.

Thoughts of hope for goodness were so inconceivable to the scourge within him that he could feel the evil losing its grip on him. His left leg came up to move forward and quivered in the air for a moment and then settled backward. He let out a scream—"No!"—and his scimitar fell from his left hand. His right hand was still just barely clinging to the mace, but he moved forward no more. He was breathing heavily, and he could barely stand. The victory had cost him much of his strength, both physically and mentally.

Voltan clutched his head in his hands, as he too was momentarily disoriented by the unexpected show of inner power from the Druid.

"Your will is strong . . . so death must come to you."

Galin watched as the Lich seemed to glide toward him, a spectral form born from some horrible nightmare. As he got closer, Galin could see the shimmering crown of surreal gems upon his ivory skull. He tried to bring his arms up in defense but could not find the strength.

Voltan, tall and menacing, looked down upon him the way a predator views its prey just before the kill.

Navarre moved cautiously, as silently as possible, maneuvering himself behind where his bodyguard was battling the half-Elven woman. He had gradually inched forward and taken position behind her. The combatants warred with such ferocity and over so wide a space that it would be foolish to come up behind her too swiftly and risk getting injured. He would wait until an opportunity presented itself, and then he would stab her from behind. Of course, that was if his deadly bodyguard didn't kill her first; the blood from the woman's wound had splattered all over the ground where they fought. Perhaps it would not be necessary to intervene at all.

Elenari parried the dark assassin's swings, skillfully blocking the twin short swords on every stroke. Though she bled heavily, she danced around her attacker, ducking, weaving, and spinning as if her blade were an extension of her being. She baited the assassin who pursued and pressed her, attacking powerfully and swiftly, unrelenting. However, his movements were more exaggerated, requiring more movement and greater exertion to perform. Hers were subtle and swift, but less strenuous, as she remained ever on the defensive to his multiple attacks.

Elenari anticipated a pattern of attacks coming and decided it was time to expand her strategy. The assassin attacked downward with his left hand while stabbing with his right. Elenari parried the left-hand stroke while coming forward and, turning into him so that, with a swift spin, she suddenly had her back against his chest, she grabbed his right wrist as he attempted the stabbing attack. She stepped away from him, beneath the arm she held in her grasp, and with a snapping motion, flipped him onto his back, causing him to drop his right-hand sword. Though he quickly bounced back on his feet, he rose only in time to see Elenari mockingly kick the blade away. Now, they had one sword each. Now more enraged, the dark assassin charged at her with renewed fury.

Archangel and Lark crossed swords and circled each other, weapons locked in midair.

"Lark . . . please," Archangel pleaded. "Don't do this. We're family; I love you, brother. Can your oath as a Paladin allow you to strike one who loves you—your own kin?"

"I will not forsake Prince Stranexx," Lark replied coldly, "and allow your unjust attack upon him to go unpunished, even for the sake of my kin. My Paladin's oath does not recognize the bonds of brotherhood where good and evil are concerned. While you fight on the side of evil, you fight against me."

Lark swung his great sword in a downward cleaving stroke. Archangel fell to his knees and blocked the killing blow, looking desperately into his brother's eyes, seeking some sign of humanity or compassion. Lark's pupils had become fuzzy and hard to see, clouded by a gray haze. Even his voice lacked its old conviction. Clearly, some devilry of the Shadow Prince controlled him. Whatever was to happen, Archangel could not bring himself to harm his brother. He pushed Lark's blade away and quickly scrambled to his feet.

"Fight it, Lark . . . please . . . for all our sakes, fight it brother."

Still, Archangel's pleas fell on deaf ears; Lark continued to advance.

In the forest, the Stygian Knight captain shouted to his cavalry, "Retreat, ride for your lives!"

The horses rode in a tight column with all speed away from the hail of arrows, which cut down the infantry of their army without mercy and with a precision so deadly that only Elves could have been the ones firing them.

Somehow, the Elves had been ready for them. They had lost the element of surprise; cut off from the Shadow Prince and Voltan, they had no option but to retreat and regroup. The arrows came from nowhere and everywhere all at once. Even some of the Knights on horseback were picked off as they rode at the full gallop toward the eastern clearing, which led out of the forest and to safety. Madly the black-armored warriors and horses rode, like a festering malignant disease driven from the purity of the forest by thousands of hidden Elven bowmen.

The Stygian Knight cavalry emerged from the Vineland Woods to the open grasslands and continued to flee. They stayed in a long, tight column, riding straight out across the plains, until suddenly, an unfamiliar noise caused them to slow and falter in their flight.

Loud trumpets and horns rang out on both sides. They were neither Dwarfish nor Elvish. The long column of Stygian Knights slowed to a near halt on the plains and looked frantically around. There, in great columns numbering in the thousands, stood the cavalry of the Sentinels of Averon, blowing horns of attack that had rarely been blown in the Sentinels' history.

Captain Etienne Gaston drew his sword and urged his men forward to attack the startled enemy. Their long great columns closed on the Stygian Knights, like a metal vise ensnaring a trapped wolf. The silver chain mail and shields of the Sentinels reflected the sunlight like heaven's own fury as, with a blinding flash, the two forces clashed.

Still in tiger form, Kael raked his claws deep into the chest of the Shadow Prince and then struck a blow across his golden helmet, ripping it off his face. The black, twisted, rotting flesh of the Shadow Prince's face, wrought with exposed blood vessels, was taut over his skull, and he stared at Kael's animal form with black, bloodshot eyes. *His eyes,* Kael thought. *There is something different, terrible, behind those eyes.*

An unseen force pressed on Kael's mind. He suddenly seemed lost in time. Unimaginable visions of pain and suffering crowded his mind. He saw the torture and death of thousands, including his friends, Elenari, and Mya—all of them. He saw a world without sunlight, without forests, without green grass or water. He saw a world without life, without hope. He felt a resonating satisfaction emanating from the Shadow Prince; with each death and every act of evil Kael saw, its power became greater and more fearsome.

As Kael became aware of the here and now once more, he realized that the shock of what he had seen had caused him to change back into his human form. Suddenly, the clawed hands of the Shadow Prince were around his throat, choking the life from him. They had switched positions; Kael was now on his back with the Shadow Prince on top of him.

Fire came from the Shadow Prince's hands and seemed to envelop Kael's head for a moment. Then, without warning, the Shadow Prince cried out and released Kael. He stood, leaving Kael lying prone at his feet, and slowly turned to see Mya, clutching the bow of a fallen archer. Kael looked up through pain-blurred eyes; an arrow protruded from the back of the evil prince. Slowly, the Shadow Prince pulled the shaft from his back and walked away from Kael, retrieving his iron mask from the ground where it had fallen.

Mya ran quickly to Kael's side. She helped him up; his face was burnt and blackened though not as damaged as she expected.

"No," he rasped, trying to regain his breath. "It is not over between us . . . stay back."

Kael dragged himself to his full height and waved Mya gently away from him. He stood some ten feet from the Shadow Prince, who slowly turned to face him, his mask of iron back upon his face.

The dark form raised his hands before him, palms up. The ground trembled, and several stalagmites protruding from the floor broke off and rose into the air. In an abrupt motion, the Shadow Prince directed them toward Kael. They streaked through the air toward the Druid.

Without hesitation, Kael dropped to one knee and brought both his arms up in a wide, sweeping motion, creating a circular shield of green fire before him. The rock formations struck the green flames and disintegrated upon impact.

The robes covering the Shadow Prince's chest had been torn and tattered; his black, rotting blood stained them. He stared at Kael, and then slowly smeared his fingers into his own blood and let droplets fall to the ground. The ground upon which the blood fell ripped open in many places, and living skeletons—children of the Shadow Prince's blood—began digging themselves free and rising from the cave floor. Half a dozen of them slowly marched toward Kael.

Voltan closed the bones of his skeletal hand and fingers around Galin's throat and lifted him carelessly off the ground. The touch of the Lich's hand wracked Galin with pain to the core of his being. Coldness paralyzed him as he released a blood-curdling scream.

Whether by instinct, reflex, or force of will alone, his left hand rose, still holding the sacred mace. The moment the weapon came close to Voltan's face, it flared to life once again with its brilliant light, causing the Lich to release his grip, crossing his arms before his face to block the blinding light that seemed to burn him as he himself let out a shriek of pain.

Galin had staggered backward, feeling his life force drained. There was no strength in his arms, but his will had become powerful. The Lich backed away, in fear of the mace.

Galin no longer hesitated. With a cry of rage, he lurched forward and, clutching the haft of *Livinilos* in both hands, he struck Voltan furiously on the right shoulder. As the weapon touched the Lich, a white light spread out from the affected area, covering his shoulder and shooting down his whole arm. Voltan shrieked and howled; this pain was like none he'd ever felt. A moment later, his right arm had completely disintegrated.

Voltan, outraged beyond madness, wheeled around and, with his out-stretched left hand, shot a lightning bolt from his skeletal fingers straight at Galin's chest. It struck dead-on with such terrible force that it lifted the Druid off the ground and threw him backward, smashing his weakened body into the cave wall.

The Lich, somewhat hunched over to one side, glided forward toward the inert body of the Druid. As he reached him and looked down, he saw that the priest was still stirring with life, barely moving. *So much the better,* he thought, as he reached down for him with his remaining arm.

Galin knew he was closer to death than he had ever been in his life and that if the Lich touched him again, his demise was certain. Though unable to see clearly, he was able to make out a blurred vision of the creature reaching down for him. He breathed inward deeply and held the breath, savoring its strength. Releasing his last cry of fury, Galin swung his right hand upward into Voltan's remaining arm, destroying it in a burst of white light.

The Lich released an otherworldly cry, its pitch so piercing the sound alone may have been the only thing that kept the Druid from passing out. Galin, his back against the wall, used his legs to push himself to his feet so that he was face-to-face with the undead Prince of Mystaria. If an animated skull was capable of expression, Galin knew Voltan's would be that of panic-stricken hatred. Bringing the mace behind his shoulders with both hands, Galin struck the skeletal head.

It connected with a flash of light and energy that threw Galin back against the wall one last time. An explosion of white light illuminated the cave enough to momentarily bring all activity therein to a screeching halt. Prince Broderick Voltan had been destroyed at last.

Elenari had seen the flash of light and energy from the cave entrance. Though she did not know its origin, it seemed to give speed to her sword, which now moved so swiftly and with such fury that her opponent found himself driven ever backward barely able to defend against her attacks.

With a reverse, one-handed stroke, Elenari batted her opponent's blade down and away and used the momentum to spin completely around. With a downward, two-handed stroke, she cut diagonally across the dark-clad form. Though not a lethal blow, it took him completely off guard. He responded by trying a weak, off-balance, one-handed attack.

This was the moment Elenari had been waiting for. Easily, she parried his sword upward, nearly dislodging it from his hand. She shifted her weight to her back leg and, with two unbelievably swift, zigzagging strokes, carved a deep Z into his chest.

The Brother of the Shadow staggered, barely able to remain standing, and feigned a weak attack that Elenari parried with a glancing blow, spinning herself around so that she stood behind him, and with a powerful two-handed, stroke, she slashed downward between his neck and right shoulder. Her sword buried itself within his torso all the way down to his waist, literally splitting him in half. The assassin's hands went limp as his sword fell. A moment later, he dropped to his knees.

Standing behind him, Elenari leaned down to whisper in his ear, "You were better trained than my last opponent," she sneered, "but not well enough."

She placed her boot on the back of his neck and dislodged her sword from his body as he fell lifelessly to the ground.

The Shadow Prince had also seen the flash of light; he had felt Voltan's death. Somehow, they had found the power to destroy his general.

With his hands outstretched above him, he levitated himself to see over the rock wall, and realized with disgust that the White Elves had stopped fighting amongst themselves and had taken to helping their wounded on both sides. Soon, the other Druid and the Elven girl would come to join with Kael and the High Priestess. He let his gaze fall upon Lark Royale, who was still fighting with his brother. The Paladin would be of much greater use at a later time. He looked back toward Kael and Mya. *"Enjoy your petty victory for now, you fools. It will be shorter lived than you can imagine."*

A glowing light suddenly encircled him, covering him completely, and disappeared just as suddenly, taking him along with it.

Just as Lark was about to attack his brother again, he stopped in mid-stride. Archangel watched as his clouded pupils became clear.

"Archangel," Lark said, dropping his sword in shock. "Is it really you brother?"

Archangel stepped forward and grabbed his brother's arm. "It is I, Lark. Are you all right?"

"When last I saw you . . . they took your eye," Lark said with a low gasp. "Oh brother, forgive me. Forgive me that I could not stop them."

Archangel embraced his older brother and felt his strong grip close about him in return. "I am well just the same," he said, "and better for seeing you as yourself once again. There is nothing to forgive now that we are together and a family once more."

The brothers held each other for a moment, but a shout from somewhere behind them caused them to halt their embrace and look up. They saw the Shadow Prince's skeletons approaching Kael and Mya.

Lark quickly rushed forward and placed himself between the monsters and his allies. He removed the silver pendant from his neck, his sacred holy symbol. He held it out proudly, strong in his faith.

"Be gone, foul creatures!" he roared. "You have no power against a holy knight!" Suddenly, the pendant began to glow, and white fire shot forth from it, striking each of the skeletons, turning them to dust.

Kael, swaying on his feet, his face blackened and dirty, grabbed Lark by the shoulder. The Paladin turned, and Kael looked at his old friend with bewilderment and joy, for he saw the strength of his friendship in his eyes again.

"Lark, are you well?" Kael asked breathlessly.

Lark's lips curved in a broad smile. "Kael, my old friend. My dear old friend . . . I am well for the first time in a long time, but clearly you are not."

Lark gently sat him down and, holding his holy symbol in one hand, placed his other hand on Kael's face. Slowly, the burns began to heal.

"He's finally free of the Shadow Prince's devilry," Archangel said to Kael.

Kael felt his hand being held. He turned his head and saw Mya. She had never looked more intoxicating to him; her emerald eyes met his, and all the pain, fatigue, and anguish no longer mattered. As he looked over Lark's shoulder, he saw Elenari walking toward them with Galin at her side, his arm slung across her shoulder. Immediately, Archangel moved to help the Druid. As they sat Galin down, Kael gasped in dismay.

"Galin . . . your hair! What has happened to you?"

"The evil that has failed to destroy me . . . has made me stronger," Galin whispered. "Fear not, my friend." With that, he drifted into unconsciousness.

"He killed the Lich, Voltan, in single combat," Elenari told them proudly, and they gazed at him with awe.

Kael stared at Galin in dismay; his hair had become as white as snow, and harsh lines were etched upon his face. Though still somewhat youthful in appearance, it was clear something of his life force had been taken from him—something he could likely never get back. He still clutched the sacred Mace of Many Blessings in his hand; the weapon had become his alone to wield, and it had served him well.

Elenari embraced her father, and Kael scowled at the sight of the large cut on her thigh. "It's nothing, Father," she said with a brave smile. "Do not worry." She looked closely upon Mya for the first time. "You're right, Father; she is beautiful."

Mya nervously reached out her hand toward Elenari. Elenari stared at Mya's hand for a moment, then pulled her into a warm embrace, which surprised the High Priestess but imparted a warmth she could not deny.

"My father has told me how you saved him," said Elenari, pulling back to meet Mya's eyes. "I can never thank you enough, and I am most honored to meet you."

Mya's eyes lingered on Elenari's, then turned their gaze upon the rest of the companions. "I think I owe you and your father and all your friends a great deal more than he owes me," she replied thoughtfully.

Navarre had crouched down in a dark corner of the cave near the entrance. Quietly, he dug at the stones blocking the way; he hoped he could make a hole large enough for him to crawl out unnoticed. After observing Voltan's death and the Shadow Prince's escape, he felt his best option was to flee.

As he pulled another rock away, he suddenly felt a blade at his throat. Slowly he raised his hands to show he was unarmed and turned to find himself face-to-face with Lark Royale.

"Get up, worm!" Lark ordered.

Navarre spoke sincerely, suddenly feeling very anxious. "Royale, there's no need for this, surely. I am your friend; I fed you and trained you. Don't you remember? We're friends, not enemies!"

Lark looked at him strangely for a moment, his expression almost confused, and then slowly he smiled. He lowered his sword. "Ahh . . . of course," Lark replied. "Put your hands down, my friend. I remember now."

Navarre eagerly nodded and placed his hands at his sides.

"I remember best when you took my brother's eye," the Paladin said, his voice deadly calm.

Navarre's blood ran cold. Lark raised his arm and delivered an open-handed slap across Navarre's face with such force that it drove him rolling to the ground.

"How dare you lay hands upon me," Navarre spat in rage. "I'm Viscount of Shadowgate and a noble of Mystaria! You will die for this, Royale!"

He pushed himself up, drew his sword, and charged at Lark. In one motion, Lark knocked Navarre's sword from his hands with his own weapon and slapped him across the face again, knocking him back to the ground.

This time Navarre rose with blood dripping from his mouth. "Royale, you pig!"

Suddenly he lunged at Lark quickly, drawing a hidden dagger from his boot.

Lark dodged the attack easily and grabbed the wrist of the hand that held the dagger. The weapon fell from Navarre's grasp. Lark grabbed hold of the viscount's fingers and slowly bent them back until he heard them all snap at once.

Navarre screamed and fell to the ground. He curled his hand to his chest and crawled toward Lark, still determined to kill him. Lark bent down, grabbed a handful of his hair, and pulled him up so they were face-to-face. He grabbed Navarre's throat with his free hand and placed the other over his former torturer's mouth.

"You . . . filthy," Lark snarled, shaking him furiously. With that, he lifted Navarre off the ground and threw him over his back.

Navarre struck the cave floor with a gut-wrenching moan. Lark turned and walked to where he lay, surprised to see that the viscount had landed on a stalagmite. It had impaled him through the left side of his back and now protruded through his stomach.

Lark stood with Navarre's head between his feet, looking down at him, his sword poised to slit the assassin's throat.

"Lark," Navarre begged, blood trickling from his mouth. "Lark . . . I beg for my life. I ask for mercy. You . . . are a Paladin. I have asked for mercy. Will you kill . . . a helpless . . . unarmed man?" He gagged on the words, unable to move.

Lark hesitated, standing over him. "Since I am a Paladin and a knight of the code," he said at last, "I must grant you mercy."

Slowly, he lowered his sword and, looking down at his enemy one last time, turned to walk away from him.

"You are . . . a true man of honor . . . Lark," Navarre gasped, attempting in vain to free himself of the impalement. "Now, perhaps . . . you could help me?"

Several steps away, Lark suddenly stopped and turned, looking down at Navarre for a long moment. "The code that dictates my actions," he said, turning and continuing on his way, "does not apply to everyone here."

Navarre's face contorted, his eyes closed tightly, but he let out a sigh of relief. He opened his eyes a moment later to see Archangel Royale standing menacingly over him, the tip of his blade turned down toward his head. Navarre's eyes bulged and he screamed the final word he would ever speak, "No!"

Archangel drove his sword down right through Navarre's mouth, penetrating out the back of his head.

Chapter 24

Dark-clad bodies lay strewn throughout the forest floor, their blood soaking the earth.

Slowly, the Elves emerged from the overgrowth of the Vinelands. Many of them knelt, their heads bowed in respect and reverence at the ending of even their enemies' lives. The death toll was immense. In war, fighting for the preservation of their race, they knew it was necessary to give no quarter during battle, but the loss of life affected them deeply. Still, they sensed this was only the beginning.

Many of the Elves worked to remove enough stones from the cave entrance so Kael and the others could make it safely out. As they appeared from the cave, they leaned on one another for support. Both Lark and Elenari supported Kael from each side, while Mya and Archangel supported Galin as they slowly limped forward to gaze upon the thousands of the Stygian Knights' corpses. Having just left the horrors of the cave—full of hundreds of White Elves wounded and dying from having fought one another—the slaughter weighed heavily upon all of them.

The green-clad members of the Emerald Watch escorted King Aeldorath forward to the scene of the battle with the Stygian Knights. There was a look of anguished disgust drawn upon his face.

"How many lives will this Shadow Prince sacrifice to destroy us?" the Elven King whispered. "And what is yet to come?"

At the sight of the King, Galin released his hold on Mya and Archangel and struggled to stand on his own power in his presence. He saw concern in the King's expression; Aeldorath was in shock at his altered appearance.

"All is well, my lord," Galin said, struggling valiantly to remain standing. "What you see is a small price to pay for the destruction of the evil that has been vanquished by the sacred mace, which you delivered into my keeping."

The King, seeing the effort Galin was putting forth, grabbed him by the arm and helped him to sit. "The mace alone did not destroy that evil, my young Druid," Aeldorath said. "You destroyed it with your strength of goodness and your great courage. Never forget that."

Captain Gaston and some of the riders of Averon appeared. The Captain dismounted and bowed to the King as he approached, all the while looking at Kael and the others, whom he'd come to know as comrades and friends.

"My friends, are you all well?" Gaston asked as he went to each of them and shook their hands. He spent an extra moment with Galin, who assured him he was as well as he had ever been.

Kael then took Mya by the hand and approached Aeldorath. Bowing low, he introduced her. "My Lord Aeldorath, allow me to present High Priestess Mya, leader of the White Elves, your kin beneath the surface."

Mya bowed. "Mya Almentir, my Lord."

"Because of her help and courage their people did not attack Alluviam this day. I think at the proper time, the two of you may have much to discuss." He bowed to both of them and silently walked away.

Aeldorath took Mya's hands in his own. "My lady, as you may know, I've known of the plight your people for some time, and instead of dealing with you honorably as our kin, like rulers before me, I pretended you did not exist. On their behalf and my own, I now humbly beg the forgiveness of you and your people." He kissed her hands.

She looked at him, a tear forming in her eye. "You are not at all what I would have imagined, my lord. We would like to come home . . . we want finally to come home."

With that, they embraced.

Galin pushed himself up and nearly fell, but Lark was there to catch him, and together they walked to where Kael stood alone, looking to the sky beyond the green treetops.

"What is it, Kael?" Lark asked.

"He's still out there, Lark," Kael replied. "I couldn't stop him, and now his evil endures further still. We dealt him his first great defeat, yes, but I fear he still commands vast forces, beyond even what we suspect. I fear for Cordilleran. I fear for us all."

At that moment, they all turned to see Aeldorath shaking hands with Captain Gaston.

"From this day forth," Aeldorath said, "let it be known that Elves and Men shall fight together with free peoples everywhere against evil until it is utterly destroyed and freedom and peace are restored to our world."

Cheers rose from the ranks of Men and Elves.

"I wish Algernon were here," Kael said. "I wish he could have seen and heard that."

Galin placed a hand on the Grand Druid's shoulder. "He was here, Kael . . . he did see."

"Indeed, my friend," Lark added. "The one god has granted us victory this day with the blessings of all who have fallen and suffered for such a battle. We shall cross paths with this demon again, Kael, and on that day, he will pay for the death and destruction he has visited upon the world. I swear it."

Kael nodded, turned, and walked away to stand with Mya. The two of them joined hands, and she looked at him, smiling.

"Kael Dracksmere, you have brought hope for me and my people beyond my wildest imagining."

Kael pulled her to him and kissed her, gently but passionately. When he drew back to look at her again, his face became serious. "You know we must leave now. You're staying here, aren't you?"

"I must stay, now more than ever," she replied, "to heal the wounds of my race and prepare them to rejoin our kin. There are still many who feel as Turnia does, and they will not be easily swayed. However, I will follow behind you, with as many soldiers as I can, as soon as possible. We will join this war on the side of light—the right side. Where you go, we will soon follow."

Kael kissed her again, softly. No matter how far he traveled from her, he knew at this moment he would never forget the taste of her lips, the feel of her hair, or the sight of his own reflection in her eyes. He kissed her hands, and just as he was about to let them go, she held fast to his hands for another moment. She quickly spoke a few words in Elvish to him, smiled one last time, and let her hands slide from his grasp. A moment later, she vanished into the blackness of the cave.

While Kael certainly knew some Elvish, he did not recognize the words she had spoken.

Seeing the confusion in his friend's face, Galin came to his side and smiled. "It was an old saying among the Elves, spoken between men and women who loved each other and must be parted. To ease their sorrow, that is what they would say to each other. In the common speech, it means, *"For one day we shall know such happiness, you and I, always and forever as we did this day such as dreams foretell."*

Galin patted him on the shoulder. Elenari came quickly to his side, and he placed his arm around her shoulder as they walked toward the captain and the King. Captain Gaston mounted his horse and ordered his men to bring horses for Kael and the others.

"Forward, riders of Averon," the captain cried. "We ride to Cordilleran, the Kingdom of the Dwarves."

"Come, my Elves," King Aeldorath commanded. "We march now to aid our Dwarven allies in the east."

Kael, Galin, Elenari, Lark, and Archangel rode alongside one another to the front of the column. The first of the alliance forces turned toward Cordilleran . . . and the unknown.

Here Ends Book I

Join the further adventures of these brave companions in Book II: *Secret of the Emerald Star.*

CPSIA information can be obtained
at www.ICGtesting.com
Printed in the USA
LVHW080258240919
631982LV00012B/452/P